Highland Wrath

MERCENARY MAIDENS
BOOK THREE

MADELINE MARTIN

OLIVERHEBERBOOKS

Prologue

S ylvi's entire life had built up to this one moment. She'd sacrificed, she'd trained, she'd gone without. And now she *would* learn to kill.

The noblewoman she watched stood alone in the courtyard, her dress vivid red against the somber gray stonework of the castle behind her. She moved with the grace of a mountain cat and could be just as lethal.

The woman spun once, her skirts lifting out like the petals of a poppy, and slammed her fist into an invisible enemy before bringing her elbow upward. My Lady. The woman who held the life Sylvi desired.

How many times had Sylvi watched this careful practice, only to return to her humble lodgings and mimic those very moves?

Far too many to count, but they were in her mind now. In her blood and her soul and her heart.

Determination flared through her. She was ready.

Her feet were silent on the uneven cobblestone, her body pressed to the shadowed wall behind her. Her heart pattered in her chest at a speed she could not control. With a deep, even breath, she slid the dagger from her pocket and aimed.

"You think I don't see you there, Girl?" My Lady crossed an

arm in front of her and brought it down, severing an attack from her invisible partner. Her gaze did not shift to the shadows. "Throw it."

She turned her back to Sylvi with such nonchalance that it could only have been done as a challenge.

Sylvi kept her fingers loose on the blade and let finesse rather than strength free the cool metal from her grip. It sailed smoothly through the air toward the bright red back facing her. My Lady swept from its path and stared through the veil of shadows directly into Sylvi's soul.

The movement had been so abrupt that My Lady's skirts swayed around her still body. She lifted a finger and curled it, beckoning. "Come here, Girl."

This was it. Sylvi grit her teeth against the tensing anxiety screaming through her and forced action into her stiffening limbs.

My Lady nudged the fallen blade with the toe of her satin slipper. "I see you finally have a proper weapon." The smirk on her lips told Sylvi she remembered all too well the last time Sylvi had used a bit of wood in place of a dagger.

The weapon had come at a high cost. Sylvi's cheeks burned at the recollection of how it'd been procured, but she shoved the memory down. She never wanted to think about that again.

There were many things she never wanted to think about again.

She stooped to pick up the dagger. The leather braid on its hilt settled warm against her palm despite the chill in the air. Her breath came short and shallow with what she was about to say.

She squeezed her hand around the dagger. "I'm ready."

My Lady lifted her head and regarded Sylvi for a long moment. While not particularly beautiful with her narrow lips and sharp jaw, she somehow presented an allure, an air of mystery and danger.

Silence widened between them and begged to be filled with justifications. Sylvi had endured loneliness to maintain discretion, sustained deprivation to practice her training, maintaining the determination she'd held steadfastly to all these years in her clutch of hope.

But arguments and pleas would not work with My Lady. No words would.

Sylvi tucked the dagger into the battered belt at her side and threw a punch at the woman she sought to have as her mentor. Never before had Sylvi been so bold.

My Lady ducked to the side, easily avoiding the blow.

"How long have you been following me now, Girl? Seven years?" She lunged forward, and her fist flew at Sylvi's face.

Sylvi threw her hands up to block the hit. Something hard and strong slammed into her stomach, nearly knocking the wind from her.

"Ten years, My Lady." Sylvi backed up and straightened, recovering easily after having built up the necessary strength in her abdomen for such a blow. "And I'm no girl anymore."

My Lady's gaze slipped down Sylvi's body. "No," she conceded. "You're not. You've gone from being a foreign gutter rat to something becoming. In fact, you've grown to be rather lovely in that savage way these Highland men like." Her forefinger wagged the air between them. "Yet your manner of speech is fine enough to land you in the heart of James's court without arousing a lick of suspicion. How did you manage?"

Sylvi had not realized how roughly she'd spoken until My Lady had pointed it out. She'd been only a girl then, one who easily blended into crowds, as unnoticed by the wealthy as rubbish heaped in a dark alley. "I followed the noblewomen of Edinburgh," she replied. "Same as I followed you."

"Clever girl." My Lady's eyes narrowed. "Clever *woman*." She swept her leg toward Sylvi's feet, but Sylvi leapt into the air and easily landed without her balance rocking. With footing so sure, Sylvi did not need to wait to recover and drove her elbow in the direction of the other woman's temple.

My Lady caught her arm and held it in a merciless grip. Her

blue eyes were chips of sapphire when they met Sylvi's. "Clever women are dangerous."

"Clever women are advantageous with the right alliances." Sylvi wrenched her elbow free. "You know that better than most." She pulled back and slammed her fist into My Lady's jaw too fast for the woman to block her.

A smile quirked at My Lady's lips. "You're better than I thought, Girl." She touched a finger to her mouth and looked down at a smear of bright blood. "If I train you, there will be rules."

Sylvi's heartbeat doubled at those words. Never had they even begun to discuss Sylvi truly joining her. For years, it had all been a list of reasons why she couldn't. A long list.

But she hadn't accepted defeat. She'd adapted, addressing every "no" and improving herself until every excuse had been struck from the list.

"I understand." Her voice was stronger than the quivering mass of her insides.

My Lady held her gaze. "If you do not abide by those rules, you will pay with your life."

"I understand," Sylvi repeated. "But I also would like to make a request."

My Lady stared at her for a long moment, and then a laugh erupted from her red-painted lips. "You would make a request of me?" Her hand waved in the air with an embellished invitation. "By all means..."

Sylvi's breathing went shallow, and her lips tingled. This one request was bold. It could be the one thing that ruined her chances. But it was also the one thing that had driven her so far. "When I find the man I'm looking for and the men who follow him, I want permission to leave so that I may pursue them."

The sun overhead was blotted out with a swell of graying clouds. Sylvi refrained from allowing an ominous shiver to trickle down her spine.

"The man with half an ear." My Lady said it casually, but her knowledge jabbed into Sylvi's heart.

"How do you know?" Sylvi whispered above the pounding of her pulse.

"Do you think I'd allow you to follow me and act as my page without learning more about you? After so many unsuccessful years, you most likely will not find him." My Lady paused and regarded Sylvi. "What would you do if you did?"

The kindling of hatred roared through Sylvi at the very thought. "I'll kill him."

"You're very determined for one so young. What happened to you?"

The image flashed in Sylvi's mind before she could stop it. Her family, all with the same white-blonde hair as hers, their eyes pale blue and seeing nothing. The slashes at their necks, gaping like macabre second mouths. Their screams echoed in her skull, her mother's pleading to spare the children.

Sylvi jerked her head to the side as if she could fling the memories out.

The scar on her throat burned with the memory. Her fingers found the coarse ribbon tied around her neck before she realized what she was doing. "You have your secrets." Her voice came out so rough it was nearly unrecognizable. "And I have mine."

My Lady's gaze fixed on the ribbon, and for a moment, Sylvi worried she might be told to remove it. The blood roared in her ears.

"You may have your request. I will agree to train you but not work with you. I work alone." My Lady's stare softened. "You must know he will be hard to find. And know killing will not bring you what you seek. Death brings consequences, not solace."

Rain spit down at them from the swollen skies. My Lady bent to retrieve her belongings. "Get your things, Girl. You'll stay here from now on rather than that hovel you call home."

"My name is—"

"Girl." My Lady straightened. "And I am My Lady to you."

Sylvi nodded in compliance and gazed up at the towering height of the stone manor. Bits of stone and mortar had flaked away, and the structure had gone dark with age, but it was the most beautiful home Sylvi had ever seen.

She would be living there, training with My Lady.

And regardless of what the death of her enemies would bring her, they would still be dead, and her family *would* be avenged.

One

APRIL 1608, ELGIN, SCOTLAND

Night was a cloak Sylvi wore well. She possessed none of the alluring seduction of My Lady but instead favored the silent discretion of her more recent instructor, Connor. He had acquired her to be part of an elite group of women to spy for King James. After all, Sylvi had required a job of her own once she had grown. She couldn't rely on My Lady's generosity forever, and My Lady had made it clear from the beginning—she worked alone.

Her stealth was not the only habit Sylvi had acquired from Connor. She also kept the girls who worked for her from the ugly task of killing.

Assassinations were not something she liked to take on, but this particular one had been at a price she could not refuse. It was no cheap task to run a spy ring of women. Especially with a recent blunder in which one of her clients lost their daughter and refused to pay. While Sylvi did not blame Delilah for the botched mission, the hit to their coffers had been hard enough to lead Sylvi to accept the abysmal task. She would have readily refused if it weren't for the other women counting on her for their survival.

Sylvi eased through the empty street with the comfort she

only found in the shadows. Her breath came faster than she liked, not from nerves but from the discomforting tension in her chest.

Killing was nasty business.

The image of the massive bag of coins on her desk sat in her mind like a stone. She'd scratched every coin with the tip of her dagger, the way her father had shown her as a girl. None of the gold had scraped off to reveal a false coin beneath.

It was a silly thing to do, she knew, but old habits were not easily lost, and the ritual summoned the memory of her father.

She quickly picked the lock of the flimsy door to the inn and slipped inside, allowing herself to be swallowed into the blackness. This would be done and over soon, then she could move on as if it had never happened.

Death brings consequences.

The phrase had stuck in Sylvi's head and lodged in her heart.

She went quickly up the stairs. The man's door was the second to the left. She had noted it when she'd pretended to be a paying customer earlier that day.

Her hand curled around the cool door latch, and she pulled in a deep breath.

She was Norse born, descended from a long-ago line of shield-maidens who had savagely fought in the centuries before. Her veins ran with cold blood, and her body was forged of iron.

She could do this.

She *would* do this.

With a silence she'd gleaned from her years under Connor's tutelage, she opened the door and entered the room.

The moon cast a silver glow within, alighting on the bulk of a man lying in his bed. He was alone. For that, Sylvi was grateful. Having one additional soul staining her hands was bad enough. Two more would be borne with greater difficulty.

The tip of her blade had been dipped in poison. A slight scratch and the man would be in a death sleep within seconds.

Seconds, however, could last a lifetime, depending on his skill with a blade.

Slitting his throat would be far easier, but she could not bring herself to do to someone else what had been done to her. To her family. She could not again witness the unnatural split of the skin or be surrounded by the odor of hot blood.

He did not move as she approached, save for the steady rise and fall of his chest. She carefully slipped the dagger from her belt and crouched beside his bed.

"Ye're no' the first man to try to kill me." The man sat up abruptly, and his leg kicked out, catching Sylvi hard in the chest.

Were she not squatting, she could have easily kept her footing. But the move was so unexpected and so sudden that she succumbed to the impact and flew backward. Her body rolled with it, and she somersaulted before stopping and lurching upright.

Moonlight fell over his face, showing up close what she'd only seen from a distance during the past few days she'd followed him. Straight brown hair to his shoulders. Sharp cheekbones. A close-cropped beard. Amber eyes widened in surprise.

"Ye are the first lass trying to kill me, though." His smile was quick and easy, as if this were a jest rather than the impending end of his life. "Usually, women come to my bed for a different purpose."

He winked, the fool.

He wouldn't find this so amusing for long. Sylvi darted at him, and the poisoned blade flashed in the moonlight.

He sank low and ducked from the path of her dagger. She spun around to attack once more and found him holding a chamber pot like a shield. His léine hung down his body and stopped below his knees.

She stopped and furrowed her brow at the man in his under-garments holding a chamber pot as a means of defense.

He glanced down at the cheap pottery and shrugged. "At least it wasna full."

She swiped the blade at him, but he shoved the pot in the way, so the dagger pinged harmlessly away. She repeated the act, and he blocked it thus once more. They did this several times before the frustration of the ludicrous act sent Sylvi to the floor to sweep his feet from underneath him.

He fell along with the chamber pot, which crashed near her head, narrowly missing her face. Her ear hummed with the force of the clatter, but not enough to miss the hiss of metal. A sharpness nipped under her chin.

She followed the path of the long sword from where it touched her throat all the way up the blade. The man stood over her with his weapon, pinning her into place. His chest pumped up and down as he caught his breath from their exertion, the same as hers.

A hammering pound sounded on the wall. "How many nights do I have to tell ye to keep it down? Some of us are sleeping, ye arse."

He grinned down at her. "I'm developing a reputation around here."

"Apparently, a lot of people try to kill you." She drew back her leg and kicked him hard between the legs.

The impertinent smile crumpled from his face, and he staggered forward with his hands clasped around his crotch. A high-pitched groan squeaked from his throat.

"Ye've no idea how bad that hurts." He shot her a wounded glare. "Who does that to a man?"

She caught the backs of his feet with hers and shoved him to the ground. He fell on his side, his body still curled around the weakness of his injured member.

"Someone who will do whatever it takes to win." She fell on top of him, her blade drawn. "And I always win."

He made a snorting sound somewhere between pain and scorn. "Was it Reginald who sent ye?"

She put the poisoned blade to his throat. She would only need to nick him. Just a scratch.

"He's a handsome fellow, easily picked out in a crowd. Short and fat." The man's mouth lifted at the side in a show of mirth. "Couple of teeth missing along with half his left ear."

Half his left ear.

Sylvi's blood went cold. "What did you say?"

The man squinted his eyes up at her. "He's handsome?"

She pulled the blade back and shoved the heel of her hand onto his throat instead. "The other part."

"Short. Fat." His speech vibrated in his throat beneath her hand. "Missing a couple teeth."

"The other part," she ground out. She pushed harder with her hand.

His voice came out strangled when he spoke, but she heard it well enough. "He's missing half his left ear."

IAN CAMPBELL STARED UP AT THE WOMAN WHO evidently wanted him dead.

No, she had most likely been paid to kill him. Doubtless, it was Reginald who wanted his death. The bastard. Ian should have killed him when he'd had the chance. It was obvious Reginald's band of men were still sore about how they'd parted ways. Ian had expected the mercenaries to find him and try to kill him. After all, several others had been sent before—none of them successful, of course.

Perhaps they assumed he would not suspect a woman.

"Who is this Reginald?" she asked. "How do you know him? Where can I find him?" The woman pressed harder on his throat.

She was a skilled fighter, even though her moves were dirty. His bollocks still ached where they'd been knocked under the brutality of her slender food. But she wasn't very smart if she thought he could speak through a crushed throat.

He loosed one of the hands cradling his offended manhood and jerked a finger at his throat.

She eased the pressure. A bit.

A caring lass, this one.

"I thought ye knew him." The words rasped out of his throat and brought on the urge to cough. But coughing would make his stones hurt worse than they already did. He swallowed thickly, easing away the rough need to clear the ache. "Are ye no' working with him?"

"Why the hell would I work with a man like him?" She shoved her hand harder into his throat again. God, the lass must be made of iron.

In a swift move, he caught her wrist, twisted and flipped her onto her back.

Her hair was white in the moonlight, but her face was young. A very fair blonde, perhaps. Pale eyes glared up at him with resolve from an angular face and broad forehead. Her mouth stretched into a hard, determined line, but he could see the sensual line of a cherub's bow shape.

Ian Campbell knew a beautiful woman when he saw one, and his would-be assassin was definitely...well...pretty. Even if she was mad as a cat caught in a Highland storm.

"I canna talk with yer hand in my throat," he ground out.

"Who is the man with half an ear?" Evidently, she was going to ignore his pointing out her oversight on basic anatomy.

"A man who makes bad choices."

"How do you know him?"

"Because I make bad choices." It was true. Running with those jackanapes was one of the worst of his life decisions. And now they were all after him.

So much for a fresh start on life. He should have known it would not be so easy.

"Why does he want you dead?"

"He doesn't like me."

"I can see why." She glared at him. "Do you think you're amusing?"

Her anger was evident in the darkening of her cheeks and the stiffening of her body.

He couldn't help the grin pulling at his lips. "Entertaining, aye. Amusing, perhaps."

Now he was just being humble.

A dagger jerked up to his hand, the blade cool where it rested near the heel of his thumb.

"One scratch from this, and you'll draw your last breath."

"I canna speak if I canna breathe." He managed to level his stare at her. "And ye have more questions."

He set his sword aside and held up his free hand, palm facing her in surrender. "I propose we set aside our weapons and talk like gentlem—er, civilized people."

She slid the dagger into the belt at her waist. "I don't need a dagger to kill you."

"And no more kicking either, aye? I'd like to have sons someday."

He thrust a hand down to help her rise, but she ignored the offer and leapt gracefully to her feet.

Really looking at her now, there was very little about her that appeared civilized or ladylike. Her pale hair had been braided back from her face and tied behind her head in a thick mass. She wore a man's black léine and breeches, as well as a small belt around her waist with various pockets and sheaths affixed to it.

"Do you know where the man with half an ear is?" she asked.

"His name is Reginald. He's head of a band of dangerous mercenaries."

She hissed in disgust and paced across the room. At second glance, he found he rather liked breeches on a woman. The fabric hugged the curve of her round arse, and he could discern the shapely lines of her slender legs beneath the fitted cloth.

She turned and eyed him as if she knew what he'd been thinking. And might cut his cock off for having thought it.

"No man with half an ear came to me," she said. "Or I wouldn't be here with you now."

Ian didn't doubt that a lick. "Describe the man who came to ye to hire ye."

"Tall, lanky, long silver and black hair split down the middle and tucked behind his ears." She paused with obvious thought. "There's a scar just under his eye and one on his jaw."

"Large ears?" he pressed.

The woman tilted her head in consideration. "They weren't small."

Ian scoffed. Figures it'd be Gregor handling Reginald's business. He was the cruelest of all. "Aye, I know him," Ian said. "His name's Gregor, and he does indeed work with Reginald."

On second look, he couldn't help but notice how the subtle swell beneath her léine hinted at the bosom beneath. Were her breasts bound or loose within?

She bent down and put her eyes where her chest had been. "Do you know where Reginald is?"

"No." He cleared his throat. "Sorry, I've no' ever seen a lass dressed like ye are. Ye wear it well."

She rolled her eyes. "Your flattery is unnecessary."

"Ye still look verra nice in it."

She slid him a warning glance.

So much for earning a smile of appreciation.

In fact, her expression went hard with concentration. "I need to find where they're staying. And you need to get these men to leave you alone. There's only one way all that can happen." She slid the dagger from her belt and studied it carefully before returning her pale stare to him. "I'm going to have to kill you."

Two

I an stared at the mad woman who dressed like a man. Like a killer.

Although his attire was of finer quality than hers, the long léine without his kilt belted around him was a sad thing indeed, making him look as if he wore a lass's nightclothes.

"If I'm dead, this plan willna help me."

She flicked the length of her white hair over her shoulder in a short, irritable motion. Only then did he notice she wore a black silk ribbon tied around her slender throat, just feminine enough to look almost ridiculous.

Almost as ridiculous as him in nightclothes.

She huffed out a sigh. "I'm supposed to leave your body on the outskirts of town. I can take your body there, collect the coins they owe me and follow them when they take you wherever they intend to take you."

Ian eyed his surrendered sword on the ground beside him. "I'm still failing to see how this might help me."

The woman followed his gaze toward his weapon, but she didn't move. Not to tense for an attack or to move closer to guard him. She was confident in her skills. More so than most men. And that made her a frightening opponent.

"You wouldn't actually die." She spoke to him as if he were a child. "It's a forged death."

"A forged death." He nodded slowly and then eyed her warily. "Explain, if ye will, how does a 'forged' death work to the point of being convincing, and more importantly, no' killing me?"

Despite what her answer would be, the twist in his gut told him this plan would not be good.

For him, at least.

She indicated the dagger she held. "This is poisoned. One scratch will immediately put you into a state of very deep sleep. So deep you will appear dead. It would eventually lead to certain death within three hours." Her gaze swept over his body, much as his had done over hers earlier. "Most likely four for you since you're bigger than most, but I wouldn't want to push it past three and a half to be certain."

He couldn't help the cocky grin. "Well, ye know how to flatter a man into interest."

"I'm discussing measurements for preventing your death, not issuing a compliment." She unlatched a pocket of her belt and pulled out a slim vial full of clear liquid. "This is what will save you. It's a counterbalance to the poison in the dagger."

He eyed the liquid in the vial. It looked like water to him, and everyone knew water was dangerous to drink.

"Does it work?" He reached for it, but the woman closed her fingers over the glass and tucked it back in her belt.

"Yes."

"So it's been tried before."

She busied herself with her belt. It was extraordinary. Many pouches, sturdy with room for several weapons.

Then he realized she still had not spoken.

"It hasna been tried before, has it?"

She looked up, and her expression turned pensive. "No. But I trust the woman who created it with my life."

"But it isna yer life," he pointed out. "It's mine."

"Then you have my word that I'll keep you safe." Her face was open in a way he wanted to trust.

He'd been trying to run from the bastards for several months. Ever since he'd rebelled against them when they had attempted to rape a woman. They hadn't appreciated his defense of her and had their bollocks in a knot over it ever since. He'd saved the woman, but it had won him some enemies. Dangerous ones.

And to think he'd only been trying to escape his old life with a new one. Now he was always running, always looking behind his back.

Still, it was better than being home. His gut twisted around the thought of Simon. Ian tried to push it from his mind, but the reminder rose painfully forefront in his mind.

Nay, he couldn't go home. There was no facing what he'd done. And the sooner he could get these men off his arse, the sooner he could find a new life. Maybe even find a way to do a right to offset so much wrong.

Home or death or...this—forged death and trusting a woman sent to kill him.

Not good options, to be sure.

The cool metal of the blade touched his throat and pulled his thoughts from his futile options.

"You don't have many options." The softness of the woman's gaze had frosted over, leaving her eyes hard and cold. "Either I kill you for good right now, or I give you my word to keep you safe and ensure you come out of this alive. I have been looking for these men for a long time, and I will *not* let you keep me from them."

The look in her eyes told him if he didn't choose fast, the choice would be made for him. And not in his favor.

"Verra well. I'll let ye do it with my permission so long as ye keep me safe, but I require two more things."

She cocked her head in silent invitation for him to continue.

He cleared his throat and eased back some from the blade. "First of all, I'd like to know the name of the person I'm conspiring with. I'm Ian Campbell." He gave her his most charming grin. The lasses always loved that smile best.

"Sylvi."

A lass of many words.

Sylvi nodded at him. "What's your second request?"

He pointed to her waist. "I want one of those belts."

An unladylike snort came from her. "Very well. I'll ensure you get one. Now get dressed. It's impossibly cold outside."

She glanced out the window, where the night was beginning to lighten and glow deep blue with the onset of early dawn. "I have to meet them soon and will have to poison you here to make it look believable in case someone is watching me."

Ian's heartbeat thumped faster. He wasn't ready now. He wanted to fight against the woman and escape this bad situation that had suddenly worsened. Even as he thought it, his hands worked to fasten his plaid around his waist and over his shoulder.

It was one thing to fight and win. It was another altogether to fight and avoid being scratched by the wicked blade. At least this way, he had her word he'd be safe.

If she kept her word.

He couldn't think of that possibility now. Instead, he gave a short nod and met her gaze. "Keep me safe, Sylvi."

She hesitated a brief moment before resting the dagger against his forearm. Her eyes narrowed with conviction. "I will."

"If ye dinna keep me safe..." The blade pressed against his skin, and a line of blood welled up around the sharpened edge. "I'll come back to haunt ye."

A thick fog welled around his mind and sucked him toward the lure of a dreamless, black nothing.

His life was in the hands of a woman he'd just met, a woman who had come to kill him, no less. Of all the bad decisions he'd made in his eight-and-twenty years, this certainly was the worst.

Time was precious, and Sylvi had just lost an hour.

The men were late.

Anxiety edged up her spine and left her body charged with restlessness. She was not often subject to the pressure of such nervousness and found she did not at all care for being so helpless in its grip.

Her feet carried her in a back-and-forth pace in front of the large tree just outside of town, where she'd been told to meet the mercenaries. The air froze around her sigh in white fog in front of her face. Ian lay immobile in the thick blanket she'd wrapped him in. She'd been careful to ensure no part of his skin touched the frozen ground where he lay, yet she could not help but worry about the cold.

She'd been precipitous in her decision to poison Ian early. True, she hadn't noticed signs of being watched, but Ian had said Reginald and his men were dangerous. Surely, they'd seen her enter his room and leave half dragging, half pulling his blanket-wrapped body under the cover of early dawn. Percy's little two-wheeled cart she'd fashioned had been invaluable; the apparatus was small enough to navigate with only minimal difficulty down the stairs.

Why the hell had these mysterious men hired her to do a job they could do themselves?

And why so much coin to do the job?

It didn't make sense, no matter how many times her mind ticked over it.

Her gaze slid to the heap of blanket once more.

The answer was Ian. Something about him, something valuable.

He certainly was heavy. If she hadn't had Percy's tool, she would never have gotten him out of that inn without waking every person.

His clothes were incredibly fine. The linen of his léine had been impossibly soft beneath her fingertips, and the wool of his kilt thick and well made. The remaining items she'd gathered from his room, and now held in the pack tied to her back, had all been of high quality as well.

She'd glanced briefly through Ian's bag. There was a considerable amount of coin within but nothing to indicate his identity. Aside from a clean léine and another length of plaid, he had not much else. His sword was exceptional. A boar's head was etched into the hilt, but then, he had said he was a Campbell.

Were these items stolen, or had they always belonged to him?

The hollow wooden bump of an empty cart going over the thin cold air of the forest met her ears, and the tension around her heart eased somewhat. They were coming.

She crouched beside the man who lay in the arms of death and flicked aside the blanket. Ian's face was relaxed in the soft light of an early day. Small creases showed on his skin at the corners of his eyes and mouth, evidence of a man who smiled often. No doubt at his own jests.

He was handsome, though. She would grudgingly admit that. Though only to herself. His arrogance needed no polishing.

The cart was close now. Sylvi replaced the blanket, rose and turned to face the same man she'd spoken with initially when securing the assassination. The man Ian had told her was named Gregor.

"I knew I could count on ye." The Gaelic rasped from his throat, deep and gravelly.

There'd been something about him when she first met him—his voice, his face. Something. Now that she knew he was with Reginald, it nipped at her awareness with more insistence.

Two other men stood several feet behind him with the cart, all men with intact ears from what she could tell.

Reginald was not there. But she *would* find him.

"I see ye made quick work of his fine things." Gregor nodded at Ian's sword at her side.

Sylvi narrowed her eyes in reply.

The light of a new day fell on the world with vivid golds and reds while turning the world seemingly dreamlike. It left the man's face darkened and hard to see. But his voice.

What was it about his voice?

He strode past her to where Ian lay and nudged the blanket aside with the toe of his boot. He regarded Ian for a long moment, then heaved a kick into the prone man's side. Ian's body rolled back slightly with the impact, but he did not make any sound. Sylvi clenched her teeth at the brutal impact and hoped he could not feel it beneath the poison's sleep.

"He's already dead," she ground out in Gaelic.

"No' by my decision." Gregor spat on the ground. "I wanted to enjoy him a little more before he died." He motioned for the other men to come forward.

They did as they were bidden, grabbing Ian's bulk, thankfully keeping him wrapped in the blanket, and tossing him into the back of the cart as if he were a sack of flour. Sylvi turned toward Gregor rather than see the painful thwack that she could not help but hear.

She held out her hand expectantly.

Gregor pulled a sack the size of a man's fist from his belt and threw it at her. It smacked hard into her palm with the weight of considerable coin. She closed her fingers over it and made her way to the surrounding woods, where she would wait and follow.

The carriage would make them easier to follow. They were slow and noisy. The journey would not be as difficult as she'd initially thought.

She sank into the snow-speckled bushes between two large trees and waited. The men continued to speak to one another as they swung up on their horses.

Sylvi closed her eyes and focused on the sound of their voices, letting them scrape through her mind and ravage the memories she never let surface.

The only man she knew by sight was the man with half an ear. *The burly man stood in front of her, his grizzled beard making* him look very much like a troll from a story meant to frighten children. The knife in his hand dripped with her father's blood.

Sylvi was scared. Frozen by fear—her body, her mind, even her heart.

This had to be a dream, and yet she could not allow herself to wake.

Sylvi stared down at her father, always so strong and powerful, as though nothing could ever hurt him.

A horrible gurgling sigh hissed from the wound at his neck, and blood swelled out. Growing and growing and growing until the puddle licked hot at her naked toes.

A shriek echoed in her head, awful and unending. Someone grabbed her hard from behind, and the noise stopped.

She had been making the sound.

"Do we really have to kill the bairns?" The man behind her said, his voice deep and gravelly.

The troll in front of Sylvi slid her a look of contempt.

"What is unseen hasna been done."

Sylvi's mother screamed—a raw, animalistic sound. She ran at the troll and slashed a dagger at his face. He ducked to the side, but not before her blade sank into his ear and sliced. The hunk of it fell to the floor.

The arm holding Sylvi tensed, and she knew she was going to die, just as her father had.

Something cool drew across Sylvi's neck, and she was dropped to the ground. She landed on the hard floor, facing her father. A pool of blood bloomed from under her and crept toward the puddle her father had made.

Her mind whirled with confusion. Had her throat been cut? Why had she not felt it? Why could she not get up and fight?

Their puddles of blood touched and became one. Her mother's scream was cut short, and something heavy fell to the floor, a sound frighteningly similar to the sound her father made when he fell.

Sylvi closed her eyes, succumbing to the scrabbling fear pumping *her life from her body, and pretended to be dead. For soon, she knew she would be.*

A cracking whip pulled Sylvi from a hole she had never allowed herself to crawl back into. Her eyes flew open. The carriage was leaving.

The man that day had been hesitant to kill a child, and so his cut had been shallow. It had saved her life.

But he had meant to take it.

And he had taken the lives of her family. She'd heard them all stop screaming, one by one. After her mother was her sisters, Inka and Alva, their pitched squeals of fear cut short almost at the same time. Only little Einar's cries remained at the end, breathless and pathetic with confusion and fear he did not understand. It had been hard to keep her eyes closed when he finally fell silent.

She tore herself from the pain blazing in her heart and slammed shut the door to her memories. Her hands balled into fists, and she welcomed the surge of hate to balm the rawness of loss.

Gregor was not Reginald, but she knew that gravelly voice. While she hadn't seen him, that deep voice had rumbled against her small back.

Oh, yes, she knew him.

He was one of them. One of the men she had been looking for all these years. His voice had caught at something within her when he hired her, but she hadn't placed it until just now.

She fixed her gaze on him as she strode soundlessly through the dark forest, no longer merely following but stalking.

He would *die*.

Three

Sylvi wanted Gregor dead.

The desire to kill him pulsed hot through her veins, taunting her. Her muscles burned with the pace she'd kept with the carriage, her world focused entirely on the head of black-and-silver hair. No longer registering the cold biting at her face or the breath huffing easily from her lungs.

She could run out and swing up on the horse behind him. It would be so easy; she could *feel* it. The heat of his back against her chest, the constriction of his body in surprise. She would curl her arm around his torso before he could even react, her dagger ready to sink into tender flesh.

She would go deep enough to let the blade scrape his neck bones. His blood would gush over her hands, hot as her father's had been, when it washed over her toes that horrific day.

The air came alive with the thought of Gregor's blood, a coppery odor floating above the wet, earthy scents of the forest. The odor coursed through her like a spell and left her body crackling with energy.

She wanted to fight.

She wanted to kill.

She wanted vengeance.

Her mouth prickled with the metallic taste of it, and she clenched her teeth to revel in the savage effect.

Gregor had come to kill a child all those years ago. While he had hesitated then, Ian had described him as the cruelest of all the men. Clearly, he had overcome his trepidation.

She had been weak when Gregor had attacked. Only someone weak would cower in a pool of shared blood and pretend death while the cries of her family fell forever silent.

She was no longer a child. Her life had been defined by those horrible moments, lost in the shadows of a darkened heart.

She was no longer weak.

The edge of the sun burned atop the peaks of trees and bled its brilliance into the clear, cold sky. Time tapped insistently in her mind as it passed.

Two hours had passed since she had given them Ian. The time from the room at the inn to the time they finally arrived had been nearly a full hour.

She was running out of time.

Her pinprick focus on Gregor widened to include the other two men and the jostling cart.

Not now. Her mind, the trap that held her nightmares and cajoled her toward vengeance, screamed for her to stop.

Now. Now. NOW! Her heart, the endless hole where her hurt and her family had been cast, shrieked for her to continue.

She could take on three men at once, but she wouldn't be able to kill them all. If she did, she would never uncover their location.

There was also the possibility of failure.

If she attacked and failed, Ian would die, and she wouldn't find Reginald.

The hate curling in her gut drew taut. She would *not* fail. She could not allow Reginald to live.

Her gaze fell on the limp figure in the cart. She'd made a promise to Ian, one she intended to keep. There had already been enough death without his blood staining her hands.

But where the hell were they?

The forest twisted and tangled far into the distance. Wherever they were going, most likely, they would not arrive soon.

Another glance at the high sun confirmed Sylvi did not have much time. She'd failed her family in the face of these brutal men. She would not fail another.

First, she needed a plan. She eyed the cart. One man rode on the horse pulling it, and the other man rode beside it, nearest her. Gregor headed the front of their small retinue on horseback. As much as she'd like to ensure he died during Ian's rescue, she could not make him her focus.

She gave him one last long look and tried to shove the weight from her heart.

Poison still laced the blade of her dagger. Only a small amount had been used on Ian, and she'd been careful not to wipe the blood from the blade lest she lose the poison. She pumped her legs harder to run faster, to get ahead of the party. Her steps were careful on the ground as she picked her way through patches of snow, light and easy, quiet enough for her efforts to be masked by the rattle of the carriage's great wooden wheels.

Her breath came hard but steady, and she slowed. The carriage was several paces away. Perfect.

She edged closer to the trail and crouched in the low brush. Her breath fogged in white puffs, and the cold burned a path down her throat. She knew she ought to go for Gregor first, yet if there were complications, the man with the cart could get away. With Ian.

She waited until they passed before launching from the foliage. The man on the horse, beside the cart, was caught off guard at her attack—an easy victim for a swipe to his thigh with the clean side of the blade.

He cried out, but she did not stop. She ran around his horse, blocking herself from the view of the remaining two men, and leapt onto the cart, careful to avoid stepping on Ian. The telltale *whump* of a body sliding from a horse sounded to her right. A horse began to gallop somewhere in front, the thundering hoof beats muffled by the forest floor but nevertheless discernible.

Gregor. Her heart tried to lurch from her chest. The coward.

Sylvi gritted her teeth. She could not think of him now.

She steadied herself against the sway of the carriage and pulled back the poisoned dagger.

The man on the horse pulling the cart turned, but the dagger had already been loosed and sailed at him. It slammed into his shoulder. A cocky smirk lit his face, and he reached for his sword. The poison was quicker.

His arm fell limp, and the arrogant smile melted from his face before he, too, slid from his horse.

Sylvi jumped from the wooden frame of the cart and raced in front of its horse, who had easily stepped over the body of its rider. Gregor's retreating back showed in the distance.

A split-second decision needed to be made. Grab the horse from the first man she had killed, catch Gregor and force him to tell her where Reginald was. Or save Ian.

Both could not be done.

A curse tore from Sylvi's throat. Damn her and her promise.

At least she knew Reginald and the other men must be near. This area would give her a better place to begin her search for him than she'd had in all these years.

She reached for the cart horse's reins and carefully stopped the beast before the cart could roll over the body on the trail. Ian had already been abused enough without being knocked to the ground.

Sylvi's body quaked with the energy spent on the battle, every muscle once powerfully strong now almost slack. Her breath dragged in and out of her chest.

Gregor would not be back, or at least she assumed so. Cowardly men did not return, at least not alone.

She fell beside Ian on shaking knees and tried to shove aside the incredible weight of regret. The gilded morning light splayed over his colorless face like a death shroud. She pulled the vial from her pocket and sucked in a breath, stilling the trembling of her fingers to slide the stopper free better. Spilling the chances of his survival would not do. Especially with what she'd sacrificed to save him.

She lifted his head and pulled his lower lip down with her thumb. His flesh was still warm and pliant beneath her fingertips. Like the living.

With careful precision, she dribbled a small amount of the liquid into his mouth. It was a painfully slow process, delivering only several drops at a time, but she could not risk spilling any.

Percy, not Sylvi, knew all the proper measurements and calculations of the concoction she'd devised. Sylvi would not see Ian dead for her ignorance.

Thoughts of Gregor clawed at her mind while she administered the antidote. Her head and heart warred over her decision like two dogs tearing at the remains of something ravaged. She'd kept her promise and had done the right thing.

What if this had been the one chance to question Gregor? What if he could not be found later?

What if the opportunity had teased over her fingertips before slipping away?

Regardless of what the answers might be, she had made her decision. Gregor was too far gone even to try to go after. If he came back with reinforcements, she would handle them. In fact, she rather hoped they did, and that one of them might be Reginald.

Her ears strained to pick up sounds of horses making their way toward her while she carefully fed Ian the antidote and found none. Damn.

The last liquid fell from the vial and disappeared between Ian's parted lips. Not a drop had leaked from the corners of his mouth.

She waited.

Nothing.

She looked up at the sky, where the sun boldly proclaimed a

solid three hours had passed. Had she miscalculated the time? Her blood chilled. Had she been too late?

She stared at his handsome face.

He did not move.

She braced herself over him, every part of her begging him to be alive. He had trusted her, putting his life in her hands. Surely, she had not failed him.

She had sacrificed so much to keep her promise. She could not lose a life she'd intended to save.

"Don't be dead," she muttered through clenched teeth. "Don't be dead."

Minutes ticked by. Ian lay there, unmoving, and her heart crumpled further into her chest.

She had failed him. Just as she'd failed her family.

Ian was dead.

Everything hurt. Ian's ribs blared hot rays of pain through his body, his head pounded and damn it if his bollocks weren't still aching.

Exhaustion lay on him like a heavy blanket, tempting him to remain in slumber forever. There, he could easily forget all the pain. His heartbeat came in long, slow, lulling pounds.

Sleep.

He let himself glide toward it.

A muffled garble interrupted his relief as if someone were yelling underwater. Far away and too thick to comprehend.

Pain exploded on his cheek. He'd just been struck.

He forced his eyes open at the affront. Brilliant golden light burned into his eyes and seared his aching skull, and everything was cold. He sucked in a breath and slammed his eyes shut. If he were dead, at least he'd gone to heaven.

But he wasn't yet ready to be dead.

"Ian." A woman's voice sounded—her accent like those of the wealthy English, her voice husky and commanding.

He kept his eyes closed. "I'm no' ready to die."

"Then you should probably open your eyes." Her reply came out dry and slightly sarcastic.

"Are all the angels in heaven as cynical as ye, or are ye the only one?"

The angel sighed. "You're not dead."

He scrunched his eyes tighter. If he did not see the golden light, he could avoid the truth he knew in his soul—that he was indeed dead.

At least he'd made it to heaven, a feat he hadn't thought possible with the stains on his soul.

"If you were dead, would you hurt so much?" she asked.

A valid point.

He grunted and squinted his eyes open to the blazing gold.

"Ian." Gone was the dry sarcasm, and in its place was a breathless relief.

His sight adjusted to the blinding light, and a woman came into focus, only inches away. Pale blonde hair framed her face, her cheekbones high and angular, an authoritative appearance to match the voice. Her lips and cheeks were flushed a warm pink, and her eyes were pale blue and wide with concern.

Concern for him.

God, she was beautiful, his angel. Not the soft-mouthed innocent type, but a vigilante—powerful and strong.

"My beautiful angel," he whispered. "Kiss me."

She pulled back slightly, her brow furrowed. "No."

He hadn't expected that. "Please?"

"No." She did not come closer.

"I think..." He swallowed, slathering on an extra layer of pity as he'd done as a lad trying to get sweets. "I think I might have died."

Her breath sucked in. "But you're not dead."

"I'll know I'm real if ye kiss me."

"Hell wouldn't be this bloody cold." She propped a hand on her hip, her fingers framed over the hilt of a dagger jutting from her belt. "You're being ridiculous."

"But I might be dead."

"You're not," she answered firmly.

He raised his brows at her. "I should be sure."

She grumbled in irritation and leaned over him to press a quick kiss to his forehead.

He pointed to his lips and almost regretted the effort for how much it hurt.

She rolled her eyes but bowed over him to touch a kiss to his lips. Her mouth was soft and warm against his, and when she sat back, her cheeks were an even brighter red than they'd been before.

Ian liked that he'd had that effect on her.

She crossed her arms over her chest, the restlessness evidence of her obvious discomfort. "Are you happy?"

He grinned.

His angel scoffed and grabbed him by the armpits. She hauled him upright, and pain blazed through his body. He loosed a curse.

"Told you you're not dead," she muttered.

They were on an open forest trail in a rough-hewn cart. Though the sun had come up, patches of snow still clung to the tops of bushes and the forest floor on either side of them. The woman in front of him, his angel, wore black trews and a black léine. Her hair was drawn back in a wild tangle of white-blonde braids. A single black ribbon adorned her neck.

It all came rushing back to him then. The fight they had when she'd tried to kill him, the deal they'd made.

"Ye kicked me in the bollocks," he declared.

She gave him a pointed look. "That was hours ago. You're fine."

Sylvi. Yes, her name was Sylvi. His thoughts were sludgy and thick. Most likely an effect of the poison. And hopefully not a long-lasting one.

"Ye owe me a belt," he added.

She glanced around them. "You'll get it later. I want to search for Reginald's camp. Can you walk?"

He leaned forward, and pain shot through his ribs. "How much did they pay ye for killing me, anyway?"

"You don't need anything else to make you cockier." She caught him under the arms, more gently this time, and helped pull him to his feet without answering his question.

A body lay in front of the cart, and another lay behind them several feet away. A vengeful angel indeed.

"Did ye kill them all?" he asked.

After he was to his feet, she hopped off the cart, obviously ready to relinquish care of him. "No, Gregor got away when I attacked. There were only three of them. Him and these two." She nodded to the bodies. "That was over an hour ago. You took a long time to wake up." Her voice held a slight strain.

He slanted a glance at her. "Were ye worried about me, my angel?"

Her face darkened into a scowl. "Don't call me that."

"Ye were worried."

She stared up at him, and he tried not to waver on his unsteady legs. "Don't make me regret my decision to stay any more than I already do. I let him go to save you."

He couldn't help the grin pulling at his lips any more than she could probably help the grimace of irritation. "Then ye'll regret it even more now that I'm awake."

"I already do." She made her way to the horse attached to the cart and began to unhitch the beast. "We need to hurry so we can try to find them."

"If it was over an hour since Gregor left, as ye say, then it won't matter where Reginald and his men were camped. They are already gone."

Four

Reginald and his men were gone.

Sylvi stood up from the scorch of earth where a fire had once been; the charred remains still warm. Their encampment was a mere twenty minutes from where she had attacked Gregor's party. If she had abandoned Ian, she would have found them.

Instead, she'd gathered him onto one horse with her and trailed the second horse at their side as they followed the trail to the remnants of the abandoned encampment.

She glanced to where Ian lay propped against a tree with the tethered horses while she examined the area where her enemy had recently been. A glossy sheen of sweat glistened on Ian's pale skin, and his eyes kept fluttering closed. At least he was wrapped in the thick blanket to keep him from the biting chill.

Still, guilt twisted in her stomach. He had trusted her, and she had almost failed him by waiting too long. And even still, she lamented her choice.

The coins she'd received in payment from Gregor hung heavy at her side. The desire to scrape her dagger over each one left a restlessness dancing over her nerves. But she dared not do it in front of Ian.

He'd have questions. And would probably be incessant about them. The very thought sent an irritated tightening over the back of her neck.

She strode over to him and put a skin of ale to his mouth. "Drink."

He turned his head to the side. "I canna drink anymore."

"Drink."

He squinted up at her. His light brown eyes were the color of honey in the sunlight. "Ye're trying to kill me with drink."

"No, I'm trying to get you to purge the poison from your body." Percy had often spoken of the benefit of drinking considerable amounts of liquid after having ingested a tonic one no longer wanted in their body.

His jaw tensed with a grimace, but he took the ale from her and took a swig of it.

"Keep it. Keep drinking and try to stay awake."

His hand fell limp in his lap, fingers gently curled around the neck of the skin. "I wouldna need to purge it if ye hadna poisoned me."

"They won't be looking for you anymore."

"Nay, but now they'll be looking for ye." He punctuated his statement with a steady stare up at her.

She looked around the encampment, where wheat-colored grass lay in dented patches, indicating something large had been placed there. Like tents, carriages. They had obviously been there for several days, but it was impossible for her to tell how many men. Ian had said they moved fast, and they were already well over an hour ahead of her.

A single trail led from the camp into the woods, riddled with multiple pockmarks where hoofprints dented the shallow snow.

She regarded Ian in his miserable state. While sympathetic to his condition, she could not let this opportunity pass. She untethered one horse and swung up onto its back. "Stay here."

"Ye're leaving me?" he asked, his tone incredulous.

"I need to follow the trail. Either I return to help you, or you can take the horse when you feel able."

She glanced down at him and regretted doing so. The sickly pallor of his skin indicated he would not be getting on his horse anytime soon. She hissed a command from between her teeth and plunged out of the clearing to the trail.

The marks were easy to follow for a good hour before they met at a crossroads on the main path. Many wagon wheels had etched the soggy earth, as well as countless shoes and hooves. The three other directions had similar indentations, making it impossible to figure out which way they had gone.

Sylvi ventured into each of the three other directions but without success. She was not skilled enough at tracking to discern from other wagon wheels which ones belonged to Reginald's group.

Dejected but determined, she returned to where Ian remained propped on the tree. His lips had a slightly bluish tinge. He needed to return to his room at the inn.

"You need to get warm." She knelt at his side and slid her hands beneath his arms to help him up. His body was firm with muscle and flexed against her grip in an effort to help.

"It would appear we're no' the only ones after Reginald and his men," he said.

"Oh?"

He braced his hand against the rough bark, wobbling slightly. "Two men were looking for them. I told them I dinna see anyone in the group and was taking a rest as I'm ill." His bloodless lips lifted in a ghost of a smile. "They got close enough to me to see my clothes were finer than that of a marauder, and then they were all too eager to leave me be. I guess yer potion has several benefits, aye?"

Two men. She'd seen two men on her return but had given them little thought as they had seemed well dressed and were alone. Reginald clearly had many enemies. Or perhaps if he was still dealing in fake gold, he was on the edge of being found out.

Sylvi wanted to scrape the coins. She rubbed her fingers together at her side to obliterate the pressing need. Had she not been so concerned about Ian earlier, she would have done it while he remained asleep. Only she'd not once considered the coins when she'd thought him dead by her doing.

Her voice was hard when she spoke. "I hope you are well rested on the morrow, for we will leave at first light."

"We? Ye like me enough to keep me around, my angel." He winked up at her.

The name crept up her spine and clenched at each muscle along the way. He had been so foolish when he woke, calling her his angel. Demanding a kiss.

Her face went hot.

Why the hell had she kissed him anyway?

To get him to stop talking about her being an angel. Or maybe out of guilt for having put him in that situation. Or maybe even curiosity.

He'd been a pathetic thing when he first woke. Eyes glassy, face still pale.

But also handsome, if she were being honest. His lips were full beneath his beard. Full and soft. Warm eddies swam low in her stomach.

"Don't call me that," she snapped. She hated the weakness of emotions. They pulled her from her task. Had she not allowed herself to be drawn into promising Ian his safety, she would be tracking Reginald now, and Gregor would already be dead. "You know more about these men than I do, and they have evaded me for far too long."

"And what of me?" Ian asked in a bland tone. "What if I have somewhere to be?"

She rolled her eyes. "You spent the last week wandering the town from tavern to tavern. You're aimless."

He went quiet for a moment, and when she finally looked down at him, he drew another sip of ale from the skin. His gaze on the surrounding area was thoughtful.

He wasn't looking at her. She could scrape one coin now.

Just one.

"I need to relieve myself of all this ale." He hefted himself to an unsteady standing position.

"Dare I ask if you need my help?" she offered warily.

The quirk of his mouth told her a foolish reply was on its way before he could even open his lips. She put up her hand to stop him. "Just go."

He staggered away, at least offering her the courtesy of not doing it in her presence. His gait was wobbly but not tipping to either side enough to warrant concern. He'd be fine.

She turned away from him and opened the sack at her side. Her fingers trembled. With haste or need, she did not know.

An image of her father flashed in her mind, as large and strong as Odin, his eyes ocean blue and his hair the same white blonde as hers. He held a coin in front of her, his hands seeming too large to do the skilled work of a goldsmith. But he was a master of his craft, creating the most intricate pieces of jewelry.

His latest commissioned masterpiece had been perched between his thick thumb and forefinger. The gold winked at her. More money than she'd ever held. He lifted a tool shaped like a miniature pick and scraped it over the top of the coin. The expertly applied gold had peeled back to reveal the flat, gray metal beneath.

Those men had paid her father so dearly over the prior year to create batches of those perfect coin imitations and then killed her family. Those men had known where the coins were stored in the shop, and they had taken every last one of them.

Though it'd been over seventeen years ago, she still scraped every coin that passed her hand, seeking a path to the killers.

She grasped the first coin in her palm and dragged the tip of a new dagger over its shiny surface, scoring the gold to reveal gold beneath. She pulled up the second coin. Gold.

The third. Gold.

She clutched the fourth in her dampening palm and scraped.

The gold curled away in a wiry strip and revealed the flat, gray metal beneath.

*

IAN LET HIS BODY SWAY IN TIME WITH THE HORSE. IT was easier to give in to the motion than fight it.

His breath huffed out in front of him in a white fog. The cold prickled against his skin despite the heavy plaid he'd wrapped around his shoulders. No matter how much ale he drank or how many times he pissed, his muscles still refused to cooperate with the same strength and ease as before.

Sylvi rode ahead of him, her back straight, her face locked in determination. She had peppered him with questions about Reginald and the men earlier in their journey.

"Where did Reginald like to go?" Everywhere, not visiting the same place twice.

"How many men were in the camp?" Around two dozen.

"What sort of weapons and specialties did they have?" They were mercenaries and marauders with various tactics.

"Did he know much about Reginald?" He knew enough.

"Had he traveled with them?" At a time.

She had grown suspicious then, her gaze hard and her following questions asked with such an edge to her tone he'd decided to scale down his replies about his association with the men.

When she'd asked about the gold coins, he'd declared himself ignorant of any activities. For the most part, he had been. He knew of them and that Reginald had been involved for some time. In truth, Ian was being brought closer into the inner circle before he'd left, only days away from uncovering what Sylvi wanted. And he was damn glad he'd left when he did.

After a while, when Sylvi evidently had enough information to placate her frantic mind, she went completely silent as though digesting all the information he'd provided.

Ian had wanted to protest coming on this journey, but Sylvi had been right about the week prior to her attacking him. Painfully right. He *was* aimless.

Lost, alone and aimless.

Ian clung to his horse while his mind wandered over his predicament. Despite the burn of used muscles, his grip was too light, and he rocked dangerously from side to side on the beast. His body was too weak, too uncooperative. He glanced at Sylvi, but she had not seen his lack of balance. He gritted his teeth and righted himself before collapsing against the horse's neck from the effort.

It wasn't the leaving of his home Ian regretted—it was how hard it was to find a new place in the world. Being a mercenary should have been so easy, but not at this cost. Ian had not left a place of barbarous punishment for a life where the weak suffered.

He was no farmer, no innkeeper, no blacksmith or baker. The various jobs he had picked up on the road had taught him all that. He was nothing more than the wayward eldest son of a cruel laird, stained with the crimes he could not stop.

Ian pulled himself into a slouched sit, feeling slightly recovered from the exhaustion of steadying himself on the horse. He would not have Sylvi look back and find him weakly slung over the animal.

She might not be his future, but he might find something while assisting her. If nothing else, he could help her right some wrong. His angel, indeed. She might ease his soul more than she realized.

After all, there was a reason she hated Reginald and his men. And with Reginald being the arse he was, Ian had no doubt it was something bad.

He wanted to ask what the affront had been but knew he'd have better luck getting his angel to dance with him than he'd likely have at getting her to speak to him.

All the women he'd been with in his life had spoken without seeming to breathe between their prattling. Now he'd finally found a woman who didn't care to speak at all, and it made him near mad to know what hummed in her mind.

She looked back at him. "It will take us six days to arrive if you don't hurry."

At least now Ian knew what she was thinking.

Ian was glad he'd expended the effort to sit up and tried to straighten his back, but his body was suddenly too heavy for even that. "Maybe I like spending time with ye." He winked to cover the grimace.

"There are better ways to spend time together than on the open road in the middle of a Scottish February."

"If that's a suggestion, I'll gladly take ye up on it." He paused and grinned at her. "My angel."

She turned away in disgust, just as he'd hoped, and he let his body sag forward on the horse. Holding himself upright while she looked back at him was a nearly impossible feat. His charm had no effect on her as it did on other women. At least it worked to his advantage this time.

He'd rather die than let her see him still so weak.

Truth be told, even if she had been suggesting a tumble, he wouldn't have the strength for even that.

Frustration knotted in his gut. He'd always been strong, skilled with a weapon. He'd relied on it for piquing the interest of tavern lasses, he'd used it to keep himself safe and protect others, and he'd used it to provide food and work after leaving home.

His body seemed like the damn ale skin Sylvi kept forcing on him, a floppy casing with naught but liquid inside.

He looked up and found her staring back at him, her brow furrowed. She turned her horse right so abruptly that Ian struggled to get his to turn in time as well. Streams of smoke billowed trails over the distant treetops. A village was nearby.

He hoped to God they were going there.

"Is this yer way of suggesting..." he asked with a bawdy grin.

"You're too weak to ride."

Her blunt reply lanced through his pride and staggered his ability to parry with a witty response.

"I can keep going." He hoped he had the grit to match his words. Ordinarily, he would. He had always been able to take on physical challenges with ease.

Sylvi did not so much as turn back to glance at him.

"In fact, I can go all day and all night." He winced at his awful jest.

If he lost his strength from the poison, it would be one thing. But if he lost his sense of humor, death might as well take him now.

Within the lesser part of an hour, the hooves of their horses met the churned snow and mud of the small village. With only two inns to choose from, Sylvi had selected the one with its door properly hung and the sign new enough to still have visible grain in the wood.

He hadn't bothered to speak anymore on the way inside nor as they made their way to their room. Not even to make a flirtatious comment about them sharing a room. He was too damn tired.

She nodded toward the narrow bed when they arrived. "Rest."

He did not protest. Weariness pulled at him with such insistence that he barely noticed the simple room's appearance, noting only the thick blue plaid laid out over the bed.

He collapsed onto it, barely noting the creak of ropes beneath him before sleep claimed him.

It was much later when he woke. He was unsure how long he'd slept, but the room had gone dark and cold. The hearth did not glow with so much as a single red ember. He could not see to tell if Sylvi was still inside with him. He pulled his arms to his chest and squeezed, testing his weary muscles.

The strength there constricted, and hope flickered through him. Was he stronger again?

He straightened his legs until his muscles flexed, and a whisper of his former power sang through them. He swung his legs over the edge of the bed, and his stomach contracted with the easy effort. He wanted to stand and perform his battle exercises and feel the life in his body. He pushed out of bed and hit something soft and warm in the dark. His feet went out from underneath him and sent him crashing to the ground.

The chill of an icy blade touched his throat.

"Sylvi?"

The weapon pulled away from him. "What the hell are you doing?"

His face went hot, and he was grateful for the darkness. "What the hell were ye doing next to my bed?"

"Sleeping." Her footsteps were heavy on the floor, suggesting she still wore her boots. The splintering shift of wood sounded, followed by the familiar clacking of flint. Sparks glowed in the hearth. A pop and crackle came from the same direction, and the warm glow of a new fire lit the room.

The heat of a fresh fire washed over Ian's chilled skin like the glow of heaven. He frowned at her. "Why were ye sleeping there?"

Sylvi set the flint on the small table, away from the fire. "I was protecting you."

Five

Whatever foolish reply Sylvi had expected from Ian did not come.

"I dinna need yer protection," he said after a brief silence.

She almost laughed. He had been damn near sliding off his horse when they finally pulled into whatever this cluster of homes called their village. Like hell, he didn't need her protection.

His face held a solemn look, and it kept so much as a smile from her lips.

Apparently, he did not see a jest in everything. Perhaps he was not the fool she'd initially assumed. Although now that his joking had ceased, she craved it over the serious expression.

Perhaps she ought to apologize for having stripped away his humor with her bluntness. And she might have if she were the apologizing type.

Which she was not.

But then, neither was she the type to share a room with a man. The circumstances were, of course, different now. She had to ensure he didn't leave, not when he had more information. What was more, she knew even if he were at his full strength and tried to accost her in the night, she could easily put a blade in his heart.

Yet now he challenged her in his weaker state. It was almost endearing. She slid the dagger from her side. "Prove it."

"I've had my time with yer poisoned dagger." He eyed her blade. "Let's just say I willna be jealous if ye save that trick for another man." He winked, and his serious expression lifted to be more jovial.

"It's not the same dagger." Truth be told, she'd had enough of the poison herself. Still, she put the weapon back into its sheath on her belt. "But I don't need a blade."

"Nor do I." He crouched low in preparation for their battle.

Weak firelight flickered over his face. The orange glow masked the pallor of his skin, making it difficult to discern if he was still pale. Regardless, she would go easy on him.

She waited for him to strike first. He ducked low and swung for her stomach. She swept her hand down hard and knocked his hit off target. His attempt had been a strong one.

He threw a punch at her face with enough speed that she narrowly avoided it. She darted out of his way. His foot flew behind her feet, and his body knocked against hers, so she tumbled backwards.

She would no longer go easy on him.

She grasped his arms as she fell, hauling him to the floor along with her. He fell on top of her with his full weight. The breath fled her body in an *oof*.

He pinned her beneath him and grinned. "How much coin did ye get for me?"

It wasn't only the weight of him keeping her in place but the power of his muscles. He was indeed a strong man. She'd noticed it the previous night when they fought. It was not often Sylvi was taken down by anyone. Then again, she'd underestimated him just now.

She knew better than to underestimate. Doing so had been a foolish oversight.

"Come on then." He cocked his head toward her as if they were in on the same shared secret. "How much did ye get for killing me?"

"More than you're worth." She whipped her legs from under his and flipped him, so she sat atop him. The warm eddies in her stomach whirled into a chaotic flurry. His legs were firm with muscle where they pressed against her inner thighs. She'd meant only to hold him to the ground, but now the awareness of their position scorched through her.

She straddled him just below his crotch, her hands spread over his strong arms in her attempt to pin him. Still, the position was primal. Sexual.

The quiet wrought by her sudden realization charged the air with a crackling and completely unexpected attraction. That damn arrogant smile quirked at his lips, and she remembered all too well how soft his lips were beneath the prickle of his beard.

She had been with several other men before, a sweaty battle of bodies seeking to slake the fires of lust. Encounters as quickly left as they had been made, with no thought to them after. The hungry pulse in her center demanded as much now. But she was far too pragmatic to give in to such weakness.

"Ye've got me, my angel." The grin spread over his face, unabashed and bold. "What will ye do with me?"

"Maybe I ought to use another poisoned dagger." She bit the words out rather than give in to what made her cheeks burn hot.

She shoved off him.

He rose from the ground in a fluid, graceful movement and caught her hand. She jerked back from him, her arm cocked back in preparation to continue their battle.

His brown eyes were honey-warm in the firelight, and his lips were full and tempting. "Thank ye for keeping me safe, Sylvi."

His nearness clutched at her chest and squeezed out all the air. But not before she noticed the draw of his scent, spicy masculine and sunshine and something like pine.

She pulled away from him, putting the necessary distance

between them. "Thank you for not using a chamber pot when we fought this time."

His face split in a wide smile, and he laughed, the sound a deep timbre, so lighthearted that she could not help the pull of lightness at her own heart. She realized then that for all the jests he'd told, she'd never once actually heard him laugh.

She found she rather liked it. Grudgingly, of course.

"I dinna know ye actually did jest." He winked at her. "Ye've a bit of humor in ye after all."

"Don't expect it from me again." She turned from him and made her way to the bed. "If you're thus recovered, I'll take my time in the bed."

"We could share it." His voice was silken in the quiet and teased a ripple of decadent chills down her spine.

"I think not." She flopped onto the bed. Darts of the straw beneath the rough sheet jabbed into her skin, but it was far better than the hard ground. She slid her feet beneath the covers and found it still held his warmth.

And his smell.

Though she told herself she didn't want to, she discreetly breathed in and held her breath, savoring. Her body hummed with the closeness of him. The hot pulse between her legs pounded with insistence, a raw need unlike any base desire she'd experienced.

The rustle of his clothing behind her told her he was settling on the ground with her pillow and the spare blanket she'd laid there.

What would it be like to have him in her bed?

The thought flitted in her mind before she could stop it.

She clenched her eyes as if doing so might prevent the idea from settling there. But laying in the bed, still so reminiscent of him, breathing in his scent, having him so damnably close, she could not stop the thought from rising forefront once more.

Her thighs were warm with the memory of his powerful body between them. What would it be like to allow his hands on her body, his full lips on her skin, those powerful hands peeling away her clothing...

Her breath hitched in the darkness, and she rolled to the other side so the pillow beneath her blazing cheek was cool once more.

She tried to will away her desire, the ridiculousness of it. The man who murdered her family, the one denoted with the half ear, was close. Vengeance was within her grasp. The last thing she needed crowding her thoughts was lust for a man she would never see again when this was done.

But no matter how hard she tried, she could not stop the insistent hum of desire from blazing through her veins and keeping sleep at bay.

A SOFT CRY SOUNDED THROUGH IAN'S SLUMBER. His eyes flew open to find the room lit with the gray light of fresh dawn.

"*Mor.*" The feminine voice was small. Scared.

Ian sat up straight on the hard floor, and his back gave a stiff couple of pops for his effort. God, he hated sleeping on floors.

"*Mor.*"

Ian looked to the bed and found Sylvi curled in a ball, her face scrunched with pain. Tears shone on her cheeks.

Tears.

Shock shook away the groggy effects of sleep. Sylvi seemed the kind of woman to drink the tears of her enemies, not make them herself.

"*Min mor.*" Were it not for the parting of Sylvi's mouth in time with the frightened whimper, he would never have believed it to be her who had spoken.

He wanted to sit on the bed and wrap his arms around her to protect her from the demons in her dreams. But he'd slept along-side enough warriors to know waking a skilled fighter mid-nightmare was a bad idea. At the very least, it was a damn good way to get punched.

Ian knelt beside the bed and crossed his arms over his chest to keep from touching her. "It's all right, lass."

A sob choked in her throat, and she began to weep, a soft, pathetic sound like a child.

Ian's heart squeezed so hard that it shoved the breath from his chest. "It's all right, lass. Ye're safe."

Her face relaxed slightly, and her quiet crying ceased.

He tensed his arms where they were crossed over his chest. He wanted nothing more than to curl her against him and soothe away all her hurt.

"No' only are ye safe," he said quietly, "ye could take on anyone who fought ye."

She rolled over. He could no longer see her face and stared at her white-blonde hair, a mix of glossy strands and plaited braids. She made no more sound, and so he eased himself to the firm floor once more. But sleep did not come.

Instead, he lay awake, cradling Sylvi's pain in his heart and wondering what could cause such a strong woman to break.

Sylvi was watching him again.

Ian knew this, of course, because he had been unable to take his eyes off her.

The forest had thinned around them, giving way to the small town they sought for rest. His body was stronger now, still not restored to his former glory, but definitely stronger.

Sylvi sat atop her horse with her back straight and her shoulders squared. Her chin slightly lifted as if daring the world to try to take her on.

And God help the world if it tried.

Several people gaped up at her as she passed, and Ian's chest swelled with pride to be with her.

She was powerful and magnificent. Not at all the kind of woman who sobbed in her sleep.

Yet after he'd witnessed it, she seemed so much more than a cold warrior, and he liked her all the more for it. And he had already liked her a considerable amount.

Her cool blue gaze slid over to him and darted away. Caught.

Ian grinned. Warmth flowed through him despite the merciless bite of the wind. He knew attraction when he met it—a hum of mutual need, a sweet taste in the air melting between them.

Theirs was a careful dance of discretion and inescapable curiosity. The most delicious kind.

"You made it an entire day on the road." Sylvi threw a glance in his direction. "It appears you are recovering well."

"I've always been a man with good vitality." He winked at her to give his words a flirtatious slant.

Color blossomed in Sylvi's cheeks, like red berries against snow—impossible to miss and incredibly beautiful.

She looked away quickly. "This one." She nodded toward an inn near the back of town with a clean facade and no intoxicated patrons slouched at its entrance. An absence of drunks and whores usually meant cleaner, more hospitable accommodation.

Ian hopped off his horse when they arrived and turned to Sylvi. He held up his hand in a mute offer to assist her from her steed.

She raised a pale brow. "What the hell are you doing?"

"Being a considerate man as my ma taught me." He tilted his head. "And possibly trying to get the opportunity to caress the waist of an angel in doing so."

Sylvi scoffed. "Not much of a gentleman."

But she placed her hand in his and let him catch her as she slid from the horse to ease her descent to the muddy ground. His hands went beneath her thick mantle to ensure he held her firmly. Her body was warm and strong against his palms.

Her gaze met his, and heat blazed between them. But there was no shy glance of interest like Ian was used to with other women. Not Sylvi, not his vengeful angel. A predatory look glinted in her eyes and sent a wicked tremor of excitement coursing through him.

His hands lingered on her slender waist. She kept her eyes locked on his and gently pushed his hands down to her hips and off her body. "I'll go secure the room while you handle the horses."

Without waiting for a response, she turned and left him standing there in the mud.

He swallowed.

The room.

Meaning only one.

All the heat in his body rushed to his cock at the prospect. He was glad for the large mantle he wore lest he make quite the spectacle of being blatantly aroused while tending to the horses no less.

Ian led the horses to the stable and tried to think of many other things: the steps for securing the horses overnight; the careful battle moves he practiced regularly; Agnes, his mother's maid, and how her jowls quivered like jelly. All things decidedly not sexual. Anything to discourage the roar of lust swelling at his crotch.

If he entered their room with his poker pointing directly at her and he was mistaken, she might try to cut it off.

Besides, if he were right, he'd have no problem being at the ready for his angel.

He tended the horses faster than he'd ever done and was most likely more thorough than ever with his intense concentration on the task. His efforts had paid off, and the discomfort of arousal had softened into something far gentler.

Still, his heart pounded as he climbed the stairs and headed to the door where the tavern wench had directed him. The lass had given him the shy smile of interest. One he easily ignored in favor of Sylvi's predatory glance.

Six

Sylvi's mind pulled in too many directions and yanked her heart along with it. The palpable frustration at having lost Reginald and the opportunity to avenge her family was forefront. Always forefront.

Urgency grappled at her nerves to get to Kindrochit in case Reginald sought her out for her failed mission. She didn't know who the two men were who had attempted to find Reginald and his band of marauders, but she would not put the ladies of Kindrochit Castle at risk. Not that she needed to worry about her girls. They knew well how to defend themselves.

Yet through it all, she had a nagging fear she'd pushed Ian too hard on the trail, and it warred with her need for expediency. He wouldn't admit to needing time to recover, even if he had fought well.

Hell, she didn't blame him. She was never one to admit to weakness.

Then there was the lust.

Her skin still hummed with the memory of his touch, and her blood pounded through her veins. Everything in her seemed fixed on recalling the details of his charming grin and the softness of his warm mouth. Her mind even dredged up every suggestive comment he'd made and tethered it to the excitement robbing her of breath.

It was obnoxious, this distraction.

She'd never experienced lust on this level before. The other men had been easily enjoyed and left without complications. Not like with Ian, who stoked the heat of her interest to a searing need, and whose damaged relationship could cost her dearly.

Footsteps sounded outside the door and stopped. Her heart fluttered with uncustomary nervous anticipation. The latch creaked, and the door came open.

Ian came in, his cheeks and mouth red beneath his beard from the February chill. He'd still worn his kilt beneath the heavy mantle. Surely, his legs must be chilled.

She wanted to press the warmth of her body to the coolness of his. Her face, her mouth, her legs and the insistent heat throbbing between them.

"I don't like this." She spoke so abruptly that she startled even herself.

Ian raised his dark brows and scanned the plain square room with an exaggerated gaze. "We can get another room if ye like. Or go to another inn. There was one—"

"What's going on between us." Her face burned, and she inwardly stumbled over herself, all words and thoughts now an awkward, clumsy tangle.

"There's no' anything going on between us." His velvety tone teased over her nerves. "Yet."

Chills prickled pleasantly over her skin.

She unfastened her belt. "You're a ridiculous distraction."

His eyes followed the belt's descent to the wooden floor. "I personally like it." He did not move as if he feared he might somehow set her off.

Which he surely might.

Sylvi didn't know what she was capable of right then. Her hands shook with pent-up energy, like being ready for a battle that did not come.

"You like it?" She stalked over to him. "This anxiety? This obstruction to our task? This weakness of the body?" She didn't stop until she was directly in front of him.

He stared down at her with hot, hungry eyes. "Do you mean the way our bodies are savoring each other when we havena so much as touched? The way being near ye makes my skin warm with the awareness of ye?" His fingertips brushed the back of her hand, setting her skin on fire. "The way each innocent caress is as intimate as making love?"

Sylvi's nipples drew taut. She remembered to breathe, yet her head spun with a lack of air. "I do not like it," she whispered.

"Because ye canna control it." He stared deep into her eyes.

"Then let us have one another and be done with it." She shoved him back onto the mattress in the corner. He fell upon it with such ease he might have tossed himself there of his own volition. The bed ropes gave a long, low squeak.

She pulled off her boots, keeping her gaze fixed on him. Then the trews and the hose she wore beneath them for warmth. Next, she jerked the léine over her head and unwound the binding over her breasts until it was loose enough to shove down over her hips.

She let the tendril of cloth fall away and stepped back from her clothing, entirely unashamed of her nudity.

His mouth lifted in a lazy grin and her heart flipped into her stomach.

He nodded at the ribbon around her neck. "What about that?"

"No." The word came out in a hard snap.

He shrugged, unfastened his belt without getting up, and pulled open his kilt. His cock jutted in eager anticipation, and a thrill spiraled low in her stomach.

He sat up and tugged his léine off, his powerful abdominal muscles flexing and bunching with the movement.

He got to his feet. "It's only fair ye see me too." It was a comment made by a man who knew all too well how he looked naked.

And he *was* fine. His body appeared more chiseled from marble than wrought with mere flesh and bone. She could appreciate the effort such a body took.

Hours of practice. The willpower to do it regardless of the weather or any life events. Heat scorched through her, and her chest heaved for air.

Discipline.

A body like that took discipline.

Determination.

Fortitude.

The pulse of desire quickened.

She stepped forward and grasped the back of his head in her hand. Their mouths connected with a shared breath of eager passion. His lips were still cold from his recent venture outside, a thrilling contrast to the heat of his exploring tongue.

He growled and jerked her hard against him. The coarse hair on his naked chest brushed the sensitive tips of her nipples, and the link smoldering between them ignited into something wild and hot.

His hands roved over her body, skimming over her waist and sliding down her bottom. His touch made her body flame with heat and lust. Husky moans slipped unbidden from her throat, encouraging his brazen hands.

Her hands were greedy in their exploration of his body as well. His flesh was cool beneath her hands, cool and hard and great.

He was so damn strong, his body so beautifully honed by dedication to battle. She lowered her head and dragged her lips over the swell of his chest. Her teeth closed gently over his skin, nipping at his strength. Power and desire mingled within her into something uncontrollable.

His head fell back, and he groaned before grabbing her face and slanting his mouth over it once more. His lips were no longer cool but hot and savage with lust.

He bent over her, lowering his head, and flicked a tongue over her nipple. Delicious tingles of need slammed through her.

She sucked in a breath. The warmth of his mouth closed over her, and he sucked. Pleasure needled through her. It drilled into her brain and made her want nothing but his touch, his tongue, his cock.

His fingers slipped up her inner thighs and met the wetness between her legs. Her body almost exploded at his touch.

She wanted more. She wanted him. Her knees trembled with the desire for him to take her.

He slid his digit over the slit of her desire several times, rubbing at the place she sometimes touched when she was alone. Having someone else do it was far, far better. None of the few others she'd been with had tried to stoke her arousal like this with tender touches.

He groaned and slipped a finger inside her. Her body tightened around him, squeezing at the delicious sensations. She clutched his shoulders and gasped at the pleasure of it.

He kissed her with ravenous need. His beard rasped over her chin, but she barely noticed when his skilled hand kept her so distracted.

While it was obvious that he was an accomplished lover, she did not want the intimacy to be drawn out. She had a base need to be sated, pounding between her legs. It needed to be slaked, and their shared desire extinguished.

She slipped her leg over his waist and jerked him against her.

This would be done.

Now.

Ian clutched Sylvi's round bottom in his hands and stared at the lust shimmering in her eyes. His cock was clumsily shoved against her stomach, hard and jutting between them. He wanted to draw out his time with her, to love every inch of her body before claiming her.

Sylvi's leg tensed, pulling him more snugly against her.

First, he would lift her to the bed, lie her down, and—

Her hand wrapped around his cock and positioned him at the entrance of her wet heat. Pleasure raked greedy hands over him and shredded his thoughts of drawn-out lovemaking.

Her hands slid up his back, and she flexed her hips forward, teasing his cock inside her where they stood. Just the slightest bit.

Enough to drive him wild.

He widened his stance and lifted her other leg to his waist. She gripped him with her thighs and held her arms around the back of his neck. Holding her upright by her bottom with her wrapped perfectly around him, he thrust deep inside her. She gave a husky cry of pleasure, the sound beside his ear where it mingled with his own savage groan.

She was tight and hot and wet. He arched his back, easing slightly from her before thrusting back in, so the thrilling friction tingled where they were joined. Every flex of his hips drove him deeper into her. She tensed her thighs where she held to him, and the muscles of her sex squeezed around him, teasing him toward the edge of release far faster than he would like.

His bollocks went taut with the impending release.

"Yes." Her whisper was breathy in his ear and tickled the skin of his neck.

His entire body was alight with prickles of blissful sensitivity.

But, no, he was not ready to be done with her. Not yet.

He took two steps back while still holding her to him and sat down hard on the bed so she was in his lap. His thigh muscles burned with the effort, but he barely noticed.

Ian pulled her bottom forward, and she rolled her hips with the action, grinding him deeper inside her. So warm.

So tight.

A groan rasped from his throat.

She put a hand on his chest and pushed his torso down. A wicked smile lit her face.

She had the power now.

His cock jerked in anticipation and her eyes closed with pleasure.

He held her hips in his hands and guided her movements, slow at first. Very slow, lest he release too soon.

She rocked her body over him, her small breasts with their pert pink nipples bouncing with her effort. And her squeezing around him, clenching with each movement.

He wouldn't be able to last much longer.

Her breathing came faster, more frenzied.

She opened her eyes and watched him as she moved. God, she looked like a queen riding him. Beautiful, powerful. So tight.

His cock swelled with the need to release. He clamped his eyes shut.

He would not release before she climaxed.

Agnes's jowls.

Agnes's jowls.

Agnes's jowls.

Her sex constricted around him, clenching in telltale spasms, and her cries sounded the pitch of her fulfillment. His eyes flew open to capture the moment of her release. Her back arched, so her beautiful breasts pushed forward, and she watched him with red cheeks and sparkling eyes.

At that very moment, all the memories of Agnes's quivering jowls could not have held him back.

His body unleashed, and a roar edged through his gritted teeth. He held her to him until their bodies relaxed and their breathing finally slowed.

Sylvi watched him with hooded eyes, a light sheen of sweat glossing over her body, so she appeared to glow.

"Ye're so damn beautiful, my angel," he said.

She tilted her head in chastisement. "I told you not to call me that."

He didn't miss the whisper of a smile on her lips as she said it.

He pulled her down to him to cradle her against him, and silence descended. Usually, women became chatty after being loved, wanting to know about his scars, his adventures, his dreams. Usually, such conversations led to further arousal and more rutting. It was a cycle he much enjoyed.

But Sylvi lay quietly at his side. If not a bit rigid.

"How did ye come about being a mercenary?" he asked. "I mean, ye dinna meet many female assassins."

She remained quiet.

Bad topic, apparently.

"Have ye always lived in Scotland?" he asked, trying again.

"Yes."

At least it was a reply. Was it his imagination, or was she pressing herself away from him? He strengthened his grip on her shoulders ever so slightly. "What does minmore mean?"

Her body stiffened. "*Min mor?*"

"Aye."

She swallowed. "It means 'my mother' in Norwegian."

My mother. What had happened to her mother? "I dinna know ye spoke—"

"Where did you hear that?"

He hesitated. "Just around. Why dinna ye tell me ye spoke Norwegian?"

"Why would I have?" she asked.

"Ye're from Norway then?" It made sense now that he thought about it—her pale blonde hair, light blue eyes and fair skin. Her ferocity and wildness. How could a woman descended from Vikings be anything but beautifully potent?

Silence thickened the air again.

He cleared his throat. "I'm from deeper south. Oban. I've always been in Scotland. If ye canna tell by my accent." Though she couldn't see his face, he still grinned at his jest.

"A noble, correct?" The way she asked it bespoke contempt.

His gut gave a slight twist.

"A laird's son. I grew up in Dunstaffnage Castle. My da is Donald Campbell of Oban, Laird of Clan Campbell." Once he'd finished speaking, he realized his voice was lacking pride.

He was not proud of his father. He was not proud of what he'd left behind. Obviously—or he'd be there now.

She turned slightly toward him and regarded him with a wary stare. "Why are you not there now?"

"I left over a year ago." He winked at her. "I appreciate yer concern."

Her gaze flicked up in a halfhearted eye roll. He couldn't help but chuckle at the response he'd almost come to expect.

Here, most women would press him for more information. They'd want to know why he left. If he was still going to be laird someday. If they might have the opportunity to be lady of a fine castle.

Sylvi lay beside him without speaking. A chill descended on their bodies, and Ian pulled the thin cover over them both. Immediately, their shared heat blazed to life and warmed his cool skin.

"What are ye thinking?" he asked. Never had he needed to work so hard for a post-rutting conversation with a lass.

"The castle you lived in. Dunstaffnage is highly defensible," she replied. "The entire mass of it accessed only by one small door, and even that only reached by a drawbridge. It's impressive."

Her blatant disregard for his personal story and the admiration of the damn castle rankled him more than he cared to admit. "Aye. The laird is an arse, though. It's why I couldna stay."

"And why is that?"

Finally. She wanted to know about him. And he suddenly found himself hesitant to share more, especially when so much was shaded with the ugliness of shame.

Seven

"I gave up my lairdship." Ian said it like a boast. For surely it was, in his opinion.

She rolled against him with more interest now. "That's a powerful position. Why would you do that?"

The fire in the hearth was beginning to die. No wonder the chill seemed to be pressing deeper into him.

"My da had been grooming me to be laird, to take over for him someday." Ian eased himself from the bed. The hair on his arms and legs rose with the cold air embracing him. "It was no' exciting work. Settling squabbles, collecting rents, ensuring farmers were happy."

He strode over to the waning fire and added a split log to the hearth. The flames woke with hunger and licked over the dry wood. He added two more for good measure until the heat blazing against his skin was blissfully uncomfortable.

"Why did you leave?" she asked.

Ian's heart gave a familiar wrench, the way it always did when he thought of Simon and Simon's father. The old man had been doomed, and there had been nothing Ian could do to stop it.

Simon, however, had not understood. After the execution of Simon's father, Ian's childhood friend took his own life.

"I have my reasons," Ian said. He turned to the bed and stopped. Sylvi lay on her side with her head propped on one arm with the blanket draped casually over her shoulder like a goddess's cloak. The curve of her waist and hip was visible beneath the cloth, a tantalizing dip and swell he longed to skim his palm over.

She looked so damn bonny he stood there staring long enough that the fire practically singed his arse.

Her brows lifted for him to continue.

"Aye, well..." He made his way back to the bed and the beautiful angel waiting for him. "My da did something I dinna agree with."

That much was true. Ian had protested the death of Simon's aging father, but the Campbell laird would have none of it.

Ian slipped into bed beside Sylvi, eager for the press of her body and the companionship his heart ached for. She kept her head propped in her hand but shifted her leg over his, her skin hot against the chill of his own. He damn near sighed with relief.

"People in a place of power often have to do unfavorable tasks." Sylvi spoke with the ease of a woman who clearly had made such decisions herself.

Ian stared at her for a long moment. This was not the reaction he had wanted.

But then he hadn't told her all the details. He couldn't. Not now. Not when he hadn't even reconciled them in his mind and in his heart.

"Your father did something you didn't like, so you left." She paused, and her light blue eyes narrowed with perception that pierced his soul. "And you were afraid you'd have to make a decision like that someday, but without your father to blame."

Ian's blood chilled. Failing anything witty snapping to mind, he simply nodded. Like a fool. A coward.

Regret lodged like an uncomfortable stone in his chest. He should never have mentioned his past—it tiptoed too close to revealing the ugliness of himself he'd tried to leave behind.

Another in a string of bad decisions.

He nodded and clenched his teeth against the memory of Simon's father, a man he'd known all his life, swaying from a creaking rope. And then his son followed suit.

Sylvi's gaze sharpened, her expression becoming pensive. "Being a leader is a difficult role."

Ian offered a mirthless chuckle. "One I'm clearly no' made for."

"I disagree."

He tilted his head for her to continue.

She smirked. "I feel like complimenting you will only make you more arrogant." She lifted her head and bumped his shoulder with her elbow before returning her face to the cradle of her palm. "There are different types of leaders. There are those whose followers obey out of fear like I'm assuming with your father. There are ones whose followers obey because they are cared for, like me. And there are those whose followers obey because they like the person they follow for their humor and skill."

"Ye're saying I'm funny and skilled?" He grinned up at her.

She rolled her eyes and swatted him on the chest.

"And ye're saying ye're a leader as well." Finally, she'd revealed something of herself to him that he hadn't had to force out of her.

The smile teasing over the corners of her mouth wilted, and her eyes narrowed. "Why did you tell me all of this?"

He knew she meant to change the subject from her and let her get away with it. This time. "I trust ye."

She lifted an eyebrow. "You're right. You do make poor decisions."

"Why do ye say that?"

"I tried to kill you."

"But ye saved me." He drew his fingertip over the side of her breast, visible beneath a fold of fabric. "And then ye loved me."

Her eyes swept closed with pleasure.

"I figured it was worth the risk." He curved the path of his finger over the swell of her bosom. Her nipple drew into a hard bud beneath the plaid. "We have to trust each other now anyway, aye, my angel?"

She opened her eyes to reveal the lust glinting there. Her fingers curled around his cock. "I told you not to call me that."

The boldness of her touch sent a thrill of excitement tingling through him. She was as fierce in her passion as she was with her fighting. A woman unlike any other.

Now was for loving, aye, but he would eventually get her to talk to him. About how she knew Norwegian, about the men she led and why she cried out for her mother in her sleep. Through loving or persistence or both, he *would* discover Sylvi's closely guarded secrets.

SYLVI SHOVED AT THE COVERS, BUT THEY WOULD NOT move their oppressive weight from atop her. Awareness tickled her conscience and drew in the realization that the blanket was made of thick muscle.

The flesh of the arm holding her was prickled with dark hair and created a layer of moist sweat where his body touched hers.

Ian.

She shifted in an attempt to escape his smothering embrace. He tightened his grip on her. She tried to wriggle away, but he flung his leg over hers.

An irrational vein of panic scrabbled through her at his unintentional battle to hold her against her will.

She pushed at his hands and slipped free, her breath coming hard. He reached out, caught her pillow and replaced her with it as his captive.

It had been a mistake sharing a bed with him, sharing a room with him. Allowing him to be close. She never allowed anyone to be close. Certainly, no one knew she was Norwegian unless they happened to guess it. He had pressed her as though she were in an inquisition, desperate for information she shared with precious few.

She cared for the ladies back at Kindrochit—they knew her past out of necessity.

But not like this. Not so near as to share sweat while they slept. Not so bonded as to have a connection, share regular conversations and push for secrets.

Discontent fluttered in her chest in erratic, frenzied beats as if a moth had been trapped in place of her heart.

Ian had wanted more from her when they had last coupled. His touch was tender and gentle as if he'd wanted to make it last through the night. She'd rushed him, the same as she had the first time. Where she had wanted her lust slaked, he had tried to draw out the seduction.

Things would be easier when they arrived at Kindrochit. When he saw Percy's beauty, he would no longer find interest in Sylvi. And when Isabel tempted him, as she did all men, he would not resist.

Sylvi would be glad to be free of the burden of his attention. He wanted more than she would ever be willing to give.

She looked to where he slept alone in the bed, clutching a pillow. The fear thrumming through her ebbed.

He was a man like any other. Laird's son or not, she would not allow herself to be swayed from who she was or her true purpose.

But it wasn't his being a laird's son that tugged at her. It was the desire to have him again.

The memory scorched through her mind of how he'd held her upright while he pleased her, how she'd balanced on the sheer strength of his body. Prickles of desire swept over her skin and pooled low in her stomach.

A far cry better than her first time, indeed. She pulled the dagger from her bag. A beam of moonlight shone brightly on the blade. It was not the best weapon she owned by any stretch, but it had been the costliest.

The blacksmith set the dagger on the anvil with a plinking sound and latched the door with his meaty fist. "Ye've no' been touched before, aye?"

Sylvi's pulse went jagged with dread, and it was all she could do to stand her ground, to keep from backing away. "I am a maid, as said."

The man's hand moved under his thick leather apron. A grin spread over his face.

She kept her eyes open, but she scrunched her mind shut and thought only of her family: her strong father, her kind mother, her two sisters and baby Einar.

And she thought of those she would kill with that very dagger.

A shudder wracked through her at the memory.

She tucked the dagger in her bag with the care one might enlist when putting a child to bed and pulled a léine free from the pack. The cloth fell over her body like a drape, large and concealing. Exactly what she wanted.

She strode to where Ian slept and tried to free her pillow.

Ian gave an aggravated snort, his arms as locked on the pillow as they had been around her.

He was naked still, and his strength glowed in the silver light. She wanted to run her hand over his flesh, to reassure herself such raw power was indeed real.

She did not, of course. Not when doing so might wake him. The last thing she needed was hurt questions as to why she didn't want to sleep with him.

Instead, she pulled out the plaid they used while traveling and spread it on the ground. The upturn of her forearm folded beneath her head was pillow enough.

She lay there on the hard floorboards and was beginning to let herself be swept into the caress of sleep when something thunked down behind her.

She jerked awake and rolled over, her arm braced for a strike.

Ian gave her a lopsided grin. "It is a verra soft bed. This feels much better." He lay on his back on the ground beside her and wriggled his bottom on the floor. "It's only hard enough to leave half of me frozen with pain tomorrow."

The tension left Sylvi's body, and she let her raised hand fall away. If any beatings would ensue, they would only be for bad jests.

"Will ye come back to bed with me?" Ian sat up and held his hand out to her.

Sylvi looked at his open palm. Was he always so ridiculously trusting? "I don't want to go to bed."

His brow furrowed in concern. "Is it yer nightmare?"

"What?"

He held up his hands. "It's cold enough in here without ye trying to turn me to ice with yer stare."

"I don't have nightmares." If he thought her stare was cold, her voice came out even frostier.

He waggled his head. "Well, that's no' exactly true."

Sylvi opened her mouth to protest.

"That's where I heard minmore." He said it softly, but it still hit her heart like a dagger.

Min mor.

My mother.

Her wounded heart crushed in her chest. The pain was nearly overwhelming. It sucked the air from her lungs and left her breathless.

"Sylvi?" Ian asked. He took her hand into the warmth of his own. "Ye can talk to me."

"Why do you need to know?" She snatched her hand free and leapt to her feet. "Are you working for them?"

She knew the claim was most likely unwarranted, but anger was a far easier emotion to handle than the weight of sorrow.

He caught her hand again. "That isna fair."

She tried to pull away, but he held fast. "Isn't it? What do you know about Reginald and his men that you aren't telling me?"

He pulled her onto the floor, his tug firm but not painful. She fell on her knees in front of him. Desire immediately warmed to an eager pulse between her legs.

"Maybe I've told ye everything already." His eyes raked over her face, and he pulled the léine over her head.

The cool air of the room kissed her naked skin and brought a wave of chills prickling over her skin.

"And maybe you haven't."

He tilted her head back and his mouth slanted over hers, hungry and possessive. A kiss she answered back with the force of her rage.

She would not ignore their shared lust, not in this short time they had to enjoy it, but she would not sleep with him. Especially when she understood now exactly how much the night, and the darkness of her memories, left her vulnerable.

Eight

The additional day and a half of travel to Kindrochit Castle passed in a blend of eagerness and anticipation, a bittersweet combination.

Sylvi looked forward to Ian's misplaced affection being redirected at women deserving of such doting. A woman who could return the warmth Ian so generously bestowed upon her, a woman both lovely and sweet.

And yet she could not help the heady rush whenever they slowed their horses for a break. Expectation would nip at her control and leave her nearly shaking with desire. They would fly from their steeds and soar into one another's arms. Clothes were shoved aside rather than wasting time removing them properly, and passions were lit with explosions that left them both reeling and panting.

Sylvi had enjoyed it, enough to have made an extra stop that morning. One last bit of sport before they arrived at Kindrochit, and Ian realized the error of his wayward flirtation.

She led the way over the aging bridge without speaking. There had been no warning of the miserable state of Kindrochit, where she and the girls trained and lived. The king had long since given up on trying to maintain the castle and then later, eagerly relinquished it to the care of Connor Grant to save his own royal neck.

She hadn't advised him of Percy, Liv or Isabel nor of the manner of their true state of being within Kindrochit. Now, as the hollow clatter of hoof beats echoed around her, she wondered if she'd made a mistake.

Perhaps she ought to have told him more.

Perhaps she ought not to have brought him at all.

She looked back at him. He glanced up and gave her the same crooked grin that left his gaze so tender that it dragged a smile to her lips. She turned from him lest he see it.

The portcullis began to lift with a savage groan of protest coming from the other side of the castle wall. As Sylvi had expected, the other women had seen her and prepared for her arrival.

A gray-and-white cat darted from between the gates and danced in daring scampers between the hooves of Sylvi's horse. Sylvi slid down from her horse and scooped the feline from the ground. "That's a fine way to get yourself trampled, Fianna."

The cat gazed up at her with wide blue eyes. Her nose had gone extraordinarily pink in the cool weather, but her body was warm beneath the pelt of soft fur.

"You know how curious she is." Liv took the horse's reins from Sylvi and cast a glance back at Ian. "Isn't he supposed to be dead?" She asked it in a lowered voice, but the snap of Ian's attention indicated he'd had no trouble overhearing the question.

Or perhaps it was the woman who had spoken that stole Ian's attention.

Sylvi regarded Liv as Ian might. Liv wore her black training outfit, her long, shapely legs encased in black leather trews. Her waist was cinched into a corset. Cat-like gray eyes sparkled out from a fair face flushed with rosy cheeks and full, pink lips, all framed with gleaming copper-colored waves.

Liv was the perfect blend of beauty and power.

"He has information I need," Sylvi muttered.

"Won't the marauders be displeased?" Liv was the only woman at Kindrochit who was brave enough to voice her concerns and questions. Sylvi had always respected her for it, even if the questioning of her decision rankled her now.

"They think he's dead," she replied. "I was unable to maintain cover and killed two. One survivor remained."

"They will come for you."

"That is what I am counting on." Sylvi paused and met Liv's eyes before she continued, "They are led by the man with half an ear."

"I'm Ian Campbell." Ian appeared at Sylvi's side and bowed low to Liv. "It's fine to meet ye, lass."

Liv continued to stare at Sylvi, her eyes wide, before she finally allowed her gaze to fall on Ian. Her slight nod bordered on civility but by no means crossed the line into anything polite. "Liv."

"Ah, yes." Ian clapped his hands once and held them clasped together. "Sylvi had a lot to say about ye."

Liv's brow furrowed. "She did?" She shot a questioning glance at Sylvi.

Ian laughed. "No, of course no'." When neither woman laughed, he rotated his forefingers around one another. "It was a jest—she doesna really talk, does she?" Neither woman replied nor laughed. His brows lifted. "That's why it was funny."

Liv eyed him as if he'd lost his mind and held out her hand. "Give me your horse. I'll see them both cared for while you go inside and get comfortable."

Ian handed his reins over with a shrug, and Sylvi had to tamp down a smile before it hinted its presence on her lips. His humor had gotten under her skin so often it was beginning to take root there.

Sylvi marched her way across the courtyard with Ian trailing behind her and saw the castle exposed in a new light, the way he might see it. The high walls had been beaten at by time, leaving bits of pale stone exposed beneath a time-blackened facade like wide, gaping wounds. Training and the constant repetition of battle had flattened whatever might be left of the meager grass.

Sylvi and Ian pushed inside the massive doors together and let them bang shut. Darkness swallowed them and emphasized a beam of sunlight glimmering from a high window. Motes danced an excited frenzy in the ray.

"Sylvi." The soft, feminine voice was so familiar.

Sylvi squinted up into the light as Percy descended the stairs. Her golden hair glowed around her head like a halo and shone around her lithe figure.

The smile on her face reached her blue eyes with such genuine happiness that one could not help but smile likewise. Her step faltered, and Sylvi realized Percy must have seen Ian.

Percy dipped her head forward and obscured most of her beautiful face behind a curtain of gilded curls. "I was unaware you wouldn't be alone." She stepped onto the landing and kept her head lowered.

Despite her attempts not to be seen, Sylvi knew it would have been impossible for Ian not to have noticed the woman coming down the stairs. Even less possible for him not to have noticed her beauty.

"This is Percy." Sylvi kept a discreet stare fixed on Ian, waiting for his gaze to skim down the other woman's body, nestle in her full bosom, or even fix on her lovely face.

Ian bowed low, as he had done with Liv, his face hidden by the action. "It's nice to meet ye, lass. Ian Campbell."

"Um, thank you." Percy stared miserably at her feet. The poor girl was an easy target for leering. And still, Ian did not stare at her any more than he would a fishmonger's wife or a priest.

"She's the one who makes the belt you seek," Sylvi said.

Ian's eyes lit up. "Ach, that's the finest belt I've ever seen. Of course, anything Sylvi wears looks bonny." He tossed one of his easy grins in her direction.

Sylvi's face went warm at the compliment in spite of herself.

Percy tilted her head. "You liked the belt?"

"Aye—I only agreed to let Sylvi kill me if I could get one for myself." He shrugged. "Well, that and obviously her promise to bring me back to life so I could enjoy it."

"Percy created the potion and antidote as well." Sylvi wanted to pull her gaze from staring at Ian, to stop watching him so possessively. He was not hers. He would never be hers. He couldn't be.

Why the hell wasn't he gaping at Percy? Couldn't he see how beautiful she was? Was he daft?

"You used the antidote?" Percy's head came up, her beautiful blue gaze drifting between Sylvi and Ian.

"Worked like a witch's charm." He spread his arms wide. "I'm alive."

Percy studied him for a long moment. "Fascinating."

The word had been whispered, but Sylvi still heard it and was startled to realize she had been more confident of the antidote than Percy had been.

Percy ducked her head suddenly. "You've traveled a long way. I'm keeping you from resting." She bit her lip and inclined her head politely. "Um...it was nice to meet you." Her fingers twisted against one another.

"You'll see him at supper," Sylvi said.

When they strode away, heading up the stairs, it was not Ian who watched Percy with interest, but Percy who watched him.

IAN MADE HIS WAY THROUGH THE BATTERED HALLS OF Kindrochit, encouraged by the briny scent of roasting meat and freshly baked bread.

For all the excitement Ian had expected at Kindrochit, his day had been dull. He did not see much of Sylvi as the preparations for an attack on Kindrochit by Reginald consumed her day. Nor did he meet anyone else who lived there aside from Percy and Liv. Both of whom had been polite enough, Percy in a sweetly shy manner and Liv with cool civility.

The castle was well worn, and Sylvi was a woman fond of discretion. Perhaps she had no more than the two women living there with her.

He entered the large room of the great hall to find one table set near a roaring hearth. Like the rest of the castle, the room might have been grand once were it not for the scoring of time upon its cracking walls.

Sylvi and Liv sat at the table already. They both looked up at him, and the quiet conversation humming between them fell into a flat and abrupt silence.

Were he a less confident man, he might be intimidated by such a welcome. Lucky for him, he was not.

"Two bonny lasses to accompany me at supper." His voice echoed in the otherwise empty great hall, and he plunked down on the hard bench opposite them.

"Liv." He nodded in the direction of the redhead, who narrowed her eyes suspiciously at him and returned his gesture. "My angel." He winked at Sylvi.

Sylvi's face went pink. The daggers coming from her gaze might have pierced his heart, but he knew her fondness for him well enough. Very well, in fact. "I trust ye were saying no' but good things about me when I walked in, aye?"

"Is he always this arrogant?" Liv turned to Sylvi.

"Indeed." Sylvi sipped from the metal goblet in front of her, but not before Ian saw a smile flinch at the corners of her mouth.

Aye. She couldn't resist him.

Sylvi set the cup down and glanced up at the doorway, the mirth slipping from her face.

"Who is this?" A woman's voice, tinged with an unusual accent, so her i's sounded like e's, echoed from across the room. "Are you keeping more secrets from me?"

Ian turned in his seat toward the sulky tone and found a woman with vivid red hair sauntering toward him. Her dress—if one could call it that—had been sliced to reveal flashes of her fair, shapely legs beneath with each step. The firelight caught the brilliant red of her hair and made it appear as though it were part of the roaring flames. Kohl lined her eyes, and her vibrantly red lips curled into a lush smile.

"I don't think we've met." She extended her hand, and a slash in her sleeve fell open to reveal the creamy, smooth skin of her arm beneath. "I'm Isabel." Her name came out like a purr, a whispered seduction.

He took her hand and brushed a kiss over her small knuckles. The spice of her perfume was as unique as her appearance. And as overly applied.

A row of gems twinkled across her large bosom, winking at him with every movement she made.

"Ian Campbell." He released her hand, and she slinked into the seat beside him.

The warmth of her thigh brushed against his. Her interest was noted.

And unwanted.

He shifted in the opposite direction to avoid her touch. She leaned into him, covering the space he attempted to put between them. Sylvi's stare fixed on them with an unreadable intensity. It made him want to scramble away from the painted woman and the fog of her perfume.

"We've never had a man in the castle before." Isabel stared up at him, her eyes wistful beneath the smearing of kohl.

"Connor was here before you even were," Liv countered.

"We needn't speak of Connor." Sylvi's abrupt tone put an end to the conversation before it could continue.

Both girls shifted their gazes away and fell silent. Ian, of course, immediately wanted to ask about Connor but decided to do so later when he was alone with Sylvi.

A rhythmic squeaking sounded in the distance and grew louder until it echoed from the walls. Percy appeared in the doorway with a small handcart containing several levels, each laden with food. First, she served a golden-skinned pheasant, which looked both crispy and juicy, then a plate of bread so fresh that yeasty-scented steam rose in a tempting curl. A few plates of stewed vegetables completed the feast.

She reached into her cart and withdrew one more item. A belt with many loops and pouches, which she handed to Ian. "I hope it fits." She glanced down. "I guessed on the size."

Ian leapt from the table, as eager for the hard-won gift as he was to be free of Isabel's cloying closeness. He wrapped it around his waist and fastened the buckle. "It's a perfect fit." The sword and dagger loops were well placed for quick access in the event of a battle.

"Ye did a fine job, Percy." He nodded his appreciation. "Thank ye."

"I'm um...I'm glad you like it." She hunched her shoulders and hid her face behind a curtain of golden hair.

While she was a lovely woman, her shyness was so powerful it threatened to overwhelm everything else about the lass.

Someone tugged at the center of the belt. "That is a fine belt," Isabel purred.

He wanted to step away from her but knew doing so for a second time might cause offense. And an offended woman was a dangerous thing, especially in front of a woman he genuinely cared for.

He slid a glance toward Sylvi, hoping for her intervention. She lifted her brows in bland amusement.

He was on his own then.

"If ye try to take my belt," Ian plucked her fingers from his belt and quickly sat down, "I may fight ye for it."

The lusty glint in Isabel's eyes darkened. She'd taken his words as flirtation. Her bosom pushed out at him as if it had a mind of its own. "Would you punish me?"

The stares from the other ladies rested heavily upon him, awaiting his answer. "Eh...no." The question had so taken him aback he couldn't even dredge up a witty remark to offset the awkward conversation.

This was by far the most uncomfortable dinner he'd ever attended.

Isabel blinked up at him, her expression innocent, which was almost laughable considering her obvious lack of innocence.

He turned his gaze from Isabel and heaped a mound of food on his plate. "But what I would like to do is eat some of this delicious food. Thank ye for making it, Percy."

Percy pushed her hair behind her pink ear and smiled.

"I'm sure you are not used to eating such peasant's fare." Isabel skimmed her eyes over his léine and kilt. "It's obvious you are a man of great wealth." Her breasts thrust upward and toward him.

"I don't think ye've had true peasant's food." Ian took an extra helping of food.

Percy glanced away, her cheeks red at Isabel's unkind comment.

The gray-and-white cat he'd seen earlier hopped up on the table and greedily licked her mouth.

"It appears I'm no' the only one looking forward to eating this incredible feast," he said.

The ladies all laughed. The sound echoed in the empty stone room and broke apart the tension.

"Fianna, off the table now." Liv lifted the cat with the chastising tenderness of a mother. Fianna settled on the ground with a little songlike chirp.

Liv tore a piece of pheasant from her plate and tossed it to the floor beside the cat, who greedily devoured it in jerky, purring bites. Ian chuckled at the cat and looked up to find Sylvi watching him, a fragile smile on her own lips. She held his gaze for a moment before turning to Liv and speaking softly about something he couldn't hear.

Ian bit into the meat and found it so succulent and perfectly spiced that he practically purred himself. "This is the best pheasant I've ever eaten."

Percy looked up from her own food with genuine surprise, and the worry smoothed from her brow with a quiet smile.

A bang snapped through the air, loud and sudden enough to make Ian jump.

"The southeast tower." Percy leapt to her feet. "Sylvi, the trap. Someone has set it off."

Nine

Ian followed the women down corridors he had not yet seen, all lit by the flickering light of a candle dancing a frenzy in their haste. Up several flights of stairs, through more corridors, until they arrived at a door that Sylvi shoved open with savage anticipation.

Freezing night air rushed in and whisked out the candle flame, plunging them into darkness.

Ian knew without being told who the trap had been set for and why Sylvi was so eager to see for herself. The landing on the castle wall was wide enough to easily accommodate all five of them.

All four of them.

Isabel apparently hadn't bothered to join them. Of that, Ian was grateful.

Percy pushed a hand to his shoulder. "Be careful." She dropped her hand quickly, as if touching him burned her, and pointed to the ground. Large cages lay open, their hungry metal mouths stretched wide, ready to snap closed on an unsuspecting victim.

Ian followed the line of them to the end, near a tower, where one cage was upright and locked with something in it.

Sylvi was already there, peering inside, her body tense. A long, drawn-out silence filled the air.

"He's dead," she said at last, her voice flat. She slapped her hand against the wall and gave a loud curse.

Ian made his way carefully around the traps to where Sylvi stood. Blood pooled on the ground, an eerie purple red in the darkness. A majority of the man's body was in the cage, but a shoulder and an arm dangled out where it had closed over him.

Percy gave a sharp gasp. "It wasn't supposed to kill him." She shook her head. "No. No. How could this happen? How could he have died?" She edged closer, peered inside, and gave a strangled cry.

Her shoulders sagged forward, and she backed away, still shaking her head. "The locking mechanism," she said miserably. "It shouldn't have gone through as blunt as it was, but it went so fast..."

Ian stepped over the rope of the man's grappling hook and studied the body's shadow in the moonlight. Sure enough, a thick bar protruded from the man's back, dripping with blood.

"Let's get him out." Liv pushed around Percy. "You probably don't want to be here." She said it in a gentle tone, which spoke of her affection for the other women.

The man jerked, a reflex of the recently dead.

"I'm so sorry, Sylvi." Percy's voice trembled with tears. "I know what this m-meant to you."

Sylvi's jaw flexed. "It wasn't your fault." She put a gentle hand on Percy's shoulder.

Tears shone on Percy's cheeks.

"This was an accident," Sylvi said. "I know you didn't mean to kill him. I know how you feel about death." She pulled Percy close and hugged her in the way a mother does a frightened child. "It's all right."

It was so tender and so gentle that Ian wondered if the darkness played tricks on him and only made him think the woman holding Percy was Sylvi.

A wild thought slid into Ian's mind. What kind of mother would Sylvi be? She was stoic and tough, aye, but he hadn't seen this softness in her before.

Sylvi released Percy and gently turned her toward the open doorway. "Go on inside. I'll come speak to you when this is dealt with."

The body jerked again.

Ian narrowed his eyes against the darkness. A river of blood from the man's chest shimmered in the meager moonlight down his torso to where his hands were clasped near his belt.

Something hung from his fingertips. The length of his plaid had fallen over whatever it was, blocking it from view. A breath wheezed out from the man, and he wrenched his arms up, exposing a crossbow aimed directly at Sylvi.

Sylvi lay on her back, staring at the star-speckled sky and a madman.

Ian had lunged at her. Before she could fend him off, he'd slammed into her and taken them both to the ground.

Her body remained still for a moment, frozen in shock before pain flashed through her body. She shoved his chest, knocking him off her. "What the hell is wrong with you?"

He stumbled back but maintained his footing. Sylvi sat up to find Liv drawing a hand back from the dead man.

"What is this?" Sylvi demanded. Her voice was hard and loud in the soft night.

"He wasn't dead." Liv held up a crossbow. "Ian saved your life."

Ian shrugged. "Guess we're even now, aye?"

An arrow jutted from the roof of the southeast tower, directly where her head had been. She stalked over to it and pulled it from where it stuck fast between the shingles. A fine white strand clung to it like a length of cobweb. She plucked it free and examined it.

Her hair.

The bolt had come *that* close.

Her heart squeezed with the realization. Ian *had* saved her life.

"It appears we are even, indeed." She nodded her thanks to Ian and received a wink in return.

The man was impossible.

"The prisoner is still alive then?" Sylvi asked Liv.

The other woman tossed the crossbow on the ground, where it landed with a solid clatter. "Long enough to fire at you. Looks as if that was the last of what he had in him." She pried open the cage, and its great metallic squeal filled the otherwise silent night. The man's body held for a moment before sliding off the locking mechanism and landing at Liv's feet in a bloody pile.

Sylvi stared at the body in revulsion. "Long enough to try to kill again. No doubt one of Reginald's men. All those bastards do is kill."

She grabbed a handful of his léine and flipped him, so he lay on his back. His body was still warm beneath the fabric, and the scent of blood swam around her.

Revulsion threatened to shudder through her, but she pushed her disgust away for the weakness it was. Death always reminded her of her family, of the finality of loss. It was indeed fortunate she did not deal with bodies often.

"Do you know him?" She looked pointedly at Ian.

He knelt beside the body and pulled away a length of dark hair which had fallen over the man's face. "Aye. And so do ye. It's Gregor."

She jerked her attention to the waxy face, studying it with renewed interest. Ian was right. It was Gregor who lay still at her feet. Regret slashed through her. She had wanted it to be her blade that took his life, not the mistake of a locking mechanism.

"We need to get him inside," Sylvi said. "Perhaps he has something on him we can use to determine where they are hiding."

Liv turned away from where she'd been scouting over the wall.

"There aren't more below from what I can see. He must be the only one."

Disappointment edged into Sylvi's heart. She hadn't expected the men to all come together. But it would have been so easy if they had.

She bent and grabbed the body's feet. "They will once he does not return."

Ian took the dead man's wrists in his hands, and together they hauled away the body of the man whose mistake had saved Sylvi's life. The man she had meant to kill.

Gregor's body contained nothing helpful.

Sylvi quietly closed the door to Percy's room and stood for a long moment in the hallway. Percy had been upset at the impact her trap had on the man, but then she always was sensitive.

The hallway was dark and cold.

Sylvi was alone.

Her throat tensed in an unexpected knot she could not swallow away.

Gregor's death had upset her as well. Because she felt nothing. For years, she had dreamt of his voice, his hand on her shoulders, his blade at her neck. For years, she'd wanted to see him dead.

But his death had been an accident, not fueled by the force of her vengeance. She hadn't gotten to tell him who she was or see the expression on his face.

She'd whispered it into his ear while he lay stiffly on the floor, but it was not the same. The lack of satisfaction settled in her heart and left it hollow—left *her* hollow.

She swallowed hard again, but the ache in her throat would not dissipate.

Ian.

Her mind screamed his name. Because of the need to find out

any additional information he might have, of course. For no other reason.

She walked briskly. Her footsteps rang out on the naked stonework around her, reminding her how very alone she was.

Her steps hastened toward Ian's room.

So alone.

She wanted one of his foolish jests to lure a smile to her lips and his strong arms around her, offering her support he knew she didn't need.

Didn't she, though?

She wrapped her arms around herself and squeezed. Thin muscle against thin muscle. No warmth.

No comfort.

But she didn't seek him for comfort, she reminded herself. She sought him for answers. After all, she'd gone this many years without a man to offer consolation.

Answers—she was going to see him for answers.

She rounded the corner of the hall to his room and stopped.

Isabel stood at his partially open door in a white gown so thin her flesh was visible beneath. Her hair blazed in the darkness like a vibrant ruby. She did not look behind her when she slipped inside and closed the door.

Sylvi's heart sucked down into her gut. The lock turned with a heavy click, and she flinched.

She jerked herself against the wall, under a blanket of shadows, lest someone see her and assume her foolish intent.

The tightening of her throat further increased until she wanted nothing more than to scream. To throw her head back and scream and scream and scream until her throat went raw.

Instead, she lifted her head and dropped her arms from where they hugged her body for warmth. She spun on her heel and made her way back to her room. It was a good thing she had been going to his room with the purpose of gleaning information and that she had not truly sought comfort.

She swallowed around the swollen ache in her throat and wished she could make it go away.

If she had gone to Ian for anything more, something of a more personal nature, this slap of rejection might actually have stung.

Ten

Ian was surprised Sylvi had been so loud coming into his room. But then, she clearly wanted her presence known.

He turned his attention from the fire he sat before and glanced over his shoulder to the woman in a white gown.

He'd expected his angel, dressed in cloth as delicate as a skein of moonlight. But it was not Sylvi who stood in front of him with her body on display. Vivid red locks tumbled down her slender shoulders in place of white-blonde hair, and the fog of an overwhelming perfume slammed his senses.

The warm sensual note of spices.

Isabel.

She twirled around like a dancer, putting her body on display for him. The gauzy fabric fanned around her like the skin of a ghost. "I knew you'd like it."

Ian got to his feet. "I dinna remember inviting ye."

If he could gently nudge her out, he would. No need to hurt the lass's feelings. It would not be the first time he would have to dissuade unreturned affections.

"I invited myself." She gave a little shrug, and the fabric shifted open to reveal the swell of her breasts beneath. Her nipples were a rosy pink.

Ian snapped his stare away. "Ye shouldna have come."

Her spicy scent swirled around him in a cloying miasma. The bitter taste of it lodged in the back of his throat. He tried to swallow it away, but still, his head spun with the effects.

"I had to come." Isabel caught his jaw in her hot palms and pushed her painted face to his. "We never have men here. And I can't be seen. Ian, it's been so long since I've had a man. So *long*."

A soft whimper slid from her throat, and her brows furrowed in agony.

He knew exactly what kind of agony plagued her. But he would not be the source of her relief. Ian backed up even though she still clutched his head, putting himself into an awkward bowing motion. "I appreciate yer attentions, but I think it's best we—"

She stepped closer and slid her hands down his back while he straightened. "I can't go anywhere for risk of being discovered." Her eyes widened in a pathetically obvious attempt to make herself appear mysterious.

Before he could pry her from him, she rubbed her body over his and moaned.

"Isabel." He spoke more firmly this time.

His voice did not startle her. Instead, she released him and caught his face once more. Her long nails prickled his skin, and her red lips came down on his, forceful and waxy with the grease.

He pushed his arms away and broke her grip on him. "Enough of this."

She stared at him with her dress hanging on her nearly naked body by one skimpy shoulder, the garish red of her lips smeared over her jaw. Hurt blazed in her eyes.

He shook his head and tried to rein in his patience. "I've tried to tell ye gently—"

"That you don't want me?" Isabel's sensual facade cracked to reveal the selfish ugliness beneath. "Because you want Sylvi?" She gave a harsh scoff. "If you think that frigid bitch could ever love you, then you're a fool. She doesn't love anything but that dagger of hers and her ridiculous dream of revenge." She rolled her eyes with great exaggeration.

Anger grappled Ian's chest. It was one thing to lash out at him, but he would not tolerate the disrespect of Sylvi. "Dinna criticize a woman ye havena truly taken the effort to know."

"She doesn't want to get to know anyone," Isabel huffed. Her gaze raked over his naked torso, and her teeth sank into the smeared red of her lower lip. "You are so handsome."

She stepped closer to him. "I wouldn't tell her, you know. I'm a very discreet lover."

Ian put his hand up to stop her. "Dinna do this."

Isabel glared at him. "Men in London court would crawl on their hands and knees to kiss my hand, let alone have me come to them like this. You have no idea who it is you are turning away."

Ian shrugged. "It doesna matter. I know the woman I want."

Isabel shook her head. "You're as ridiculous as she is. Perhaps you two deserve one another. You can chase after her while she's chasing after her revenge, and not one of you will end up happy. But know this..." She stabbed a finger at him. "You will never mean as much to her as those she intends to kill. Never."

Isabel spun on her heel and stomped from the room, the tendrils of her filmy garment jerking and knotting on the floor as it trailed behind her. Before she could reach the door, she turned to face him once more. "My cousin is King James, you daft fool. You could have had royalty riding you."

She wrenched the door open and let it slam shut behind her.

He stared at the closed door and gave a long exhale of relief. Cousin to the king. He chuckled and shook his head. All the more reason not to have lain with her.

And probably a good thing she left so abruptly rather than give him time to voice his opinion.

Were Sylvi any other woman, he wouldn't have cared. In fact, before Sylvi, he would have readily taken Isabel up on her offer. A couple of times, in fact. Better to be loved for the night than to be alone.

But Sylvi was like a wild horse in a stable of mares. She was power and beauty and strength where the others were meekly compliant. Unbroken horses were dangerous, and yet it was part of their appeal. To tame one created a bond unlike any other if it didn't kill you first.

Sylvi.

She would kill him for certain if she knew he'd just compared her to a horse in his mind.

Thinking of her ferocity made him crave her again.

He'd noticed her slight smiles when he spoke that evening. She was starting to warm toward him, even if she didn't realize it.

He was edging his way in, earning trust from a woman who did not give it easily. It was part of her challenge, part of her charm, all the things that drove him delightfully mad.

He strode to the door, intent on seeing Sylvi—eager to wipe clean Isabel's bawdy attempt at seduction and the ugliness of her bitter words.

Sylvi slammed her body onto the bed. Her blood pounded through her veins hard enough to leave her cheeks burning with heat.

Isabel was in Ian's room.

This was what Sylvi had wanted. He would be distracted with his new conquest and would leave her the hell alone.

An unbidden image flashed in her mind of him locked in an embrace with Isabel, his gaze devouring her beautiful face and lush body.

Sylvi's heart wrenched, and energy swelled through her.

She wanted to fight someone, to swing her blade with all the anger raging through her and feel something break beneath the force of her blows. Ian had been so charming. He'd paid her such attention—she should have known his affections were false.

She was not an attractive woman. Not like the sensual softness of Isabel or the quiet mystery of Liv—and nowhere near the infallible beauty of Percy. She was battle-scarred and irreparably broken.

What man would need her for anything more than her skilled blade?

With Ian, she had been available. She had filled a basic need. *She* had been the one to initiate the first of their lovemaking. No —not lovemaking. Rutting. They had not made love, and now she was glad for it.

She rolled her body over to lay on her side. His angel, indeed. What a fool she would have been to believe him.

And, after all, wasn't this what she had wanted? For him to leave her alone, to turn his attention to someone more willing to return it.

She squeezed her eyes shut against the wall she faced and tried to wrestle sleep into taking her. A quiet knock sounded on her door. Her eyes flew open, and damn him if her first thought wasn't of Ian.

Renewed anger blazed through her at the ridiculous hope.

Of course, it wasn't him on the other side of the door. He would still be busy with Isabel.

But perhaps it was Percy. The rage faded to a simmer. Percy would not bother her sleep unless it were of great import, and the woman had been extraordinarily upset over the death of Gregor.

The knock sounded again, just as soft but more insistent.

Sylvi pulled herself from the bed and opened her door.

Ian stood there with a smear of red over his mouth.

His presence hit her like a gut punch, and the emotions poured through her with more speed than she could stop.

Excitement.

Horror.

Outrage.

He nodded as if confirming something to himself. "As I thought. Ye were too busy to come to my room."

"Did you want me to join you and Isabel?" she asked in an icy tone.

At the very mention of the other woman's name, the spicy foreign scent of Isabel coiled around her like a serpent.

Ian's jaw flexed. "How did ye know?"

"I saw her enter your room, as I see now the color of her lips smeared on your face and smell her perfume on your skin." She pushed her door to close it.

He shoved his palm against the wood, stopping her. With his free hand, he dragged his fingers over his mouth, looked down at the brilliant red wax, and cursed.

"It isna what ye think," he said.

"So she wasn't in your room?" Sylvi lifted a brow in an invitation for him to continue. Her grip, however, remained on the door in the event of a ready need to slam it in his face.

Ian sighed and shook his head. "Nay, ye're right. She was in my room. I dinna open the door—she came in and..." He tapered off.

"Offered herself to you."

He nodded.

She eyed the red wax smeared on his face and hand. "She was not enough, and so now you need more?"

His eyes widened. "Ye canna think I would abandon my angel so easily."

"Can't I?" She pushed at the door, but he caught it in his hands and held it in place.

He gazed down at her with so much sincerity that her heart swelled with the effect. "If I wanted her, I would have had her," he said. "And I wouldna be here."

Her pushing faltered. Perhaps he meant it that he truly wanted her. The relaxed hold on the door worked to Ian's advantage, and he pressed it open several inches wider.

"Is it so hard to believe I want ye, Sylvi?"

Yes.

The word lodged in her throat, and the fight bled out of her. She dropped her hands and stepped back. He could take it as an invitation if he wished. She no longer cared to fight.

He stepped in and left a smear of red on the door, where he held it before letting it gently close behind him. He dragged his hands over his mouth in a continuous sweeping motion, rubbing at the red lip wax.

Sylvi watched him carefully, not yet eager to welcome him into her room despite his presence.

"Isabel is beautiful," she said.

"I'm going to assume yer girls are not whores to let out."

He might as well have slapped her. Sylvi sucked in a breath. "Of course not."

He shrugged. "I know what ye expected of me. I'd prefer to be flattered that ye know they'd find me attractive rather than offended ye dinna trust me well enough not to pull my cock from my kilt for every bonny lass I see."

"That isn't what I thought. I—" Except it *was* what she thought. Shame burned at her cheeks.

"Aye," he said. "Isabel is bonny."

She slid her gaze slowly toward him.

"And a bit odd, if I'm being honest." His dark brows rose, and he grinned at her from beneath his well-trimmed beard. "But she isna Sylvi."

He stepped closer to her, and all the air in the room sucked away, leaving her breathless. She looked up at him. She wanted to believe him. "And what is it about me that draws you?"

He gave her a lopsided smile that lodged into her heart. "Yers is a trust worth winning. Ye're fierce and beautiful in your power, and—" He paused. "Ye're my angel."

The word that had once rankled her nerves now tickled relief through the tension of her uncertainty. "You know I hate it when you call me that." She couldn't help but smile as she spoke.

"Ye know that's why I do it." He winked at her, his golden eyes dancing with mischief. "It's part of my charm."

His arms came around her, warm and wonderfully masculine. She didn't pull away or push at him. No, she melted into the embrace with a sigh locked in her soul and rested her head against his large chest. His heartbeat was steady and sure beneath her ear, a rhythmic thumping she wanted to fall asleep to.

"I want to love ye, Sylvi." His whisper washed warm over the skin of her neck and left gooseflesh prickling her flesh. He increased his grip on her, and she closed her eyes to savor the wave of euphoria.

She was the last woman who needed protection, but damn, he made her feel safe in a way even her dagger never could.

Ian nuzzled his nose against her neck, and the warmth of his tongue flicked against her earlobe. "I thought I was going to lose ye when I saw that bastard aiming his crossbow at ye."

A little shiver of anticipation wound through her.

His teeth nipped where he had so teasingly licked. "I couldna lose ye. We've no' had enough time yet. We have no' yet killed Reginald. We have no' spent an entire week lost in a haze of love-making. We have no' had an evening under a moonlit glen."

She laughed and leaned back to look at him. Mirth twinkled in his eyes. "An evening under a moonlit glen?"

He shrugged. "It sounds verra romantic, dinna ye think? I'd like to experience it with ye."

"I'm not much of a romantic, and anyway, it's too cold."

He slid her a sly glance. "We'll keep each other warm. And I did save yer life." He looked away in a show of innocent help-lessness.

She laughed again and pushed at him. "You don't fight fair."

"I'll take it that's an aye, then?" He grinned, his teeth brilliant white against the darkness of his beard.

"Is there even a glen nearby?"

"If there is, I'll find it." His hands slid around her waist, and his gaze darkened with a desire she knew so deliciously well. "And

I'll make love to ye there beneath the moon tomorrow." Then his mouth opened over hers, and he was kissing away her protest to his silly request.

Right then, with her body pulsing with want and his strong hands caressing her skin, she found it impossible to say no to Ian Campbell.

Eleven

The search through the neighboring towns near Kindrochit had not revealed Reginald or his men. The sun was still high enough for Ian to make out Sylvi's stern expression beside him. Disappointment blanketed her in a shroud.

Were he a typical man and she a typical woman, he would have asked how she fared. But he was not the kind of man who broached such topics any more than she was the type of woman to share. Especially when he knew well enough what lay heaviest on her heart.

"We could scout the outlaying area of town." Ian scanned through the surrounding forest. The trees had thickened around them—the perfect location for Reginald to set up a camp. "The men stayed on the outskirts."

"Wouldn't they have taken their drink and whoring within?" she asked.

A valid point.

Sylvi turned in her saddle to regard him. "How is it you know the men and their habits so well? You never explained exactly why they want to kill you."

He kept his gaze fixed on her rather than let his stare slide away, a sure sign he was keeping something from her. And he had been. She'd asked several times, and he'd evaded her questions. He should tell her, he knew.

He should.

"And ye never told me how much they paid ye." He tried a smile, but it was not returned. Humor would not work in this case.

"It was after I left home," he said finally. "I met them at a tavern." He waved a hand dismissively. "They looked as if they were having fun."

"Fun?" Her stare hardened.

"It'd been a while since I'd had fun." He couldn't keep the cynicism from his voice any more than he could stop the memory of Simon and his father from flashing through his mind. Faces bloated and blue, eyes bulging. The creak of Ian's saddle was suddenly reminiscent of the long, low groan of a swinging rope burdened with a corpse.

"Raping women and killing children is fun?" The anger in Sylvi's tone scraped into Ian's awareness.

"I prefer my women willing," he countered. When the tension in her shoulders didn't ease, he tried again. "Ye know I dinna do such things, Sylvi."

She shook her head. "That's the thing, Ian—I don't."

She turned away from him, her gaze fixed on the trail. An abrupt command erupted from her lips, and the black steed beneath her raced forward into a thundering gallop, propelling her away from him.

Ian snapped his reins and bellowed at his horse. Like hell would he let her run from him. The lass was fast. He'd give her that. She'd put quite a bit of space between them, but he managed to get closer to her. He hugged his body to his steed to gain additional speed.

It worked. He pushed forward far enough to be able to spin his horse to a stop in front of hers on the narrow forest trail and force her to stop.

She jerked the reins of her horse and stared at him. Her chest heaved with her effort, her breasts round and high and deliciously evident in her bodice. She looked every bit the part of the lower-born noble she played, her blue gown and wide black cloak plain but of sufficient quality. Several ribbons fluttered in her pale blonde hair, tousled free by the recklessness of her ride.

She glared. "Move."

"I dinna think ye'd ever be one to run from anything."

"I wasn't—" She clenched her jaw.

He was right, and they both knew it.

He pushed off his horse. A risky move, perhaps. She could easily bolt again, and it'd be all the more difficult to catch her. He made his way to her horse and stood beside it. If he offered to help her down, he knew she'd refuse. And if he didn't approach her, she might not feel inclined to join him on the forest path.

His angel always was a game carefully played.

Now she knew what he wanted and would make her own decision.

She slid from her saddle and landed softly beside him.

The subtle rustles of forest life came from deep within the surrounding trees. He let the quiet sound fill the gap between them for a moment before he reached for her hand. She let him take it but did not step closer to him. Her palm was hot and damp.

"Ye want to know why they want me dead?" he asked. "They sought to take a woman who wasna willing, and I stopped them."

The skin around her eyes tightened.

"They dinna much care for me interfering," he continued. "They tried to kill me. Luckily, I'm too good to be killed by only a few men."

He did grin at this, and Sylvi's wary expression eased. His charm was working once more.

"Ye say ye dinna know if I would kill children or rape women. But ye do, dinna ye?" He met her eyes, and the hardness there softened.

"You wouldn't." There was a conviction to her tone that stroked his wounded pride. "I..." She shook her head. "I had this fear you'd worked alongside them, lived with them, I don't know —been part of them."

A cold ball knotted itself in Ian's stomach. He *had* worked alongside them. For only about four months. Enough time to take several mercenary positions, fighting for coin, gleaning information when necessary. It was something to fill in the gap leaving his family had made—the wide, gaping hole he hadn't expected. Leaving Dunstaffnage Castle was supposed to shove it all away, the same as his light jests did.

Roaming with those men only exacerbated the hollowness in his chest.

Sylvi, with her resolve and fortitude, had given him a sense of purpose again—a fight for vengeance, something noble, something honest. A way to make some right to all the wrong he'd done.

He should tell her of his true involvement with them. Crack the trust she'd given him now rather than render it shattered later. Cracks could at least be mended in time.

"You are a good man, Ian Campbell." She stepped toward him and pressed a kiss to his lips, sweet and delicate with a shyness he would never expect from Sylvi.

The kind of kiss one gave when they cared too much, and it left them frightened with uncertainty.

Warmth glowed to life in his chest and quickly cooled. He was not a good man. Or at least he hadn't been. And even now, he was not opening his mouth to speak the truth.

Tell her.

She kissed him again with more confidence. "Nothing to say? Have I finally brushed past your charming arrogance?" She gave a soft laugh, a husky, throaty sound.

Tell her.

He opened his mouth, but nothing came out. Not a confession, not a thought, not even a mindless jest fired on reflex rather than consideration.

He knew then, as he stared deep into the warming depths of her cool blue eyes, he could not tell her. And he knew himself to be a miserable coward for it. He had run from his home, he had run from Reginald's men, and he was still running.

He couldn't do it now, but he would.

Later.

When they went to the moonlit glen—after she had softened from their lovemaking—when they were fully and completely alone. It would be then that he would be honest with her.

"So, ye think I'm charming?" The quip came out flat to his own ears, but her broadening smile told him she didn't notice.

"Are you ignoring that I called you arrogant too?"

He cocked his head. "Did ye say something?"

"Apparently not." She turned from him, but not before he caught the good-natured eye roll.

Regret twisted around him and held him in place where he stood. The smile on his face was tight and nearly cracking as if it were made of plaster.

For so, too, was his heart.

Sylvi left Ian at the stable to care for the horses and warred with her decision to meet him later for a tryst outdoors. It was foolish, really. Cold and pointless and a waste of time better spent seeking Reginald.

Sylvi had considered telling Ian she wouldn't do it, but when he'd declared himself eager for their romantic interlude, she could not bring herself to tell him no.

She knew she ought to, especially with the possibility of Reginald returning to the castle with his men. Really, the entire thing was absurd, ludicrously romantic and wasted on one such as her. And yet, there was a part of her she had thought long since dead

—a tender, fledgling piece of her—and it craved the sweet words and adoring affection. Everything Ian was so willing and eager to give.

The sun slipped between the hills in the distance. It would be nightfall within the hour, and soon after, the moon would show her face in the sky. Sylvi shoved through the main door of Kindrochit and was met with the warm, savory scent of roasting stew. Her mouth watered.

A moonlit glen indeed.

Sylvi almost laughed. It was so foolish a thought.

"What are you thinking of to put such a smile on your face?" Percy appeared at her side and pulled the cloak from her shoulders.

Heat scorched Sylvi's cheeks. She cleared her throat and smoothed at the dress she wore. "A jest I heard earlier."

"From Ian?" Percy probed, her grin widening.

Sylvi cast the woman a warning look. "I'll be gone for a while this evening but would like to speak to Liv and Isabel before I depart."

For all the lifetime she'd waited to find Reginald and his men, she suddenly now hoped Liv and Isabel had found nothing. Then, for one blissful night, Sylvi could set aside her rage and her vengeance and focus on the mundane. Possibly even romantic. Moonlit glens.

If they had found something, of course, Sylvi and Ian would not leave. But in truth, how could such a large party as Reginald and his men leave no mark? If they found no indication of Reginald and his men nearby, Sylvi and Ian would be clear for a night of shared freedom.

Percy pointed to Sylvi's mouth. "You're doing it again."

Sylvi gave a playful swipe at the offending digit and spun away. "Enough."

Percy's good-natured chuckle followed Sylvi's departure. "I'm glad to see you happy," Percy said behind her. "You've been sad for far too long."

If Percy was grateful for Sylvi's happiness, then she did not begrudge Sylvi the man she was with. And truthfully, Sylvi was grateful Percy did not want Ian for herself.

What woman could compete with Percy's beauty?

Sylvi pushed into her room and closed the door behind her. She ran her hands down her dress and considered if she ought to change or stay as she was.

Ian had seemed to like the gown.

Her cheeks went warm again. She stalked across the room toward her clothing trunk and stopped in front of the window. The darkness outside allowed her reflection to show. Her waist was clipped impossibly narrow in the gown, and her small bosom pushed up high and... She turned to the side, admiring the swell of her breasts—they appeared almost...lush.

While uncomfortable and impractical, the gown did become her.

She damn near felt pretty.

Pretty. At the very thought of the word, she scoffed. She certainly was playing the fool, indeed. She ought to take off the gown and put on her old trews—

Something moved in the darkness behind her. A shadow. A person.

Alarm prickled through her, late in its warning. She spun around to defend herself, and something whistled past her cheek. The dagger sank deep into the fine wood of the bedpost behind her. Sylvi jerked her blade free from her belt and regarded her attacker.

A woman stepped from the shadows. Her slender body was encased in a fitted black corset, and her skirts flared wide with the latest fashion. A smile spread over her handsome face.

"Distracted?" My Lady asked. "I never took you as one for preening."

Sylvi stared at the woman the way she might a ghost. And of all times she could have been snuck up on, Sylvi had been caught admiring her reflection like some simpering court girl.

Heat blazed in Sylvi's cheeks. She thrust up her chin and straightened her back to hide her embarrassment. "I never took you for one to skulk through the shadows."

"You are right, Girl. Sneaking about was never my forte. I figured you might appreciate the effort." She stepped closer, and her skirts rustled in the quiet room, accompanying a snapping pop from the fire in the hearth.

"I'm growing weary of weapons being thrown at my head." Sylvi grabbed the hilt of My Lady's dagger and pulled it free from the wood.

"Do you have so many enemies?" She stopped in front of Sylvi. Silver strands shone in the ebony black hair, and a fine sifting of powder lay over My Lady's smooth skin. Regardless of the effects of the last seven years, she was still a beautiful woman with an air of seduction. Something Sylvi had never been able to master.

My Lady's sharp gaze swept over Sylvi, assessing with as much detail, if not more. "I don't blame you for looking at yourself. If I still had a waist like that, I don't think I'd be able to walk away from a mirror."

Sylvi did not notice anything amiss with her former instructor's waist but did not correct her. Seeing her former mentor brought a wealth of memories surging through Sylvi. The hours they'd spent training. My Lady's patience with Sylvi's novice skills, her care in honing such amateur attempts into perfection.

My Lady had laid the foundation for the strength Sylvi possessed. Without her, Sylvi would still be an orphaned gutter rat scuttling through the streets, aimless and lost and broken.

"Where have you been all this time?" Sylvi asked, unable to keep the wistful note from her tone.

"I liked it better when we kept our secrets to ourselves." My Lady patted Sylvi's cheek. The powdery sweetness of My Lady's perfume was still the same as it had been seven years prior. "You've been doing well for yourself, from what I hear."

"I've heard nothing of you."

My Lady's red smile widened. "Exactly as intended."

"For a woman so blatant with her seduction, how do you remain hidden so well?" Surely, hers was a skill Isabel would appreciate. "And how the hell did you get into the castle without setting off the traps or being caught?"

"Secrets. Do you not wonder why I've come now after all these years?"

Sylvi lifted her brows.

"I'm here with news I knew you'd be eager to hear. News I did not trust to a page."

"You kill them all anyway."

My Lady shrugged dismissively. "Perhaps I wanted to see you again."

Sylvi held her hands out at her sides. "Here I am."

"You've become something amazing, Girl." The older woman's voice went soft. "Truly amazing. I'm proud of you."

The words sank into her heart, soothing a place Sylvi had not known was raw.

I'm proud of you. She lowered her head in silent gratitude, and My Lady placed her hand on the top of Sylvi's bent head—the way a parent does to a child at night to give them their blessings before bed. Emotion welled within Sylvi, but she tamped it down. She would not have herself appear weak now.

"What news do you have?" Sylvi asked, lifting her head.

"What news have you spent a lifetime wanting?"

Sylvi's heart stilled. "The man with half an ear. Reginald."

"Yes, I see you know his name now."

"I still don't know his exact location, though we do suspect he is near."

My Lady nodded. "It would appear he knows yours." She examined the backs of her hands. As always, her nails were perfectly shaped and beautiful. "I was warned by an acquaintance that a man had been sent here to kill the inhabitants of Kindrochit. It had been some time since I communicated with this acquaintance, as he assumed I still resided here."

"The man who came is dead," Sylvi said.

"Of course he is." My Lady lowered her hands. "But I know the location of the others. If you hurry, you can arrive before they realize their comrade has been slain. It's more than two days from here, near the Isle of Skye."

Sylvi's pulse roared in her ears. "They won't leave until he comes back."

My Lady clasped Sylvi's face in her hands, her palms dry and warm where they caressed her skin. "You will have your revenge, Girl."

"Yes," Sylvi said with all the enthusiasm pounding through her. Her head swam, and her breath was almost impossible to catch.

She had to tell Ian. The excitement that swirled through her stilled.

He expected to take her on a romantic tryst. But he knew what this meant to her. He appreciated practicality. He would understand.

Sylvi rushed toward the door.

"Where are you going?" My Lady asked.

Sylvi paused, her heart thundering a rhythm in her temples. "To cancel plans."

This opportunity could not slip through her fingers. Not again.

Twelve

Sylvi's heart squeezed in her chest the closer she got to Ian's room. Surely, he would understand her desire to leave for the Isle of Skye immediately. Yet no matter how often she repeated this to herself, she found the affirmation harder and harder to believe.

His door opened before she could raise her knuckles to the darkened wood. He flashed a smile at her, his teeth impossibly white beneath his beard.

He'd donned a crisp kilt and léine—the extra ones from his bag.

"I see you got some washing done in the short time we've been back." It wasn't quite a compliment on her end, but he would know well enough she meant it as one.

"Aye, Perce helped perform it while we were gone." Ian held his hand out to her. "I had to look fine for my lass."

She took his hand even though she willed her fingers not to slide into his proffered palm. He had that effect on her, leaving her so entranced that she did not realize what she was letting herself do until it was too late.

"Ye look bonny." His gaze trailed down the neckline of her simple gown, dipping lower to her bosom and waist before coming back up to rest on her face. "Verra bonny. I'm glad ye kept the dress on."

She shook her head. "I can't go tonight."

His grin did not falter. "Aye, ye can."

"Ian. We can't do this. Not now. I know where Reginald and his men are." She clasped his hand tighter, wanting to share the excitement humming through her. "We can leave tonight to go to where they're staying. He's near Skye. If we ride quickly and not sleep more than—"

Ian's finger came to rest on her lips. The callous on his fingertip rasped against the sensitive skin of her mouth and prickled her irritation.

"We can leave after." He spoke in a silky tone, which might have convinced her in days prior. When she did not have so great a task on her mind.

She shook him away from her face. He was clearly not understanding. "No, we must go now. They haven't moved yet, and I don't—"

"Ye promised me." The reminder was gentle, but it scraped against her nerves.

"Promises change." She pulled her hand from him. "You know what I've been after this entire time."

He put his hand on her waist. "And ye know what I've been after."

Her anger swept through any amount of charm he threw her way. "Is everything a damn jest to you? Do you ever take anything seriously?"

He studied her for a moment, his face unreadable before a smile broke out. "Life's no' long enough to give in to anger."

Were she not so angry, she could have pushed past her ire, and they might have had a conversation without it intensifying. But deep inside her, the thread of civility snapped beneath the pressure of time's strain.

"You have no idea what these men have done." She shoved her hand against his chest to put space between them.

"To ye? Nay, I dinna know. Ye willna tell me."

She dropped her arm and stepped away. He was right. She hadn't told him. He had no idea of the importance of Reginald's death. He didn't know her hurt, her loss, the rage that was so much easier to bear than the pain of it all.

He stepped closer and reached for her. "Calm down, my angel. We'll put this aside—"

She pulled away from him, and her veins blazed with the desire for vengeance.

"'Tis only a stroll in a moonlit glen." He gave her a peddler's smile.

"With time we do not have, all wasted on a foolish venture." She spoke in a harsh tone. "I lost them once because of you. I won't lose them again. It's not worth it."

His brow furrowed, and the realization of what she said settled into Sylvi's heart like the prickle of winter's first chill.

Sylvi's mouth fell open, but Ian put his hand up.

"Ye know how to win a fight. I'll give ye that." His smile was sharp and feral. "I'll go pack my things and meet ye in the stable."

Sylvi swallowed. "In an hour, we ride."

It was perhaps not what she ought to say. But she had never been a lover, and she'd thought her heart too incapable of any softness to coddle.

She turned on her heel and left Ian standing with his brittle grin and disappointed acquiescence. She couldn't be who he wanted her to be or what he expected. She would always just be herself. A leader, a fighter, a seeker of vengeance.

No matter the cost.

Despite the short notice, the lot of Sylvi's household, including Ian, was on the road within the designated hour. Even Fianna, who was little more than a bump beneath a thick plaid, huddled on the bed Percy had fashioned on Liv's saddle.

My Lady had been introduced to them all as Lady Camille, a name Sylvi knew to be fake and one she refused to call the woman she had so long referred to as "My Lady." Percy, Liv and Isabel accepted her with the same willingness they had Ian, each of them trusting Sylvi's judgement, especially when she was the most skeptical of them all. They knew My Lady to have been Sylvi's former instructor but had been doing discreet work long enough to ask no questions despite their unspoken curiosity.

The constant clink of Percy's many bottles of potions and tonics accompanied the crunch of the horses' hooves over the frosted landscape.

It was uncommon for all the women of Kindrochit to venture out together, especially Percy, who preferred to hide and was uncomfortable with the action, and Isabel, who had tricked all of Scotland and England into believing she was dead. Both women had their own skills they could bring to the fight, but it was more than that. Sylvi hadn't wanted to leave them back at Kindrochit. If one man could find them, more could as well. She would not leave anyone there to fend off a band of marauders on their own.

My Lady had said there were well over twenty men. Ian was skilled, as were Sylvi, Liv and My Lady. But more than twenty men spread over an encampment were a difficult target to wipe out with only three people. She would need the assistance.

Sylvi glanced to where Ian was chatting with My Lady. He gave his lighthearted laugh and jested as if he hadn't a worry in the world.

If only Sylvi could believe the front. But she knew better. His smiles were too bright, his voice too loud—all of it a mask for the flash of hurt when he flicked his gaze in her direction. Had she not known him so well, she would never have noticed such things.

But she knew him intimately, and the realization stuck in her heart like a dagger. What she had said had been cruel.

She ought to have apologized, but she couldn't bring herself to do it, to form the complexity of it on her tongue. And while she hurt for him, she could not compromise her mission for him. Not again.

Perhaps she was truly incapable of love.

The thought settled into her mind with a chill.

Ian had his own problems, to be sure, but he'd grown up with a family, a home, people who had looked up to him and held expectations. She'd clambered through survival, assuming everything was lost until she happened upon My Lady by chance. The bud of vengeance had given her life meaning while it blossomed and grew.

But in a world so centered on anger and hate, was there any room for love?

IAN'S BACK WAS NEARLY BREAKING, AND HE'D HELD THE reins so long his fingers were frozen into claws. It was almost dusk the next day before they finally stopped at the edge of the forest. The cluster of several buildings was so small it couldn't even be referred to as a town.

Sylvi, who had remained silent much of the trip—especially regarding him—turned toward them all. "Stay here. I'll go secure our rooms."

Ian nudged his horse forward. "I'll go with ye."

She cast him a long, considering look, and he tried to ignore the barb of discomfort her gaze cast into his chest. "Very well."

Together, they rode the short distance to where the inn came into better view. It seemed to sigh into the wind and lean a bit in the same direction. Its pock-marked sign swung by only one side.

Rutting Inn.

He tilted his head to follow the path of the sign until an *S* and a *T* were revealed to him.

Aye, Strutting Inn sounded more appropriate for a proprietor. Depending on the clientele, of course.

"We've no' had much of a chance to talk." There. He'd extended the courtesy of conversation.

"I haven't." She swung off her horse. "You've apparently had plenty of opportunity."

He leapt from his horse and followed at her side.

So she'd noticed him talking with the other ladies—except Liv, whose cat seemed to hate him as much as its mistress did. Both had stared balefully out from under the folds of a heavy plaid at his every attempt to speak with them.

He studied Sylvi's profile for a hint of jealousy. He'd always hated jealousy in women. It made them needy and drove them to the point of unnecessary distraction. But he *wanted* jealousy from Sylvi. He wanted her to have seen the conversations and noted his feigned inability to be affected by her harsh words.

She glanced up, and her step faltered. Her gaze narrowed on the dancing sign. "Does that say Rutting Inn?"

He caught the edge of the sign and held it up. "Strutting Inn. What have ye got on yer mind, my angel?"

"Don't call me that." The warning edge to her voice had returned.

She shot him a glare and shoved through the door of the inn. The room was dark with the shutters closed, and the air was thick with a haze of smoke from tallow candles and peat.

A large woman in a dress stood beside several men at a table midway into the room. She slapped down the rag she was holding and strode toward them.

"Can I help ye with something?" the woman asked in a brusque tone. She was most likely one of the tallest women Ian had ever seen.

"Do you have any rooms available?" Sylvi asked.

"I've got three," the woman said.

"Is there another inn nearby?" Sylvi asked.

The woman shook her head. "No' anything less than a day's ride from here."

"We'll take them," Sylvi said, handing her some coins before

Ian could pull out his coin purse to do so. "Is there a back door leading to the rooms?"

The woman jerked her head to the right. "By the stables."

Sylvi nodded her thanks, and Ian turned with her to go. Once they were outside, he leaned closer to her. "Does that mean ye'll be sleeping with me tonight?"

"That means the rooms will be crowded for the lot of women, and you'll have a room to yourself." She marched forward through the overgrown grass.

She'd quickly changed out of the dress before they left, opting for her men's trews and léine as she had before. While he had enjoyed her in the dress and the idea of how easy it would be to lift her skirts, he appreciated the snugness of the fitted cloth against her round bottom and long legs. Aye, the lass had a fine arse.

He quickened his pace to keep up. "What if I'd rather sleep with ye?"

She stopped and glanced into the forest where the rest of their party waited. "What started between us should never have begun."

His heart flinched against her words. "Because I'm too charming, and ye fear ye might fall in love with me?" He forced his most enchanting smile even though his insides had gone hollow.

The stern expression on her face slipped to the softness of vulnerability for a brief moment. She licked her lips and opened her mouth to speak. But then she said nothing and resumed her march toward the other women.

He reached out and caught her by the arm. "Come see me when we're inside."

She turned slightly to him, looked at where he held her arm and turned her hard gaze on him. "Why?"

"To talk." He shrugged. "To offer me protection from Isabel."

She pulled her arm from his grasp. "Very well." Then she turned away from him and headed to where the others waited.

If nothing else, he could at least determine why she had

suddenly gone so cold with him. He hadn't done anything wrong. Of that, he was certain.

It had all changed when she'd received word of the location of Reginald's men. Perhaps Sylvi truly would choose vengeance above all else.

Thirteen

Sylvi's heart should not be beating so hard. Certainly, her hands should not be shaking.

She was stronger than this.

She faced a door. A plain, simple door with the grain running downward in long, stretching loops. The other ladies were settled in for the evening, their food eaten within their rooms to avoid being seen.

In truth, it was mainly Isabel and Percy she had wanted to keep hidden away. Some secrets were best kept shielded.

The candle flame flickered in the simple wooden sconce she carried. She had promised to speak to Ian, and she had to do it now.

She rapped softly upon the wood and waited.

What she had said to him back at Kindrochit about the moonlit glen and their time together being a waste had been wrong.

But then, did he not deserve to know?

The door opened, and Ian was there with that damn charming smile. Their eyes met, and everything unsaid was laid out in the small space between them. The hurt Ian hid behind his smile, the nervousness rattling Sylvi's body. The longing to push aside her fears and fall into the blissful affection they shared, easy and carefree.

But Sylvi could never be easy and carefree.

The moment held too long and passed into a nervous energy that left them both shifting their gazes away.

He opened the door wider in invitation. Firelight burned in the hearth behind him, and the smoky warmth of peat lured her forward.

Sylvi's stomach gave a nervous twist. This anxiety was something to which she was unaccustomed. Emotions were complicated, messy things. She did not like being a victim to them.

Even through it all, her heart knocked hard against her ribs when she turned back around and faced him.

"I wasna sure if ye'd come." He closed the door and locked them both in the room together. "But I'm glad ye did."

The intimacy of the silence weighed on her and threatened to break apart her wits. She needed to stop everything with him while she still could stop it. Before he got hurt. Before *she* got hurt.

Her mouth was dry, and the speed of her pounding heart was driving her to distraction. Why was this so damn hard?

"I believe the word ye're looking for is 'sorry,'" he said.

She stared at him, incredulous. "What?"

He laughed and held up his hands defensively. "Ye'll feel better after ye apologize to me."

"For what?" She knew what she'd done, but an apology would bring them closer. And she'd come to end this foolish behavior with him.

He lifted one shoulder in a careless shrug. "Anything ye feel like apologizing for. I've got all night unless ye've got better ways for us to spend our time."

She rolled her eyes and made for the door. "It's always a jest with you, isn't it?"

His large hand settled over the door, and he blocked her path. Gone was the charming smile, and in its place was a serious expression. "Sylvi, I care about ye. Far more than I have ever cared about a woman."

She stared into his amber eyes, and her heart went warm in spite of her resolve.

"Perhaps it's me who should apologize as I've clearly offended ye in some way. I'm just..." He shook his head. "I'm no' good at apologizing."

Her heart twisted in the complexity of the situation. She could not allow him to take full responsibility. Not when it all truly rested on her shoulders.

"I'm not good at apologizing either," she said quietly. "And it's me who owes you one."

He relaxed away from the door and motioned for her to sit on the bed, one they would have eagerly used for different purposes the day before. She sank to the firm mattress and resisted the urge to cross her arms.

The bed ropes gave a long groan of protest when Ian sat on the stiff, thin bedding beside her.

"I regret that I lost Reginald in the beginning," she said. "But I am glad I saved your life."

"Thank ye for that." He gave a soft chuckle, his good-natured mood restored.

"But I cannot apologize for having chosen to come here over a tryst with you." She looked hard at him, determined to explain how she felt. "I have been looking for Reginald and his men for most of my life. To kill them." The frustration knotting her muscles pushed out in a great sigh. "And now, with my goal so close, I can't let it be jeopardized by anything or anyone." She nodded in his direction. "Including you."

"What will ye do when it's done?"

She blinked. The resolution of her goal had always seemed like such an impossibility—one she never lost sight of, but one she never expected, either.

"I don't know," she finally said.

He studied her for a long moment and gave her a lopsided

smile, boyish and hopeful. "Then perhaps we can keep being together until ye know."

"I will never love you, Ian." She wanted to look away when she said it but knew she could not. He needed to see the honesty in her gaze. For in her heart, she knew she was not capable of love. Not anymore. Not after what Reginald and his men had done to her family.

"Good thing I'm no' asking ye to marry me, or that might have hurt." He offered a thin chuckle and glanced away.

She tried to ignore the inward wince in her chest. "And what of you? What will you do?"

He shook his head. "I dinna know either. Perhaps return to hiring out my sword for coin until I find a place to settle."

"You could go home." She couldn't help but think of her own family when she spoke any more than she could stop the heart-aching wish to have the opportunity to see them all again. "I lost my family. You shouldn't lose yours."

He was quiet for a long moment and then finally spoke. "Ye say ye've spent yer whole life focused on finding these men and killing them. Why?"

She clenched her hand into a fist and let her fingernails bite into the flesh of her palm.

"Talking about it will help ye heal."

Sylvi scoffed. "You're one to talk with how you brush every-thing off with playful wit."

He cocked his head. "My angel has a point. Very well. I'll agree to be honest with ye, free of jesting if ye are honest with me in return." And indeed, his face did go stern with sincerity. "I'm about to kill a lot of men for ye, Sylvi. I'd like to know why."

Sylvi drew a deep breath. "You're right." Her heartbeat thun-dered in her ears, and her stomach twisted into knots. "Reginald and his men...they killed my entire family. They tried to kill me too. But I survived."

His gaze went to the ribbon on her throat, and she touched

her hand to it as if she could prevent him from seeing it and the understanding that dawned in his eyes.

"What happened?"

Her throat constricted. Suddenly, she wanted the jests and lack of sincerity. And she wanted this conversation over with. She'd never revealed anything more about her family's deaths— only that they'd been killed. "I can't—"

He gently touched the underside of her chin. "There's no' anything my angel canna do."

She let herself bask for a brief moment in the power of his stare before lifting her chin from his fingertips. "I don't even know where to begin." She crossed her arms over her chest. "I've never told anyone more than I just told you."

He untucked her hand from where it was folded snugly in the crook of her arm and held it. "Tell me what happened. Please, Sylvi, I want to know all of it."

"We were poor," she said softly. "My parents came from Norway for a new life in Scotland. I don't know how it started, but my father made replicas of coins."

She remembered her father's large hand with a gold coin shining as if all the treasure in the world was within his ruddy palm. "We had so little money," she said. "The idea of someone being wealthy enough to pay my father to make money was incredible, like God making the heavens larger. I didn't realize at the time counterfeiting was considered treasonous. My father knew it was wrong, but he didn't care. He was a goldsmith in a foreign land, seeking to feed his wife and four children."

She glanced at Ian, but he remained silent, his expression soft. Weary lines creased his brow. She was nearly numb with exhaustion herself. They'd all foregone a night of sleep to ride into the next day.

Perhaps this was why she was telling him now. Her mind was too impacted by fatigue to put up a fight. And perhaps that was why the scene in her head played out more vividly now than it had ever before—a wooden floor the color of honey and the small stool etched with an ornate shield atop its darkened surface.

"He kept a bag for us to use, hidden under the floorboards beneath a stool, with spare clothing for each of us inside," she said. "It also held most of the coin he'd earned. Real coin— nothing imitation. He always told us if something happened to him, we were to take the bag and live off the money until we were safe and able to work." She looked down at where her hand was clasped within Ian's. Her skin had begun to sweat where it pressed to his, but she reveled in the strength the simple gesture gave her. "That bag saved my life."

"Do ye think he knew something bad was going to happen?"

Her father had always been so large, so powerful, like Odin himself. He protected his family against all things: nighttime fears, hunger, hurt. But even Odin could not protect everyone all the time.

She nodded once. "Yes. Yes, he knew, but I don't think—" Her throat squeezed and cut off her words. "I don't think he thought we'd all be there when it did." Her eyes went hot, and her nose tingled. A tear slid down her cheek, and for the first time since she was a little girl, she could not keep herself from crying.

IAN HELD SYLVI AGAINST HIS CHEST. HIS HEART ACHED anew with each beat at the pain of her loss. She'd kept her sobbing silent, an element of control even when breaking.

Holding women while they cried was a thing he'd done many times before, but it had been for simple things. Someone whose ire had parted a friendship, frustration at a father who had rules too strict, sadness at a man they would need to marry and did not care for.

Sylvi's hurt ran far deeper. She stayed on his chest for only a moment after her back stopped trembling, her tears lasting little more than seconds. She sat upright and gently pushed at his chest. He wanted to pull her closer and let his comfort balm her hurt.

"I'm fine." Her voice was all the huskier with emotion. "I shouldn't have—" She cleared her throat and met his gaze with her reddened eyes. "I haven't cried in a very long time."

"I still think ye're one of the toughest warriors I've ever known." He pushed aside a tendril of blonde hair from her face. Her cheek was warm and still wet from her brushed-away tears. "I dinna realize this would be so hard for ye. Thank ye for sharing with me."

"You ought to know." She took a deep, shuddering breath. "And what better person to tell than the man who trusted me enough to let me temporarily kill him?"

It was on the tip of his tongue to throw in a quip, but he merely nodded in understanding.

She looked down at her hands. "It was a spring morning. Mamma was tending to Einar with my sisters, and Pappa was working on several coins for the man who paid him to make them gold. I was sitting near the door when it flew open."

She paused and drew a deep breath. "A man grabbed me and held me in place while another man, Reginald, rushed forward and swiped his blade at my father. It was so fast that I thought he'd missed. But then Pappa's neck opened up, like a wine bag being split along the seam, and blood came out in great gushes. So much blood."

Ian reached for the hands she stared so intently at and clasped them in his own. But she wasn't looking at her hands. She was seeing what he could not, a horrible event long ago passed.

"Mamma ran forward. She had a dagger in her hand and slashed at Reginald. She missed his face, but something flew from his head. I didn't realize what it was until the chunk of his ear landed in front of me. The man holding me had been nervous about killing a child but was told to obey orders, so he did."

She looked up and met Ian's gaze. What he saw in the depths of those winter-blue eyes wrenched at his heart. Beyond the horror and sadness, he saw the scared little girl whose father had been killed in front of her, whose mother had fought to save her children.

"He cut my throat. But his uncertainty left his attempt half-hearted." Her lips lifted in a sad smile. "I didn't know any better. I was only eight. I thought I was dying. He threw me to the ground. Blood was everywhere. Hot on my skin, salty and metallic in my mouth, clogging my nose with the coppery thickness of it."

She fell silent.

Ian's stomach twisted. The last thing he wanted was for her to relive it all. "Sylvi...ye dinna—"

She squeezed his hand and shook her head. "I've come too far now. Don't make me stop."

She drew a soft breath, and a tear spattered on the back of his hand even though she was not sobbing as she'd done earlier. "They were all killed after that. Momma. My two sisters, Alva and Inka. Even little Einar, who wasn't even able to talk yet." She pursed her lips. "I heard it all."

"I was a coward." She growled the words out through clenched teeth, and her hands tensed on his. "I was alive, yet I lay there pretending to be dead while my family was slaughtered around me."

Her anger at herself knotted in his chest. "Ye were a girl." Ian freed one hand to cup her face and wished he could pour his reasoning into her, make her understand what would have been so apparent to anyone else. "Ye couldna have stopped them."

Ian swiped away a single tear trailing down her cheek with his thumb, where it melted against the pad of his finger.

Sylvi took his hand once more and drew it back to her lap where it'd been. "They took all of Pappa's coin replicas, and there was a considerable amount. Bags worth. My body lay over the secret loose floorboard, and I was glad for it. I waited until they had left and lay there for longer until the sun stopped burning a red glow behind my eyelids. And then I opened my eyes. I thought my family might be playing at death like me." She balled her hands into fists against his palms. "They were not. They were all dead, their bodies stiff and cold and empty."

She shook her head as if to clear it. "Reginald and his men took everything from me, Ian. They took my life and left me with nothing. And I lay there and let them do it."

Her gaze met his, glossy with unshed tears and hard with hatred. "That is why I crave vengeance. I know it won't bring back my family, but it will make them pay for what they've done. And I will finally stop being the cowering little girl who let her family be murdered."

Gone were the tears, and in place of the self-hatred burned a gritty determination unlike anything he'd ever seen. It lit her from the inside and promised to destroy all in her path to see her purpose done.

And he did not blame her.

"Sylvi, I—my God, what ye went through."

"Now you know why I wear this." Sylvi touched the ribbon at her neck. "To hide the constant reminder of how I so gravely failed my family."

"It's no' failure at all. Dinna ye see? It's a banner of yer survival. It tells the world a bastard could slice yer neck, and ye'll still be there the next day."

He reached for the ribbon at her neck, his movements slow and careful. She did not stop him. He caught one edge of the flimsy silk between his fingertips. Still, she did not stop him. He met her gaze and pulled gently.

A breath whispered over her lips, and he looked down.

The skin of her throat was milky white and smooth, bisected by a jagged pink scar. He looked into her eyes, the pale blue no longer cool but an open door into a soul as wounded as her throat.

Every day she hid her pain behind an impenetrable mask of strength, and every day she woke up to face the loss again.

Now he finally, truly understood.

Fourteen

Sylvi's heart was trapped in the mutilated confines of her throat. Ian stared deep into her eyes before dropping his gaze to her neck and back up again.

She was exposed. Her most tender vulnerability splayed open for his judgment.

"Sylvi." His voice broke around her name. "Ye're the strongest person I've ever known." He swept his thumb over her lips. "And the most beautiful."

Heat flared over her cheeks, and she turned away, unable to take his placating endearments. He gently turned her head back to him.

"It's hard to know what to say after hearing a story like yers. And yet all I can think is how powerful ye are. Ye hide it all day after day, but seeing it like this." He drew a finger down her throat over the sensitive line of her scar.

She closed her eyes against the caress. His touch on the tender skin did not make her jerk back as she might have thought. There was far too much acceptance in such a stroke for her to fear.

"I love ye, Sylvi."

A chill prickled through her veins.

Love.

How could the idea of love even begin to grow in a heart so damaged?

His mouth came near hers, and she let the warm softness of his lips brush over hers. But it was not the balm she needed, and her heart crumpled at his show of tenderness. She shook her head. He immediately drew back, and cool air filled the space between them.

She opened her eyes to his confused stare. "I can't love you, Ian. I'm too full of hate."

His arms came around her. "Let me love enough for us both, lass." His voice was rich and sensual in her ear.

She wanted to melt into him, to let down the constant iron she always curled around her, for it was heavy and cumbersome.

"It's not fair." Her protest was meek, beaten down by emotion and exhaustion.

"What happened to ye is no' fair." His hold on her intensified, and she realized the ferocity behind his embrace had been held back while she told her story. "After we've killed them all, yer heart will be free, and ye can love."

He had more belief in her than she held for herself. Healing would be impossible. She opened her mouth to protest when his lips came down on hers, tender and so gloriously loving she could not turn him away this time.

Perhaps it was wrong what she did, but she could not refuse the comfort he offered, the acceptance in his gaze. And when he pulled her to him, she allowed her body to mold against his. He was everything warm and safe, everything she had not allowed herself to feel in far too long. She would allow herself the concession of his affection before giving everything up once more in her desperate race for vengeance.

Sylvi woke the next morning to find the room still cloaked in darkness. The comfortable warmth behind her pulled her closer in an embrace.

Ian.

"Good morning." His voice was a deep, delicious rumble in her ear. He nuzzled closer to her, and the scruff of his unshaven jaw scratched against the sensitive skin at the back of her neck.

Her mind came to awareness with a snap of realization.

If it was morning, she'd slept the entire night with him.

Sylvi rolled over to face him and found him smiling. "Good morning."

He propped himself up on his elbow and regarded her, his smile widening. "Ye stayed through the night."

"I didn't have any other place to go." She winked at him.

"Look at ye, no' being so serious." He brushed a hand over her cheek. "Ye're actually verra good at teasing when ye put yer mind to it. Almost as good as me."

She smirked. "Don't get arrogant now."

"That, too, is part of my charm."

She glanced out the window. "Is the sun not up yet?"

A streak of lightning lit up the dark sky, followed almost immediately by a deafening clap of thunder.

"It's trying," Ian said. "But it's no' winning the fight."

She frowned. "What time is it?"

Ian pressed a kiss to her temple, then hopped out of bed without a bit of clothing on him. Naked and totally unconcerned, he made his way to the window and peered out. The muscles of his back flexed with the action.

Sylvi's body went warm with the memory of his powerful back, arms, legs, stomach, everything. The prior night had been unlike any other they'd shared before.

He'd been careful, tender and affectionate. He'd made her feel like someone special and beautiful.

He'd made love to her in the slow, gentle manner he had been trying to implement since their first tryst, and she had allowed it. His tenderness had fed her hungry soul.

When it was all done, he'd wrapped her in his arms, and she'd fallen asleep finally feeling whole.

"I believe it's about the middle of the morning," he said.

Her heart leapt. "So late?" They'd slept longer than intended. "We should have left over an hour ago."

Ian turned back to her. "It will be slow going today. The rain is coming down hard."

A faint light from the window shone over his flat stomach, highlighting the rippled muscle beneath. It would have been distracting were she not so preoccupied with the delay they already faced. The rain would cause them to slip farther behind.

Damn.

"The others should be up by now." Sylvi threw the covers off her and nearly gasped at the chill of the air on her naked skin. "No doubt they've been waiting on us."

Ian pulled his léine on and set to work, fastening the kilt around his waist while she dressed. "Let's divide to save time. I'll go round up the others. Ye can get food from the innkeeper for the journey today."

He dug out the coin pouch from his bag and tossed her a couple of coins. "Ye paid for the room. I'll buy the food."

Sylvi made a face. "You don't have to do that."

He shrugged and opened the door. "I know that, but it's only fair."

Fair.

The word hung in the air for a moment, recalling the conversation from the night before. How it was unfair that she would not be able to love him, and he'd insisted on loving enough for the both of them.

"And it's already done because I'm gone," he added quickly before closing the door.

The coins were cool and heavy in her hand.

It was a kind offer, though she'd find a way to get the coins back to him regardless. After all, this entire trip was for her to get her revenge finally.

She shook her head to clear it of the smile creeping over her lips. Percy was right. Sylvi did keep smiling. But today would require concentration.

Sylvi glanced out the window, and the lightness in her heart went dark. The mud below was thick as pottage and deep enough to have sucked a man's leg in up to his calf.

Today would be difficult, indeed.

She looked at the coins in her palm and reached for her dagger, the habit so ingrained she did not even realize what she was doing until she scraped the first coin. Her hand paused over the second coin.

It was a pointless exercise. They knew where Reginald was.

Her pulse came a little faster. This would truly all be over soon.

She scraped over the coin. It was so silly, yet it always brought her closer to her father. She couldn't help but cherish that thought as she dragged the tip of her dagger over the last and final coin. Her heart stopped mid-beat, and everything in her went cold.

The gold had curled away to reveal a flat, gray metal beneath.

THE WIND OUTSIDE HOWLED, AND THE WALLS OF THE shabby inn creaked. Ian made his way down the darkened corridor toward the other rooms Sylvi had rented. It was almost dark as night despite the window near the stairs.

Rain spattered the window, and a low groan of wood sounded from somewhere in the building. Hopefully, the thing would wait to break apart until after they'd left.

He knocked on Lady Camille's door. She opened it before he'd even drawn his hand back. Behind her, all the other ladies were dressed in heavy traveling clothes.

"I see you were both quite exhausted." Lady Camille gave him a knowing smile. "No doubt from our extensive travels yesterday."

All the eyes in the room fixed on him. "Aye, yesterday was quite...strenuous."

She welcomed him into the room. All the women's bags were piled in the center of the room.

"I can see why ye dinna go to the stables," he said. A growl of thunder rumbled overhead.

"We just got ready." Liv jabbed a pointed stare at Isabel and stroked a hand over her cat's sleek back.

Isabel cast a hard glance back at Liv. "Some of us don't care what we look like, so it's easier to prepare."

"Some of us are going to freeze in our inadequate clothes not meant for rain or wind or anything in Scotland," Liv shot back.

"Ladies." Percy's patient voice interrupted the catfight before the claws could come out. The large green cloak hood draped down her back, and for the time being, her face was visible.

She eyed Isabel's flimsy gold-and-red dress. "It might be prudent to wear something a little...more in light of the weather."

Isabel shot a pout in her direction and turned her kohl-slanted gray eyes toward Ian. "What do you think?"

Ian opened his mouth to speak when the door to Lady Camille's room flew open, and Sylvi stormed in. Her hand was thrust in front of her with a coin nestled in her palm.

"Where did you get this?" she demanded.

He held his ground and stared at the coin. "Sylvi, I dinna know—"

She curled the metal into her fist and swung at him. He jerked out of her way.

"I said, where did you get it?" she snarled.

Lady Camille ran to them in a flurry of blue skirts and grabbed Sylvi's arms to pull her back. "What in God's name are you doing, Girl?"

Sylvi flung the older woman off her and threw a kick at Ian.

He blocked the blow and shifted backward once more. His ankle met the hard wall, and he realized he had nowhere else to go.

"The coin?" Ian asked. His mind whirled. "I dinna remember where I got it."

"You're lying." Sylvi threw her weight into him and trapped his body against the wall, leveraging herself against his neck.

The "strangle until they can't talk" questioning routine again. Wonderful.

An arm flew up between them, and a woman with copper hair stood in front of him.

"This is wrong." Liv put her hands on her hips and stood her ground before him with a wide, stubborn stance. "You're attacking a man who has no idea why."

Sylvi glared at him over Liv's shoulder. Her gaze was once more as hard and cold as ice.

Ian sidled from behind Liv's protection. He would certainly not cower behind a woman. "Much as I appreciate yer assistance, I can handle myself." He nodded his thanks.

Liv shrugged. "If she kills you, your death won't be on my conscience."

Sylvi's eyes narrowed with accusation. The ribbon was not on her neck, and the scar showed an angry red against the white of her throat. "You knew. This whole time." She shook her head. "You didn't tell me. Not even after I told you..."

A flash of hurt showed brilliant and cutting in her stare before she slid behind her cold exterior once more.

Guilt twisted in Ian's gut and locked his tongue in place.

"How do you know this, Sylvi?" Percy put a hand on Sylvi's shoulder.

Sylvi flinched but did not strike her gentle friend. She held out the coin once more.

Now Ian was close enough to see the scrape of gold missing from its center and the metal beneath. His stomach churned with disgust.

"A counterfeit coin," he said softly. One of those stolen from her family after they'd been murdered.

Sylvi did not meet his eyes. "There's only one place you could obtain this." She threw the coin at his feet. It spun on the hardwood floor in a ringing warble for a moment before settling next to the toe of his boot, its scratched face glaring up at him.

"Did you lie to me?" Gone was the harshness of her anger, replaced by a tone so quiet and sad that it punched into his gut with more force than her fist ever could.

Lady Camille reached out as though she meant to put her hand on Sylvi's shoulder, then thought better of it and let her arm fall. "He could have gotten that from anywhere."

Sylvi stared at him with vulnerability and pained betrayal on her face. "But he didn't."

He swallowed hard, knowing all eyes were on him but caring only for the pale blue ones watching him. He'd known he probably had some on his person, yet he couldn't bring himself to tell Sylvi. That had been a mistake, and he had realized as much far too late. "I dinna want to hurt ye."

She stiffened. "I'd have to care about you for you to hurt me." Then she turned on her heel and left the room.

Fifteen

I an left the confused party behind and found Sylvi in the room they'd shared together.

The ribbon she'd forgotten earlier draped around the back of her neck in preparation to tie it into place once more. She remained turned away from him when he entered.

Her fingers shook while she attempted to secure a small bow in the black ribbon. "Of all the things to lie to me about. Of all the men you could be..."

The ribbon fell to the floor in a resigned wisp, and she spun around to face him. Her cheeks flared red with anger. "Why?"

She curled her hand over the scar on her neck, blocking it from his view. What they had, the trust he'd built with her, was ruined.

And he had no one to blame but himself.

He swallowed and looked at the ground where the ribbon lay in a sad slip of black. "Because I'm a coward."

"Yes, you are," she replied in a hard voice.

"I'd hoped ye wouldna agree with me."

He wished he were indeed as small as he felt so she could crush him under her boot and be done with it. He raised his gaze to her. "I'm sorry, Sylvi."

She lifted her chin up a notch.

"I dinna tell ye in the beginning because I dinna have a part in making the coins, and even knowing it happened while I was there is treasonous. And when ye told me everything..." He wished she could see the depth of his regret, experience how great the pain seared. "Then I wanted to, but ye looked at me so gently, I dinna want to lose that. I couldna bring myself to admit it. I planned to tell ye everything when we had the tryst at our moonlit glen—when we were completely alone."

"Which is why you were so upset when I said I couldn't go." She frowned. "You wouldn't have told me then either, though. You could have done so last night when we were alone, but you didn't. I shared with you what happened to my family, and you held me and loved me. You comforted me." Her lip curled with disgust.

She was slipping from him. He could feel it as surely as he'd felt her cold absence in bed when she'd left him in the middle of the night in evenings past.

"I never did any of the things they did. I was only with them for four months. Ye knew all of this."

"Knowing it and seeing it are two separate things. Seeing that coin..." She broke off. "It only took minutes to kill my entire family." Her voice was like a blade slipping into his heart. "How many families were killed in those four months? How many women raped? How many lives destroyed?"

Rage flashed through Ian, defiant and defensive. "I dinna do any of that. I wasna lying when I told ye I saved a woman from being hurt by them. I hadna realized what they'd been doing until that day. I put a stop to it immediately and left them."

"What had you been doing for them?"

"I delivered messages, negotiated for them. Sometimes I had matches with other swordsmen for money." He shook his head. "Nothing like what you said."

His words came out rushed in his attempt to make her understand. He needed her to know so she wouldn't leave.

She bent and picked up her ribbon from where it lay discarded on the ground. "Go home, Ian." She turned from him and worked the slender black silk around her neck with fingers that no longer trembled.

Go home.

As if it were so simple. As if his da wanted him back.

As if he could face the guilt he'd left behind.

Rain splashed against the window, and the sky seemed to darken further. The weather matched the ugly emptiness of his mood.

"This is my fight, too," he said fiercely.

She turned to him with a smirk. The ribbon had been successfully secured around her throat, the scar hidden from view. Her shield had once more been raised. "Of course, I forgot you have to protect yourself. If they discover you did not die, they certainly will make reparations."

He didn't like the snideness of her tone. "I meant, I am still at yer side to fight against them. I want to help ye avenge yer family to make things right."

She opened her mouth to speak, but he rushed on. "Ye are already outnumbered. I can help even the odds in yer favor more. And ye know I'm a good fighter. I also know their habits better than ye might."

She studied him for a long moment, and he could practically see the calculations spinning in her head. "Very well. But when this is done, you will leave."

Her gaze slid to the bed they'd shared, with its crumpled blankets and memories. "You will sleep in a separate room, and after this is all over, I will never see you again."

Those final words slammed into Ian like a throat punch. He'd expected her anger, of course. He'd even expected it to hurt. But not as much as it did.

"If that's what ye wish."

"It is." Her answer came swiftly, a lethal blow to the budding bond he'd worked so hard to cultivate.

Without a whisper of emotion showing on her composed face, she strode toward the door, her boots thundering over the hardwood surface, and then she was gone.

The rain was damn miserable. Like a mirror to Sylvi's soul, it was cold and driving and abysmal. The ground froze in patches, leaving the parts of the trails not sucking with mud slick with ice instead. Heavy clouds hid the sun as well as its light, leaving the world cast in an unreal gray that kept much of the forests they passed concealed in shadows.

Everyone in their wretched party was huddled beneath the additional blankets they'd brought with them, so they appeared nothing more than six shapeless masses plopped atop equally gloomy horses.

There was a solemnity to the party, and Sylvi knew it had some to do with the storm and even more with Ian's silence. His jovial personality added more to the overall mood than she'd given him credit for. Without his wit and their smiles, the awfulness of their journey was all the more tangible.

What was more, the unrest between Sylvi and Ian had caused disquiet among the ladies. For all but Isabel, who grinned with an annoying smugness.

Sylvi was not responsible for his silence, however, and refused to allow a slip of guilt to nip at her. He had made his choices. He had kept pertinent information from her.

He had deceived her in the worst of ways.

The very thought of it brought a surge of energy to her muscles and left her wanting to slam her fist into his handsome face. At least such rage brought a semblance of warmth with it. She flexed her frozen fingers, and prickles of protest tingled up her arm.

My Lady's horse appeared beside Sylvi's. The fine beast had once been beautifully white and was now a pathetic gray, spattered with flecks and chunks of mud. My Lady regarded her from a narrow slit in the folds of her blanket, nothing more than a slash of skin and two eyes. "We cannot keep traveling like this."

Sylvi pushed away the blanket from her face and was hit hard by a rush of cold wind and smattering rain. "We are only an hour away."

"Yes. In good weather." My Lady's horse slipped in the mud. Her hand shot out—bone white against the darkness of blankets so sodden their color was indiscernible—and grabbed the reins. The beast steadied itself, and My Lady slid a look of annoyance in Sylvi's direction. "You may not be affected by this weather, but the rest of us are near mutiny."

Mutiny was a strong word. One Sylvi knew My Lady added for exaggeration. Still, Sylvi cast a glance over her shoulder to regard the bundles on their horses. The trail was wide despite the dense forest around them. White puffs intermittently fogged in front of each person's face as their breath froze once it hit the air.

She knew they were miserable.

"Even if we were to arrive in an hour," My Lady said, "we are not in any condition to fight."

"If we arrive and do not attack, they could find out about our presence, and we will lose our advantage." A thread of icy air slipped down Sylvi's back, and she shuddered. "We could lose them again."

"Better to have to find them again than have us all slaughtered for naught."

Sylvi regarded her mentor and found the other woman nearly glaring at her.

My Lady jerked the bottom of the blanket from her face in a show of high irritation. "You are responsible for your ladies, Girl." Her face was white and pinched, every line of age evident. "They look to you for guidance and care. Leading them to slaughter is not what a leader does. Do not let your need for vengeance over-rule your judgment."

Sylvi's heart thundered in her chest, and her breath came fast.

"Do not presume to tell me how to lead my ladies. They are tougher than they appear."

My Lady scoffed. "I came here to help you put an end to what has haunted you most of your life. These ladies, and Ian, are here for that reason as well. I'll tell you this one time to have a care for them and will leave it to your discretion."

Damn it.

They were so close. Reginald and his men were practically beneath the point of her blade.

Sylvi pulled up the thick blanket around her face. The wind was starting to make the insides of her ears ache. Or perhaps it was My Lady's words. Regardless, their conversation was done. When Sylvi glanced beside her, she found the spot empty.

Her sigh of relief warmed the blanket wrapped around her face for a moment before the wind chilled it, leaving it wet and cold against her nose. A fresh torrent of rain whipped around them. Sylvi couldn't feel her hands anymore. In fact, the only things she could feel were the ice forming in her bones and the maddeningly rhythmic blossoming of wet, hot and cold in the fabric over her face with every breath.

Guilt constricted in her chest, and she glanced back at those who so diligently followed her.

Every one of them kept pace. Not a one had complained, except for Isabel, who offered growling complaints from beneath the layers of blankets where she was nearly frozen in her tissue-thin clothing. My Lady was the only one to approach Sylvi and did so on behalf of the group. My Lady had been in the right—a realization Sylvi grudgingly admitted to herself. She knew her fortitude to be unique, and if she struggled with the cold, she knew the others were indeed suffering.

My Lady had also been right in that they all looked to Sylvi to make the right decisions.

Frustration squeezed through her, and she blew it out in a great cloud of aggravation. She would never live with herself if she got them all killed.

She would have to put off killing Reginald. So she risked losing him again.

Sixteen

Ian's body shuddered at the savage tear of wind and the fresh pelting of freezing rain. He clenched his teeth against the chill and tried not to think about how cold he was, how wet, how miserable. Yet somehow, trying not to think of such things only made him focus on them more.

He kept his gaze fixed on several feeble curls of smoke in the distance, a beacon of hope to be warm once again. Closer and closer and closer it came until finally, a small cluster of buildings became visible. No one walked the sludge-thick roads, and not a soul could be seen. But they were there. No doubt, all tucked inside their sturdy homes with a slab of peat smoldering in the hearth.

By his estimation, they were less than an hour from where Lady Camille had indicated Reginald and his men would be camped. Which made it all the more surprising they were stopping.

The hard mask on Sylvi's face indicated she was none too pleased with her decision. She swept from her horse and strode toward the inn without so much as casting a glance back at him. Ian's gut wrenched at the clear dismissal, and he hated it.

"I told you she'd choose her vengeance over you."

He turned to find Isabel sitting on her horse, a self-satisfied smile on her uncovered face. The kohl she lined her eyes with melted down her face, so the hollows under her eyes appeared deep and dark. For all the beauty she attempted, she now looked like a wraith.

"Aye, but she chose our comfort over her vengeance. Maybe ye should appreciate what she's sacrificing for ye."

Isabel rolled her eyes and fell into sullen silence. A petulant sign of grudging acceptance.

Sylvi was a good leader and an incredible woman. Passionate, formidable, beautiful. And she was slipping from his grasp. A knot of longing worked its way into Ian's chest.

He had a habit of losing everything in his life that meant something.

And losing them only made him want them back more.

His family, whom he had nothing to offer. Simon and his father, neither of whom could be brought back. Sylvi, whose trust had been shattered.

Perhaps he ought to leave as Sylvi suggested, but not toward home. He couldn't bring himself to return and be the type of man he knew his father wanted him to be. He could return to the road. The thought soured as soon as it entered his mind, bringing with it the memory of the hollow emptiness of such an aimless life.

And he didn't want to leave Sylvi. Especially not after what she'd told him with the utmost trust. He wanted that trust back.

He wanted her love back.

He wanted her.

Because with her, he didn't feel so worthlessly lost.

She exited the inn and made her way to them, her stride confident and sure as if the ground were not thick with sucking mud. "They have enough rooms but do not have a door at the rear, nor do they deliver food to the rooms. We'll have to eat in the main area." The downturn of her mouth indicated she was not happy about this as she reached up to her horse's bridle and led it toward the stables.

Ian should speak to her. He knew this, and yet he could not bring himself to summon a thing to say, not when they got to the stables nor when they left their horses with a stable lad, who took their coin with red, chapped hands.

All the ready sayings that easily sprang from mind to mouth had suddenly gone quiet, weighed down by regret and guilt.

He kept under the narrow roof of the stable as he made his way to the inn with Sylvi directly in front of him. A soft touch on his arm pulled his attention. He looked down to find Percy's blue eyes gazing up at him from beneath her wide hood.

"Give her some time." She pursed her lips and glanced to where Sylvi's back disappeared through the inn door before speaking again. "I know she cares very much for you."

Ian nodded his thanks, grateful for Percy's ever-present consideration, and opened the door for her. A remarkably nasty gust of wind tried to wrench it from his grasp, but he held it long enough to pass through before letting it slam shut behind him.

His body prickled with the warmth of the room. Everything once cold only a second ago was now stinging with the introduction of heat. He unwound the plaid from his face.

It was curious how every inn seemed to be identical to the last. With the exception of how clean a place was, they all were the same. Long wooden tables with sputtering candles set at their centers, a door in the back leading to an unseen kitchen, and a staircase to the rooms above.

Not all were so warm. He knew well enough to be grateful for the heat.

Several other patrons sat at the tables throughout the room, their voices mingling with one another to create a deep hum. Sylvi led the way to a table near the back. Percy and Lady Camille sat closest to the wall, where their faces might remain shadowed, Liv and Sylvi sat opposite them, and Isabel quickly grabbed the spot beside Sylvi.

There was nothing quite like the ire of a rejected woman.

Ian sank into the remaining spot beside Liv, who cast him a look as cool as the woman she modeled herself after. The lass might have offered to save him, but she was not inclined to forgive his transgressions.

Sylvi's gaze settled on him once and flicked away. Enough of a look to set his pulse racing.

A brown-haired barmaid approached the table. Lines creased her comely face from a lifetime of smiles, and the easy sway of her hips told him she was comfortable in her role at the inn. "Sorry to not deliver food to the rooms. Rats." She winked down at him. "Miserable day to be out, eh?"

Sylvi straightened on the other side of the table.

"It's a frozen hell out there," he conceded. "Thanks for getting the place good and warm for us."

"We aim to please." Her smile was one of invitation.

"We'll all have ale and stew," Sylvi said abruptly.

The woman nodded and turned away to comply with Sylvi's request, nonplussed with the sudden halt to her casual flirtation.

The skin around Sylvi's eyes tightened, and she glared at a spot over Ian's shoulder.

"Um...I'm looking forward to the stew." From beneath her hood, Percy spoke softly at the end of the table.

Usually, it was Ian's place to break up the discomfort of quiet at a table. Yet since his conversation with Sylvi that morning, he'd found his well of witty conversation had run dry.

"I'm sure our horses are glad we stopped as well," Ian added in a halfhearted attempt.

A muscle worked in Sylvi's jaw. He hadn't meant it as criticism, but she seemed to take it as such. Especially when she was already near to wanting to eat his soul and spit out the pieces.

Their food came without fanfare, though the brown-haired

woman did pause to give him a smile when she set his steaming stew in front of his face. The meal was eaten in near silence, with only Isabel appearing to be enjoying herself with continually coquettish grins and winks in the direction of a man sitting by himself at a nearby table.

Better him than Ian.

With a belly full of warm food and the last chill of cold stripped from his bones, a deep exhaustion settled over him. The door to the inn burst open, and a small group of men came in, their voices boisterous. One of them spoke, and the lot of them burst into raucous laughter.

"We should get some rest," Sylvi said. "Especially considering tomorrow."

Tomorrow, they would be attacking Reginald. And facing the storm if the weather proved as nasty as it had that day.

Together they trudged upstairs, with Isabel lingering in the back before finally following them. Ian's pulse came a little quicker while they waited for Sylvi to tell them which room belonged to whom. All strategically selected, of course. No doubt he'd be placed as far from Sylvi as possible. Even knowing this did not stop the dread from balling in his stomach.

The second floor was a simple corridor of doors with wooden walls and floors. It was cooler there than below. The perfect temperature for bundling under a set of heavy covers and letting sleep steal away all one's worries and hurts.

"The first room is where I'll sleep." Sylvi spoke loudly to be heard over the men below, who were now singing a song so out of tune that he couldn't name it.

She pointed to each room as she spoke. "Then Percy, Liv, My Lady, Isabel and Ian."

As far opposite of hers as it could be—just as he'd expected. Nor did he miss how she'd placed Isabel's room next to his.

"I forgot something downstairs," Isabel said casually. "I'll be back in a moment."

Sylvi cast her a wary look before nodding. Isabel eagerly dashed back downstairs, and they all knew she wouldn't be back anytime soon.

Lady Camille poked her head into her room and strolled to Sylvi's room. "I want this one instead," she said. "There are two windows here since it's at the corner. I like to see from all directions when I can."

Sylvi's irritation was obvious. "Fine. Anyone else have issues with their rooms?"

Ian bit his cheek to keep from speaking up. Of course, he wished to have his room by hers instead. In hers. With her.

He waited until they had all cleared to their rooms, intentionally stalling so he could speak with Sylvi. She didn't so much as look at him until they were left alone.

"Sylvi, I—"

She put up a hand to stop him and met his eyes for the first time that afternoon. "We need rest, and we need to be prepared for tomorrow. I will not allow you to interfere with any of it."

"Then tomorrow, I—"

"You've already done enough, Ian." She turned from him then and closed her door behind her with finality.

Ian stared at the thin wooden door for a long moment.

Aye, tomorrow they would fight, but no matter how they won, he knew he would still lose. For he had indeed lost his angel.

The night had been a hard one.

Sylvi squinted her eyes open and flinched at the glare of sunlight streaming in through the window. Her head screamed with a hollow ache pulsing behind her eyes.

The men who had come in as she'd brought the others upstairs had been loud through the evening and into the early morning. In fact, they'd grown louder as the night pressed on into early dawn. Now the silence was so heavy it seemed stuffed and thick in her ears.

If Ian had come to her door in an attempt to speak again, she would not have heard him.

Her heart flinched. Why had she even thought that? Wasn't it splashing vinegar on the freshness of her wound?

After all, she'd already turned him away. Surely, he would not attempt to return after their previous conversation.

No doubt he'd found solace with the wench who had served them. She had been none too discreet in presenting her interest for him to enjoy. And damn if he hadn't given her that charming smile right back.

Sylvi could have kicked him.

Not that any of it mattered. After today, she wouldn't see him again.

Today.

When Reginald would die under the bite of her blade—when his men would pay the price for having killed her family, and all the other wrongdoings they'd surely done.

Her pulse sped at the thought. After almost seventeen years, her family would be able to rest in peace with their murderers punished. Now fully awake and with her eyes adjusted to the light, she sat up to look out the window. The sun shone through the feathered wisps of clouds, and only a light drizzle fell upon whatever town it was they had slept in.

She leapt from her bed and dressed with trembling hands. Fatigue from a poor night of sleep and a heady mix of nerves left her insides quivering. She drew in a long, slow breath and then exhaled. Of all days, today was the most important, especially with such powerful emotions at play. She needed to maintain control.

By the time she'd splashed cold water from the basin onto her face and twisted her hair back, her hands no longer shook. A quick touch of the warm plaid by the hearth confirmed it was nearly dry. After her fast had been broken, it'd be ready for another bout of travel.

She exited into the hallway and found a door open to the far right. Was it Ian's room?

The nervous pounding of her pulse resumed. She needed to face him only a while longer, just these last few hours, and then she would be done with him forever.

A brown-haired woman backed out of the open door with a throaty giggle. She looked at Sylvi and immediately straightened. The wench from the night before. Only now, her hair was mussed, and one naked breast peeked above her corset.

She flushed and shoved at her flesh, tucking the bright pink nipple from sight.

Sylvi's stomach swirled, but she tamped down nausea. It was better if Ian moved on.

If only she could stop the wrenching squeeze every time her heart beat.

A man's arm appeared in the doorway and wrapped around the woman's waist, pulling her back inside. The woman laughed and pulled away. He stepped forward, naked, with a crop of red hair so wild and tousled one couldn't tell where his beard met his hair.

Not Ian.

Sylvi breathed out with relief she shouldn't feel.

The woman laughed again and pointed at Sylvi. The man waved and swatted the woman on the rump before letting her leave.

"Men, eh?" the wench said as she passed with a wink.

"Indeed," Sylvi murmured in reply.

She waited until the woman had swept down the stairs before going to each of the rooms and knocking to rouse her army. Hopefully, they'd slept better than she had, for today, they would battle.

My Lady did not answer. She'd always risen early, but perhaps age was beginning to show itself. "I'll come back in five minutes,"

Sylvi said through the closed door. No reply came from the other side.

Percy opened her door immediately, a wide smile on her face. She clasped Sylvi's hand in her warm ones. "Today is the day, Sylvi." Tears shone in her eyes. "I'm so happy you will finally have your heart set at peace." Then she threw her arms around Sylvi. The sweet scent of violets—of Percy—surrounded Sylvi and lent comfort to her soul that threatened to bring tears to her own eyes.

Sylvi squeezed the other girl and quickly released her lest she fall prey to soft emotions.

Liv's door opened before Sylvi could knock on it. She nodded once at Sylvi. "I'm ready."

The three of them went to Isabel's room, but their knocks were unanswered. Sylvi suppressed a sigh of irritation. Isabel typically did what she wanted, including her obvious indulgence with the man downstairs the prior evening.

Sylvi had not stopped her, of course. No one was in danger if Isabel's identity was discovered, save Isabel herself. If she wanted to put herself at risk, Sylvi would not intervene beyond the warnings she'd already issued.

"Five minutes," Sylvi said through the door. No reply from her either.

Liv slid a knowing look to Sylvi. One that Sylvi did not acknowledge. She would not have her forces divided on the day of the fight.

Next was Ian's room. Sylvi's heartbeat came a little faster. She could not get from her mind the sickening horror she'd felt when she thought the serving wench had come from his room.

She might not be capable of love, but Ian still held a hard grip on her emotions. She shouldn't let him have that effect on her.

It was an easy thought, at least before he pulled open his door and met her with a handsome smile. As if the betrayal had never happened—as if Liv and Percy were not there beside her. As if everything had remained the same, and he was greeting her with the intimate comfort they'd shared.

Her heart dipped into her lower stomach, and her gaze drifted toward his mouth, his lips pink beneath the darkness of his beard. Soft and full. Warm.

She flicked her stare from him. "It's time."

He stepped out into the hall, but she didn't stay with him. She couldn't, not when being so close to him allowed his scent to tease over her memories and recall too much she'd rather forget. Suddenly Isabel sleeping in gritted at her nerves all the more.

Sylvi made her way back down to Isabel's room and knocked once more. No answer. Again.

"Isabel, if you don't open this door, I will." The warning in her tone would be unmistakable—even to Isabel.

The door still did not open.

Sylvi slipped the pin from her hair and used it to pick the lock. It clicked open. Sylvi opened the door and stepped inside.

The room was empty. The blanket on the bed was unrumpled, and none of Isabel's bags sat within. Sylvi looked behind her to where Percy and Liv took it all in at the same time, concern furrowing their brows.

"Did either of you see her come up here last night?" Sylvi asked.

They both shook their heads. And if they hadn't seen anything, surely no one had heard anything either with how damn loud it'd been.

Sylvi uttered a curse.

Of all days for Isabel to decide to find a male suitor and disappear.

She heaved a sigh. "You ladies stay here and see if you can find any hints of her even having come into the room or where she might have gone. I'm going to go wake My Lady."

A sudden wall of dread smacked into her. Sylvi shook it off and made her way to My Lady's room. Isabel's disappearance left a disconcerting edge cutting through her. Nothing more.

Sylvi knocked gently on My Lady's door.

No answer.

Her heart started to pound. "My Lady?"

Still no answer.

"I'm going to open your door." Sylvi pulled the pin from her hair once more but found it unnecessary. The door was unlocked.

She pushed the door open, and the sight that met her eyes dragged her to her knees.

Seventeen

A hollow thud came from somewhere nearby, followed by a low, moaning cry. Ian turned toward Liv and Percy. They all met each other's gazes, and together they ran from Isabel's room to Lady Camille's.

The sound became louder.

Ian was the first to arrive. His heart jerked into his throat, and he stopped in the doorway.

In the center of the room, Lady Camille lay on her stomach, the white of her nightrail soaked a brilliant red with blood. It pooled around her in such an amount the unseen wound could only be fatal. Her hands were bound awkwardly behind her back, and her fingers tipped with blue.

Sylvi curled over her protectively as if she could prevent what had already been done. A low moan came from her, so hollow and painful it pulled at Ian's heart.

"Sylvi." He said her name softly.

Percy had begun to sob beside him. "Please go to her," she whispered.

Ian made his way into the room and found two men lying face up, one with a patch of blood over his heart, the other with a dagger jutting from his neck. A chair had been smashed to pieces, and the small table by the bed had been overturned with a splintered ewer beneath it. Clearly, there had been a struggle.

"Sylvi," Ian said again.

Her shoulders curled around Lady Camille's body. "Leave us." Her voice was emotionless and flat.

"Sylvi, I'm here for ye." He touched her back, and she bowed her head low over the body.

"*Min mor*," Sylvi murmured. "*Min mor.*"

Ian knelt beside Sylvi. His knee sank into the blood, cold and congealing. Lady Camille had died some time ago. He pushed back a thread of hair from Sylvi's face. Her cheek was smeared with blood, and it had soaked into her clothing.

"Just like my mother." Sylvi looked up at him. Her eyes were dry, but her throat rasped with emotion. She leaned back and revealed Lady Camille's pale face, her vacantly staring eyes and the gaping hole where her throat had been slit so savagely that it had cut her neck almost completely in half.

"Just like my mother, and my father, and my sisters and Einar. Sweet baby Einar." Sylvi shook her head, her gaze distant on a horror Ian could not see but could guess well enough.

Sylvi caressed her former mentor's white cheek, smearing the thick blood there. "She did all this for me. She wouldn't be here if it weren't for me."

"She knew what she was getting into, Sylvi. Ye canna blame yerself."

"She died helping me, and the last words we had were not kind." Sylvi pursed her lips, and Ian realized she was keeping back tears. "We would never have stopped if it were not for her. After all this time, she still had so much to teach me. So much more I'll never learn."

Heavy footsteps and the rattling of pans sounded from below the room. People were starting to rouse.

"We need to get her out of here, aye?" he said.

Sylvi closed her eyes for a moment before opening them once more, revealing a glossy sheen of tears. "We have to bury her."

"Aye, we'll bury her, my angel." He carefully eased her away from Lady Camille and put his arms around her to lend her his support, his strength. He knew how desperately she needed it.

She allowed herself to be pulled to a standing position. Percy and Liv stood in the doorway, silent and wide-eyed. Ian gave them a reassuring nod, and Percy's shoulders relaxed.

Sylvi said nothing for a moment, casting her gaze on the death in the room, her clothing glistening with it. "We will leave the others. Liv, bring me any identifying information and ensure they have nothing on them to signify who they are or where they've come from. Let them be found alone and unnamed."

Liv nodded.

"Percy, ask after Isabel." Sylvi pulled in a deep, pained breath. "I fear she may be in grave danger."

THE WORLD HAD SLIPPED AWAY FROM UNDERFOOT. OR so it seemed to Sylvi.

She stared into the gaping hole cut into the soft, rain-swollen earth where My Lady lay. All white skin and bright red blood. Such a vivid contrast to the darkness in which she rested.

Sylvi hoped this was what My Lady would have wanted, though she could almost hear the purr of My Lady's pragmatic voice in her head. "If I'm dead, what would I care what happens to my body?"

Because Sylvi cared.

Because Sylvi had loved her with the optimistic affection that she'd held for her father when he'd been alive. My Lady had been a mentor, a caretaker, a reason to live.

"It's time," Ian said softly.

He had insisted on staying by her side while Liv and Percy went inside to gather their belongings and question the staff about Isabel.

He held the shovel out to Sylvi. She let her hands curl around the cold wood, wet from the persistent rain. Her clothes were streaked with a runny mix of mud and gore, but she did not care.

"She saved me." Sylvi regarded the body of her mentor once more, knowing she needed to bury her but unable to bring herself to go through the movements to do so. Her heart squeezed at the thought of putting so much dirt atop her, blotting her out of existence.

Burial was so final.

Forever.

Ian's arm came around her, respectfully distant yet comforting enough for Sylvi to wish he would break through the boundaries she'd erected and curl her into the protection of his strength.

"I was a shell of a person after my family died," she said. "I had no purpose. I ate when I couldn't stand the gnaw of hunger anymore. I skulked in the shadows of the streets, wishing death would find me and reunite me with my family."

Rainwater ran over his head, slicking Ian's dark hair to his skull and dripping from his nose. Yet he remained silent and at her side.

"Death never found me," Sylvi said. "But My Lady did. Or rather, I found her. I heard a scuffle in an alleyway and ran toward it. What I found was My Lady fighting another man." Sylvi's heart swelled with the memory. "She wore a yellow dress, so bright in the dinginess of the alley, so elegant, like something fine ladies would wear. But she was a warrior. So beautiful, so graceful."

A knot tightened in her throat, but she swallowed it away. She would not cry. My Lady would not have wanted her tears.

"I knew the man—he was the one who had been taking children from the streets." She grimaced. "He fought like a cornered cat, and she like a lioness. This man was a nightmare, and she defeated him with such ferocity."

Sylvi closed her eyes to clear away the sting of impending tears. "She gave me something I never thought to have again. She gave me hope."

When she opened her eyes again, she saw My Lady resting in the dirt. Her face was wet with the soft rain, as if glossy with a sheen of sweat, her empty stare closed forever.

Forever.

It was time.

"I love you, My Lady," she said quietly. "For everything you taught me and all you gave back."

She gripped the handle of the shovel in her hands and hefted the first spadeful of dirt into the hole. It spattered over the center of My Lady's dressing gown like a defilement. Sylvi winced but forced herself to fill her shovel once more.

The first one would be the hardest. It would get easier.

It didn't. No matter how hard she tried to focus on only the task itself or the burn of her muscles, she could not get My Lady's slowly disappearing body out of her mind—out of her heart.

Percy and Liv emerged beside them.

"I know her name," Liv said solemnly and held out a book to Sylvi. "Do you want to know it?"

Sylvi stared at the leather-bound book, fat with parchment, and shook her head. "No."

"It was her journal, from what I can tell. Take it," Liv said. "I think she would want you to have it."

Ian took the shovel from Sylvi's numb hands, and she accepted the book from Liv. The leather was already slick with the drizzle of rain. Sylvi quickly tucked it into her bag, the one Percy had treated with wax to keep the contents dry.

Perhaps the journal ought to be buried with My Lady, her secrets disappearing with her body. But Sylvi could not bring herself to toss that part of My Lady into the grave.

Sylvi hadn't had the presence of mind that fateful day to take any personal effects from her childhood home to remind her of her family. She would not make the same mistake again.

They buried My Lady's clothes with her but kept her weapons and the book. Ian aided with a shovel borrowed from the stable. He'd been able to work far faster than her—not due to physical strength, but emotional fortitude. It was easier to labor with a lighter heart.

Within several minutes, My Lady was gone.

Forever.

Sylvi stared at the plot of churned wet earth, unable to drag her gaze away. "What news of Isabel?"

"The innkeeper said she left with one of the men," Liv said. "He didn't indicate there was any trouble."

Sylvi gritted her teeth. "That doesn't mean there wasn't any."

"Liv, show her," Percy said softly.

"The men upstairs had nothing on them but this." Liv held out her hand to reveal a coin with its surface scratched to reveal the bland metal beneath. "They had several coins on them, but only two peeled back."

One would have been a coincidence, but two were enough to tell her who had killed My Lady.

Reginald's men.

Sylvi regarded the three remaining in her party. Who would have told? Was it one among them?

Percy wouldn't have done it. She still couldn't bring herself to lift the hood of her cloak in public. Liv had always been loyal. Then there was Ian. The man she had loved and lost. The man she had rejected.

He'd lied once before to save his neck. What would stop him from lying again?

It was too late for inquisitions, not with the fight on the horizon. She would keep her eye on Ian to ensure he did not turn on them. If he were with Reginald, he would not admit it to her, no matter how she asked.

And if he were not, she could not risk him going into battle rattled by her accusation.

Sylvi clutched the bag holding My Lady's book to her chest. "We must save Isabel while we still can." She looked pointedly at Ian. "Perhaps they knew we were coming."

Eighteen

Ian had not missed the pointed accusation in Sylvi's tone nor the weight of her careful gaze. She didn't trust him.

The four of them had returned the shovel to the stable and taken their horses, leaving Lady Camille's. It wasn't needed and would at least compensate the innkeeper for the two bodies they'd have to dispose of on the second floor. Surely not the first time bodies remained for disposal in an inn.

The short time from the grave to the stable had brought a shift in Sylvi's mood. From the somber, reverent woman who had stared with red-rimmed eyes into the grave of a friend to a woman set on vengeance.

Liv had found a map at the back of Lady Camille's book indicating where Reginald and his men were. She led the way, with Sylvi following closely at her heels. Blood and dirt streaked Sylvi's body and face, turning her beauty into a nightmare.

His avenging angel in her full glory.

The four of them rode as hard as the soft ground would allow. The rain did not abate through the course of their journey. While it never poured upon them, it misted and spit, slowly soaking them. But they were well rested and had enough food to fill their bellies for the morning. At least to make it through a battle.

Liv motioned at the rocks ahead of them, indicating they were near.

Large, gray boulders jutted from the ground, shooting up above tender, green grass only several feet ahead. The trees beyond were heavily grown, far too close together to bring the horses.

Ian's body tensed for the onset of war, and energy blazed through him. He was ready to help Sylvi, to prove his loyalty. To do the right thing for once in his damn life.

They slowed as they neared the rocks and leapt from their horses. Sylvi looked to Percy and nodded.

Percy slid behind a large boulder with a pile of small clay pots at her side and slung her bow from her back. Liv waited beside Sylvi, impatiently bouncing on her toes.

Sylvi looked at him, put her arm in the air and dropped it.

It was time.

Ian sprinted forward. His muscles practically sang from engaging the energy firing through him. He made sure to stay at Sylvi's side, his senses sharp and aware. No matter the cost, he would see her protected.

They ran through the surrounding trees, the clearing immediately becoming visible.

Something wasn't right.

Liv and Sylvi breathed deep and even in their running beside him. Even still, the sounds were too loud.

It was too empty. And too quiet.

All three sprinted faster, running to the thing they all knew but could not bring themselves to say.

They did not stop until they reached the clearing only a second later, revealing the truth.

Reginald and his men were gone.

Sylvi dropped to her knees, lifted her face to the sky, and screamed—a long, savage cry of rage directed at the heavens and all else who would listen. The sound was worse than seeing her cry. A woman blazing at the peak of her power and yet so helpless.

Ian stepped beside her. "We'll find them."

Liv shook her head at him, but he would not listen. He would not cower behind Sylvi while she wallowed in such pain.

"We'll find them." He said it again with all the conviction that pumped through his heart. "We will not rest until they are found."

"Was this you? Did you tell them?" Sylvi spun to face him, her gaze large and wounded and angry.

He kept his stare locked on hers. "I dinna know how they found out, but I can promise ye it wasna me who told."

"Just like you didn't tell me about the coins before." She scoffed and pushed herself to her feet as one did in preparation to fight.

His body still hummed with the unspent energy of the battle that hadn't come. He knew she felt the same way; only she was always charged with the added fuel of rage.

"I dinna tell ye everything before, no," Ian said. "But I've no' lied about anything and have told ye everything since. I swear on everything I hold sacred I'm telling ye the truth now."

"I don't think you hold anything sacred." She shot him a hard look and then turned away toward the empty campsite.

He grabbed her arm. She swung around, and her fist flew at his face. He stopped it with his palm and curled his fingers around her hand, trapping her. "I hold the life I gave up as sacred. I hold what we shared sacred. I hold ye sacred. Sylvi, I care about ye—I wouldna ever want to see ye hurt."

She jerked her arms free and turned from him. Something nearby on the ground caught his eye, bright red and glinting, perhaps an item intentionally left behind by men who were otherwise so damn careful.

Sylvi obviously saw it as well as they both began running toward it simultaneously. She got there first and bent to retrieve the garment. A dress.

Sylvi sucked in her breath and crumpled it to her chest, but not before Ian could determine how very fine the fabric was and caught sight of the numerous paste gemstones sparkling along the neckline.

It was the kind of dress only one woman would have worn. Isabel.

ISABEL WAS MISSING AND PRESUMABLY NAKED.

Sylvi had been desperate to find Reginald and his band of marauders, but after hours of searching, they'd had to give up. Again.

Like the last time she'd tried to track them, she followed the clearly marked trails from the camp to where they blurred with many others on the main road. Once more, there were too many tracks to follow their path.

Determined, they had followed all paths to see if one branched off with the wagon wheels and footfalls of twenty men. As the afternoon grew later and thunderstorms drenched them, they were forced to give up their efforts.

She hadn't wanted to relinquish their search, not when Isabel was missing, not when My Lady had been murdered. And yet she'd had no choice.

They'd found an inn not far from the main road and had easily secured four rooms, though it pained Sylvi to have to stop. The floorboards of Sylvi's room at the inn were grayed and soft from a lifetime of people walking. Perhaps pacing as she did now. Her mind was churning, her feet moving back and forth through the narrow room, while Percy and Liv watched on in solemn silence.

The red gown lay upon the dark blanket of her bed, a slash of color in a blend of gray and black and dirty wooden walls. But it did not inspire an idea as she'd intended. It only served to unsettle the concentration she sought and rattle her nerves.

Isabel was missing and might die if not found in time. If she were not already dead.

But then, would they bother to leave a message if they'd killed her?

Though Sylvi had bathed and changed into fresh garments and was far away from the original inn where the bodies had been left, she could not stop the scrabbling restlessness from chasing over her nerves.

"They left the gown there for a reason." She turned to Percy and Liv. All that remained.

Ian was with them in his room, but she could not bring herself to face him yet.

Her head ached as if it were trapped in a vice.

"We know it was a warning," Liv said. "But how? What are we supposed to do?"

"I hate that she's out there somewhere with them," Percy said softly. She'd pulled back the long hood she used to conceal her appearance.

All Sylvi's girls cared for one another. Even though they'd had their issues with Isabel, her loss was still tangible among them. The loss of any one of them was devastating. They were women who had no one left to care for them or love them in the world, save each other—a band of broken lives bonded by desperation.

"What of Ian?" Liv asked. She'd been casually looking out to the busy street below the window.

Sylvi's heart flinched at the mention of his name.

"He should be planning with us," Liv said. "He's risking his life. It's only fair—"

"He's the only of us who could have told the men where we were." Sylvi fought to keep her voice controlled. "Who else could have done it?"

"It could have been Isabel," Percy said. The room went quiet, and her cheeks stained a deep red. "Men who have no qualms about hurting children and women have ways of getting the information they need." Her suggestion hit the room like a blow. Of course, she was right. It was an awful thing to imagine Isabel, beautiful and soft, under the duress of torture.

"It makes sense when you think about it." Liv bent, lifted Fianna from the floor and stroked the cat's soft fur. Fianna arched in appreciation, and her vibrating purr could be heard from where Sylvi stood.

The pain in Sylvi's head echoed in on itself as if someone were beating at her temple with a blacksmith's hammer. She pressed her fingertips into the tender spot, unsure if the pressure relieved or exacerbated the discomfort. "How does it make sense?"

"Isabel was not as strong as the rest of us," Liv stated bluntly. "Her flirtation made her easy prey. It was all too simple to separate her, then take her." Liv hesitated. "And then there's Lady Camille."

Sylvi's heartbeat slammed with splintering volume in her head. "What about her?"

"I think they didn't mean to kill her." Liv met her gaze from across the room.

Sylvi's throat went tight as she accepted the fear niggling in the back of her mind for the first time. "They meant to kill me instead."

Liv nodded slowly.

Silence settled in the room, a hot, suffocating blanket.

Percy gave a soft gasp. "Isabel left before Lady Camille switched rooms with you."

Sylvi's mind whirled. Had she been the intended victim? If so, My Lady had paid the price instead. An image from the room came to Sylvi's mind—the way My Lady's hands had been bound, tied behind her, unable to stop the blade in its path to her neck. The two dead, left behind by the man or men who had killed her. My Lady had fought for her life based on the disruption in the room, yet no one had heard. It appeared there had been a struggle, and two had been slain before she could finally be bound and subdued. Despite her strength and her bravery, no one had come to rescue her.

"You may not want to hear this, Sylvi," Percy said. "But I trust Ian."

Liv sighed and crossed her arms. "I do too." It was said grudgingly, but Liv was not the type of woman to say what she did not feel.

"What if you're wrong and it is him?" Sylvi let her gaze linger on each of them. She could not lose these brave, loyal women. They'd found a place in her heart and burrowed there, replacing the family who'd been taken from her. She had not realized the impact of her attachment until she had begun to see them disappear, one after the other.

The pain was considerable. She could not bear the idea of also losing them.

The glance Percy slid Liv said they had already discussed as much between themselves.

"If it is him, then we're all dead anyway," Liv replied. "At least this gives us a chance to stand. *United.*"

A carriage drove past on the street outside. Sylvi stalked over to the bed and lifted Isabel's dress to her chest. Sweet, spicy notes of a familiar foreign perfume wafted up from the silky fabric. Sylvi's heart crumbled. She was willing to do anything to save Isabel, wasn't she?

Even work with someone she suspected might be a traitor. But Liv was right—to go at this united and equal made for a better team.

Resigned, she nodded. "Very well. I will allow Ian to join in the preparation. I'll trust him." But even as she said the words, she knew she could not clear the suspicion in her heart. Any form of trust in Ian would only be an illusion.

Nineteen

Ian had been shut up in his room like a lad who'd stuck toads in his Ma's slippers. Not that he'd ever been a lad to have done such an awful thing. At least not any more than he'd been a lad who'd laughed at the horrified expression on his ma's face when she discovered the prank.

The memory drew a smile.

He leaned back in the bed and crossed his arms under his head to compensate for the lack of support offered by the thin pillow. It had occurred to him more than once to venture out on his own and seek out Reginald and his men.

But then, if he found them, he would appear all the more suspicious to Sylvi. After all, who better to "find" them than a man spying for them? No, it was better to wait in his room, staring up at the mottled plaster ceiling, than do anything further to splinter Sylvi's trust.

He continued to stare upward. There were seven cracks, three splotches of something dark that might or might not be mold and a section toward the right with enough flaking pieces to entertain him for at least several minutes.

Of course, he could devise a plan for his next move after they eventually killed Reginald. The future's bleakness made the ceiling as appealing as cards.

He sighed and began to count.

Just after 269, a knock came at the door, so firm and abrupt it pulled him from his dull game with a start.

He looked up from his bed, lazy with his forced sedentary existence. "Who is it?"

There was a pause long enough to invite him to reach for his dagger. "It's Sylvi."

He freed the dagger from its sheath at his belt. Experience had taught him it was unwise to be in her presence unarmed. He unlocked the door and pulled it open.

She'd washed and changed into a fresh black léine and trews. Only a few braids were twisted back and secured behind her right temple, while the rest hung loosely around her face.

"Coming to check on me?" He held both arms open.

She glanced at his dagger.

"Do ye blame me?" he asked.

"I'm not here to harm you." Exhaustion lined her face, and mourning dulled the shine in her eyes. Even her voice was softer than usual. "May I come in?"

He stepped back to allow her to enter and faced her once the door was closed. She was no longer his, and somehow reminding himself of that made her even more beautiful.

He had always wanted the things he could never have. Perhaps that had been her appeal all the while.

But no, he knew it was not. There was so much more with Sylvi. So many more levels and depths and dimensions within her than any woman he had ever possessed.

She eyed the dagger once more in silent reprimand for its presence. "I was...not in my right mind after having found My Lady, nor still when we realized Reginald had slipped away and confirmed they had Isabel."

Ian lifted a brow and slid the dagger into one of the many wonderfully useful sheaths on his belt.

Sylvi squared her shoulders. "I may not be good at apologizing, but I'll admit when I'm wrong. I was wrong to accuse you of being a traitor."

Her expression was stern and fierce. He wanted to kiss her until her mouth softened under his and her beautiful strength opened to him.

"Ach, it isna a thing to worry over, my angel." The endearment fell from his lips and landed flat. Ian cleared his throat. "Do ye know anything new?"

"Only speculation at this point. We think Isabel was the one who gave the information to Reginald. She was the only one who didn't know My Lady and I had switched rooms." Sylvi looked away, her gaze distant. "We believe Isabel would only give this information up under extreme duress."

"They meant to kill ye—no' Lady Camille." Ian narrowed his eyes. "I'll kill any man who touches ye. I'll stand by yer side and see ye defended until I know ye're safe."

Sylvi's brow crinkled, and she peered up at him with something akin to desperation. "How can you be so forgiving and so charming to me when I've done nothing to deserve it?"

"Ye've been through enough."

Sylvi gave an almost imperceptible wince, a slight twitch of her mouth, but evident to him.

"Besides, I dinna hold grudges well. It's so much easier to be charming." He winked at her. "I'm also still hoping to find out how much ye were paid to kill me."

And then it happened—the twitch of a smile from the corner of her mouth, like the first warm spring day after a grueling winter. She rolled her eyes at him.

"Was it enough to buy a castle?" he goaded.

She exhaled a chuckle. "Don't flatter yourself, Ian Campbell."

"But I'm so verra good at it."

"Too good."

He grinned at her. God, how he'd missed this play, this banter between them. "Does that mean ye'll tell me?"

She cocked her head in consideration. "It was enough to...buy a couple of horses."

"Destriers or nags?"

She laughed and shook her head. "You're impossible."

He grinned again. "That's part of my charm too."

Their eyes met, and they fell into a comfortable silence. He wanted to pull her into his arms, as he'd done so many times before, and let his mouth come down on the softness of her lips. The need for her ached through him like the most incredible thirst.

"Thank you." She spoke with such quiet intimacy a shiver teased over his skin.

"For being charming?"

"For being more inclined to forgive than me. For staying at my side and helping me bury My Lady, and wanting to protect me even though we both know I don't need it."

She leaned closer to him as if she were drawn by the same force as he to her. As if she yearned for him with the same tangible need.

"Sylvi." He savored the sweetness of her name. "My angel." He stroked a hand down her cheek and caught her beautiful face in his hands.

Her eyes closed, and the heat of her mouth whispered against his own.

A knock came from the door, so sharp it jerked them apart and sent them racing toward the door. Liv stood on the other side, her eyes wide and a note held in her outstretched hand. "This was delivered just now."

Liv's name was written on it.

Sylvi took the folded parchment and opened it.

Come to the market to find the one you seek, or face dire consequences.

"It was addressed to you." Sylvi frowned.

It was just past midday. The marketplace would be swarming with people.

"I think we're right. They think you're dead." Liv glanced down. "And the boy who delivered it said it was extremely urgent. He raced off before I could ask him any questions. They must mean now."

"It's a trap." An icy ball of dread knotted in Ian's stomach.

"I know it is." Sylvi stared at the note, and her jaw clenched. "But I can't see how we have much choice. We've lost one of our own. I will not have another lost. Tell Percy to prepare for battle. We leave in five minutes."

Liv turned away to follow her orders with Fianna padding behind her, but Ian put his arm against the door, stopping Sylvi from following. "Let me go. They think ye're dead."

"I will not have another person I care about die in my stead." Her eyes flashed with determination.

A person she cared about. Such sweet words to say at such a bitter time.

"I dinna like yer plan, but I know better than to dissuade ye," he said.

She looked up in a long, tender glance before drawing a deep, pained breath. "Then it is time."

SYLVI THREADED THROUGH THE NARROW ALLEYWAYS OF the city toward its busy heart. Somewhere in the distance, Liv, Percy and Ian followed behind her, hidden in the shadows. She would not have them placed at risk, not until it was time for war.

The humming buzz of the market came into awareness before she met the wall of people jostling in the heavy crowd. Scents of sticky sweet buns and roasted meat flavored the air and made her glad she'd eaten earlier. She would not have herself distracted.

Her senses sharpened, and she darted her gaze around the crowd, searching for faces she might know. There had been no instructions. Would someone come to her? Was she to find something?

A sense of doubt nagged at her. What if whoever was supposed to find her didn't think to look for her since they assumed her dead?

But then, she knew she was a woman who stood out. She needed only to peruse the gawking stares of every passerby to confirm as much. Not only did the fairness of her braided hair set her apart from others, but her man's attire and the weapons she wore drew attention.

She would not be missed.

Her gaze sifted through the throngs of people, and frustration raked over her nerves. Damn it, what was she looking for?

A flash of brilliant red hair caught her attention.

Her heart lodged itself in her throat. Isabel?

She pushed her way through the wall of people to where she'd seen the glimpse of red hair. Nothing. A pebble skittered near her foot. Sylvi glanced up and found Percy's hooded face peering from the alley. She jerked her finger to the left. Sylvi turned at once and caught sight of red hair in the distance.

The crowd was so damn thick. Still, she managed to keep her stare fixed on the woman while heading in her direction. The redhead moved surprisingly fast despite the crowd.

The red hair disappeared behind a cart and did not emerge. Sylvi hissed a breath of irritation. What the hell was this stupid game they were playing?

She stood for one helpless moment in the center of the square and looked around her. A clacking bang sounded from a nearby alley. Liv peeked out and nodded behind Sylvi.

She turned and found the redhead in the distance. It wasn't until she was on her way toward the woman that a realization struck her.

Reginald no doubt suspected only one of them would be coming to the market and wanted to know how many had arrived to fight. One by one, Sylvi's army was revealing themselves from the shadows to their enemy in her attempt to find Isabel in the crowd.

If that were indeed the case, they'd played right into Reginald's trap.

Sylvi pushed through the crowd now, heedless of civility. Offended shouts rose around her, but she paid them little mind. She would get to Isabel before she lost her again. Before Ian could reveal himself.

The redhead stopped abruptly, and Sylvi immediately realized why with a sinking stomach. Ian stood in the woman's path, his charming grin doing its magic.

"Isabel," Sylvi said.

The woman spun around, her eyes wide and scared.

And not Isabel.

"I have a note." She held a bit of parchment between her fingers. The corners of the paper fluttered frantically in her nervous grip like the wings of a moth.

"Who are ye?" Ian asked, his expression no longer so inviting.

"I'm no one." Her cheeks tinged red. "A baker's daughter. I was told people would follow me, and I had to run from them, but I had to give them this when they caught me."

She shoved the note at Sylvi with determination.

Sylvi took the parchment. "And how much did they pay you?"

"They won't kill my family," the girl said with large, wet eyes.

"Then we'll go save yer family first," Ian said.

The redhead shook her head ferociously. "They are watching. You cannot. Please let me go."

"Go, but do not trust their word," Sylvi said. The girl's family was most likely already dead.

What is unseen hasna been done.

The words from when her family was slaughtered slid icily in her mind. She suppressed a shudder. She could not think of such things now.

"They were luring us out of our hiding places." Sylvi opened the parchment.

Come to the abandoned monastery north of town, and don't bother hiding. We already know where you are.

Sylvi balled the note in her fist. "Damn it. I was right."

But what was the point of knowing where they hid? They already had known their numbers—they would have gotten that from Isabel.

A sliver of something cold edged down Sylvi's spine. She turned abruptly and ran to the first alley where Percy had been. Her heart slammed hard in her chest.

Not Percy. Not her girls.

The alley was empty. Sylvi's rapid breathing echoed off the high walls of the surrounding buildings.

"Percy," she called.

No answer.

Ian gripped Sylvi's shoulder. "She's no' here. Let's check for Liv. Together."

They skirted the perimeter of the crowd and checked where Liv had been. Nothing. Not even Fianna lingered in the area.

"Liv?" Sylvi called. No sound emerged.

Sylvi's heart crumpled in her chest. "Ian, I've lost them all." No matter how hard she breathed, she could not seem to draw sufficient air. "I've lost everything."

He grabbed her to him and held her there for a long moment, so strong and *real* against her she could not pull from the embrace. Not when it was possibly the only thing keeping her together. "Ye've no' lost me."

Too late did the blare of warning prickle in the back of her mind. Something cold and pungent pushed against her nose and mouth. At the same time, a figure from behind Ian snaked an arm around him with a square of cloth.

Sylvi exhaled as hard as she could to free her body of the poison she'd already inhaled. Her nostrils burned, and her chest ached.

Ian's eyes rolled back in his head, and he slumped backward. Sylvi reached behind her, trying to grapple with whoever was holding her in place. Her body moved slowly, her muscles thick and weak. The hand pushed firmly against her face, jabbing the wet cloth into her nose and making her eyes sting.

Her body screamed for breath, and finally, she had no choice but to drag in a chestful of tainted air.

Everything waned in her vision, and her world went dark.

Twenty

A hollow clunk echoed in Ian's head. He groaned against the pain radiating inside his skull and rolled his head to the side. Another hollow clunk.

Another.

Ian forced his eyes open and winced against the daylight streaming in from above, where a portion of the roof was missing.

The clunk sounded again. Ian followed the noise to where a man sat in the middle of the room, an open sack laying in front of him. He pulled a fist-sized clay pot from it and set it on the ground with the familiar clunking sound.

Ian tried to sit forward and found his wrists and ankles bound to a very uncomfortable wooden chair. He narrowed his eyes to better fix his bleary gaze more steadily on the man.

The man's long, graying hair fell in waves over his face. He shook it free, and the half of an ear became visible.

Reginald. A man so cold and cruel he could order the death of a child and kill a mother trying to protect her babies. Disgust rolled through Ian, and then another thought hit him.

Sylvi.

He immediately looked beside him and found her bound to a

chair in a similar fashion, her head still slumped forward, the length of her pale blonde hair blocking her face from his view. Beside her were two other women, one with the same curling golden hair as Percy and the other with the copper locks of Liv.

But where was Isabel?

Ian turned back to Reginald and found him returning everything to the bag. He looked up abruptly and grinned when his small, black eyes lit on Ian. "I figured ye'd wake before the lasses." He hefted the bag up for a moment before letting it thunk back to the ground. "The archer had some good stuff in here."

"Where's Isabel?" Ian asked.

Reginald tugged his belt into place under his large belly and sniffed. He was as Ian remembered him, his body thick with the effects of a gluttonous life, his bulbous nose red with it.

"The red-haired slut? She'll be by in a minute to gloat, no doubt." Reginald scoffed. "I dinna know how ye ended up with these women, but ye've gotten yerself into a mess of trouble, lad."

"Because ye paid them to kill me." Ian lifted his fingers from the arm of the chair in a helpless gesture.

Reginald gave a high-pitched exhale that was more wheezing than laughing. "Aye, that I did. Apparently, death dinna take."

"Mayhap I'm too good for death." Ian smirked. "Dinna think ye could do it on yer own, eh?"

"Something like that. Anyway, these lasses were a quieter option." Reginald tilted his head back and forth. "Until we realized she dinna kill ye. Then it only complicated matters." He strode forward and bent over Sylvi. "And now the two of ye have been rutting?"

Reginald grabbed Sylvi's hair with a meaty fist to pull her head back and regard her face. "She looks wild." He threw Ian a grin so wide it revealed several more gaps in the back of his mouth where molars had been lost. "I bet being with this one is like riding an unbroken horse."

Ian's body tensed, every part of him screaming to protect Sylvi. And every one of those parts was hopelessly tied down.

Reginald released her hair, and Sylvi's head flopped back into place where it hung over her chest. "Dinna worry, lad. She's still alive. For now. After the heartache that this bitch has cost me, I'll be making her pay later on." He nodded to Percy and Liv. "Those others too." He scowled down at his hand, where angry red scratches showed against a smattering of black hair.

Cat scratches. Liv's cat must have tried to protect her.

Ian did not ask after the brave creature, not when he feared the answer.

Ian's hands squeezed hard on the wooden arms of the chair. They needed to escape.

Obviously, fighting was not an option currently. But if he could get Reginald to untie him, maybe even trust him, he might stand a chance at attempting a rescue.

He would do anything to save Sylvi and her ladies. Even if it cost him his life. At least it would be the one good thing he ever did in his miserable, over-privileged life.

"What about me?" he asked.

Reginald put his hands on his hips, squaring his massive belly between them. "That's what's been giving me the hardest time with all this. What do I do with ye?"

Ian shrugged as if the decision mattered little to him. "Take me back."

"The others dinna take so kindly to yer meddling last time."

Ian scoffed. "Gregor's dead, and I'm guessing the two others were the ones with him when Sylvi left me in the cart—they're dead." He looked at Sylvi. He couldn't help it.

Her body was still. Too still. Her lack of movement threaded fear through his heart, but he couldn't think on that now. Not when so much was at stake.

"Ye're a crafty devil." Reginald looked thoughtfully through a gaping window and scratched at his crotch. "How do I know I can trust ye?"

"Ye dinna." Ian chuckled. "But I'd rather be on the winning

side. I know about the coins now. I could help. And I can help ye lose the two king's men who have been tracking ye too."

Reginald's stare intensified. "How do ye know about them?"

Ian smirked as though he didn't care. In truth, he'd just remembered the brilliant red suits beneath the black cloaks the men had worn when he'd seen them. "Because ye're no' as quick and stealthy as ye think. The king's arm is coming for ye, and ye best know how to get out of it."

"And ye can do that?" Reginald asked, skeptical.

"I can talk my way out of anything." Ian puffed out his chest.

Reginald smirked. "What about this one?" He nodded toward Sylvi. "Ye take a fancy to her?"

Sylvi's forefinger shifted. She was waking. If she wasn't already awake. Ian's stomach tensed. Of all things for her to have to overhear...

He only hoped she was not yet aware.

"Of course, I've no' taken a fancy to her. She was no' more than something warm to fill a lonely night." Ian winked.

The room they were in was large, with massive arching windows lining either side. Perhaps a dining hall, a place where monks once ate.

Regardless, it was the perfect place to keep them all captive. Away from peering eyes, on the outskirts of town, in a room devoid of any debris to use in freeing themselves.

"So, ye dinna mind if I have her then?" Reginald asked.

Ian gave an easy smile despite the wave of nausea rolling through him. "Have her."

He kept his face impassive despite the hot rage boiling through his veins. God help Reginald if he so much as laid a hand on Sylvi—for Ian sure as hell wouldn't help him.

At least if he did attempt something, it would get Sylvi alone in a room with Reginald. If anyone could still manage to kill him, it'd be her.

Reginald gave Ian a wide, companionable smile and pulled a

blade from his belt. He sawed at the ropes binding Ian until they fell to the floor in broken coils. Ian rolled his wrists and elbows. His skin and joints tingled after having been immobile for so long.

He pushed to his feet, and the room spun around him, dizzying and fast, like when he'd had too much drink.

"It takes a while to wear off, lad." Reginald patted him on the back with an endearing gesture that made Ian's skin want to slither off him. "Ye better be right about getting those jack-anapeses off our trail. Ye've got a lot of making up to do."

It was just the two of them now. He could take him. Kill Reginald and save the women.

But as it was, something wasn't right. All this had been too easy.

Ian straightened and took an unsteady step. He certainly wasn't in his best fighting shape.

The not-so-subtle clatter of shoes on the stairs echoed through a dark corridor on the right. Someone was coming.

Ian's heart sank with his hopes. There was no time. He would be lucky to disable Reginald. He couldn't take on more than one person. Not with how he was.

Isabel emerged through the entryway with another man. She was not black and blue and bleeding from the torture they had all expected she had endured, but looking bright and merry in a green gown encrusted with gems.

Reginald turned to her, and his mouth slid up in a lascivious grin.

She sauntered their way. "Oh, Ian," she purred. "Don't you wish you'd had me when I gave you the chance?"

Her steps faltered, and her catlike grin melted off her face. "Is she still alive?" She nodded at Sylvi. "I thought you killed her."

Ian looked beside him and saw Sylvi's head lifting. She was definitely awake. He pulled in a deep breath to prepare himself for the pain of having her realize Isabel's betrayal.

And also his own.

He only hoped she had enough faith in him to see through his ruse.

❀

SYLVI HAD BEEN AWAKE LONG ENOUGH TO HEAR everything she needed. The coarse language, the deception. Ian was gladly handing her over to Reginald. Her head swam in a swirl, and her stomach rolled with the need to retch.

She shook her head to clear the hair from her face, and the room swayed from the effort. She clenched her fists and let her nails dig painfully into her palms. The pain. She needed to focus on the pain and stay sharp. Especially in a room so full of enemies.

Ian had sided with Reginald. After all that they'd been through, after everything he'd promised. More lies. She gritted her teeth and tried to move.

Her wrists were bound to the arms of a solid wooden chair, as were her ankles. The rope was thin but strong, and the wood beneath her was of good quality. Neither would be easy to be free of.

Her gaze settled first on Reginald, and a dagger of hate jabbed into her gut. The small dark eyes, the blubbery lips, the ear her own mother had mutilated to protect her child. Suddenly, none of it mattered. Not Isabel or her reason for betraying them all. Not Ian and his lies.

When Sylvi stared at Reginald, she saw violent death. Her father's; her mother's; her siblings', who were far too young to die; My Lady's, who fought so hard to live; and then Reginald's. For he *would* die. And by her hand.

Her heart beat deep and smooth like in battle, and the room sharpened with clarity. She was aware of everything suddenly, including the slow shifting of Percy and Liv at her side as they slowly came to.

"I want her dead." Isabel's tone was petulant.

"No' as much as she wants me dead." Reginald chuckled. As if Sylvi were a jest. "Look at how she stares at me."

"Isabel? What?" Liv's words slurred slightly. "You're all right."

Isabel scoffed. "Of course, I'm all right. Especially now that I'm free of all of you."

"You were never forced to stay," Percy said.

Sylvi knew she ought to look at the other women to ensure they were all right, but she could not pull her eyes from Reginald. He drew her, all the hate and ugliness a beacon for her need to exact vengeance and rage.

She breathed, and she watched, and she planned.

"I wasn't forced to stay...but I was." Isabel still spoke with a whining tone, her voice distant in the background of Sylvi's thoughts.

"I had nowhere else to go," Isabel said. "Of all places to end up, I was in the middle of nowhere with a bunch of women who only cared about fighting and couldn't keep me company. You made me *work* for my keep."

"You want Sylvi dead for making you work?" Liv asked dryly.

Reginald was looking at Liv, and then his gaze slid to Percy. Sylvi's heart jerked. She knew exactly what he thought when he saw Percy. What so many other men thought.

A fresh burst of energy flashed through Sylvi. She twisted her arms against her bonds. The sharp edges of the chair bit hard into her skin, but no matter how hard she struggled, she could not loosen the ropes.

Reginald stopped in front of Percy, so his belly was almost touching her nose. "I've been waiting for this one to wake. Ye dinna tell me how pretty this one was." He raked his fingers through her hair before fisting a handful of it at the nape of her neck. "Look at me."

Percy's body went stiff, and she kept her eyes fixed downward. Sylvi yanked her arms against the ropes. They did not give at all.

Reginald trailed a hand down Percy's face. "If ye willna give me the respect I deserve, maybe I should let my men break ye in. They were eager to see what I brought them."

A tear dropped from Percy's chin. Light from overhead caught it on its descent and made it sparkle like a falling gem. Sylvi's body tensed with rage, so brilliantly hot that she was surprised it did not burn away her ropes. She would not stand by while Percy was raped.

"I wouldna do that if I were ye." Ian spoke somewhere beside her.

Reginald glared up at him with irritation. "Why?"

"She's a witch." Ian's voice was smooth as it had ever been, the lie falling from his lips like gold tinkling through a thief's fingers. "She has great powers. It was she who created the potion for me to die and then come back to life. She has many potions and spells, but they only work because she is pure. Ye know what happens when ye take a witch's purity, aye?"

Sylvi had to force herself not to turn her stare toward Ian. Was he *helping* Percy?

Reginald squinted at Ian and grunted something akin to a wordless question.

"Yer prick withers and falls off, and yer bollocks pinch up into yer body." Ian shrugged as though it were common knowledge. "From what I've heard, at any rate."

Reginald's sharp gaze landed on Percy, and then he jerked his glare back to Isabel. "Is this true?"

Sylvi tensed for the reply. Isabel knew well enough Percy was no witch, that it was nothing more than a recipe of extracts and herbs.

"If she's sent down below and raped by all those men, she will lose her power, and ye'll have a band of men who are ball-less and pissed." Ian spoke carefully. He was spelling out Percy's fate, making Isabel realize the full impact of it.

Reginald pinched Percy's face harder in his hand, and a soft sob escaped her lips. Sylvi bit her tongue to keep from snarling out threats. It would only incite Reginald to make good on his claim.

Isabel watched all of this with an intense expression creasing her brows. "It's true," she said finally. The admission was spoken casually as if she found the entire matter boring.

Reginald huffed out a sigh and released his hold on Percy.

Sylvi discreetly exhaled the breath she'd been holding. The idea of sweet Percy at the mercy of ruthless men who would laugh at her pleas. The most unbearable chasm of pain opened in Sylvi's heart.

"Pity," Reginald said. "She is beautiful." He threw a cold smile over his shoulder. "Even more beautiful than ye."

Isabel's eyes narrowed, and she slowly stepped toward Percy as if she intended to see the truth for herself. "She's always had more beauty than any one woman should." Her arm lifted. It wasn't until her fist drove downward that Sylvi saw the flash of a blade.

Percy. No.

Sylvi rocked the chair savagely to the side. If she could hit Isabel, throw off her aim...

Sylvi acted without thought and tossed herself to the right. Her actions were slow, thick, like those performed through water. The drug, she realized when she finally pitched over.

Something warm splashed across Sylvi's face, metallic and salty in her mouth.

Blood.

She landed hard on the ground. Her body jarred at the impact, and her teeth clacked together. But still, the chair remained intact.

Sylvi's head swam in a murky sea of disorientation. Percy's cry brought her back, thick with pain and helplessness.

Percy.

Sylvi couldn't lose another friend. Not Percy.

The strong arms of the chair had remained solid through the fall, pinning the ropes more snuggly against Sylvi's arms. She struggled against them, her determination renewed.

She had to save Percy.

Despite her attempts, all she yielded were helpless scrapes and squeaks of the chair against the wooden floor.

Her bindings would not give.

"Percy." She jerked her head to the side to clear it of the wave of wild hair blocking her view.

Percy's face hung forward and dripped with blood. So much blood. Puddling in her lap, smearing the bit of her face that Sylvi could see.

Reginald threw his hand toward Isabel and caught her on the cheek with a resounding thwack. She staggered back, out of Sylvi's line of sight. Out of her realm of even caring.

Sylvi writhed against her bonds, barely aware of their bite into her flesh. "Fight me, you bastard. Be a man and untie me."

Reginald whirled on her and jerked her chair upright so quickly that the bones in her neck popped. He shoved his face into hers. Small, broken red lines showed under the skin on the large tip of his nose. "Dinna worry, ye'll get what's coming to ye soon."

"Ian, take the other redhead down to the lads." He shoved Ian in Liv's direction. "Ye want to prove yerself to me? Give my boys their treat and stay to watch. Make sure ye take a go yerself." He panted under the effort. "And aye, I'll be asking to make sure ye did."

Sylvi shook her head, and a cry lodged in her throat. "Don't take her. Take me instead."

She would be able to handle it. If she couldn't fight them off, she would endure it. No matter what it took, she would find a way to help her ladies. And then she'd find a way to kill every one of the bastards.

Ian glanced at Sylvi, only a skim of a look, but she saw it. And so did Reginald.

He summoned the third man over with the flick of his fingers and indicated Liv. "Take this one down with him. Dinna leave her alone with him." He arched an eyebrow toward Ian. "Until ye prove yerself, aye?"

Ian lifted his hands defensively and helped the man cut Liv's ties. She tried to lift an arm to fight, but her movements were slow and inaccurate, her body still affected by the potion. Sylvi's heart rent in her chest, and she screamed with all the hurt and anger and frustration and hate she had in her. She screamed until her throat rasped as though it would bleed. All of it for naught. The men carried Liv to the door and out of sight.

This time, Ian had not looked back.

Twenty-One

There had to be a way to get Liv out safely. Ian held her arm to keep her upright. He couldn't help but notice her footsteps became surer with each stair they descended. Or perhaps he just hoped it was so.

He wanted to tell her to be strong, to gather her wits to fight. The man who held her other arm watched him with suspicion. If Ian attempted any communication, the man would know.

He wished he recognized some of the other men. With how the marauders came and went through Reginald's band, most thieves and beggars, it was not surprising how many did not stay.

The chatter of many voices came from below, and Ian's heart slid a couple of notches downward. There would be more men than he could fight himself. The volume alone told him that.

Conversation ceased as they neared the end of the stone staircase and was quickly replaced by whistles and leering jeers at the impending entertainment. The bitter taste of bile welled in the back of Ian's throat.

He could not allow this to happen.

He scanned the abandoned church around him, seeking out the demons who resided in what was once hallowed ground. There were easily fifteen men in the room, including the one who held Liv with him. Now he recognized a few, the men he had fought against before he left the group. Several others he noted as looking familiar, but no one he could appeal to for help.

"We've brought ye a lass to love," a bald man said. "Be gentle." It was the arse who had held down that woman the day Ian attacked them.

Ian tensed.

The men all started to laugh. They pressed closer, their eyes sparkling with interest and lust.

Liv's pulse raced beneath Ian's fingertips. He could only imagine what was going through her mind. It all made him sick to his stomach.

This could not happen.

"I'll get through this," she said softly. "I'll be fine."

It wasn't until she squeezed the hand that he used to hold her up that he realized she was talking to him. She was trying to reassure him.

He gritted his teeth.

If only he could have killed Reginald. If only he'd been able to attack the other man and somehow prevent them from even coming downstairs, if only—

But all the "if onlys" in Ian's head did not stop the men from stalking forward, eager to see their prey.

The other man shoved Liv forward, and she was wrenched from Ian's grasp. She staggered but caught herself and immediately stood upright, a look of defiance glowing in her gray eyes.

Ian's awareness prickled. Someone was behind him. Yet he did not turn. He did not want to pull his gaze from Liv. The person grabbed his hand and pushed something long and solid into his palm. A hilt.

Ian jerked around.

"No," the man said.

Ian snapped his head forward but could not stop the kick of his heartbeat at the familiar voice. Kyle. His brother, two years his junior, who stood to inherit the estate with Ian gone.

"I dinna know what ye've gotten yerself into," Kyle whispered. "But I've got yer back, brother."

Ian gave a subtle nod and tried to shove aside all the questions welling in his mind. Why Kyle was there, how long he'd been with the men, what he was willing to do to help, if he knew what he was getting himself into. But none of that mattered now.

Liv mattered, and dealing with the men who were circling her and fighting over who would be first.

Ian leaned his head to speak discreetly to his brother. "Claim her as yers before anyone else and give her a dagger. She can handle herself."

Kyle shoved past Ian and strode out toward the men. Ian's little brother had always been one of the largest warriors. Well over a head above all others and with a body roped with muscles most men would only dream of possessing.

"I dinna think I've had a chance to play this game." Kyle squared his shoulders. The act seemed to make him swell even larger. "I want to go first." He put a hand to his sword. "Unless one of ye lads has a problem with that."

Ian's heart pounded as if he were the one out there challenging all those men.

"Yeah." A man with pale blond hair and a singed beard stepped forward. "I do."

He was a big man as well, but not big enough. Kyle smirked and waved him over.

The man didn't step toward Kyle but toward Liv, catching her arm. Kyle opened his mouth to speak, but Liv's arm flew up and caught the man in the face. A hearty crack filled the air, and blood poured from his nose.

Kyle stomped over to the man, his steps deliberately slow and heavy to accentuate his size. "I said, she's mine first." He lifted his fist and brought it down on the injured man. The mercenary dropped like a stone and did not rise.

That was one down, at least.

Kyle turned back to the others and raised his arm. Blood smeared his right hand. "Anyone else?"

Not a single objection came forward. Even the bald man who had held down the woman those months ago held his ground and would not come forward. Some of the more grizzled men stared with hatred at Kyle, wanting to fight but not stupid enough to try. Several of the weaker ones cast their gazes away as if they didn't even want to be caught looking at him and have it mistaken for a challenge.

Liv tensed and tried to step back, but Kyle grabbed her to him with a hard laugh. They were so close that her body pressed against his. He caught her hand and thrust it to his crotch. "Do ye feel that?"

Ian tensed, and fear blasted through him like ice. Was Kyle—

All at once, Kyle and Liv broke apart, both of them with blades glinting in the sunshine.

Ian caught an easy breath before brandishing the blade Kyle had snuck him. He'd almost forgotten what a convincing liar his brother could be. Lucky for them all, Kyle was an even better fighter.

Gone was the heavy slowness he'd exaggerated, and in its place were lightning-fast strikes and the agility of a man half his size. Already one man had fallen, and Kyle was on another.

Ian lunged at the man who had helped bring Liv downstairs. He had his blade out, too, but was still easily overtaken.

Ian said a quick prayer between swipes of his blade. For this once-holy place would soon be filled with death.

SYLVI FOUGHT AGAINST HER BINDINGS AND TRIED TO block out the sounds coming from below. The shouting and grunting.

Tears burned in her eyes. She'd hoped Ian somehow could have prevented Liv from enduring such misery. Perhaps he'd tried.

A cold thread of fear tightened through her.

If Ian had tried, he might already be dead.

Percy had stopped crying, but her head remained bent. Sylvi stared hard at her and prayed she was not also dead.

So much death.

All because of her.

She'd sacrificed too damn much, and it left her soul leaden.

Reginald spoke to Isabel in low tones, too quiet for Sylvi to make out what he said. He stroked a hand over Isabel's cheek, and she nodded. Sylvi didn't know what the hell they were planning, but she didn't like it.

In the time they talked, she had taken advantage of the opportunity to scan the room thoroughly.

The sunlight overhead indicated it was late afternoon. The room was large, with old bits of furniture pressed along the back, away from the stairs. In one far corner, she recognized their confiscated bags.

If she could get away, even for a fraction of a moment, she knew she was fast enough to make it to her bag and grab a weapon. She could kill Reginald and escape Isabel. She could go to Ian. Down to help him and Liv and either free them from capture or aid them in battle. She couldn't stop thinking of them, wondering what transpired downstairs. Battle? Or their demise?

Her heart flinched.

The hum of Reginald and Isabel's conversation fell quiet. Their gazes turned to her, and they approached. Sylvi's body tensed.

"We're discussing the best way to cut your bindings." Reginald smirked. "I can't have ye flying out at me like a hellcat, now can I?"

"Are you afraid of me?" Sylvi challenged.

Reginald scoffed. "I just want to ensure ye canna get away."

Isabel lifted a heavy mallet and swung it at her. Sylvi jerked, but not with enough force to rock the chair nor keep her from being struck. The mallet slammed into her arm, and something deep inside cracked. Pain splintered through her arm and radiated outward, searing as glowing embers.

No matter how hard Sylvi gritted her teeth, she could not bite back the scream. It rasped from her throat and brought hot tears to her eyes. She blinked them away and glared through the clearing blur to where Reginald watched with a smug smile on his face.

She would kill him.

Even with a broken arm.

For what he had done to her family and to My Lady. And now also what he'd done to Liv and what Isabel had done to Percy. All these years, she'd been so careful not to let anyone too close. Yet he'd still found those she cared about and hurt them all.

Reginald yanked the rope from the wrist of her injured arm, and spots of white danced in Sylvi's vision. Her breath became shallow, and her lips prickled. A cold sensation washed over her skin. She floated above her body for a moment, vaguely aware of him shifting her arm but no longer feeling any pain.

Sylvi was being moved, her consciousness fluttering between an exhaustive black and a fuzzy white awareness. Something hard pressed against her back. A floor. She was on the floor.

"Isabel, hold her down." Reginald's voice sounded in the distance.

It wasn't until the jingle of a belt hit her ears that realization slapped her back into reality. Isabel leaned over her, and her grip settled hard on Sylvi's good arm, securing her to the ground.

She looked up at the woman she had once called friend. The woman she had risked the remainder of those she loved to save. "Why would you do this?"

Isabel turned a cold look downward. "Because you had everything I did not. Power, strength, comradery."

"You have to earn those things, Isabel." Sylvi tried to pull her arm free, to no avail. "We thought you were one of us. It's why we came here—why we risked our lives. To save *you*."

"I'm not one of you," Isabel ground out through her teeth.

"Not as strong as you, not as skilled as Liv, not as beautiful and talented as Percy. Always rejected, always used. I'm nothing with all of you, and I was never meant to be nothing—I'm the king's cousin." She tipped her head upright as if it bore the weight of a crown.

A rustling of fabric sounded from near Sylvi's feet. She didn't look to see what it was Reginald was doing. She didn't want to see, could not see.

"If you felt like nothing, it was your own doing. We cared for you," Sylvi said. "We risked everything for you." She tried not to think of the immobile form of Percy nearby. Doing so ached too deeply in her heart.

Tears glistened in Isabel's eyes. "It's too late to say such things now."

"How can you do this?" Sylvi gritted through her teeth.

Isabel shook her head and said nothing further.

Reginald's hands moved over the ties of Sylvi's trews. A shudder of revulsion wracked through her and sent a fresh wave of pain radiating from her arm.

"In that case," Sylvi said, "I won't feel bad about this."

She thrust her foot upward and caught Reginald between the legs with the hard toe of her boot. Before Isabel could react, Sylvi drove her head upward and slammed her forehead into Isabel's jaw. Without looking to see how weakened either was, Sylvi leapt up, cradling her injured arm, and ran.

Twenty-Two

A scream had come from above, loud enough to be heard over the grunts and clangs of battle. The man in front of Ian dropped to his knees and folded to the ground. Dead.

No matter how quickly Ian moved or how many men he killed, more seemed to come. The original surge of his energy before the fight had waned and left his movements more methodical, more rhythmic. Duck and slash, stab and parry.

He'd made his way into the throng of fighting and put his back against those of Kyle and Liv. In the middle of the battle, he found the small gray-and-white cat huddled close to Liv's ankle, hackles up and hissing.

"Are ye doing all right?" Ian chanced a glance at Liv.

"I know ye are no' talking to me," Kyle said.

"And I know you aren't talking to me either." Liv tossed him an angry glare. Sweat glistened on her brow, and dots of blood showed vividly against her pale skin, but she did not appear tired. Somehow, she'd even acquired a sword. Most likely from the dead.

He smirked. "Of course no'. I like to talk to myself when I fight." He thrust his stolen sword into the chest of a man before him. "Ach, that was a bonny hit, Ian. Ye've done well, lad!"

Something heavy landed on the floor above. Ian's heart jarred in his chest.

What was going on up there?

If ever there was a woman not to worry about, it was Sylvi. And yet he could not stop himself from doing exactly that.

Only a few men remained. The fight was nearly done. Ian's sword arm burned, as did a long cut on his leg. Nothing serious, but enough to leave a sting.

What was going on up there?

The question buzzed in his mind, insistent in its plucking at his thoughts.

Shouts came from the side of the room Ian could not see.

"We've got a few more coming," Kyle said. His body tensed behind Ian.

Liv blew out a long, slow breath. The kind one took when they needed to stop their heart from running too fast—when they were getting tired.

"Liv, are ye—"

"I'm fine," she snapped.

A roaring of voices echoed off the stone walls, and Ian knew the men who had not been present downstairs previously had finally arrived.

Ian closed his mouth and took a breath of his own before the new mercenaries slammed into them. He hoped there weren't many, that the fight would be over quickly, and he could go upstairs and see for himself.

What was going on up there?

Ian cut down the last man in front of him and craned his head toward the oncoming horde. Six men. Not too bad. This fight would be over soon.

The first man appeared before him. Sunlight gleamed on the smooth skin of his bald head. He screamed his war cry, lips peeling back from straight teeth.

Ian put up his blade to block the blow and stabbed out with his dagger. A cry came from beside him.

Not Kyle, but Liv. Ian crossed his dagger and sword over one another and shoved the man back with all the force he could muster. He needed only a second, a flash of time to ensure Liv was all right.

A man staggered back from her. The cat had managed to latch itself onto the man's face. He flailed and wrenched it off him with a savage throw.

Liv launched a dagger at the man so fast it hit its mark in the center of his throat before the cat had a chance to land neatly on its four paws and return to her side.

The man flew back at Ian with renewed vigor. His arm raised to strike once more, and the door behind the man banged open to reveal four more men.

This fight was going to be longer than Ian had thought.

And what the hell was going on upstairs?

Sylvi dropped hard to her knees in front of her bag. The impact jarred her injured arm, and white-hot pain splashed over her thoughts. Pain. Pain. *Pain*.

Her breath hissed between her teeth. She needed to focus. She reached into her bag, grabbed the first dagger her fingertip scrabbled over and spun back to Reginald.

He was on his feet now, with Isabel beside him, both bent over with their injuries. Their slow recovery had given her the breadth of time she desperately needed. Reginald looked up, his face still a grimace of mottled purple and a slow chuckle wheezed from deep in his throat. "Ye canna throw that with a broken arm."

It was well and good then that Sylvi knew how to use both hands. She pulled back the dagger with her left hand and let it fly from her fingertips. It sailed toward him with practiced precision.

The world went still, and Sylvi swore she could discern every graceful turn the dagger made as it cut its way through the air.

The world moved slower still when Reginald grasped Isabel's shoulders and jerked her in front of him.

The blade stabbed its landing into the soft flesh of Isabel's chest, directly between her breasts. Blood spurted out and stained the fine green cloth of her gown.

Isabel.

Sylvi gasped out a breath of air as if she'd been punched in the gut.

God, no—she hadn't meant...

No sooner had the horror hit her mind than another thought blared at her. No time to mourn. No time to pause. *No time left.*

Sylvi plucked another dagger blindly from her bag and raced at Reginald with the blade clutched in her left hand. He backed up, dragging Isabel's jerking body with him as he went, leaving a streak of blood in their wake.

Sylvi's body burned with the need for revenge, fueled by all those she'd lost and the determination to save those she had yet to lose.

Reginald's eyes went wide with a realization Sylvi already knew. He could not outrun her. Isabel fell gracelessly from his arms, and he turned and ran toward the entryway. His pants slipped further down his hips with each step, his preparation to rape her now bringing him faster toward his demise.

She leapt forward like a wild cat and kicked out with all the power of her legs. Her foot caught him square in the back of his head and sent him backward. He staggered back and turned to face her, blubbering. Sylvi squeezed the hilt of her dagger so hard it carved into her palm.

Now.

She swept his feet out from underneath him, and he slammed hard onto the floor.

He stared up at her, his eyes wide with shock. The fabric of his trews, where they hovered below his crotch, darkened with a spread of urine.

"You took my family from me." Sylvi dropped down hard on

his chest, and a fetid breath choked out from him. "My mother took half your ear."

She waited until the flash of recognition lit his black eyes.

He shook his head in disbelief. "They're all dead."

She shoved her left elbow into his neck. His skin was sweaty and soft with fat. "All but a little girl whose neck hadn't been cut as deep as the others. A little girl who has waited a long, long time to kill you."

"Please," he rasped. "Dinna hurt me."

His eyes were large and wet with desperation, but Sylvi had nothing left to soften.

"You killed everyone I loved." Rage pounded through her body and made her voice shake.

Reginald's face went blue, and his eyes bulged. Only then did she realize she was crushing his throat. But, no, he needed to die the same way as her family.

"My mother took half your ear," she said again. She eased the pressure off his neck and gripped hard at her dagger. "And I'm going to take your life."

With all the force of her rage, she plunged the dagger into the tender skin of his neck and wrenched it right with all her strength. The tip of her blade scraped against something hard and unseen beneath, and blood erupted from the violent depth of the wound, spreading around him in a rapidly growing pool. She pushed off him.

She needed to go to Isabel and Percy to see if they could be saved. And yet she could not lift her feet from where they remained steadfastly stuck to the floor. She gazed down for a long moment while the light faded from Reginald's eyes, and then she stared another moment more at the man who had destroyed her life, who had taken her family and threatened her friends.

Her throat constricted, and all the energy fueling her body forward sagged out of her.

It was done.

After seventeen long years of training and searching and waiting—it was done.

The pain burning through her arm was enough to nearly drag her to her knees. She cradled the injured limb to her chest and waited for the simmer of rage, her constant companion for the last seventeen years, to cease.

It did not.

And how could it when so many had sacrificed so much?

She choked back a harsh sob and ripped her gaze from Reginald. He did not deserve any more of her time or consideration. But her ladies did.

She darted to where Isabel lay and immediately knew she was too late. Isabel stared upward to where the sky had gone the same stormy blue as the kohl-lined eyes Sylvi had known for so long.

How had she not seen Isabel's unhappiness? How could she have let all this happen?

A choked sound emerged from Percy's slumped form.

Sylvi hugged her arm to keep it from jostling and ran toward her friend.

Percy lifted her head slightly and regarded Isabel with one bright blue eye from a face streaked with gore. "You couldn't have saved her."

"What about you?" Sylvi asked around a hard knot in her throat. "Can I save you?" She slipped her blade through the bindings at Percy's wrists and ankles, smearing the rope with Reginald's blood.

"I'm fine," Percy said. She stood of her own volition and wobbled. "We have to save Liv."

Sylvi dropped her dagger in her attempt to catch Percy with her good arm. "Ian is with her. He will help her."

Hopefully.

Sylvi did not voice the last part. Her heart clenched around the fragile hope, guarding it. After all, Ian was resourceful. He could save Liv and come out unscathed.

Couldn't he?

She refused to think of another alternative.

"It should have been me." Percy's voice trembled with a sob. "It should have been me down there."

Sylvi shushed Percy and held her face in her hands. "Let me see your injuries. And then we will go to them."

There was so much blood. Too much. The need to go downstairs pressed at Sylvi's heart, but first, she had to confirm Percy would live.

Percy quieted and obediently let Sylvi push the hair back from her brow in a smear of crimson gold. Sylvi's tattered heart slipped to her feet.

A cut sliced through Percy's face from her temple through her right eye, which remained closed, over the bridge of her nose and beside her mouth before ending at her jawline.

"It will need to be stitched," Percy said.

Her matter-of-fact tone pulled deep at Sylvi's chest. She had to remain strong—no matter how much it cut into her to do so. Strength had gotten Sylvi this far. So, too, would it see them all safe.

She squared her shoulders. They needed to go downstairs. "Yes, your face will need to be stitched," Sylvi agreed. "But first, I'm going to go downstairs, and I want you to stay here."

She released her hold on Percy, who remained upright without issue.

"Like hell you are," Percy said.

Sylvi raised her eyes at Percy's uncharacteristic language.

The other woman ducked her head and let it bob back up confidently. "I've trained for this too."

"Yes, you have." Sylvi bent and retrieved her dagger, which had dropped when she'd aided Percy. Only then did she realize it was the very dagger she'd bought all those years before, paid for with her virginity. The one she had anticipated she would use to kill the man with half an ear. The one now wet with his blood.

Sylvi lifted her face to where the patch of sky showed through the broken ceiling. "You are avenged," she whispered.

Together, she and Percy raced over to the door, not once faltering, not even when the echo of footsteps thundering up became apparent.

Sylvi didn't know who was coming, but if they were not her people, they would die.

Twenty-Three

T he first man who emerged from the doorway was massive. Sylvi pulled back her dagger to fling it toward him when Ian appeared beside him.

He put his hands up. "Dinna throw yer dagger."

A wave of relief ran through her, significantly stronger than she would have anticipated. It was then she realized how truly worried she'd been. Not just for Liv—of course, she'd been worried about Liv. But also for Ian.

She lowered her weapon warily and eyed the beast of a man. He was taller than Ian and more heavily muscled. The kind of man who could easily kill.

The kind of man who *did* kill. Both he and Ian were covered in the evidence of exactly that.

"He's Ian's brother." Liv appeared beside Ian with Fianna at her side, both seemingly unharmed. The cat sat on the floor and complacently licked at her paw.

Perhaps it was the sight of the small cat and the knowledge that even she was safe, but a knot of emotion welled in Sylvi's throat, and she could not swallow it away. Liv was alive. Percy was alive. Ian was alive.

She hadn't lost everyone.

And a brother? Ian's brother was here? She tamped down questions that could be asked later.

"We were coming to save you," Sylvi said.

Ian grinned at her, and for that one moment, it was the most wonderful sight she'd seen in the whole of her life. Ian, alive and well and smiling.

"We were coming to save ye," he said.

He strode toward her, and the tension bled from her body. He was safe.

"Guess that makes us even," she said.

He caught her face in his hands, and his smile slid away. "I was so worried. I heard ye scream, and I thought..." His brow furrowed. "What happened?"

She looked down at the useless limb she held clutched against her. "Isabel broke my arm to subdue me."

Ian's face went a hot shade of red, and his eyes sparked. "That dinna work to their advantage like they thought, did it?"

Sylvi chuckled. "Apparently, not even Isabel knew I could toss a blade with both hands, or she didn't think to mention it." Her mirth disappeared under the burden of her guilt. "She's dead, Ian. I didn't mean to kill her. Reginald—"

Ian's jaw tensed. "I know ye never would." He hugged her to him on her left side, obviously taking care not to cause further injury.

She relaxed her body against him. He was alive. She kept repeating that in her head because it felt so damn wonderful.

He was alive.

Liv ran to Percy and embraced her. "Percy, what happened?"

Percy put up a hand to stop her friend. "I thought you were —"

"No. No, I'm fine." Liv stared down at Percy, and tears slipped down her cheeks. "Oh, your beautiful face, Percy."

Liv's tears were so rare a sight that they almost undid Sylvi's control. Her ladies looked to her for strength. She would need to continue to be strong for them all.

"My face...and Sylvi's arm," Percy said. "But we are all alive." She wavered slightly on her feet.

"I can carry ye." The large man spoke for the first time.

Percy straightened. "I'm fine." Her face had gone pale beneath the smear of gore, and blood dripped from her chin.

Sylvi pulled away from Ian and quickly ran to Percy. "This needs to be stitched up right away." She tried to keep the urgency from her tone lest she frighten Percy. "Liv, our bags are over there. Please go get Percy's."

"Outside, please." Percy put a hand on Sylvi's arm. "I imagine everyone downstairs is dead, or Liv would not be up here. We cannot stay."

Sylvi hesitated. While Percy was correct, she was losing a significant amount of blood.

"I can do this quickly." Sylvi motioned for the bag, grateful that Percy always brought a healing kit with her wherever she went. There wouldn't be as many medicines as Percy had at Kindrochit, but Sylvi wouldn't know what to do with them anyway.

"Ian's brother, please help her sit down." Sylvi nodded to the chair Liv had occupied—the only one still upright and not covered in blood.

"Kyle Campbell." He came forward and lifted Percy like a doll. This time, Percy did not protest. When he set her in the chair, her good eye started to flutter closed. Working immediately on Percy had been the right decision.

Fear tingled in Sylvi's veins. The threat was not over yet. "Percy, you need to stay with me. You need to tell me what to do."

Percy's chest swelled with a deep breath as if she were too tired to drag the air into her lungs. "The blue bottle. Wash my wound with it, but not all of it." She licked her dry lips. "Save some for Ian's leg."

"My leg is fine," Ian said. It was then Sylvi noticed the streak of glistening blood running down from his naked leg beneath his kilt.

Liv appeared beside Sylvi with Percy's bag in hand and pulled out the blue bottle.

"Is there anything I can do?" Ian asked. He was close enough to be Sylvi's shadow, and Kyle stood by Percy's side like a sentry.

Sylvi looked at his leg. She wanted to tell him he needed to care for it. When she met his gaze again, there was a hard set to his stare—one she knew well. He wanted orders, not coddling.

She knew the feeling well.

Sylvi took the blue bottle from Liv. "Go stand watch, Ian. We can't have this being interrupted."

She went to pull the stopper off and cursed her broken arm.

Liv must have realized Sylvi's inability to do the job, for her eyes went wide, and her face paled. "I can't." She shook her head. "I can't stitch her."

"I will." Kyle opened his palm for the bottle.

His hand was massive and dotted with calluses from a life handling a sword and fighting. Not a life of healing, like Percy's soft hands.

All of Percy was gentle and fragile. Giving her to the hands of the large, unknown man felt like handing a skein of silk to a tanner.

"I usually tend to the wounds for my people after battle," Kyle said.

"He's actually quite good," Ian added from where he stood across the room.

Percy's head drooped forward.

Sylvi reluctantly placed the small bottle in Kyle's hand. Her heart flinched with worry, with the uncertainty of giving up her position of control over helping Percy to someone she didn't know. Ian met her gaze from where he stood near the stairs and gave a single nod of reassurance.

She could trust him. "Be quick about it, but be gentle."

Kyle pulled the stopper from the blue bottle with an audible pop and jerked his face away with his brows raised. A sharp vinegar odor wafted toward Sylvi, strong enough to sting her nostrils.

"This is going to hurt." Kyle pulled a needle and thread from the bag. He threaded the catgut through the needle's narrow eye with the precision of a clothier despite the ungainly size of his hands and handed it to Liv to hold for him.

"Hold her hand," he said to Sylvi. "And if she sleeps from the pain, let her. It will be easier to stitch the wound."

Sylvi curled her good hand around Percy's. The pulse there was weak and left Sylvi's racing all the harder. "Do it."

Kyle tilted Percy's face back with the care of a lover and carefully poured the vinegar-smelling liquid over her wound. Percy's hand clenched Sylvi's. Her lips pressed hard against one another, and a whimper emerged from her throat, deep and painful. Percy's attempt at stifling her pain ached Sylvi worse than her broken arm.

Percy's body jerked against Kyle's hold, but he did not relax his grip on her. He shushed her gently, the way one does with a spooked horse, his voice low and soothing while he wiped her face clean with a strip of linen.

"I need the needle," he said. "Hold her head."

Liv passed it to him and came behind Percy to hold her head as directed. Sylvi knew exactly what she was feeling—a heady mix of compassionate pain, overwhelming fear and the weighty press of time.

They could not lose Percy.

Kyle carefully pinched the wound closed near her temple and plunged the needle through Percy's fair skin.

Percy's clenching hand on Sylvi's went limp. Percy had lost consciousness by the third stitch, as Kyle had said she might. If nothing else, it made the process go faster, which was necessary. Every second they spent there was another second they might be caught.

Ian stood guard, torn between minding the empty stairwell and trying not to think of Percy, who was being cared for within the room.

"Done." Kyle's words were the best damn thing Ian had heard in a while. They'd been lucky no one had wandered up those stairs in the time it took for Percy to be properly stitched.

"We need to go," Sylvi said.

Ian glanced over his shoulder to where she stood cradling her arm. "Get yer arm set first, Sylvi."

"Later." She made her way to him, her face pale and the corners of her mouth creased with suppressed pain. Her agony curled around his heart and squeezed until it was suffocating to endure.

Her breath came out in soft pants. "I'm perfectly fine."

"She refused to take anything for her pain," Kyle said.

"I'm still worried about ye." Ian helped Sylvi gently to her feet.

"I'm worried about all of us." Sylvi widened her stance and stiffened, and for the briefest of moments, he wondered if she was going to faint. "We need to leave this place." Her voice was quieter, as faded as she appeared.

"Sylvi," he said gently.

Her eyes snapped open, and the fierceness returned. The lass was continuing on determination alone.

"Percy needs rest." Sylvi glanced around the broken room, her gaze skimming the bodies of Reginald and Isabel.

Ian grabbed his bag and Percy's while Sylvi stared at Isabel's body. Evening was beginning to settle in the room, making Isabel's hair gleam purple against her white-blue skin.

"We ought to bury her," Sylvi said quietly.

Time pressed in on them and frayed at Ian's nerves. More men might come as they stood in place, perhaps even the two men who had been seeking Reginald before—men frightening enough to run the group of marauders off more than once.

"I'll come back tonight," Ian said. "I'll do it then."

Night would be best. It would be easier to sneak in and out undetected. Sylvi's mouth opened, and he knew she meant to protest, but suddenly she stopped and nodded.

"We must leave." She strode to the stairs, but her gaze remained fixed on Isabel.

Kyle lifted Percy into his arms. The woman's head fell limply against his chest, and one hand swung over his arm. He held her easily and tucked the errant hand over her chest.

Ian knew they were lucky to have had Kyle there. He had saved them all. Not only downstairs with Liv, making an impossible escape possible, but also with healing Percy. Without his aid, Ian feared she would surely have died.

But why the hell had Kyle been there at all?

The battered group made their way down the darkened stairs. Below was silent as the tomb it was.

Moonlight slanted in from the high arched windows and fell upon unmoving men splayed in their frozen death throes. A shiver wound down Ian's back, and he carefully picked his way over them, ensuring he did not step on any bodies.

A base part of him wanted to bolt from the place like a spooked horse. If it were difficult now with the rest of them, it would be far more disturbing later when he returned to bury Isabel.

A hand slid into his, cool and dry. He looked beside him to see Sylvi, her face lined with tension, and he knew she was enduring the same disquiet.

She looked back toward Kyle. "Make sure she does not see if she wakes." She spoke softly, but her voice almost made Ian jump.

Kyle nodded and strode to the front of their party, leading the way with the ease of one navigating toward home. He led the way to a set of large double doors, one of which hung open, gaping into the night like a mouth with a missing tooth.

Ian released Sylvi's good hand and moved to the front of the line. Cradling her arm, she followed at his side as if sensing his intent to ensure all was clear and refusing for him to do it without her. He put up his palm to stay her and all the others. Ignoring her glare, he slipped out of the door into the still night.

The air was cool and crisp and fresh. A sweet reprieve from the odor of death. He did a quick sweep of the perimeter and ensured all was safe before waving the others to follow.

Within minutes, he had grabbed enough horses from where Reginald's men kept them stabled, and the party quickly fled the area, leaving behind their dead and their fear.

Ian kept Sylvi with him, holding tight to her waist in front of him as he rode lest she faint from her injuries and slide off. His leg burned now from where he'd been cut; the way injuries did when the energy of battle calmed in one's blood.

He didn't push the horse as fast as it could go, opting for a smoother stride to keep from jostling Sylvi's arm. Ian regarded his large younger brother as they rode. Kyle held Percy to him as if she were a baby bird. His massive hands were as gentle as they'd always been with the many things he'd healed over the years.

Kyle had always been the more empathetic of them, the one willing to sacrifice for another's comfort. It was a trait that Ian had appreciated and had taken great advantage of in his youth.

So why the hell was Kyle, with his soft heart and high moral integrity, running with the likes of Reginald and his men?

The desire to know clawed at Ian, but he held his impatience. He'd wait until they were alone at the inn.

Twenty-Four

S ylvi's soul was not at ease.

The source of her rage had not quelled, and the calm she'd anticipated had not descended. All the expectation she'd gathered for most of her life crumpled in the pit of her stomach.

She sat on the bed in the inn and tried to rein in the force of her emotions. Ian had gone to get food and would be back soon. She wouldn't have him find her thus, tears burning in her eyes and a heart afire with—with what?

Disappointment?

Lack of satisfaction?

The need for revenge already had?

She leapt from the hard bed, and pain lanced up her arm. Kyle had been gentle setting it, his quiet care evident in every touch. Yet when setting a broken arm, all the care in the world still caused incredible agony. The ache thudded through the tincture he'd given her and intensified when she moved it. Or jarred it by jumping off the bed.

Ian's leg had been cleaned and bandaged, though he'd refused to be seen until the ladies had been properly tended to and he'd ensured Percy did not need further assistance.

She paced the room. It was small, barely large enough to hold the simple bed and a table. She took seven rapid steps before needing to turn to pace to the other wall. Everything seemed to press in on her like a cage, and her damn arm ached.

The door opened, and Ian was standing there with two trenchers of steaming stew and a smile.

Her heart twisted further still. Part of her wanted to run to him like some insipid courtier and let his arms curl around her. She craved warmth and safety and affection. Yet, the hollowness inside her begged to be left alone, to spiral downward in the pull of misery.

Her heart remained heavy, and her mind was devoid of all thought but the one pain thundering its way up her arm and the recurring reminder of how everything was so...empty.

Ian set the stew on the small table. Brown gravy coated generous hunks of meat and pale lumps of vegetables while the bread soaked it all in. The savory scent churned against her stomach. She should be hungry.

"Thank you for getting food." She didn't attempt to rouse a smile. "How is everyone?"

Ian lifted a hand to her face and gently caressed her cheek. His fingers were warm from where he'd held the hot food. She turned in to the tender embrace and wished it could warm all of her soul.

"Liv is fine," he said. "Pacing the room just like ye. Percy is awake with Kyle at her side, forcing her to eat." His warm gaze found hers. "And how is my angel?"

A weight crushed against her chest and made breathing hard. "I'm..." Her mind staggered over the right word. How could she tell him how she felt when she didn't even know? "Fine. I'm fine."

His brow furrowed, and she knew he saw right through her.

"Tell me about your brother. Why was Kyle with Reginald?" She spoke quickly to keep him from asking questions. Her words were abrupt to the point of being harsh, especially when referring to the man who had saved them all. She shook her head. "I didn't mean it like that. We're all fortunate he was

there. His skill with the needle is exceptional. Percy's stitches
are—"

"Ye dinna have to do this." Ian put an arm on her shoulders
and carefully led her to the bed to sit.

She sank onto the straw mattress and stared at the food on the
table. The fluffy white bread was halfway soaked with gravy. It
would be soggy.

"I'm no' sure why Kyle was there today, but ye know I'll be
asking him." Ian settled beside her, and the bed shifted under his
weight. "I know Percy is injured, but she'll heal." He narrowed his
gaze at her, far too observant for comfort. "But it's no' her ye're
thinking of, is it?"

Sylvi pursed her lips and kept her stare fixed on the ruined
bread. No part of her wanted to have this conversation with him
right now. It made the hollowness inside her echo in on itself.

Ian's hand folded over Sylvi's. "Killing someone willna bring
someone else back."

His words punctured her heart like a dagger. She clenched her
jaw and nodded. "I know."

"I know ye know." He smoothed a hand over her head. "But
it's harder to believe here." His hand settled on her chest, just
below the center of her collarbones. "I know ye dinna think ye'd
bring them back, but I think ye thought it'd heal yer heart."

The bread blurred, and a hard lump knotted in her throat.
She blinked the sensation away.

"Ye spent yer life planning for what happened today. And
now it's done." Ian continued in a gentle voice. "But even with it
done, ye still hurt, and it makes ye feel empty."

She looked at him, startled. "How do you know this?"

"Because I've felt that emptiness too." He looked down at
where their hands joined. "I thought leaving would make everything go away. I thought I could start a new life and be free of the
guilt. But then I wandered...and found nothing." The small smile
he gave her didn't reach his eyes, leaving it mirthless and resigned.
"I dinna join with Reginald's men because I wanted fun. I joined

because they at least seemed to be heading in a direction, even if I dinna know where that was. They were a brotherhood, and I felt like if I belonged, it would fill the emptiness."

Sylvi flinched at the thought of Ian running with those men. But this was the first time he had truly explained it to her. And in a manner that she could understand.

"I dinna know what they were about, Sylvi. When they broke into that woman's home…" He stopped speaking and clenched his jaw. Spots of color showed on his cheeks beneath his beard. "I killed two of Reginald's men and injured a couple others. After that, I was left to wander again. I did that for a bit of time. Then I met ye."

He caressed Sylvi's cheek, then dropped his hand and tilted his head. "Even if ye tried to kill me. Twice."

"Only once." She immediately missed the loss of contact with his hand against her face. "The second time I brought you back."

"Ye brought me back more than ye realize." He lifted her hand to his chest. "Ye took away my emptiness, Sylvi. Ye had such fire and such conviction. Everything in ye was so fixed on this goal to see yer family avenged. I latched onto it and knew ye'd no' only fulfill yer own need, but ye'd make me whole in the process."

His heart beat in a strong, steady rhythm beneath her fingers.

"And now it's done," she said softly.

"And now it's done." He nodded once. "I've helped ye right a wrong. I've satisfied what I set out to do. And after it's all done, ye feel lost."

"Neither of us has a purpose to aspire to," she said. The hollowness inside her echoed.

"I know what my purpose is," he said. "Ye need to find yers. But first, ye need to say goodbye to yer family. Ye've held them alive in yer heart all this time, waiting to release them. Ye need to let them go."

She dragged in a ragged breath.

"I love ye, Sylvi." He took her face in his hands and pressed a gentle kiss to her lips.

Sylvi kept her eyes closed, so she could not see his expression, and he could not see hers. For her heart was not yet open enough to accept his words, and certainly nowhere near being able to reciprocate. The bed shifted as his weight lifted away.

When at last she did open her eyes, he was gone, as was one trencher of food. She knew he understood her dilemma, and perhaps he'd even expected it. And yet still, he'd told her he loved her again.

He was right in saying she needed to say goodbye. To her family, to My Lady, even to the little girl she once was. She needed to clear out her heart.

Hesitation stuttered through her.

What if it was not enough? What if all she'd done was for naught? What if she was too broken ever to allow herself to love?

With everything else in her life, she had been brave. Now, facing the thing that could somehow take away the hurt and the emptiness, she was suddenly very afraid.

IAN HAD NOT EXPECTED SYLVI TO RETURN HIS expression of love, yet her silence had caught at his chest.

He was a damn fool.

Night had fallen, and he would need to return soon to fulfill his promise to bury Isabel. The very idea of the task made his stomach fill with cold dread.

It was not yet nearly late enough, and so he was able to put off the task for now. He made his way to Kyle's room, stopped and turned to Percy's door. He knocked softly.

The door opened to reveal Kyle's towering frame.

Ian held up his trencher of cold stew. "Want some company for supper?"

Kyle put a finger to his lips. He disappeared for a moment and reemerged with his trencher of cold stew.

"Let's go to my room." He closed the door quietly and led the way.

It was as small inside as the one Sylvi and Ian shared.

When they were alone, the brothers set down their food and embraced for a long time. "It's been too long," Kyle said when they moved apart at last. "I dinna know if ye were ever going to come back."

Ian hadn't planned to. Being lost in the world was better than being the kind of hard ruler his father had expected him to be. "I thought ye'd be glad to be laird someday." Ian clapped his brother on his shoulder.

Kyle shot him a sidelong look. "I never wanted it."

"Ye'd be good at it," Ian said in his most convincing tone.

Kyle grabbed his trencher of food and plunked down on the edge of the bed. "Da wouldna ever leave the lairdship to me, even if I did want it." He lifted a sodden piece of bread and let it hover in front of his mouth. "Which I dinna." He pushed the bread into his mouth and chewed.

Ian lifted his trencher and casually leaned against the wall. "What were ye doing with Reginald and his men?"

Kyle stopped chewing and drew a long swallow of ale from a mug. "Two things." He thrust up his thumb. "One, looking for ye." He lifted his pointer finger. "Two, looking for information."

"Information on what? Did ye find anything?" Ian drew a hunk of bread through the gravy and bit into it. While soggy and cold, it was rich with herbs and salty on his tongue.

"I found out they hated ye," Kyle said. "Looks as if ye finally found people ye couldna win over with yer charm, eh?"

Ian shrugged. "Canna win all the hearts all the time. Did they know who ye were?"

Kyle shook his head. "Nay, but they knew who ye were." He nodded toward Ian's sword. "Yer fine clothes gave ye away as noble."

Ian tried to ignore the internal grimace at the second mention in one day of how obvious he'd been. But then, he hadn't exactly known what he was doing when he joined them. Never had it crossed his mind he ought to hide his identity. "Aside from me, what information were ye looking for? And why the devil did ye care if I was found or no'?"

Kyle smirked. "Ye changing the subject?"

"Aye, to something relevant." Ian popped a juicy piece of meat in his mouth, so tender it broke apart before he even bit down.

"I was trying to find ye because I need yer help. The marauders said they'd sent someone to kill ye before I joined them. Some thought ye were dead; some thought ye were alive. I figured I'd hang about a bit to see if news of ye turned up." He swallowed the last of his bread with some more ale. "Then the men came in, yelling about lasses being taken and rewards coming to them." His lip curled in disgust. "I readied to fight to protect the lasses. I hadna expected to see ye."

He sighed and set aside the empty trencher. "A month wasted with no' much to show for it."

Ian grinned. "Ye found me."

"Aye," Kyle said dejectedly. "No' much to show for it, as I said." He raised his brows at Ian, and they both laughed.

"I'm glad ye were there today, brother," Ian said. "It would have had a different outcome without ye."

"I canna always let ye have all the glory, aye?" Kyle stood and slapped him on the shoulder. "Want me to go back with ye to bury the redhead?"

It was on the tip of Ian's tongue to say yes. It was something the old him would have readily agreed to. Someone else could do his dirty work, and he could keep them good company while they did so. But after seeing how hard Sylvi fought for everything she had, everything she did, eschewing his own promises seemed suddenly wrong.

"Stay here in case the girls need ye." Ian hesitated. "Ye said ye needed my help. What information were ye searching for? I'll look through Reginald's items to see if I can find anything."

"There's something I've no' told ye, Ian." Kyle put his hand on Ian's shoulder. He didn't speak for a long moment, enough time for apprehension to curl around him.

Ian's heart pounded. "What is it?"

"It's Mum. She's dead, Ian." He made the sign of the cross.

Were a wall not behind Ian, he might have staggered back. Their mother had been spirited and loving. To imagine such a light snuffed out—his mother dead—was unthinkable.

Kyle raised his gaze to Ian's, his eyes as sapphire blue as their ma's had been. "We need to find who killed her. Da willna look into it further, and I canna find enough to support my suspicions, but I suspect she was murdered."

Twenty-Five

Sylvi woke with a start. Her dagger was gripped firmly against her palm, her heart pounding.

A scream.

She'd been woken by a scream.

It came again, a shriek of terror.

Sylvi leapt from her bed and cursed the spike of pain lancing up her arm. Heedless of her half-dressed state in the long black léine and nothing more, she ran into the hall in time to be greeted with another wail, this one softer and less frightened.

Percy's door stood open.

Sylvi's heart leapt into her throat.

Not Percy.

She ran toward the room with her blade brandished. Nothing would happen to Percy—not if Sylvi had anything to do about it.

A soft shushing sound came from the room, and the cries began to quiet. Sylvi stopped short at the massive figure standing beside Percy's bed.

"It's all right, lass." Kyle's voice drifted from where he bent over Percy. "It was only a dream."

"What happened?" Sylvi demanded.

He turned to her, his movement slow as if he didn't want to

frighten Percy further. If he'd started abruptly like a man caught, he would be dead by now.

"She had a bad dream," he said. "Scared the life out of me. These walls are thin as parchment."

"I'm sorry," Percy whimpered. "Sylvi, is that you? I woke you too?"

Sylvi approached the bed where Percy lay, small and helpless, with a band of white linen bisecting her face. "I was awake anyway," Sylvi lied.

"You should have let him take me." Percy drew in a shuddering breath. "You should have let them take me. I've endured it before. I could endure it again." Her eyes shone brightly in the moonlight.

"Percy, what are you talking about?" Sylvi pressed her hand to Percy's uninjured cheek. The smooth skin beneath her fingers was burning hot.

"Rape," Percy said the word so easily, it shocked Sylvi more than the heat blazing from Percy's face.

"She has a fever," Sylvi murmured.

When Kyle did not move, she turned to face him. He stared down at Percy with such a wounded expression on his open, honest face that Sylvi could practically feel the pain of his empathy.

"She has a fever," she repeated quietly. "Are you familiar with making a tonic to help with that?"

"It should have been me," Percy said. "Not Liv, after all that she's been through." She sobbed softly. "Not Liv."

He nodded slowly and turned away with great hesitation.

"Percy, you're ill," Sylvi said. "Liv is fine. She was never touched. Kyle and Ian saved her."

Percy slowly released a breath of air, and her body relaxed.

What she'd said, though, stuck in Sylvi's heart like a thorn. How had she never known about Percy? Had any of them?

"I never knew, Percy." Sylvi dipped a bit of linen into the

small tub of water on the table and draped it over Percy's head. "I'm so sorry. I never knew."

Percy's eyes drifted closed against the coolness of the cloth on her hot skin. "I never told anyone." Her hand blindly grabbed for Sylvi's. "I want to tell you." She licked her dry lips. "I want someone to know it wasn't my fault. That I didn't do it."

Sylvi looked over her shoulder at Kyle's retreating form. She waited until the door clicked before speaking again.

"You don't have to tell me," Sylvi said. Already the cloth in her hand was growing hot from Percy's skin.

"I want someone to know." Percy pressed her lips together. "In case I don't live."

Sylvi's heart jolted. "Don't say tha—"

Percy caught her hand and folded it in the heat of her fever. "I've seen infections kill more men than blades. I'm sure Kyle would say the same."

"You aren't going to die." Sylvi pushed all the conviction she had into her words as if she could make them so by the way she said them. For truly, in her heart, she did not believe Percy would die.

"We all have our reasons why we came to be at Kindrochit." Percy spoke as if she had not heard Sylvi. "But I never told anyone mine. Connor saved me but never told anyone what he knew. He's always so trustworthy like that."

Sylvi nodded to herself. "Yes, he is." They had all missed him after he left Kindrochit, he and Ariana both. Their occasional visits did not fill the void the two had left behind. A void worth enduring to see them in such happiness together.

"I lived with my parents in a small country estate outside of London," Percy said. "We had a title but were by no means wealthy. When I was sixteen, they got the sweating sickness, and, um..." She pursed her lips and winced slightly. "They died."

Sylvi squeezed her hand and released it to remove the cloth from Percy's brow. "I'm so sorry."

Percy nodded in quiet appreciation. "My mother had a wealthy aunt at court who took me in."

Sylvi dragged the cloth through the cold water.

"I didn't like court." Percy's brow flinched. "The men were uncouth and the women cruel. They were uncommonly so because of…" She shifted in her bed, and her gaze shifted away with discomfort. "Because of the way I looked."

Sylvi squeezed the water from the linen. The gentle plinking of water filled the room. She understood what Percy was saying. Hers was a beauty people wanted. Sylvi had seen the reaction most had to Percy. The men with their lust and the women with their bitter jealousy.

"I hated it," Percy said. "My aunt got tired of it as well and took me from court to stay with her in her country estate. I was so relieved. Until my uncle joined her."

Sylvi patted the cool cloth over Percy's face and hardened her heart for what she knew would come next in the tale.

"He was…forceful…with me." Percy's words were flat now as if she were trying to speak of something she did not want her mind to acknowledge. "Many times. And once my aunt found us, I was so glad because I thought it would finally stop." Percy swallowed. "But she grabbed a candlestick and hit me with it. She accused me of seducing her husband, then she hit him and he fell to the ground. Dead."

Sylvi turned the compress over so that the coolest side would be against Percy's skin, laid it over her brow, then grabbed her friend's hand. For support and for comfort. For both of them.

"She said I did it, and who would question her?" The good side of Percy's lips lifted in a mirthless smirk. "I was a pauper, and she was a noble. I was taken to prison, where things were even more awful than they'd been with my uncle." She drew in a deep breath and slowly let it out. "I don't know how Connor found me, but my gratitude for his saving me is unending."

"Percy," Sylvi said softly. "I'm so sorry."

Her good eye looked up at Sylvi. "When I went out on my

first mission, I was so desperate to prove myself. The man I'd been sent to spy on...he became amorous. Not forceful, but it brought back so many memories that I-I panicked and attacked him. I was so much more powerful after my training, and I couldn't let myself be a victim again. I couldn't let anyone take—" She clenched her fists, and her voice was calmer when she spoke again. "We fought. He almost killed me, but I ended up killing him instead. It was not a fast death or a clean one. Connor never made me do another mission. And he promised never to let anyone go alone again."

Sylvi remained silent for a long moment. She held tight to Percy's hand. It all made sense now. Percy's refusal to leave, her uncertainty around others when speaking, the way she covered herself in a hooded cloak the few times they were forced outside. If only Sylvi had known all this, she never would have asked Percy to join them. She would have kept her locked in Kindrochit for all of eternity.

Yet never once did Percy protest what she'd been asked to do, nor issue forth a complaint.

"I think," Sylvi said slowly, "you are the strongest of all of us to come out of something so awful with such sweetness and kindness."

"Because of the love I've found with all of you." Percy's voice cracked. "You've given me life. You've made me whole."

Sylvi kissed Percy's hand with all the love she would have held for her own sisters had they survived. Love could not undo a life of hurt, but perhaps it could help heal.

"Thank you." Percy turned her heat toward Sylvi. "Thank you for listening to my story."

"Thank you for sharing, Percy," Sylvi said. And by God, did she mean every word. Even in such a dark time as this, Percy had helped in the most unthinkable way.

She'd given Sylvi hope.

WHO KNEW GOLD COULD WEIGH SO MUCH?

Ian hefted the bag to his shoulder and made his way up the stairs. To Sylvi.

He wanted to wrap her in his arms and forget about the dead he'd seen lying where they fell, to warm the haunted chill from his soul. No matter how those men had been in life, he would never forget the horror of seeing so many dead.

The door was open, and the room they shared was empty within. Ian dropped the bags on the floor with a frown. And then he heard it, the low murmur of softly talking voices.

He followed the sound until he was outside Percy's room and was able to discern the speakers. Kyle and Sylvi. He opened the door, and both spun around, daggers in hand.

Ian put his hands up defensively.

"Ye almost got yerself killed," Kyle said.

"I'm no' so easy to kill." It was difficult to jest with the weight of their mother's death pressing down on him and with what he'd just been through. But discussing those things would be harder still. Impossible.

He looked between them to where Percy lay sleeping. "How is she?"

"Her fever is just starting to break," Sylvi said.

Kyle nodded to the door. "Ye go. I'll stay with her."

Sylvi hesitated, but Kyle put a hand on her good shoulder. "These walls are thin, lass. I tried no' to listen, but I couldna keep from hearing." His jaw clenched. "I'd no' ever hurt her."

"I'd kill you if you did." Sylvi issued the threat with such vehemence its sincerity could not be questioned.

He inclined his head respectfully. "I'd no' expect anything less."

Still, Sylvi hesitated before leaving the room, her gaze fixed on Ian, silently seeking his trust. He nodded, and she cast off her reluctance and followed him with confidence.

She would want details, of course.

But Ian didn't want to talk. He wanted to hold her and love

her and forget the events of the night had ever happened. The cold, spongy texture of Isabel's dead skin, the stiffness of her limbs. The memories of it all played over his fingertips as if he gripped her still. A shudder wracked through him.

Sylvi pulled him into their room and closed the door behind her. She stared into his face for a long moment, and her expression softened.

"I know that was unpleasant," she said. "Thank you for doing that for me. For Isabel. I know she betrayed us. But she was so damaged, so used, like the rest of us." She frowned. "I'd have done it myself if it wasn't for this damn arm."

He let the bag fall from his hand. It hit the ground hard, the metallic contents jingling against one another like chain mail. Only it wasn't chain mail. It was jewelry. Necklaces and bracelets and brooches and rings, all the jewelry any goldsmith could be commissioned to make.

He caught her chin between his fingers. "I'd do anything for ye, Sylvi." His nails were still rimmed with black from the rich dirt despite the number of times he'd scrubbed them. He quickly let his hand fall away.

"What did you find out?" Sylvi asked. "About Kyle? Why was he with Reginald?"

He knew it would come to this. The questions burning in her mind and the answers he loathed giving. "He was with them to find out where I'd gone to. Kyle found out I'd traveled with them. He was trying to find out information, but no one would say anything."

Her gaze flicked to the bag on the floor. "And what did you find when you went there?"

"Those two men I saw the day ye killed me and gave me to Gregor. They came right as I was leaving. I just managed to escape."

It'd been a narrow getaway, with him slipping from an empty window to the soft grass below. He'd been fortunate in many ways—that he'd already buried Isabel, that he'd hidden the bag in the woods already, that he was on his final look-through and had been quiet enough in his escape they hadn't heard him despite the silence of the dead. It had been so silent that he'd heard their conversation. "They were the king's men, seeking out the coins. It appears they found out about them and finally tracked down Reginald and his men."

Sylvi straightened. "Isabel. They can't find her body."

He shook his head. "I'd already buried her. And I left the coins. They'll find what they came for."

"And that?" Sylvi indicated the bag.

She carefully lowered herself one-armed to the floor beside the bag. "If you left the coins, then what is this?" She pulled open the bag and gasped at the treasure inside.

Ian struck a flint to light the small candle on the table. It flickered to life and cast the small room in a stronger glow than the meager hearth provided. Ian sank onto the floor beside Sylvi and carefully pulled out a necklace. The craftsmanship was so fine it appeared to be made of lace. The candlelight made the gold twinkle like the stars and caught at the large red stone encased at its center.

"I dinna want to bring this at first," Ian said. "But then I remembered yer da was a goldsmith. I thought mayhap his creations might be here. I thought ye'd want that."

Sylvi pulled in a soft breath and turned to him with a wide-eyed expression. "I never took anything of my family's when I left. I was in too much of a hurry to get out of there." She stared with wonder at the necklace in her hand. "Thank you."

She turned the necklace in her hand, and the length of chain coiled around her fingers. Her gaze searched the back of the piece for a long moment. "Bring the candle closer, please."

He lowered the candle to cast a stronger light on the gold.

Sylvi set aside the fine piece. "This one is not his."

He picked it up. For something so small, its weight was considerable. "How do ye know?"

"Right here." She guided his hand to flip the piece over and pointed to where the shape of a bear's head had been pressed into the soft gold. It was so small it would never have been noticed had it not been pointed out.

"Every goldsmith has his mark, something to show as his work." Sylvi smiled softly to herself. "My father had what looked like a circle with several dots lining it. The shape of a shield since my mother's family descended from a family of Viking shield-maidens. He was always proud of that and said her bravery was exactly that of her ancestors."

Clearly, Sylvi's mother was brave. After all, she had taken most of Reginald's ear. Instead of commenting, he reached inside the bag and handed her another necklace while he took a bracelet.

He turned the jewelry over and studied the back. A square had been marked near the clasp. "This one is a square."

"This one is another bear's head." She set aside the necklace beside the other and reached in, pulling out a ring.

Piece after piece, they removed from the bag and identified out loud, piling the jewelry with its like markings.

Ian looked at the back of a brooch bracelet cuff, and his heart leapt. There, stamped beside the carefully welded gold, was a circle with dots lining it. "Is this yer da's?" He held it out to Sylvi.

Her eyes widened with vulnerable hope. She took a deep breath and folded her fingers over it. When she flipped the piece over, her hands were trembling slightly. She gave a shuddering exhale, wrapped the jewelry in her hand and pushed it to her chest, just over her heart.

"Yes." She nodded. "Yes, this is his."

Ian's chest filled with joy at the awed wonder on her face when she finally turned back the bracelet to study it. If she could not find peace with her family in her heart, then perhaps this would help.

Twenty-Six

Sylvi had never cared for jewelry. Perhaps the idea of wearing it was too painful and called to mind too many memories of Papa's large fingers carefully crafting the fragile pieces. And how they would never craft anything ever again.

But holding the bracelet in the splay of her fingers, it was as if she held all his love cradled in her hand. The pale blue stone glinted at her, and delicate coils of gold curled around its edge in an elegant casing meant to wrap around one's wrist.

She looked up at Ian to find him watching her with a wistful smile as if he took incredible joy in seeing her reaction.

"This is the most precious gift you could have given me." Her emotions, usually so locked into submission by her control, had been wrung out to the point of exhaustion.

It was unimaginable her father's piece would still be in the pile of jewelry and hadn't been sold off to buy drink and women. Really, it was astonishing they'd kept all they had. They'd gone through only the topmost portion of the bag, and already five small piles of jewelry lay about the floor, all piled up by maker.

Sylvi's blood chilled.

The jewelry. *All piled up by maker.*

"Ian..." She eased the bracelet carefully onto her good arm and scooted closer to the gleaming mounds of treasure. "Look at all this jewelry."

He nodded. "And there is probably more inside the bag from yer da."

"It's not that. Look at all of it. All piled up by maker." Her heart was pounding in her chest, its beat roaring in her ears and making her arm pulse with pain. "How did they get so much jewelry from these particular makers? If they were just stolen, there'd be all different marks."

He snapped his gaze toward her, and she knew he understood.

"Yer family was not the only one Reginald did this to," he said.

Having those words spoken made her stomach slide to her toes. Ian put a hand to her back. His palm was warm, and the gesture was meant to comfort, of which there would be none. Not now.

"We have to check the rest of these." Sylvi reached for the bag. "We have to see. How many goldsmiths might have suffered the same fate as my family?"

Ian lifted the bag and carefully overturned it. Jewelry of all kinds slid out into a careful pile between them, and they set to task—flipping, checking, sorting.

An *X*.

A square.

A bear's head.

The letter *R*.

The shield of her father's work.

One by one, each piece was put into a designated stack, the maker's mark spoken aloud each time. The medicine Kyle had given Sylvi when she was in Percy's room was in full effect, and the pain in her arm had significantly decreased. She was grateful for the reprieve, especially for this task.

While they sorted, Sylvi tried not to notice as each section piled higher and higher. After a while, she could identify the maker before turning the item over.

The maker of the square mark used flat bands of metal curling around each stone, opting for round-cut gems. The maker of the bear's head mark preferred large sheets of hammered gold with insets of dozens of stones glittering from its surface like stars in the sky.

Her father's work was so much more careful than the others, the small threads of gold so delicately woven they appeared to have been done by fairies. Many of those delicate pieces had become bent at some point, crushed by the weight of other jewelry.

Finally, she held the last piece of the collection in her hand, a ring with a round green stone at its center and wrapped in a flat band of gold. "Square." She spoke as she flipped it over, confirming the square pressed into the gold.

She set it atop a small mountain of pieces, all similarly crafted by the same maker. They'd been sorted appropriately. Now to face what they'd done—the neatly piled jewelry markers for families possibly dead like her own.

Only there were not five piles this time, but six. As they neared the bottom, where most of her father's jewelry had been, they found another mark. A sun.

There hadn't been many pieces of her father's shield or the sun, only a dozen of her father's and ten of the other.

Sylvi sat back on her heels and stared in silence at the piles. Six in all.

"Six piles. Six goldsmiths." She spoke through numb lips. "Six families."

Ian put his arm around her. The action was meant to comfort her, but it pulled her from her distressing reverie. "Think of how many we might have saved in stopping Reginald and his men."

She gazed up at him and found deep shadows under his eyes. He looked nearly ready to collapse. And was it any wonder? He and Kyle had worked to secure a safe place for the evening for all of them, and then Ian had gone back to bury Isabel.

He'd done so much already that day.

Too much.

Ian stroked a hand down her face in a gentle caress. "I thought I lost ye earlier today."

His mouth came down on hers, tender and sweet, a kiss that made her heart burn with longing. Why couldn't she just be a regular woman tonight in the arms of the man she cared for?

He loved her. She hadn't let herself think on it more after he'd said it.

She'd felt a flicker of hope after speaking to Percy. If someone who had been through as much as Percy had could still emerge as selfless and kind, it was possible.

Yet there in her lover's arms, Sylvi could think of nothing but conspiracies and stolen jewelry. And the families of other gold-smiths who might have been slaughtered.

"You need sleep." She stepped away from him.

He watched her carefully for a long moment. "Ye mean alone?"

She'd hurt him.

She wanted to tell him it wasn't his fault. But she'd already warned him her heart was too broken to mend. What was the point in saying it all again?

The stacks of gold gleamed in the flickering candlelight, and the rich scent of the congealing stew she hadn't touched filled her nostrils. She had to get out into the open air to let her thoughts free.

"I need to think." She rose and shoved through the door and let it slam behind her.

Her heart quivered like a wounded bird in her chest as she sucked in the night air. She wanted to go back inside and let him love away her pain, yet she couldn't be with him while her mind scrambled through the jewelry hoard and the lost families.

She stayed where she stood, as unsure of what to do as when

she was a lost, hopeless orphan in the streets. The bracelet on her wrist weighed heavily on her heart.

The door opened, and Ian exited. His surprised expression faded immediately and melted into a roguish grin. One of his brows cocked upright. "Well, ye made this chase easy."

"I don't have anywhere to go."

He cocked his head. "Aye, that would be a problem. Do ye..." He pulled back the door wider. "Do ye want to come in?"

"What if I run from this mess?" she asked, her heart pounding.

"It doesna make anything better. I've tried." He held his hand out to her. "Face this head-on like ye always do, my angel, with strength and courage and determination. We can find the other goldsmiths together. We can do anything together."

His words snapped through her mind, and she straightened. He was right. She didn't need to think. She needed to talk this through.

She reached out with her good arm and took his proffered hand.

IAN'S HEART THRUMMED WITH RESOLVE. SYLVI WAS back in their room, and this time, he would not let her go. Exhaustion lay in his mind like lead, but he could push past it.

Sylvi regarded him, her expression blank. So much roiled beneath the surface, he knew. So much he needed to get past.

"Sylvi." He took her good hand in his. "I love ye."

Her jaw tensed, and she looked away. He put his hand on her cheek and gently turned her face back to him. Her eyes wouldn't meet his.

"I can't love you." Her tone was sharp.

"Why do ye say that?" He kept his tone gentle.

She stared at him incredulously. "I haven't been able to love since my family died."

"No, ye havena taken the time with men until me, but ye've loved. Look at how ye feel about Liv and Percy." He paused. "How ye felt about Lady Camille."

Her brow flinched. "When you kissed me just now, all I could think about was the jewelry and those families killed." She turned away from him and stood in front of the fire, staring into its flames.

Ian watched her for a long moment. "Ye only recently found out. Of course, it's still on yer mind." He stepped closer to stand beside her. "We'll follow the marks in the gold and see if we can find their owners or what happened to them."

Sylvi turned to look at him. "You'd do that?"

Ian cupped her chin. "I'd do anything for ye."

She stared up at him with a worried expression. "Ian—"

"Let me ask ye this," he said quickly. "What did ye think when I was downstairs with Liv, and ye were upstairs with Reginald?"

The delicate, beautiful muscles along her neck tensed. "I worried you would do anything in your power to protect Liv."

"And?" he pressed.

She swallowed. "And I thought you were going to die."

He watched her face carefully. "How did that make ye feel?"

She closed her eyes against what he hoped was the pain of memory. "Afraid. Panicked." She opened her eyes, and a flash of determination showed in the ice-blue depths. "I wanted to kill Reginald as fast as possible so that I could find you."

"This man who ye've been searching for all these years, ye finally found, and ye wanted to rush his death." He lifted his brows suggestively. "To save me."

Her mouth parted softly, and the determined tension in her body relaxed.

"In a moment where you needed an immediate decision," he said, "ye were ready to choose me over yer revenge."

Her gaze searched the ground.

"And how did ye feel when ye saw me after?" he asked.

Her lips lifted in a smile. "As though I could laugh and cry at the same time, and that your arrogant grin was the most magnificent thing I'd ever seen."

He couldn't help but chuckle at that.

"What if I hadna come back? What if ye'd found me dead?" he asked.

Her brows knit together, and she shook her head. "I couldn't even think of it while I was upstairs. I refused to. I couldn't—"

"Sylvi." He gently pinched her chin and lifted her face. "Ye say ye canna love me, but I think yer heart is more open than ye're letting yerself realize." He stroked a length of hair from her face. "We're both alive. We're together."

He stared into her eyes, at the affection glowing deep in those cool depths. "And I love ye."

He closed his eyes and let his mouth come down on her sweet warmth. Her good hand curled around the back of his neck, and she returned his kiss with the hunger and passion he knew so wonderfully well. His body sang with her returned desire, and he went hard with need. Not just for her body but also for her heart, which was so close within his grasp.

"Ian," she whispered against his lips. "Love me."

He swept his tongue between her lips and let it brush hers. Shivers of pleasure coursed through his body. She intensified her grip on him, and her body arched against his.

He pulled away to look at her. Her cheeks were pink, her eyes sparkling and warm. All with desire. For him. "Ye're so beautiful, my angel."

A hesitant smile blossomed on her lips. Shy almost. He nearly laughed out loud at the thought of his Sylvi, his vengeful angel, being shy.

But it was so beautiful a sight that he would never laugh.

"Ye want me to love ye." He popped free the first button on her breeches. The corner of the front flap sagged forward. "Then I intend to love ye as I've always wanted." He liberated the second button. "Slow." The third. "Careful." The fourth.

Her jaw clenched, and her gaze followed his fingers, moving

over the loosened side of her breeches to graze the covered cleft between her legs. Her breath hitched.

"Ye know what I want." He drew his hand up her waist and higher still to graze the side of her breast. "No rushing me this time." He said it playfully, but he meant it with his whole heart.

He would take all night if he needed, but he wanted to savor Sylvi, to slow what she'd always rushed through in the past to get to sexual satisfaction. Tonight, he would show her just how much he truly loved her.

Twenty-Seven

S ylvi's body was on fire, lit by Ian's touch. Everything in her pounded to kiss him, to rake her fingers over his hard stomach to where he was harder still. She wanted the heat of his nakedness against her and him swollen and hot inside her.

Yet all he'd done thus far was halfway unbutton her trews. It would be a long time until they got to the point she so looked forward to.

He cupped her face in his hands and stared down at her with his golden-brown eyes as if he meant to look into her soul. There was so much emotion to be had in that one long, beautiful gaze that it almost overwhelmed her. It *could* have overwhelmed her if she'd let it. But the look in his eyes—the love, the resolve, the desire—was a heady mix.

He looked down, and his fingers slowly worked over the rest of her trews. Each button slipped free and nudged the snugly fitted cloth against her sex. The heat was building already there, hot and hungry.

He lowered himself to his knees, like a courtier pledging fealty, and peeled the trews from her hips.

"Ye've got the loveliest legs." He slid her léine up to see her legs better and pressed a kiss to her upper thigh, deliciously close to the sensitive spot between her legs.

A jolt of anticipation shot through Sylvi. She gritted her teeth against it and let him pull away the trews at an agonizing pace. His palms skimmed over her thighs, and shivers washed over her skin. His warm lips grazed the tender skin behind her knees, where she was much more sensitive than she'd ever realized.

He held her hand, and she stepped free of her trews, leaving them discarded on the floor. He remained kneeling between her legs and dragged his hands up her calves, teasing that wonderful spot behind her knees and up the backs of her thighs. His hands curled around her bottom and upper thighs, his fingertips inside her thighs and whispering against her sex.

He pressed a kiss to the top of one thigh, then the other. Sylvi couldn't tear away her gaze. Her heart beat in long, slow pounds that seemed to slam through her entire body. He placed a gentle kiss between her legs, over her mons. His breath whispered warm temptation across the sensitive bud, and she almost moaned. He gazed up at her and dragged the tip of his tongue over her, a hot, wet caress over her most intimate place.

This time she did moan, a low, hungry sound that came from her soul.

Ian got to his feet, and his fingertips slid up her body as he did so. The wispy fabric of the léine lifted from her waist, from her breasts, from her good arm, and over her head. Then, with great care and consideration, Ian helped free the shirt from her braced arm.

He met her gaze, his golden eyes like warm honey. There was a gentle tug at the ribbon on her neck, and its perpetual embrace slipped away.

She was wholly naked before him now, with a man for whom she'd laid bare all her fears and nightmares.

He took all of her in, from her slender ankles to the body dotted with bruises and scars to her broken arm and the mutilated skin at her neck. A thread of self-consciousness twisted through her.

He reached for her and dragged his fingertips from the line of her jaw down to her lower stomach, stopping just before reaching her sex. In that one tender touch, he took away the ugly, uncomfortable feeling and left her body glowing instead.

He pulled off his léine and let it flutter to the ground, discarded and quickly followed by the length of his plaid and the belt of many pouches. Sylvi watched his body as he undressed, the glide of muscle over powerful muscle, all carved for her pleasure in the firelight.

He was the embodiment of strength and health. Her core tightened with the desire to spread her legs over him and let his proud phallus slide inside of her.

As if hearing her thoughts, he closed the distance between them, and the heat of his nakedness surged against the hunger of hers. His hard cock nudged against her stomach. She wanted it inside of her.

She gave a frustrated moan and rubbed her body against his. The hair on his chest prickled against her sensitive nipples. She wanted him so damn badly that her body actually ached in thunderous, angry thrums between her legs.

He set his forehead against hers, and his hand glided down her back. "My beautiful angel," he whispered against her lips.

His name for her laced through her heart and softened her knees. How could she have come to love something she so loathed only weeks before?

"I'm going to love ye." His lips still moved against hers, close but not kissing. Just as his cock rested against her, close but not rutting.

She arched against him to encourage his touch. He kissed her lower lip, and his tongue brushed hers. He continued to kiss her in maddening little half-kisses and pressed a hand to her lower back. Holding her to him, he walked forward, driving her to walk back. To the bed.

They stopped, and his hands smoothed down the sides of her body. The tension winding through her body, the want, the anticipation was all so powerful that she couldn't help but cry out at even such a simple touch. He bent over her and kissed her mouth, using lips and tongue and teeth until she was breathless, and her head spun in a dizzying rush of need.

His kisses trailed over her jaw and under her ear, where his beard rasped against the delicate skin of her neck. Chills of pleasure tingled over her entire body and left everything heightened with the most delicious awareness. Sylvi closed her eyes against the bliss of it all.

"I love ye, Sylvi." He nipped her earlobe, and his warm breath washed over her ear. "For yer strength." He kissed the spot on her neck below her ear. "Yer determination." He kissed her neck down to her collarbone. "Yer passion and how much ye care." He bent over her, his mouth lowering to her breast. "How intelligent ye are."

She opened her eyes and found his hot gaze fixed on her.

"How bonny ye are." He dragged his tongue over her nipple, and prickling desire clutched her.

She increased her grip on him with her good arm and wished her other arm could do the same. His body was powerful under her touch, so incredibly strong, so beautiful. Her nipples drew so hard that the sensation of it needled through her. His mouth opened and captured one pink, pert bud between the warmth of his lips.

Sylvi cried out at the sharp pleasure, and her legs threatened to give. He sucked and licked, teasing her until she felt she might die for wanting him. The hand on her hip descended lower, lower.

Her mouth went dry.

Oh God, yes.

He skimmed the top of her thighs and swept his fingers over the cleft between her legs. Her knees buckled beneath the powerful force of the slightest touch there. Ian's arm flexed around her waist, and he chuckled. "Lay back, my love."

He guided her toward the bed. The covers were cool underneath her, a welcome contrast to the blazing heat flaring through her.

Finally, he would take her. She stared up at him. He was truly a beautiful man. His body was hard everywhere. His beard and long, dark hair were just wild enough to appeal to her, his eyes burning with the same intensity sparking through her.

Beautiful and brave and giving and so much more patient than she deserved.

He knelt between her parted legs and flashed her a wicked grin. "Lift yer arm."

Sylvi lifted her bad arm as his hands ran over her thighs. He gently pulled her toward him, so her bottom was near the edge of the bed, and his mouth was just over her sex.

Sylvi's breathing deepened with anticipation, knowing what he intended. Knowing and welcoming. If it were any bit as pleasant as when he'd sampled her earlier, she might lose herself to—

He opened his mouth, and his warm breath teased over her, wiping out all thought. A little sound, like a choked moan, came from the back of her throat. His lips quirked into an arrogant half-smile. And then he licked her.

Sylvi's head fell back against the covers, the pleasure so great she carefully lowered her arm to the bed and gave in to the sensual ministrations. His tongue slid against her sex again, a long, slow, teasing lick that stopped where her desire was swollen and pounding. He paused and carefully circled the sensitive bud.

Heat and pleasure, heat and pleasure, heat and wet, delicious pleasure. Sylvi gripped the bed covers and gave in to the storm of sensations. Ian closed his mouth over her once more, his tongue expertly finding that spot again. His beard rasped against her, the sensation adding to his flicking licks. Heat tingled at Sylvi's feet and hands, and her core tightened. She was so close, so close to sliding over the edge and losing herself to his ministrations.

As if sensing this, he worked with fervor. Heat blasted

through her, and she splintered apart. She cried out, and her body clenched and unclenched with each powerful wave, eager to be filled. Needing Ian.

NEVER WERE THE CRIES OF A WOMAN MORE ALLURING than the ready moans of pleasure from Ian's angel. He watched the beauty of it play over her face; her parted lips, the flush to her cheeks, the tensing of her brow.

He would bring her to climax again, but the next time, he wanted to be inside her, with her gaze locked on his. His cock pulsed with desire so hard it felt near exploding.

Sylvi's pert breasts rose and fell while she caught her breath from the exertion of her release. A sheen of sweat left her beautiful body glossy. Every long, lean muscle was visible, flexing with each pant.

He got to his knees so the blunt head of his hardness pointed directly at the glistening pink slit of her sex. She was so wet he knew he could slide right in. The thought alone made his bollocks clench. He gritted his teeth. He needed to calm down lest he lose himself too quickly.

Agnes's jowls.

He breathed deeply.

Agnes's jowls.

Sylvi opened her eyes and stared at him with the heat of her ice-blue eyes.

Agnes and her jowls be damned. Ian leaned over Sylvi, and his cock nudged between her legs. She watched him with a desperate need burning bright in her eyes. He braced his weight on the bed and flexed his hips forward, easing into her.

Her wet heat gripped him. Tight. So tight. So good. A growl rasped between Ian's teeth, and Sylvi gave a little scream of pleasure that almost undid him. He caught a handful of the bed covers in each fist and held on while he plunged into her with long, slow thrusts, careful not to jar her and cause pain in her arm.

She lifted her injured arm in its brace and arched her hips up to meet him, rolling with each push and pull of his pelvis. He stared down at her, unable to drag his gaze from the way she pressed her tongue between her lips to wet them and the lift of her brows in pleasure every time he flexed into her. His body burned with the need to push harder and faster, but he resisted. It was not her body he wanted to claim tonight. It was her heart.

She wrapped her legs around his waist, and her grip around his cock tensed further still. Squeezing, squeezing, squeezing with each thrust. Pleasure and love swirled around his consciousness until Sylvi was the only one in his world of existence.

She did not tear her eyes from his. Instead, she gazed up at him with the same quiet intensity, the connection between them deeper than the joining of their bodies. It drew his pleasure to dizzying heights and staved off his need to burst.

"Ian," she whispered softly.

He pushed into her, deeper than before, and held himself there for a moment, reveling in her powerful grip and the embrace of her pleasure. She exhaled in a moan.

He let his hands glide over her beautiful body. The swell of her breasts—he pulled out and thrust deep and long once more. The dip of her waist—he flexed his hips forward, and his stomach tightened. He caught her bottom in his hands, round and firm, and thrust hard and fast, letting the friction between them build to something wild and unstoppable.

Ian's body was on fire, hot and swollen and ready to explode.

Sylvi's moans of pleasure became longer, more pitched, more breathless. Her eyes widened, and she cried out. The delicious grip around Ian's cock squeezed again and again with the powerful waves of her release.

He let go of his control, and he untethered. Desire washed over him, and his seed rushed into her in euphoric pulses. Their gazes remained locked through it all, from the heat of passion to the gentle cooling of their bodies while their breaths caught as one.

Ian pulled out of her and lowered himself gently to lay at the side of her good arm. "I love ye, Sylvi." He craned his head and kissed her mouth, a chaste kiss after the explosive desire they'd just shared.

She took a breath to speak, but he put a finger to her lips. "Ye dinna need to say anything."

His heart could not handle her protests now. He wanted her to remember this night, for them both to relive it in their minds in flashing memories of heat and bliss the following day and so many more thereafter.

He wanted her to love him because of who he was and not the pleasure he gave her.

She wriggled closer to him, her bad arm carefully stationary, and he pulled her against him.

He wanted to talk, to ask her questions about herself, to see what she'd been like as a child, what her favorite foods were, all the things he usually asked the lasses after sex to pass the time. Only this time, he truly wanted to know.

His mind dragged slowly over the many questions popping up, but exhaustion kept his mouth closed. Satisfaction laid a heavy cloak over his body. Sylvi curled her leg around his and laid her head against his chest.

The clean scent of rosemary wafted from her hair. He breathed deep, savoring the delicate scent, cherishing her and what they'd shared.

At least he had this moment to look back on, this one glorious moment where he finally felt as if he'd found a home, even if all this had been for naught. Which he desperately hoped was not the case, for in trying to lure Sylvi into loving him, he found himself falling deeper in love with her.

Sylvi listened to the steady pounding of Ian's heartbeat beneath her cheek. Her body still hummed with the aftereffects of their incredible joining. While she had been resistant to losing the wildness of their rutting, the way he had pleased her this time was indescribable.

And, if she were being honest, he'd been right in being gentle. Even with such care, the pain in her arm had flared up with their motions. A discomfort worth the trade for such pleasure.

He had loved every inch of her body. He'd made her feel beautiful and cared for in a way she'd never thought possible. Even still, after it had all stopped and he lay sleeping beneath her, she could not get his touch from her mind nor his words of affection.

His praise glowed warmly in her heart and left the rest of her softer and more relaxed than she'd been in far too long.

She briefly parried with the thought of how the night would have gone had she not come back in the room. If she'd fled the inn as she'd been so tempted to do.

The hollowness inside would have consumed her. She would have been alone with the memories haunting her, surrounded by the dead, when she'd been made to feel so alive by the living. For she did feel alive, and she was not alone. She still had a purpose, and she had a partner who would help her track down those who Reginald might have also slain.

She nestled her face against the warmth of his chest, and the downy prickle of his hair rasped against her cheek. All of her wanted to be as close to him as possible, to bask in the exhilarated hope he'd given her.

She loved the heat of his body against hers and the way his jests were often said at just the right moment to bring a smile to her face when she might otherwise have fallen to anger.

She couldn't imagine him not being in her life, not having him nearby to discuss tactics and ideas.

She loved him.

Her breath caught at the realization. It was more than her reaction to the fear he might have died. He was right—she'd chosen him over her vengeance. She loved him even before he had so carefully loved her tonight.

She kissed his naked chest and spoke softly into the silence of the room. "I can't imagine my life without you." Her heart pattered a little faster, scared and excited all at once to test aloud the words resonating in her heart. "I love you, Ian."

Twenty-Eight

Sylvi woke to the steady, deep pain in her arm. The mix of herbs Kyle had made the night before had worn off and left her with a blaze of agony. She shifted to ease some of the pressure from her arm and opened her eyes.

Ian was propped beside her on his elbow, gazing down at her.

"Were you watching me?" she asked.

He grinned. "Do ye no' like it?"

"Seems like it would be boring." She tried to ignore the ache in her arm and let her eyes drift closed again into the caress of sleep.

"No' when it's ye I'm staring at." He ran a hand over her cheek. "I love seeing all the beautiful contours of yer face, the way ye look almost soft when ye sleep."

She wrinkled her nose at being called soft and squinted an eye open.

He playfully rolled his eyes. "I know ye're no' soft. Ye just look it." He trailed a finger down her jaw. "Sweet."

Sylvi opened her eyes and scoffed, regardless of the smile creeping over her lips. "I'm not sweet."

"To me ye are." He inclined his head. "And I heard ye last night."

She raised an eyebrow.

"When ye said ye love me." He grinned like a lad who'd gotten away with something when he ought to have been punished.

Heat scorched hot in her cheeks.

"First ye say ye love me, and now ye're blushing." Ian leaned over her and placed a gentle kiss on her forehead. "Ye know how to make a man feel appreciated, lass."

She smirked. He knew very well that was not her intent. "Has anyone ever told you you're arrogant?"

"All the time." He settled his chin on his hand. "How does yer arm feel?"

Sylvi cast a dismayed glance at her arm, lying immobile at her side. "In a lot of pain," she admitted.

"I'll be right back." Ian carefully shifted off the bed and pulled his léine over his head.

Without care for being nearly naked, he slipped from the room and returned moments later with a cup in hand. "Kyle was already awake and seeing to Percy. He figured ye'd need this and already had it at the ready."

Ian helped her to a sitting position and passed her the acrid scented tincture. She gritted her teeth and swallowed it down, eager for the effects to warm through her body and calm the blaze of pain.

Ian settled onto the bed and gazed at her. "What were ye like as a girl?"

She passed the empty cup to him, and her light mood slipped behind a cloud.

"Before all of it," he said. "Ye grew up too fast. I want to know the kind of girl ye were when ye were young, before the fighting and vengeance and death."

Sylvi rifled through her thoughts the way one might through old clothes. What *had* she been like as a girl?

The question was so simple, but the answer was so out of her grasp. Her immediate memories started when her family had been attacked. Surely, there were more before then. She had flashes of her father periodically. His large hands and the impossibly fragile jewelry he created. But what else?

She closed her eyes, and sunlight filled her mind.

Einar laughed beside her on the floor, his baby squeals so alight with joy, they made everyone in their small, one-room home smile. His cheeks were rosy, and his blue eyes danced with delight. Her mother held him in her lap, with both other girls sitting at her feet, working on their sewing. Father had come into the house with a wrapped parcel.

He held it up as if it were a prize. "We'll have meat tonight."

"Meat is too expensive." Mor's worried expression did not in any way diminish her fair beauty.

Sunlight played over Mor's hair and made it sparkle like pale gold. She looked like a princess there by the fire in her simple dress. If she wore the gowns of the court ladies at the market, she'd be the most beautiful one of them all.

"Do it again, Sylvi," Alva said.

"I din't know what ye're talking about." Sylvi buffed her nails with great exaggeration on her sleeve.

"Aye, ye do," Inka said. "Please."

Einar looked up at her, his eyes wide with ready anticipation.

Sylvi stuck out her tongue and curled it upward to touch the tip of her nose. Her brother's face blossomed into a smile. She crossed her eyes. Laughter squealed out from his throat and brought a wave of it from the rest of her family.

"Ah, my Sylvi." Her father strode past with his treasure and ruffled her hair. "Always so playful."

"I was playful." The warmth of the memory bathed her soul in an unexpected but beautiful light. "I had a brother, Einar. He had the most wonderful laugh, and I would do anything to make him squeal with joy."

She looked down at Ian and stuck out her tongue, letting it curl up to touch the tip of her nose, then crossed her eyes.

Ian chuckled. When she relaxed her eyes, she found him

staring up at her. "Ye know, ye're actually pretty good at humor when ye do it."

Sylvi smiled and rolled her eyes. "Thank you."

Ian studied her. "I could see ye being playful." He ran a hand down her cheek, and the lightness of the mood shifted to a more comfortable intimacy. "And kind and loving."

"I haven't thought of that little girl in so long," Sylvi confessed. "I never let myself remember any of those happy memories. Thinking of them was too painful."

He nodded in understanding. "Reginald and his men are dead, and ye're no longer a lass. Nor are ye alone." He stroked her hair, and pleasure tingled over her scalp. The muscles of his arm bulged with the simple act. "Maybe ye should remember again."

Sylvi stared down at the rumpled bedclothes. Perhaps he was right. Remembering the joy of her family would help ease the weight of her grief.

"Ye can tell me the stories," Ian said. "I like the idea of ye being a playful lass who sticks out her tongue and crosses her eyes to make her wee brother laugh."

A knock came at the door, and they both startled.

"It's Percy," Kyle said. "Her fever still isna going down. I think it's getting worse."

Sylvi sat up quickly, and the ache in her arm exploded with enough ferocity to render her momentarily frozen.

"A moment," Ian called. "We must dress."

Sylvi tried to climb out of bed and was rewarded with a sharp spear of agony shooting up her arm. "We must hurry."

The thud of Kyle's boots on the wooden floor indicated his departure.

"Nay. There is time," Ian said in a calm voice. "We still need to break our fast, ready the horses and Liv needs to be told."

Ian held out a hand to Sylvi to help her from the bed.

She looked at his offer of assistance and swung her legs over the side of the bed. "I can still get up on my own."

Ian shrugged, nonplussed. "It doesna mean I'll ever stop being a good man. My mum would be appalled to think I'd no' used the manners she forced into me."

Panic beat in Sylvi's mind despite Ian's soothing resolve. She grabbed her trews with one arm and awkwardly thrust one leg into the limp fabric. It sagged into a crumpled heap at her ankle.

Ian raised a brow.

Sylvi sighed and tossed the trews at him. "Oh, fine, you can help."

"I think I'll dress first." He pulled his léine on. "I like seeing ye naked."

Irritation rankled Sylvi. Did he not see the severity of their situation? "Ian, Kindrochit is two days away. And that's if we ride hard."

She bit off the last word, refusing to continue with her following thought: that she could not ride hard with her arm in such bad condition. No matter what it took, she would see Percy safe. Even if it meant two days of jostling on the horse. Kyle's tincture would be a huge help, but it would not be without pain.

Ian lay on the floor to buckle his plaid. "Aye, but Dunstaffnage is only a few hours."

He'd said it nonchalantly, but she knew the weight of such a decision.

"You haven't been home in over a year," she said.

He adjusted several pleats before popping upright and taking her léine from the back of the chair. "Aye, and now it's time I finally go home."

It was hard not to regret the decision to go home. Ian rode at Sylvi's side, having lost the argument to keep her on the same horse as him. In the end, he knew it would be easier on the horses to have only one rider for their journey to Dunstaffnage.

Liv rode ahead of them in a cart they'd procured. Fianna

could easily sit at her side, and Kyle and Percy could ride in relative comfort in the back. The cart had been a risk. If danger found them, their party would not fare well in their attempt to escape or defend themselves.

But it was not danger on the road that concerned Ian. It was what awaited him at home. His stomach knotted with trepidation. There was a father who would no doubt comment on his inability to stay and face responsibility and a home without the comradery of his best friend or the warm light of his mother.

It had been easy to push aside the idea of her death while he was not home. Going back to Dunstaffnage with her not being there would be like walking into a castle without a great hall.

The heart of their home had stopped beating.

"You never told me what happened," Sylvi said from where she rode beside him. Her father's bracelet still twinkled where it lay on her wrist.

"Hmmm?"

She turned slightly to regard him and kept her injured arm cradled in her lap. "Why you left home."

Ian drew in a deep breath to ward off the inevitable wincing of his heart. "Aye, I suppose it is time to share this story with ye."

Sylvi gazed forward, but he knew she listened.

"I had a friend when I was a lad," he said. "We were so close that he was more a brother to me than Kyle at times."

The two had been inseparable most of their lives, sharing the same thoughts and ideals.

Ian sighed at the thought and let the memory press heavily on his shoulders. "Simon's da had no' been paying his taxes. But it was more than that. He'd been offering to bring his neighbors' coin to my da for them. But then he kept it."

Sylvi cast a hard look at him but said nothing.

"My da found out," Ian continued, "and meant to punish Simon's da by hanging him. As an example to others."

"You can't let something like that go unpunished," Sylvi said. "Or others will see you as weak and take advantage."

"I know that." Ian tried to keep the edge from his voice. "But this was Simon. The boy I'd grown up with. Our friendship had survived many obstacles, and even as our paths split, with him being a farmer and me being laird someday, it remained intact. I tried to stop the hanging," he said. "But my da said exactly what ye did. He had a responsibility as a laird, and friendship couldn't interfere with that. It was then I decided I dinna want to be a laird. I tried to tell him, but he wouldna have it."

"And Simon's father died," Sylvi surmised.

"No' just Simon's da. Simon took his own life after as well." Ian steeled himself against the memory. "He hung himself, dying the same as his da." Though a year had passed, his stomach still knotted. "I tried. But I could have tried harder. I could have saved them both if I had just tried harder."

"I'm sorry, Ian." Sylvi's brow furrowed with her earnestness.

A soft cry from Percy pulled their attention to the cart, where Kyle bent over her with anxious determination, the way he'd done with the small forest animals he'd saved when he was a lad.

Though no one had said it aloud, Percy did not look well. The stitches beneath the linen on her face were red and glossy with swollen anger. The fever had so taken her she cried out to people no one else knew, the sounds pitiful and heart-pulling.

Their progress was slow, mindful of the injuries they'd all sustained.

For her part, Sylvi had made no comment, even when she swung up on the horse and jostled her bad arm.

Percy whimpered from the cart again. "No." Her voice was a whisper of a gasp, small and scared. "Please don't."

Sylvi tensed beside Ian.

He edged closer to her. "She'll be better when we get to Dunstaffnage."

"All her things are at Kindrochit."

Percy sobbed and was immediately quieted under Kyle's indiscernible soothing.

"Kyle has many herbs and healing remedies at Dunstaffnage,"

Ian said. The image of Kyle's small room flashed in Ian's mind—the wall of shelves with various small bottles, all shadowed with herbs and powders and liquids of varying gray, green, brown and white.

To even think of it made it seem like Ian had never left home, as if he were remembering a life lived yesterday and not a year ago. Going home became suddenly very real, and he had the urge to pull on his horse's reins and reverse their progress.

"He is skilled at caring for others," Ian said, fixing his gaze on the open road. "He willna let anything happen to her."

Ian did not state that Percy would doubtless not survive the trip to Kindrochit. It would be too far for her to travel in such a condition.

The gray-black tip of a castle showed through the trees. Ian pulled in a deep breath. They were near Dunstaffnage.

Sylvi brought her horse closer to the cart, and Ian followed suit.

"We're almost there." Kyle glanced up at Ian. "Da isna upset with ye like ye probably think he is. I believe ye'll find he'll be glad to see ye."

Kyle, always trying to make everything right.

Ian smirked. "Ach, aye. Glad to have his heir back after realizing ye'd no' be up for the task of being laird?"

Kyle smiled. "Aye."

The tip of the castle dipped behind several trees and then came into view in flashes through the trees beyond. Sea water tinged the air with the familiar salt and pine scent of home. They were so close. Too close.

Damn it, Ian did not want to do this.

Kyle glanced down at Percy. "Things are no' the same since Mum's death."

Ian nodded vigorously to rush his brother's unwanted speech along. Ian did not wish to speak of this any more than he wanted to face it.

Kyle fell wonderfully silent.

Sylvi gave Ian a worried look. "I know you're dreading this."

"Is it so apparent?" he asked wryly.

"Well, you are gripping your reins rather tight."

Ian regarded his white knuckles and relaxed his hold.

Sylvi smiled gently in understanding, and he was suddenly glad she understood him so well that he didn't have to explain what he could hardly bring himself even to acknowledge.

The trees cleared away and opened a wide path to the massive boat-like appearance of Dunstaffnage. As a lad, Ian had often wondered if Noah's ark had looked similar. A wide hull with a single entrance and everything inside sealed off from the rest of the world.

But the door was not sealed today. The drawbridge was lowered to allow the clan access to their laird. And many tenants were there, all in swaths of plaid with their heads bare against the early spring air.

They nodded their greeting respectfully to Ian and the rest of the party, curiosity and concern on their faces as the cart passed.

Even though Ian knew Simon wasn't there, couldn't possibly be there, he found his gaze skimming the sea of faces for his childhood friend. Simon's absence opened the gates to the hurt he'd dammed up, his failure to help and the crushing weight of guilt.

Damn it. He did not want to be here.

"There was nothing you could do," Sylvi said under her breath.

Her words drew him from scanning the crowd for his dead friend. Ian looked once more at Dunstaffnage Castle and the man striding toward them. His plaid was crisp, the colors more vivid than those around him. A band of gold secured the excess of his plaid over his shoulder, and he walked with a sense of authority and purpose.

Donald Campbell, Laird of the Campbell clan and Ian's father, the very man Ian had been dreading.

Twenty-Nine

S ylvi had not missed the way Ian had looked desperately at his clan. Though he had not said it, she knew how poignantly he missed Simon at that moment.

"Here he comes," Ian said from between his teeth.

An older man with graying hair strode toward him, his hands open in a welcoming gesture. "Are these my sons returned?" His gaze fell on Percy, who lay at Kyle's side in the cart. "And what is this ye have here?"

Kyle climbed out of the cart. "A woman in need of healing."

Now that they were still, Sylvi could make out Percy's form with more clarity. A flash of fear struck through Sylvi. Percy had gone white as death. Sylvi hoped coming to Dunstaffnage was the right decision.

Laird Campbell waved a man over. "Get a litter and help Kyle take the lass inside. See that he has everything he needs." He glanced at Percy and clucked his tongue in a sympathetic gesture. "Such a bonny lass too."

Liv leapt down from the cart and strode forward, with Fianna trotting at her heels. "I'll go too." The deep blue dress she wore belled out around her and called attention to the vivid copper of her hair gleaming in the sun.

Laird Campbell bowed low and took her hand. "Welcome to Dunstaffnage, Lady..."

"Lady Liv." She offered a curtsy, an elegant gesture practiced to the point of perfection. "Thank you kindly for welcoming us. Our friend is very ill."

Liv's graceful manners, the softness of her tone and the demur cast of her gaze—they were all dance steps practiced in another lifetime and gave Sylvi a glimpse of the girl Liv must have once been.

Sylvi realized then the true burden Connor must have faced in training the girls he took in. It must be a difficult thing indeed to take an innocent life, one softened with manners and civility, and twist it into something hard and focused for spying.

The longer Sylvi continued with her tasks for pay, the more she understood the mentor she had fought so tenaciously against. And the more she realized it was not a life she could pursue forever. Not when it stained souls and cost lives.

Several men arrived with a litter between them. With their help, Kyle carefully shifted Percy to the stretch of padded cloth while Liv watched them anxiously. Once Percy was secure, the lot made their way up the trail to the castle.

Laird Campbell stared after the small departing party before turning to Ian and Sylvi. Ian slid from the horse and raised his hand to help Sylvi down from hers. She hesitated. To ignore the gesture in front of his men might convey a lack of respect, even if accepting aid chipped at her pride.

She lifted her chin to thwart the discomfort of her loss and put her hand into the large warmth of Ian's. A smile immediately lit his eyes, and his fingers curled around hers, enveloping her beneath his palm.

She gritted her teeth and slid from the saddle. Just before her feet hit the ground with a jolting stop, Ian released her hand and expertly caught her waist so she lowered gently to the soft grass. He held her gaze a moment and the whisper of gratitude for both their actions warmed between them.

"My son. My eldest son." Laird Campbell clapped Ian on the back.

Ian was caught in a massive embrace by the older man. He was taller than Ian but shorter than Kyle. Closer now, the silver in his hair almost matched the darker strands, clean and cropped just below the shoulders.

Laird Campbell held his son for a long moment before finally releasing him. "It's no' been the same without ye, lad." He patted Ian's cheek. "It fills my heart to have ye home again."

Ian stepped back and put his hand on Sylvi's waist. A move of ownership. The gesture would have otherwise rankled her had she not been so keenly aware of everything behind the touch, the love, the pride. "Da, this bonny lass is Sylvi."

Laird Campbell studied her for a long moment with the same laughing, golden-colored eyes as Ian. "I always wondered if ye'd end up with a strong woman to see yer flighty ways laid to land. I see ye have." He nodded in approval at the weapons tucked at her waist. "Ye any good, lass?"

"Very." She squared her shoulders.

"One of the best fighters I've ever seen." Admiration tinged Ian's declaration and warmed through Sylvi despite the chilled wind coming off the nearby ocean.

Laird Campbell looked between the two of them. "So, have ye tried to kill him yet?"

"Only twice," Sylvi answered honestly.

Ian's father burst into laughter and clapped Ian on the shoulder. "I can see why my son cares for ye. This lad needs a lass like ye to keep him reined in." He released Ian and offered her his arm on her good side. "Let me show ye around our home."

"No stealing my lass, Da." Ian's playful tone suggested a lifetime of comfortable, friendly banter between the two.

At least Sylvi now knew where Ian got his charm.

His dad waved a hand at him. "Yer mum's no' been dead that long."

The words landed with an awkward heaviness and knocked

Ian's smile away. Indeed, it knocked the wind from Sylvi's chest as surely as a hit. Ian's mother was dead. Did he know?

"How did she die?" Ian asked with such hesitation and so little shock Sylvi realized he already knew.

He knew, and he hadn't told her. And yet, she could hardly be surprised. Ian Campbell was a brave fighter, but he did not like to face difficulties of the heart, especially when there was no way of winning.

"She was found dead," Laird Campbell said simply. "We think possibly outlaws." He settled a hand on his son's shoulder, and lines creased his face where they had not been before.

"Outlaws." The word growled low between Ian's teeth. "And there's been no looking into it?"

"Ye sound like yer brother." His father eyed him suspiciously, and then his face broke into a smirk of mirth. "Of course, we searched the area, but with no one having seen them and no' anything left behind..." Laird Campbell tapered off and shook his head. "For now, let us put the ugliness of it away and introduce Sylvi to our home. Dunstaffnage hasna been the same without ye, lad."

Ian gave a stiff nod, and Laird Campbell turned away as if the matter had been fully resolved and led the way to the castle. Sylvi caught Ian's eye and tipped her head slightly.

Regardless of the recent discovery and what Ian sought with his father in the conversation, she would be by Ian's side. They were in this together.

IAN FOLLOWED HIS FATHER AND SYLVI THROUGH THE narrow, single entrance of Dunstaffnage. Darkness preceded their arrival, a fitting swath of black cut in front of their eyes where the walls closed in on either side of them.

Above the passage, Ian knew some portals opened for hot oil to be poured through, just as there were arrow slits on either side.

The long entryway was a deathtrap for those who were not wanted. And while Ian was wanted, it felt to him crushing with responsibility.

And his mum was not there to offer guidance when he needed it most. Her loss hit him like a jouster's lance.

"How thick are these walls?" Sylvi's voice echoed in the darkness. She had given no indication of surprise when he'd asked about his mother's death. He regretted not having told her of his mother's passing before and yet could not find the right time, the right way, to bring up something so very painful.

"Ten feet in some areas," Donald said with great pride. "This is far more than ten feet deep here, though, as it is the foundation for the gatehouse above us."

In front of Ian, Sylvi's shadow lifted her hand and ran graceful fingers along the walls, her entire form limned in the distant daylight. "Amazing," she said. Her long neck arched as she looked up, and Ian knew she was noting the trap doors in the smooth stone overhead.

"Dunstaffnage is one of the most highly defensible castles in Scotland." Sylvi returned to Donald's side, and he immediately folded her good hand in his arm once more.

"Aye, ye'll be safe here, lass."

"I don't need protection."

"Well, in that case," Donald said, "ye're welcome here all the same. As family." He led them into the open center of Dunstaffnage. The sun shone so brilliantly it left Ian momentarily blind.

Ian blinked, and the world he'd left a year prior came rushing back with a flood of memories. The bustle of guards and nobles alike in the courtyard, the new house to the right, the West Tower at the far rear of the castle. And none of it changed.

Somehow, he'd expected his mother's absence and Simon's loss to have left a more definitive mark, a crater of some kind at the center of the hall. And yet it looked exactly as he'd left it.

Donald spoke at length in front of him, going over the finer aspects of the castle's defenses while Sylvi listened, rapt. Ian knew everything said. He knew every arrow slit, every advantage and detail.

Donald's voice prattled on and on, carried on the wings of pride and glee at a ready pupil, all of it grating against Ian's ravaged nerves.

"Da, Sylvi's no' had much sleep," Ian said abruptly.

Donald stopped speaking and turned to him. "Aye, son, I imagine she hasna." He winked. "Verra well, but I hope ye're planning to stay." He leaned in close and said in a secretive voice loud enough for Sylvi to hear, "I like this lass."

"I do too." Ian had meant it as a jest, but it sounded petulant. Everything inside him was tender as a raw wound. He wanted the solace of a quiet room and Sylvi's embrace and counsel. If she'd found Reginald after seventeen years, she might know how to help him identify if Reginald had indeed killed his mother.

The thought of his mother's death sliced fresh into him with pain so radiant it rendered breathing difficult. He would need to see her room, but not now. Not yet.

"Ye'll be staying in the West Tower. Ye can see Sylvi there." Donald's voice interrupted Ian's thoughts—a welcome interruption, to be sure. "But I want ye back to go over what ye've missed since ye've been gone."

Perhaps not so welcome an interruption after all.

Donald clasped his arm over Ian's shoulders and affectionately shook him. "I've no' ever named an heir after ye left. I knew ye'd be home again."

The burden of Ian's birthright fell over his heart like a boulder. He nodded. "Later, Da. After I've rested."

Donald paused, and the skin around his eyes tightened. After a long moment, a congenial smile blossomed on his face. "Of course, son. Do what ye need. I'll be here when ye're ready."

Ian nodded again and murmured his thanks, not giving voice to the resounding thought in his head that he'd never be ready.

Instead, he took Sylvi's good arm as his father had and led her to the West Tower. She followed in silence but squeezed his elbow with her hand.

And God knew he needed her support for what he faced with his return home.

They did not speak. Not until they were up in the guest room she'd be staying in, with its lush red velvet and polished wood furnishings. Though they had only recently arrived, the room had been swept clean, and a fire burned warmly in the hearth. Her bags lay piled beside the bed, slumped over one another. He knew his would be in his room, laid out similarly.

He'd carried the bag of jewelry and now set the weight of it gently on the floor. He trusted his father's servants not to steal, but he didn't trust those servants not to talk. And he couldn't have his father know about the attack on Reginald and his men. Not until he discovered how his father had been involved and how his mother's death factored into everything.

Sylvi closed the door and locked it before striding toward him. He braced himself for questions. She asked none. Instead, she widened her uninjured arm and caught him against her breast in an embrace.

Ian wrapped his arms around her lean frame and breathed in the rosemary and leather scent of her. "I couldna tell ye about my mum," he said finally.

"Because then it would be real." She spoke softly, her lips next to his ear in their embrace.

He drew in a pained breath and nodded. "Kyle told me. He was traveling with Reginald to find me so I could help him seek out our mother's killer. He said my da had given up trying to find who did it."

She pulled back and regarded Ian with the fierce, determined expression only Sylvi could give. "We'll find the men who killed her. We won't leave until we do."

"Kyle thinks it was Reginald and his men."

Sylvi's body tensed. "Why?"

"I dinna know." He shook his head. "I want to find out while Percy heals, while we research the jewelry that we found and then I want to leave. I dinna want us here longer than we need to stay."

Thirty

Ian shifted on the hard wooden bench beside his father, the same as he'd done for the entire week since their arrival. His repeated attempts at telling Donald he was uninterested in the lairdship had fallen on deaf ears. Donald had insisted on Ian at least reviewing the accounts of Dunstaffnage.

While Ian saw through his father's ruse—a flimsy attempt to get Ian interested in the lairdship—he still agreed to meet with his father for an hour a day. If nothing else, that hour had been compromise enough to still his da's constant badgering.

They were currently poring over rents, and Ian noticed Donald's careful avoidance of discussing the penalties for not paying rent. In fact, his da had not once mentioned Simon or Simon's father.

Ian flipped through the pages and tried not to think of his friend and how those very rents had destroyed their lives.

Several figures appeared on the following pages, lined neatly in the far-right column.

"What are these from?" Ian asked and pointed to the tallied amounts. The sum was considerable.

"A wise man has more than one source of income." Donald

closed the book. "But I dinna want to get into all that yet." A sparkle showed in his eyes. "It's...complicated."

The mystery and suggestion of its implied difficulty snagged Ian's interest despite himself.

Complicated.

A challenge.

Fascinating.

"Ye did well today, lad. Thank ye for indulging an old man." Donald patted his cheek, an affectionate gesture he'd done since Ian was a lad. "And I like that lass of yers quite a bit."

"Ye dinna give me much of a choice." Ian smirked. "I thought ye'd like her. She thinks like ye."

In truth, they did appear to get on well. Donald and Sylvi could discuss fortifications and army strategy at length. Despite Sylvi's stoic demeanor and air of skepticism, Donald appeared to have won her over. A feat not easily done.

"I like her all the more then." Donald grinned. "I know she doesna have a dowry, but ye should marry her."

Ian stared at Donald. His father had never been the one pressing him toward marriage as his ma always had. "Ye sound like Mum."

Donald Campbell scoffed. "Ach, just an old man who kens his time is limited. I've a mind to see some grandchildren scampering about my feet. And Sylvi would give ye strong bairns."

An image of Sylvi flashed in his mind with her head bent over their child. The idea warmed him, even if he found it unlikely. Not that Sylvi wouldn't be a good mother. God knew she'd protect their bairns like a lioness. But the confinement would drive her to madness.

The idea of her as his wife, however, curled in his heart like a band of gold. He'd thought of it before, though he was sure he'd have a beast of a time convincing her to say yes. She didn't seem the marrying sort any more than she appeared the maternal sort. But, aye, he could see her as his wife, by his side, as powerful as she was beautiful.

"I'll think on it," Ian said.

Donald caught his eye and gave a knowing smile. "Aye, ye do that."

Ian got to his feet and made his way to the large door of the solar. He reached for the handle and paused. "Have ye found any more on Mum's death?"

Several papers rustled behind him. "No' anything on my last report," his father answered.

The answer did not surprise Ian. It had taken some bartering to get Donald to resume the search for Ian's mum's killer. Even though the laird had finally acquiesced, Ian wondered at the thoroughness.

In the meantime, Ian and Sylvi had been working with Liv on the pieces of jewelry in an attempt to locate some of the families who might be involved the way Sylvi's family had been. Kyle had assisted, but between the search for their mother's killer and caring for Percy, his time had been too insufficient to be of use.

Thus far, they'd gotten nowhere.

Ian stepped from the solar and into the coolness of the hall outside. His mother's room was down the far-left corridor. On any ordinary day, he would turn right. But today was no ordinary day.

Kyle had searched their mother's room and had found nothing amiss. He'd asked Ian to do a thorough search to identify something he might have missed. Ian had put it off for two days, dreading the rush of the painful ache of his mother's loss.

Yet he knew he needed to go into his mother's room to face the memories as she had left them. He knew well enough by now running from problems only brought more. It was time to stop running.

Ian turned left, his stride determined and did not stop until he was in front of her door. He pushed on the latch. It rattled and stayed in place.

Locked.

He glanced at the framed portrait of his grandmother, whose

pinched expression did not match the beautiful blue eyes of his mother staring out from the face. Careful not to knock it from its place on the wall, he reached behind it and extracted the key his mother had kept there. At least no one had removed it from its hiding place. Likely no one even knew it was there.

He inserted the key in the lock, twisted and took a long, deep breath before pushing into his mother's room.

The sweet lavender scent of her hit him like a kick to the chest. His heart crumpled at the fragrance and the flood of memories it brought. Her soothing voice, the love shining from her gaze, the gentle kisses on his brow. Too much. He nearly staggered beneath the force of it.

He held tight to the door for a long moment before finally releasing it and stepping into the room. It looked as he remembered, the large bed with the curtains pulled back and ready for an occupant to sleep on its purple velvet. New candles perched in sconces freed of all dust from the servant's cleaning, ready to be needed and lit. Kindling and wood were piled in the hearth, ready for a roaring blaze.

All of it was as if his mother had never died. As if she were expected home that evening.

Pain drove deep into Ian's heart. His mother would not be coming home. The scent of her, initially so powerful, was growing fainter with every breath. Ian pulled in a great, greedy inhale and held it until his chest burned, savoring the last tendrils of her perfume.

He released the breath, and an ache settled in his throat.

Her hands were always so warm, and Ian's father had said it was because her heart was bigger than everyone else's. Indeed it was. Filled with kindness and love and everything good.

Her sewing lay on the table beside the bed. The gold thread angel at its center dissolved to nothing from the waist down, where his mother would never finish the rest of it. She'd always enjoyed sewing.

An image jabbed at his heart, one of her sitting beside the fire while he played as a boy, her needle popping in and out of the fabric. Between stitches, she would gaze affectionately at him and Kyle as if she had to reassure herself constantly that they were near.

Ian's heart was weighed down with regret. He'd never been able to say goodbye. His impulsive decision to leave Dunstaffnage the year prior had come with a high price.

He pulled open one of the drawers to her dressing table, and a small pomander rolled toward the front. The metal ball was barely tall enough to rattle freely through the otherwise empty drawer.

He lifted it to his nose and breathed in but was met only with the tinny scent of metal. Apparently, the item was as yet unused. And never would be.

After searching through the remainder of her drawers and finding nothing save for the simple items of face creams and combs, Ian sat before the mirror of the dressing table. Something was amiss in the drawers, but he couldn't quite place it.

He opened each in turn, noticing again how the pomander ball rolled forward. Something nipped at the back of his mind. He opened the matching drawer on the other side and placed the small pomander inside. The ball sat high enough on the velvet-trimmed bottom that the drawer would not close.

Ian ran his finger along the fine fabric base and discovered a corner of ribbon the same deep blue as the velvet lining. He caught the edge of his blunt fingernail against the ribbon and pulled upward.

The bottom of the drawer lifted to reveal a hidden compartment beneath made of plain wood. A gold ring stared up at him.

Strange when, despite her high station, his mother seldom wore jewelry. He pinched the cool band between his fingertips and lifted it to see what memories it revealed.

His blood went cold.

The stone was round and blue with a flat band of gold securing it to the ring. He'd seen so many pieces almost identical to this that he could not help the word as it slipped from his mouth. "Square."

With shaking fingers, he flipped the ring over and found the goldsmith's mark beside the backside of the stone, pressed into the soft gold. A square.

Just like so many others in the sack hidden in his room.

Ian's heartbeat roared in his ears.

He carefully replaced the false bottom in the drawer and slipped the ring into his pocket. It would appear Kyle had been right—Reginald most likely did have something to do with their mother's death. And Kyle's flippant assistance with the search for the goldsmiths would be increasing in earnest.

Once they uncovered the secrets within the bag of jewelry, Ian had a strong feeling they would uncover the secrets about their mother's murder.

THREE WEEKS LATER, SYLVI WORE THE RING WITH THE blue stone on her good hand alongside her father's bracelet. It had taken this long to get enough information on goldsmiths in the surrounding area for the square marker to be identified.

And, finally, it had. Not only had they learned the location of the shop, but they also found a daughter had survived.

The small goldsmith's shop was located in Glenuig, a village four hours northwest of Dunstaffnage. To arrive, Sylvi and Ian had to ride over land and ferry over the sea. Kyle had remained at Dunstaffnage with Percy, whose wounds had begun to heal nicely.

Liv, whose wounds had been minor, had healed within two weeks of their arrival and had found a place within the ranks of warriors in Dunstaffnage. The position had been hard-won and well-deserved.

The briny ocean air whipped Sylvi's hair around her face, and the humidity left a salty wetness against her skin. At long last, the thatched roofs of a village came into view, and Sylvi straightened in her saddle. Nervous energy rioted through her and made her heart beat as though she were preparing for battle rather than meeting the remaining daughter of a dead goldsmith.

"It was easier to keep up with ye when yer arm was in a brace." Ian appeared beside her on his horse.

Only then did she realize she was practically racing the poor beast. She pulled back on the reins slowly and let her horse come to a frustratingly slow trot. Once they finally arrived, they found the village small and quaint, with only a blacksmith's shop, a bakery and several other undiscernible shops, as well as a handful of fish peddlers in the center of town.

Which was exactly where the small white cottage stood that had once been a goldsmith's shop. Sylvi cast Ian an anxious glance and rapped on the door, the sound almost muted beneath the calling of vendors behind her.

Hette Schmidt had written a letter accepting their request to speak with her, though the time between their missive and hers had indicated her trepidation. The door in front of Sylvi did not open.

"This is the correct day, aye?" Ian asked.

Sylvi shot him a stern look. "Of course it is."

He shrugged, nonplussed. She raised her fist to knock once more when the rattle of locks being undone sounded before the door finally creaked open. A woman with dull brown hair and bright blue eyes appeared. She waved them in and cast an anxious glance about.

The door slammed shut behind Sylvi and Ian, followed by the clinks and thunks of several locking mechanisms being twisted into place.

The heat inside the home was stifling, almost suffocating, compared to the nipping coastal winds outside. Piles of items were stacked around the small interior of the home. Various pieces of clothing cluttered the floor around an unmade bed, pamphlets were stacked on one end of the home's table beside bits of wilting vegetables, and a distinct odor of rot permeated the air. Sylvi swallowed and kept her face indifferent.

"Thank you for having us," she said. "We have been eager to speak with you."

Hette stared at Sylvi's hand, the one with Hette's father's ring. "Yes. Yes. Please, come sit." There was a foreign staccato to her words. Prussian, most likely.

Her anxious gaze flitted up to Sylvi, then to Ian, and back again before she backed up and nudged at a fat tabby lounging on one of the two seats at the table. Sylvi settled onto the seat, still hot from the cat's generous body. Sweat prickled at her palms and brow.

Hette glanced apologetically at Ian. "I have only two seats."

He grinned with his usual ease. "I prefer to stand, lass, especially after having been on a horse for the better part of the day. Dinna worry after me." He lifted his arms and stretched to demonstrate.

A nervous smile flicked at the corners of Hette's mouth. She nodded, a short, vigorous movement, and settled into the remaining seat. The brunette's skin had the sallow cast of one who did not often see the sun, and lines creased small folds in her brow. Worry lines.

Sylvi removed the ring from her finger and held it out to Hette. "I came because of this."

Hette reached for the ring and took it with the same hesitant care with which a wild animal might accept proffered food, skittish with an expectation of malintent. "You know this ring?"

Sylvi nodded. "Your father?"

"Yes." Hette's stare fell on Sylvi's wrist. "And this?"

Sylvi swallowed before replying. "My father's."

Hette's pale gaze snapped up and met Sylvi's. "Is he dead too?"

"Him. My mother. My brother and sisters. All of my family." Sylvi touched her neck where the black ribbon remained tied over her scar and pulled the bow free. It slipped from her neck, and Hette's eyes went wide.

"They tried to kill me too." Sylvi touched the mutilated skin at her throat.

Hette sat back in her chair and stared at Sylvi. "They have not come back to kill you?"

"I killed them." Sylvi couldn't keep the pride from her voice. "How did you survive? When did they..."

"Five and twenty years ago. My father was told to send me away. What hasn't been seen hasn't been done." Hette leapt to her feet and sent the cat skittering from its place beneath the table.

"What is unseen hasn't been done." The Prussian began to pace, her words blurring into more of a mutter than clear speech.

But Sylvi still heard her. And she knew those words.

What is unseen hasna been done.

A chill slipped down her spine. "What did you say?" she asked.

Hette was not listening. She paced frantically, her loose slippers slapping the dirty floor as she repeated the phrase over and over with a breathless frenzy. "What is unseen hasn't been done. What is unseen seen hasn't been done. What is unseen—" She fisted her hands in her hair and went quiet.

Her ranting did not continue. Instead, she darted to the window and secured her fingers over the latch as though ensuring it was indeed locked. "You cannot be here."

"Who said that to you?" Sylvi asked.

"You cannot be here," Hette repeated. "They might come. They might find me." She stiffened. "If you found me, they can find me."

"Who said that to you?" Sylvi said firmly.

"Leave." Hette lowered her head and charged at Sylvi as though she meant to ram into her.

Ian grabbed Sylvi and pulled her toward the door. "We should go, angel."

"Was it the man with half an ear?" Sylvi stopped her question abruptly. Hette's father was killed before Sylvi's family. Reginald would have had a full ear then. "Was he fat and short?"

"A fine man with fine means," Hette bellowed. "A bore."

Sylvi reeled. "Was it a group of men, then? Led by one man?"

"Sylvi," Ian said in warning in her ear.

"I—"

Hette pointed to the door. "Out. Out!"

"Was it a group of men?" Sylvi shouted at the madwoman.

"One man," Hette flicked open one of her locks as she said it, repeating it over and over as she opened the remaining locks. "One man. One man. A bore."

Before Sylvi could ask more, Ian dragged her from the stuffy room. Outside, she gasped for fresh air before pulling from Ian. "How could you draw me away? She was telling me what I needed."

The door slammed closed, followed by the thuds and clatters of locks being slipped into place.

"She's mad." Ian stared at the door in disbelief.

"There is someone else, Ian." Sylvi pulled him from the door back to the edge of town where they'd left their horses. "She said a 'fine man.' Neither Reginald nor the rest of his men were noble or fine." Her brain rattled over the woman's words. "A 'bore of a man,' though?"

"Dinna pay any mind to her." Ian waved a dismissive hand behind them. "The woman is out of her mind."

Sylvi stopped and stared back at that house. "Don't you see it, Ian?" She suppressed a shudder. "If I had not met My Lady—if she had not allowed me to become who I became—Hette Schmidt could have been me."

Thirty-One

The journey home to Dunstaffnage had been quiet while Sylvi's mind spun and spun and spun around what Hette had told them. There was someone else. A nobleman. A bore. But what did it mean?

She'd posed the question to Ian, who had deemed many noblemen bores. To which she had grudgingly agreed. Kyle and Percy were not to be found, at least not until later that evening when Sylvi and Ian headed to the great hall for supper after having told Liv everything they'd discovered.

Kyle and Percy emerged through the castle's single entrance, glowing with joy. Sylvi's heart lifted with recognition of Kyle's towering frame and the slight form of Percy beside him; her attention was momentarily pulled from the mystery of the nobleman. Percy did not wear her cape and hood, her golden hair loose and glinting with the gilded cast of the setting sun.

Percy with no hood. It was a sight to behold, indeed.

"Sylvi. Ian." The smile of greeting on Percy's face was mirrored in her sweet voice. The scar running over her face was a raw pink, but the stitches had been removed without issue, and the line remaining was thin. Even her eye, which Sylvi had thought lost, was undamaged and twinkled with happiness. Kyle had performed a miracle.

Sylvi stared openly at her friend as if she were seeing some mythological creature in the flesh. "You went out?" It was a stupid question, she knew, but she could not stop herself.

Percy nodded. "It's lovely here. So lovely." She looked up to Kyle, who smiled down at her with all the affection any man ever held for a woman. "Kyle convinced me to go, and I'm so glad he did."

"Aye, I'm glad he did as well." Ian nudged his brother. "Every now and then, this lad has fine ideas."

"And without a hood." Sylvi nodded approvingly at Kyle.

He put his hands up. "That wasna me. That was Percy's bravery."

Percy clasped her hands over her heart. "Watch." She boldly reached for Sylvi and pulled her close. "We're going to go into the great hall together. Through this crowded courtyard."

Sylvi allowed herself to be led by the incredible new Percy, who strode through the bustle of people with her back straight and her scarred face lifted with pride. They did not stop until they were near the entrance to the great hall.

Percy released Sylvi and pressed a kiss to Kyle's cheek. "I'll join you in a moment."

Ian shot Sylvi a wink, and the brothers entered the great hall, leaving the ladies to their privacy.

Percy turned to Sylvi. "Did you see that?"

Sylvi gave a rare grin. "You were so brave, Percy."

Percy laughed and shook her head. "Not me. *Them*." She nodded toward the faceless crowd behind her. "Women were kind to me. They moved out of my way. Men took no more notice of me than they did you. Less even." Her eyes shone with tears, and she lowered her voice to a whisper. "This is not a face women envy. This is not a face men want. This is not the face of a woman arrested for murder."

Sylvi's chest went tight with Percy's admission. Isabel had

thought she was destroying Percy by ravaging her exquisite beauty, but it would appear Isabel had set her free.

Percy glanced into the great hall to where Kyle's head rose above the others making their way between the tables. "And he loves me for who I am, not as an accessory on his arm, but as a woman he respects for her knowledge and her heart."

"Percy, I'm so pleased for you." Sylvi wrapped her arm around her friend and hugged her close. "It lifts my heart to see you so happy like this."

"And mine also." Percy leaned forward and whispered in her ear. "We are to be wed tonight after all have gone to bed. We want you and Ian there to bear witness. Liv has already said she will come. Please say you will be there as well."

There would be no time for banns or the planning of a ceremony. But of course, Percy would not want a massive affair where crowds of people would come to observe her as a spectacle of a bride. It made sense she wished for a private ceremony. Even with her newfound comfort among the masses, she would still not care for the attention the wedding of a laird's son would provide.

"I wouldn't miss it for all the coin in Scotland," Sylvi said earnestly.

Percy slid an excited glance to where Kyle stood, chatting with several men. "He says he will not have me until we are wed."

"He's a good man," Sylvi said.

"As is his brother." Percy gave her a sly look, glanced over Sylvi's shoulder and slipped away.

Sylvi turned to find Ian striding toward her. He caught her face in his hands and gently kissed her mouth, the movement sweet and tender. Warmth washed over Sylvi's cheeks despite herself.

"We have a private wedding to attend tonight." He lowered his voice to a whisper. "It's a secret."

"I know," Sylvi whispered back. "I was invited too."

"One never knows what may happen at a secret wedding." He

lifted his brows, and something twinkled in his eye. Ian clearly had something on his mind.

☙

IAN HAD SYLVI IN A MOONLIT GLEN. AT LAST.

And what was more, he had a surprise.

The priest flipped through his prayer book while they waited for Percy and Kyle to arrive. The pages made a dry, crackling sound with each careful turn. Ian took Sylvi's good arm and gently pulled her behind a tree to afford them some privacy.

His heart hammered in his chest with a force even battle could not produce. He hadn't expected to be so nervous.

Sylvi looked up at him, and her brow flinched. "What's wrong? Did you figure it out? What Hette said? Or discover any more information about the other jewelry?"

He shook his head. "Sorry, lass. No' any of those things as yet."

Her hair looked almost white in the moonlight, her skin milky blue. She wore her usual trews and black léine with the ribbon tied at her throat. He ran a finger down the softness of her cheek and tipped her chin toward him. And the strong, willful woman in front of him obediently, trustingly, lifted her face to him.

"I wanted to tell ye..." The depth of his love constricted in his chest and made his whisper hoarse. "I love ye."

She searched his eyes, and her lips lifted in a smile. "And I love you."

He cleared his throat and suddenly found himself without words. A rare and very uncomfortable problem. Especially considering what he was about to say.

She tilted her head questioningly. "Your behavior is strange."

"Because I love ye so verra much." He winced at the awkwardness of his words.

Sylvi chuckled. "And I love you. I think we've already had this conversation."

"Marry me." It was said abruptly and without the finesse of all his attempts in the mirror that evening. "Now," he added.

She regarded him as if he were mad. "Tonight?"

"Aye, unless ye want a formal ceremony with a dress of gold and flowers in yer hair."

She wrinkled her nose, and he laughed.

"I don't want a gold dress or flowers in my hair," she said. "Or the display coming with such ceremony. Tonight is for Percy."

He shook his head. "I asked Percy and Kyle if they minded. Percy was so excited that she started to cry. Ye know how she is."

Sylvi smiled and nodded. "I do."

"Sylvi." He touched the edge of her jaw. "Ye're brave and beautiful and the only woman I've ever loved. Ye challenge me to face my problems, then ye stand by my side to battle them with me. Ye're my angel. Marry me tonight. Please."

"If you don't say yes, I'll be forced to pull my blade." A woman's voice came from the trees.

Liv emerged with her arms stubbornly crossed over her chest and her stance braced wide, every bit the proud soldier. Fianna glided around Liv, sat stubbornly before her mistress and gave an expectant look up at Ian. Liv looked down at the small gray-and-white cat and tilted her head. They were all waiting for the answer Ian was eagerly anticipating himself.

Sylvi scoffed and shot Liv a smirk. "I'd beat ye and still marry him all the same."

Ian pulled her face back to him. "Is that a yes?"

Sylvi rolled her eyes playfully. "It is."

Ian's heart swelled in his chest—with love for the woman in front of him, with pride that she would be his wife.

"Perfect timing." Liv glanced over her shoulder to where Percy and Kyle appeared, their hands locked together.

Within minutes, they were all standing in front of the priest, with the light of the moon glowing off his balding pate. His voice droned on through the ceremony of binding Kyle and Percy, who said their vows with joy shining in their eyes.

Ian watched his younger brother, whose heart was as large as their mum's had been, marry a woman whose soul was as pure and good as Kyle's. They would be a good couple, the two of them.

He held Sylvi's hand in his, the warmth between them comfortable and fulfilling. Soon it would be their turn. Soon Sylvi would be his wife.

At long last, Kyle bent over Percy and pressed a kiss to her lips. It was a soft, sweet kiss, exactly the kind he expected from Kyle and his gentle bride. They turned together to where he, Sylvi and Liv watched, and Kyle nodded toward Ian. "It's yer turn, brother."

Ian caught Kyle in a fierce hug. "Congratulations."

Kyle pushed at him. "Aye, get up there, and then we can congratulate each other."

Ian pulled Sylvi with him, and she came readily, only stopping when they arrived in front of the priest together.

Her chest rose and fell with what he hoped was the same giddy excitement leaving him breathless. The priest started the ceremony, his thin, reedy voice high in the night air. Ian did not pay much mind to what was said. How could he when Sylvi kept her beautiful soft blue eyes on his while their souls were bound together for all eternity?

The priest stopped talking, and Sylvi nodded. "Yes, I will." Her voice was huskier than usual, the tone tender and beautiful. The priest continued on once more.

Ian's heart nearly burst from his chest. Sylvi had agreed. She'd tied herself to him in life, in sword and in heart.

The moonlight seemed to glow around her, lending her the same brilliance as the angel she truly was. God, she was beautiful. And she was his.

The priest stopped talking, and the recognition of silence nipped at Ian's thoughts.

Sylvi smiled at him, and he smiled back, his heart warm and full.

She raised her brows, and he winked in reply.

A finger jabbed into his shoulder. He jerked his head to find Kyle beside him. "Ye're supposed to say ye will," Kyle whispered.

Ian glanced toward the priest, who stared expectantly at him down the beak of his nose.

"Aye, I will," he said quickly as soft laughter rose around him, kind and well-meaning.

"And ye are now man and wife," the priest concluded.

Ian caught Sylvi's face between his palms and gazed at his beautiful wife. "I was staring at ye so hard, I wasna listening," he whispered.

"I know," she whispered back.

"I love ye," he said with all the passion blazing in his soul.

Her eyes shone. "I know."

Then he lowered his face and closed his mouth over hers, letting the love in his heart pass between the heat of their mouths.

He was married, and never had his life been happier. No matter what challenges they faced from this moment on, they would face them together.

And he knew there were many challenges on their horizon.

SYLVI HAD NEVER BEEN ONE FOR HAPPINESS. BUT THE following morning, with her body practically glowing from the tender lovemaking she'd shared with Ian the night before, she was truly happy.

She'd woken beside him, content and more cheerful than she ever remembered being. Ian cradled her close to him, enveloping her in his warmth and his love. Beautiful though it was, the late hour of the day pressed on her. Hunger snarled in her stomach, and there were still more goldsmiths to find.

"I wish we could stay here until tonight," Sylvi said wistfully.

Ian intensified his hold on her. "We can."

She laughed and pushed off him before the temptation to

never leave became too great. "And yet we have much to do today. Many people to tell. Food to eat." She did not mention the goldsmiths or the nobleman, not now while the mood was light. But she certainly would once they'd broken their fast.

Ian caught her hand and tried to pull her back toward him, but she resisted playfully. "We cannot stay in bed forever."

His stomach rumbled, and he chuckled. "I confess food to eat does sound good."

He sat upright, and his gaze roamed appreciatively over her naked body. Pride heated through her.

"What do you think people will say when they find out?" she asked.

"That it's about time. For Kyle and me both." He got out of bed, and it was Sylvi's turn to admire.

Her husband's body certainly was one worthy of admiration. The power of his muscular build rippled and flexed with each small move and left desire pulsing anew between her legs.

"My da will be especially happy," Ian said. "He likes ye."

He moved to swat her on the rump, but she blocked him and stepped back with a grin.

He reached out again but swiveled left and managed to grab her this time, trapping her against him in a fierce hug. "Someday ye'll be Lady of Dunstaffnage."

"That doesn't require a dress, does it?" She made a face.

"For some lasses, aye." He pressed a kiss to her brow and plucked his léine from the floor. "For ye, it means a powerful woman at my side, working with me through negotiations and war, wearing whatever the hell she wants."

She pulled on her trews and fastened them. "I like the sound of that."

"Aye, me too." He grabbed his kilt, but she stopped him.

"I'll get food from the kitchens. Let's break our fast together and then start our day."

"Ye dinna—"

"My trews are easier to put on than your kilt." Before he could protest further, she kissed his lips and was out the door.

She hadn't walked more than ten steps from the West Tower when a booming voice called her attention.

"There is my bonny new daughter." Laird Campbell sauntered over to her and caught her in a firm embrace. He smiled down at her with his kind, amber gaze. "Welcome to the family, lass. I couldna be prouder."

His exuberance warmed through her. He had accepted her so readily, and now his welcome to the family was just as heartfelt and genuine. It was then she realized, for the first time, she had a family once again.

Hette came into her mind, an occurrence Sylvi knew would happen most likely for the rest of her life. For Sylvi had been far more fortunate than the Prussian woman. Sylvi had not only had training to give her strength, but she had the love and acceptance of her friends and her husband. A family.

And all those things had kept Sylvi from becoming as frightened and alone as poor, dear Hette.

"Thank you, Laird." Sylvi inclined her head respectfully.

He squeezed her good shoulder. "Nay Laird to ye, daughter. Call me Da." He nudged her and gave a wink. "Go on—say it."

"Thank you...Da." She smiled as she spoke.

His signet ring sparkled in the sun as he lowered his hand. The boar's head winked up at her.

Her heartbeat faltered for a brief moment. A boar. Not a bore.

What if the nobleman was a Campbell?

"Da." Donald nodded appreciatively. "That sounds like music to these old ears. The only way I could be gladder is if I'd been there myself."

Sylvi's face warmed. "It was so sudden—"

He put his hand up to stop her. "Dinna fash over it, daughter. I know ye and Percy are no' the kind of lasses who want all the..." He swirled his fingers in the air. "Frills of wedding ceremonies.

I'm just glad ye had witnesses. After all, what is unseen hasna been done."

Ice chilled through her soul.

He clapped her on the good shoulder once more, that damning ring glinting, and said something with a jovial smile before turning to go. She stood there with feet rooted to the ground and stared after the man she had so readily considered family, the man she'd only moments ago called Da with a smile on her face.

The man who might very well have ordered the death of her entire family.

Thirty-Two

Somehow Sylvi managed to stagger back toward the room she shared with Ian. Her muscles moved of their own volition, her entire body numb, yet one foot had stepped in front of the other over and over. They carried her to the door, where she stopped. Hesitating.

The betrayal scorched her heart, seething beneath the muted blanket of shock.

Lies.

Hate.

Murder.

Her family.

Her family.

The emotions scrabbled over themselves inside her, clawing to escape. Her fingers slipped over the latch twice before it caught. Her heart blazed, and her mind whirled. She shoved through the door, and it smacked hard on the stone wall.

Ian jerked from his place beside the window, his hand immediately grabbing for his dagger. Recognition stilled the action, and he was at her side in only a moment. "Sylvi? What is it? Has someone hurt ye? Have ye injured yer arm?"

He kicked the door closed and gently led her to the bed. She stared at him.

All this time, it might have been Ian's father. Her greatest love, spawned by her greatest hate.

A ball of ice curled in her gut.

How could she tell him? After all, if it were indeed Donald Campbell, it would mean he had killed Ian's mom as well.

She sucked in a hard gasp of air and realized she'd forgotten to keep breathing. She would be the one to break the news to him, to hurt him when already he suffered from his mother's death. One parent dead, and the other a murderer.

"What? Sylvi?" He held her face in his hands, and the heartfelt tenderness of his regard slipped into her heart like a hot dagger. "My angel, what is it?" Desperation made his voice hoarse.

"Your da—Laird Campbell." Revulsion shuddered through her; she had embraced the man only moments ago.

"Is he all right?" Ian asked. "My da. Sylvi, please."

"It was him," she whispered. "This whole time. It has to be him."

Ian's gaze turned wary, and he backed away ever so slightly. "What do ye mean?"

"What is unseen hasna been done," she spoke it with the soft accent of Ian's father. "I heard that phrase before—Reginald said it when they killed my family. Hette said it as well. And now…Ian, your father said it to me."

Ian's jaw clenched beneath his beard. "Sylvi—" His stare slipped away and darted around the room, chasing invisible thoughts.

"It wasn't bore, as in uninteresting, Hette was saying." Sylvi grasped Ian's hand with her free one. "It was a boar." She nodded to where his sword lay on the table, its hilt facing them with the image of the Campbell boar at its base.

He frowned to himself, piecing it together, she knew. "The accounts that were too complicated to discuss." The color drained from his face. "The ring in my mum's room." He issued a low curse and swept his hand over his face. "My mum."

She curled her fingers into fists and squeezed. Her arm ached from the effort, but she didn't care. She welcomed the pain as a necessary distraction from the rage threatening to tear free inside of her.

"Ye are certain?" Ian asked.

"I have no proof, only suspicions, but I feel it in my soul."

"Everything points in that direction, aye?" Ian lifted his head and dropped it back.

"I don't know what to do," Sylvi said through clenched teeth. "If he were any other man, I'd kill him and be done with it. But he's your father."

"My God, ye do love me, my angel." Ian met her gaze and caught her fists in his. "Let me talk to him, see if I can get him to admit it, then we can turn him in to the king."

"Counterfeiting is stealing directly from the king and an act of high treason." She didn't say more than that. It was not necessary.

They both knew what happened to men guilty of high treason—they were hanged, drawn and quartered.

Ian cursed again and jumped up from the bed to pace the room with renewed fury. He stopped mid-pace and shook his head. "Let me talk to him. I need to confirm this."

"What if he tries to kill you?" She got to her feet. "I'm coming with you."

He shook his head. "I'm his heir. He wouldna kill me."

"He has Kyle as well."

"Trust me, aye?" Ian stared hard at her. "Let me have this one conversation and see what I can gently press from him. He still sees me as his ally, his heir. I need to see his reactions when he doesna know I know. If we interrogate him, he'll no' ever speak."

Sylvi nodded. It was a good plan, even if she didn't like it. It was all she could do—to allow any emotion would undo the dam she had built against the surge of her rioting emotions.

He fell to his knees in front of where she sat on the bed and took her hands in his once more. "I'll make this right somehow. He will face punishment for his actions." Ian bowed his head and pressed his forehead to his knuckles. When he lifted his head, tears glistened in his eyes. "I know how hard this was for ye to do, to bring this to me rather than immediately strike him down. Thank ye."

He kissed her hard on the lips, looked down at her one last time and strode from the room.

It wasn't until the door was closed and she was alone in the silence of their shattered happiness that she regretted her decision to come to Ian. It could all be over by now had she done as he said—cut Laird Campbell down. Issue the final strike of justice.

She had made her decision. She had chosen her husband over vengeance for her family, and now all she could do was wait.

IAN CLIMBED THE STAIRS TO HIS FATHER'S STUDY. His nerves drew tight with every step, and his palms dampened with sweat.

What if Sylvi was right and his father was behind her slain family? If he'd killed her family, then had he also had the others murdered? And Ian's mother, Lady of Dunstaffnage...had his da truly killed her as well?

It would explain Donald's lack of interest in finding her killer. Ian's stomach churned with bile.

The questions rose in his mind like nightmares, ugly and unstoppable.

He knocked on the door and waited.

"Enter." The distracted grunt told him his father was busy.

Ian pulled in a deep breath and pushed into the solar. Donald's face brightened with joy. "Ach, son, congratulations on yer wedding."

"Thank ye, Da." Ian grinned. "I suppose I took to heart what ye said about marrying the lass."

His father pushed up from the large wooden chair behind his desk and opened his arms to embrace his son. Ian allowed the fierce hug and only straightened when his father finally released him.

"Ye've only just wed," Donald said. "Do ye really want to resume yer studies when ye've got a bonny new wife?"

Ian shrugged and hoped he appeared nonchalant despite his racing pulse. "Well, I'm a married man now, Da, as ye say. Married men need homes. Futures."

Donald's eyes brightened. "A lairdship?"

"I may be considering it."

"Aye, of course." Donald put a hand to Ian's shoulder and led him over to the chair beside the great desk.

The slightness of Donald's touch was like a weight against Ian's back. Was that truly the hand of a murderer?

It was hard to imagine Donald, the charismatic man who everyone loved, the leader who kept his people safe and cared for, killing families and wives.

And yet, there was Simon and his father.

These thoughts crowded Ian's mind as his father pored over the accounts with him, offering more explanation and detail than before. When they got to the rents, Ian saw his opportunity to do what he had come for.

"Da, what is the right column for in the accounts?" Ian pointed to the line of numbers he'd been told before was too complicated.

"Something only a laird would know." Donald slid Ian a sly gaze.

"Then I should learn it."

Donald beamed at his son. "This is something I've been building up for years. I've been exceedingly careful in ensuring all of this is secure. Ye must understand my telling you will require discretion on yer part."

Ian nodded once and hoped his face was as calm as he intended it to be.

His father rubbed his hands together and puffed out his chest with great pride. "I've been having coins commissioned."

Ian's heart slid a long, slow, painful path into his gut. He hadn't wanted any of it to be true. "You mean counterfeited."

Donald shrugged. "It's a means of providing greater wealth than any land could produce."

"And who makes the coins?" Ian asked.

"Goldsmiths, of course. Discreet ones."

Discreet ones. Dead ones. Ian ground his teeth to stop the whirling of his thoughts. Now more than ever he needed to keep his wits about him. "How long have ye been doing this?" Ian dreaded the answer as soon as he'd asked the question.

"Since before ye were born."

Ian's chest constricted. So many years. So many goldsmiths. Was Hette Schmidt's father the first?

His father flipped through the pages. "Do ye see what it's done for our wealth?" He pointed to an exorbitant figure.

It was a large figure. No doubt many had died to create such a sum. Ian swallowed. "Did ye deal with the goldsmiths yerself?"

"Ach, no." Donald hesitated. "Well, initially I did, when I dinna have enough coin to afford to hire someone. It took a while to build up wealth, son. I kept my dealings in the northernmost parts of the Highlands, paying for investments with a blend of counterfeit coin and true coin."

The northernmost parts of the Highlands. Where the king did not try to expend his forces. A crafty plan. And clearly an effective one.

Ian asked. "Then ye hired someone to speak for ye?"

"Aye, mercenaries. They ensured the goldsmiths and their families stayed quiet. I put enough money in their pockets that they'll never seek me out. And they know I have enough connections not to suffer an attempted extortion."

The room spun around Ian. "How did ye keep them all quiet? Did ye have all of the goldsmiths killed?" he said it in a forced jest.

"Of course I did." Donald scoffed. "Men become greedy." He closed the book. "They see what ye profit and they ask for more, or they ask questions, seeking safety in case we all got caught." Donald folded his hands behind his back and strode across the room. "After the first two goldsmiths, I found a pattern. Ye see, after about four years, they would begin to question the agreement, ask for me. And so, when ye resume this, ye know at four years ye must put a stop to yer work with them."

Ian watched his father's back pace away from him. "Ye mean have them killed."

Donald turned back toward him and nodded slowly. "Aye. To be caught would be certain death. It's high treason to replicate the king's coin. I've stopped now and havena done it in several years. No' worth the risk."

Disgust swirled in Ian's gut, and the anger, the injustice of it all, snared at his heart. "Did ye kill children?"

"I dinna kill them." Ian's father twisted his lips. "But, aye, I ordered their deaths. Being a laird isna easy, my son."

"How can ye order the deaths of children?" Ian leapt from the chair, unable to control the intensity of his rage.

"Because anyone who knows anything could come back and implicate us. All it takes is one." His father thrust a finger in the air. "One," he snarled. "A vengeful brat who knows what ye did to their da and a lifetime of work is destroyed."

Sylvi rose forefront in Ian's mind, her face wild with determination, her body and mind honed into a warrior's, perfectly primed for vengeance.

Donald had no idea how right he was.

Ian had most of what he needed. Now he had to figure out what the hell to do with it. His father could not be allowed to continue. There were many wrongs to right. Too damn many.

And yet, possibly one more Ian had not asked after. His mother.

"Ye dinna understand, Ian." Donald squeezed a hand on Ian's shoulder." Ye dinna know what it's like to be hungry, lad. I've made sure of that."

Ian swept his father's hand away. "Ye killed children, families."

Donald narrowed his eyes. "Did ye know, when I was a lad, my da died a disgraced man? We were forced into the woods, my mum and three sisters. I was only ten, but I had a family to feed, to care for." He pushed Ian backward and blocked the door with his body. "I know hunger and fear and uncertainty. I know what it's like to watch someone ye love die because ye havena enough food and they got too weak, but ye've no coin for a physic."

Donald shook his head, and the anger of his expression softened into affection. "Ye've never known that life, Ian. Nor has Kyle. I made sure of that. And ye never will." He gestured to the closed book on the desk. "I restored my da's favor. I made a life our blood is worthy of. I've given ye everything I dinna have."

Ian stared at his father. All of this, the act of high treason, the murder of families, all of it Donald had done for his own children. The blood of Sylvi's family was on Ian's palms as well as on the hands of his own father.

"It's no' right." Ian shook his head. "Ye canna do this."

The lines on Donald's face deepened. "Yer mum said the same thing."

"Is that why ye killed her?" Ian asked quietly.

His father was silent, but his face reddened. "If ye want to be laird, ye need to understand there are secrets—"

"Ye mean the death of my mum." Ian shook his head again. "Ye killed her."

"I dinna do it."

"But ye paid someone, aye?"

Donald glared at Ian. "Ye're too bloody softhearted, like yer ma. Ye and that damn brother of yers."

"Was it Reginald?"

His father stilled. "How do ye know who that is?"

"Because we killed him."

Donald's face remained expressionless. "It was ye?"

"In retaliation," Ian replied slowly. "For what Reginald and his men had done to Sylvi and her family."

The skin around Donald's eyes tightened.

"Aye, Da, ye ordered her family killed. They tried to kill her too."

Donald lowered his head and gave a sardonic laugh. "The Norseman."

"This is no' a jest." Ian glared at his father.

"And what will ye do with me now?" Donald asked. "Send me to the king for a fine traitor's death? Ye'll have to be laird then."

"Ye canna go unpunished."

Donald's face purpled. "I built us up, ye entitled bairn. Ye dinna know what it's like to nearly starve. To have nothing. I'll no' ever go back to that life again."

Ian's father tensed, giving enough of a warning for Ian to know the hit was coming. He lunged at Donald and threw a punch at the older man. Donald moved with far more speed than seemed possible.

"Ye may have youth, lad, but I've got decades of experience." He feinted left and right several times before throwing his fist toward Ian.

He moved too damn fast, and his punch hit Ian in the chest like a blacksmith's hammer, knocking the wind from him. Ian staggered back and immediately leapt forward again. He jerked his blade from his belt and swiped at Donald, catching him in the side. Blood blossomed on the white fabric of Donald's léine.

Ian crouched low and circled his father. "This ends now."

Donald shook his head. "It never ends. Or ye willna live to tell." He leapt at Ian, who darted out of his path and swiped at the air again. This time Ian's blade caught nothing.

His mother's face flashed in his mind, gentle and kind and beautiful. He would avenge her.

Rage roared up through Ian's throat, and he charged at his

father. He landed a punch on Donald's face, somewhere hard and solid. Pain lanced through his fist and up his arm.

His father recovered first and hit Ian just under the chin, sending his world into black.

Awareness did not leave him long. The world swam back to greet him with a vicious bite of reality. His face lay on the worn wooden floor; an unseen force on his back pushed down his chest. Someone wrenched his arms backward and secured his wrists with something rough.

The confusion stilled him for only a second before he bucked wildly against the person binding him. Not just any person. His father.

"I told ye ye're nay a match for me, lad." Donald panted around his words and gave a great groan as the weight lifted from Ian's back.

Ian wriggled on his side to flip over. His knuckles pressed into the ground, but he ignored the discomfort. "What are ye going to do? Tie me up until I agree to go along with yer madness?"

Donald squatted beside his son, and one of his knees popped. "Tie ye up while I go see to yer wife."

Ian's body went cold as ice, and he stopped struggling.

Donald rose and stood over Ian. "I've got unfinished business with the lass."

Ian twisted against his bonds. The rope was securely fastened. "Stop. Dinna do this."

Donald strode to the door and stopped. "Ye'll forgive me one of these days. Ye'll understand."

"Dinna hurt her." Ian writhed against the ropes holding his arms behind his back, and tried to kick his legs. His ankles were tied as well.

"I dinna intend to hurt her," Donald said. "I mean to kill her."

The door closed, and Ian was alone, bound and helpless to save his wife.

Thirty-Three

A knock at the door set Sylvi's heart racing. If the person on the other side were Ian, he would have entered.

She slipped a dagger from her pocket and approached the door. Her pulse thundered in her ears, and her skin tingled with such heightened awareness, she felt as if it'd leap from her body. She drew a long, slow breath and pulled open the door.

Laird Campbell shoved into the room and kicked the door shut behind them. "I know who ye are."

Sylvi had time to snatch her dagger from her belt before Laird Campbell stalked toward her. The kindness she had found in his brown eyes had burned away into glinting anger. "Ye Norse bitch."

Her brain raced with tactics to fight, to flee, and through it all —worry for Ian. Sylvi readjusted her firm grip on her dagger and backed into the room. There would be more open space for her to fight in there. She knew well her room, the layout, what was where—it was an advantage she might need.

"Where's Ian?" she asked.

Laird Campbell narrowed his eyes at her. "Ye tried to turn him against me."

Fear prickled like ice over her skin. "Did you kill him?"

Laird Campbell stepped into the room and kicked the door shut with a slam. "Of course, I dinna kill him." He reached into the excess folds of his plaid, where it was slung over his shoulder, and withdrew a pistol. "He'll come to understand, and he'll forgive me." He raised the pistol. "Even for killing ye."

Sylvi had put as much distance between them as the room would allow, with him at the door and her on the opposite side of the bed. The pistol pointed directly at her.

He cocked it back with a loud mechanical click. Before she could duck, sparks flashed bright with an audible pop, and the muzzle emitted a cloud of black smoke. Sylvi flinched, but she hadn't needed to.

Splinters of wood flew at her from the bedpost, easily three feet away.

Sylvi lifted her head. Her arm was still injured, but she was a damn good fighter regardless. "That's why I never use pistols. Completely untrustworthy."

She launched her dagger toward Ian's dad with her left hand, but a piece of splintered wood she had landed on when she changed her stance for the throw rocked her balance at the last moment. The blade sank deep into his upper thigh. He heaved a grunt, and the pistol dropped to the ground with a heavy *thunk*. He curled his hands around the handle of the blade and jerked it from his thigh. Blood ran in a stream down his leg.

Sylvi came around the bed toward him—an old man quickly taken down without his pistol.

It was almost too easy.

Her heart twisted around a spider web of powerful emotions: her need to end this, to kill the man who had slain her own family and so many others. Her love of Ian. All of it stayed her hand.

Donald fell to his knees and put up a bloody hand. "Please dinna hurt me."

Sylvi pulled another dagger from her belt. Only a fool

approached an injured enemy with confidence. "I want to talk to Ian. Now."

He nodded. "Aye, we can go to him."

"You killed all those families," Sylvi said. "You killed my family." Her voice trembled, this time with the power of her sorrow rather than the vehemence of hatred. "I trusted you."

Donald shoved himself off the ground with the hand he'd been bracing himself with and flew at her with the pistol held backward like a bludgeon. Sylvi jerked back, but not before he managed to clip her with the heavy butt of his pistol—directly on her injured arm.

Pain shot white sparks through her vision, and she had to bite down hard to keep from crying. She cradled her arm and staggered.

Donald roared and threw himself at her. She ducked his attack, but he followed, pursuing. Determination gleamed like bloodlust in his gaze. "Ye will die," he snarled. "No one can be left alive who kens what happened. I willna die for the likes of ye."

Sylvi ran into him and swiped her blade at his throat. "I want to see Ian."

Donald arched backward, evading her strike. She slashed again, this time at his chest, and he dodged the blow again. The large man moved way too quickly.

"If you don't take me to him," Sylvi said. "I will kill you."

Donald lunged at her and pinned her against the wall with his elbow on her throat. "No' if I kill ye first."

She pulled her knee up with all the strength she could muster and drove it into his bollocks. He gave a feral growl, and his hold slackened enough for her to slip free from his grasp. Her forward momentum suddenly snapped backward, and pain exploded at her scalp.

The bastard was dragging her by her hair. He flung her against the wall she'd just been pinned to. Her body slapped the unyielding stone and bounced off. The ache in her arm pounded ferociously and left her stomach roiling with nausea.

Donald shoved her back against the wall and locked her into place with the heft of his body. Sweat dotted his brow, and his skin was hot from their fight.

No matter how much he tried to hide it, he was panting—from the effort, from his injuries—and the odor of his musty breath mingled with the metallic scent of his blood. He was weakening.

"I order that the families be killed quickly." He tugged the ribbon from her neck. "A slit to the throat."

She shoved hard at his chest, and he edged back beneath the force of her hit.

"No' this time," he vowed. He cocked his arm back, and before she could duck, his fist slammed into her face.

Ian's wrists were on fire from constantly wrenching at them. The floor dug into his hip, and the burning at his wrists told him he'd long since sawed the rope into his flesh. Still, he held on to hope, especially with the bindings beginning to loosen.

Was he too late?

The thought spun through his mind on an endless loop, encouraging him as much as dragging his heart to a heavy, hurtful place in his gut.

"I'm coming, Sylvi." He said it more for himself than for her, to counteract the voice in his head.

But was he too late?

Was she dead?

He jerked his wrists in the opposite direction and cried at the searing pain of the rough rope cutting into raw, flayed skin. It sagged to the heel of his hand, a fraction of an inch more, but perhaps it was enough.

More carefully this time, he wriggled his right hand and sucked in a breath against the burning pain. With slow precision, the rope slipped over the base of his thumb. He curled his hand inward, touching his pinky to his thumb to make it all small enough to slip through his bonds.

Was he too late?

"I'm coming, Sylvi." His voice echoed around him, full of determination as much as it was full of fear.

His heart thundered in his chest, demanding he go faster, but he kept his mind fixed on the task, carefully shifting his hand back and forth, back and forth, back and forth. The rope was at the back of his hand now, nearing his knuckles. He panted with concentration. He could do this.

He had to.

For Sylvi.

The rope slid over his knuckles, and his hand was free. He gave a strangled cry of relief and pulled his arms around in front of him. Little pins and needles seemed to shoot through his limbs as the blood flowed back into them. He forced himself to only look at the knot at his left hand and focused on working it loose. It was better than letting his gaze wander toward the broken skin on his wrists, the flesh pulled back and bleeding, where every touch made his breath hiss.

As soon as his hands were free, he redirected his focus to his ankles. His fingers trembled with his haste. The rope had gone slippery, with the blood trickling freely from his wrists. He gave a growl of frustration and tried to force himself to go slow—to concentrate.

What if he was too late?

"I'm coming, Sylvi."

Finally, he caught the rope between the pinch of his fingers and shook the knot loose enough to pull it apart. The rope flopped uselessly to the floor, and his feet were free. He rose slowly, knowing doing so quickly might result in him falling over. His legs were numb beneath him as if they were not there at all.

A drum of pain thrummed in his skull, and the room spun. He caught himself on the desk. The world around him faded into a glow of white. He clenched onto the edge of the desk, holding on for dear life.

Breathe.

Slow and steady. Deep and even. He tamped down the urgent voice in his head, the one questioning Sylvi's safety, and focused on his breathing until the neat rows of meticulously lined books came back into view.

He pulled open his da's drawer, where he knew a pistol had been kept and loaded it with shaking hands before limping to the door. The floor shifted under his feet, but he was able to walk. And if he could walk, then he could get to Sylvi.

He went down the stairs as quickly as possible and let his hand drag over the scrape of stone for support, careful to avoid his ravaged wrists. His feet were clumsy and clattering on the stone stairs, but he forced his way down. Closer to Sylvi.

The courtyard was almost empty. The morning meal had finished, and most of the castle's people had set about their daily tasks. Perfect timing for killing someone with discretion.

Ian's muscles cramped with the effort of running, yet everything seemed to move too slowly. Was he too late?

He didn't know who was involved with this scheme of his father's, who might be there now, aiding Donald in silencing Sylvi.

Was she already dead?

"I'm coming, Sylvi." He didn't stop until he reached the door of the West Tower, expecting it to open beneath his touch, as it always did, with such ease. Instead, he slammed hard into it and stopped. He shoved at it for good measure, but it did not move.

The door to the West Tower was locked.

Thirty-Four

I f Sylvi's arm hadn't still been injured from the break, Donald would be dead. Now, she was pinned up against the wall and fighting harder than she'd ever had to fight. The slow mend of the bone blazed with agony once more.

He lifted his hand and swung it down toward her face again. This time, she darted right and drove her elbow into the wound at his thigh. He howled with pain and caught the side of her jaw with his massive fist.

Sylvi's head snapped right, and the world spun around her as she was knocked to the floor. She tensed, expecting another blow.

"Ye're a tough bitch—I'll give ye that." Donald nodded to himself and spat a wad of blood foam onto the ground next to her where she lay beside the wall.

"You haven't seen what I can do yet." She reached for the dagger, which had fallen near where she lay. Her fingertips grazed the cool metal of the blade. Just outside her reach.

So close, and yet it might as well have been back at Kindrochit for what good it did her now.

Donald drew his bad leg back with obvious intent to kick her. She could stay and grab her blade, which would risk injury, or roll away farther from her dagger.

With a grunt of irritation, she rolled away.

This needed to end. Now.

She caught his boot with both her hands and pulled hard with all the strength of her left arm. Her right one sent flames of agony licking through her, but it was a necessary sacrifice. Donald's boot slipped forward, and the one foot he was standing on went out from underneath him.

He flew into the air, arms and legs flailing, before landing hard on the ground. His breath whoofed out of his lungs.

Sylvi bent over to grab her dagger and threw herself on top of him. He needed to die for what he'd done. She lifted her blade high, ready to plunge it into his heart. "This is for my family."

His eyes, the same warm brown as Ian's, widened beneath the blood spattering his face. "Mercy."

She hesitated. Had he just asked for mercy?

Could she actually bring herself to grant it?

Donald's arm came up, and something solid slammed into the side of Sylvi's head. She stiffened against the dazzling pain of it, and her body slumped to the side. She tried to rise, but her mind refused to connect with her body, still stunned by the unexpected hit.

She realized her mistake then, her stupidity in allowing her heart to intercede where her mind should have been. She knew better than to hesitate.

Donald threw his heavy weight on top of her, pinning her to the hard floor. Her arm shot brilliant rays of agony where his hand pressed her down. He snatched a dagger from the ground, *her* dagger. The very one she'd traded her virginity for to kill her family's killers.

She knew then he intended to finish the job started almost seventeen years ago.

The door flew open. Footsteps of someone unseen ran toward them as Donald jerked the blade up and angled it to strike.

A shadow appeared over Donald's shoulder and aimed a pistol

down at the two of them. Sparks flared to life, and the firearm went off.

🌼

IAN HELD THE SMOKING GUN IN HIS HANDS. HIS FATHER had ceased fighting and had collapsed on top of Sylvi. Ian reached toward his father and hefted him backward off of his bride. Donald's body rolled away, limp, his eyes gazing at nothing from a blood-smeared face.

Dead.

He had killed his father.

The realization gripped Ian's heart. He turned from his father, as much with the inability to face what he'd done as concern for his wife.

Sylvi—his Sylvi, his beautiful angel—lay motionless. Blood glistened on her black léine and trews. Her blood? There was so much. From her? From his father?

Damn it. He couldn't tell.

"Sylvi?" he choked out. He moved his hands over her chest, seeking out a bullet hole. Finding nothing, he moved to her neck, where her ribbon was missing. Beneath the gore on her face, her skin was swelling black and blue. She'd been beaten.

God, what had his father done?

Ian pulled Sylvi into his arms and held her to him. "Sylvi, please say ye're all right. Please, my love."

Ian could not look away from Sylvi's battered face. He could not allay the ache in his heart from the idea he might have lost the woman who meant the world to him. His beautiful angel. The woman who fought so hard to bring peace to those she loved. She couldn't die. Not now. Not when happiness might finally find them, not when they had just started their life together.

He couldn't lose her, for he had nothing without her.

"Sylvi, please." His voice cracked beneath the tension in his throat. "Please don't leave me, my angel."

He gathered her more firmly in his arms and squeezed. Why was no one coming? Had they not heard the blast of the gun?

Her body jerked, and a moan sounded from her lips.

"Sylvi?"

He stared down at her, and her beautiful crystal-blue eyes blinked open.

"My arm," she whispered.

It was then he remembered her injured arm and quickly eased the pressure from her limb. "I thought ye were dead." He bent over her, curling his body around her as if he might protect her forever.

Tears ran from the corners of her eyes and streaked through the blood on her face. "I couldn't kill him." She shook her head. "I couldn't kill him."

"I did it for ye, my love."

Her lashes swept over her cheeks, and her head lolled toward him.

Panic clawed at Ian's heart. "Sylvi, stay awake."

"I'm so tired." Her words slurred together.

Footsteps clattered through the hallway toward the room. People were finally coming. Perhaps they could help. Perhaps Kyle or Percy had some method of healing to make this better.

"Stay with me, my angel." His throat clogged with emotion. "Dinna leave me, my love. Help is coming."

He curled his hand over her slackening fingers.

"I love you," she whispered, and her eyes closed.

THE SHARP SCENT OF VINEGAR AND ROSEMARY PRICKED Sylvi's awareness.

She wrinkled her nose and immediately winced at the pressure of pain all over her face. All over her body. A slow groan rose from deep in her throat.

It all came rushing back to her then, the discovery of Ian's father, the fight, the fear. And Ian had been there, cradling her, his body strong and safe.

She opened her eyes and found the room either shaded in the early evening or lit by very early morning. A chair creaked and pulled her attention to the right of her bed.

Ian.

Sylvi's heart soared at the sight of him, healthy and handsome. He leaned toward her from a plain wooden chair. Shadows of exhaustion showed beneath the eager gleam in his eyes.

"Sylvi?" His voice was the same wonderful deep timbre she knew so intimately.

Her throat constricted at the sound of that beautiful voice, at the wonderful sight of him.

He slipped off the chair and onto his knees beside her bed. "Thank God ye're awake. I've been so worried." He caught her hand in his and pressed his mouth to it in a long, loving gesture. The prickle of his beard against her skin was as welcome as his affection.

"Ian." Sylvi's voice rasped with disuse.

His hand lifted to her face, but he stopped and dropped his hand to clutch her fingers in his once more instead. She flinched inwardly. Her face must look a fright if he wouldn't even touch it.

"Ye dinna need to talk," he said. "I'm just—" He looked away, and when he returned his gaze to hers, his eyes were glossy with unshed tears. "I'm just glad ye're awake finally."

Finally?

She cleared her throat to eliminate some of the hoarseness. "You act as though I've been asleep for days." She tried to smile, but doing so made her face pound in time with her heartbeat.

Ian bent his head over her hand. "Ye have. Three days, my angel." His voice cracked. "This morning would have brought the fourth." When he raised his head, a tear crept down his cheek.

Sylvi's nose tingled, and her eyes went warm with tears. Three days. Almost four.

"I thought I was going to lose ye," Ian said softly. "I thought—"

"No." Sylvi squeezed her hand around his. "No, I'd never leave you. I love you too much. I would fight the angels of heaven rather than let them take me from you." She touched his face and tried not to imagine what her own must look like. "You taught me to love. You made me whole again."

Ian pressed her palm into his cheek. "I couldna live without ye, my angel. I know it's difficult to see how broken I was beneath this charming exterior." He winked at her in a way so familiar it almost ached. Certainly, it did ache when she laughed. "But ye saved me. From a life of running, from always being alone."

He looked down and hesitated. A bit too long, in fact.

Sylvi straightened. "What is it? Is it my face?" She gently touched her cheek and found the skin there warm and tender to the touch. Her fingers were ice cold in a contrast so soothing that she wanted to press her open palm to her entire cheek.

He put his hand over hers, caressing her face through her touch. "Even bruised, ye're beautiful, Sylvi. I dinna touch ye because I dinna want to hurt ye." His brow flinched. "It's just— why dinna ye tell me?"

The sun rose outside the window and cast a golden slant of sunbeams through the shutters. It fell over Ian's arm and made the skin of his forearm glow with warm light.

Sylvi regarded her husband with a sudden edge of wariness. "Tell you about what? Your father?"

He shook his head. "Though he is now dead."

"If you had not done so, I would not be here."

"Ye mean ye'd be beating angels in heaven to make yer way back to me?" Ian winked, and her heart swelled with the familiar gesture.

Sylvi chuckled. "Of course, that's what I meant. How is the clan now that your father is dead?"

Ian smirked. "They're looking to me as their new laird. Word spread quickly about how we'd been found, with ye near death and my father killed. He was a friendly man, but he made a lot of enemies through the years because of the harshness of his punishments. Like the one that he meted out to Simon's father." He paused and pressed his lips together. "He is now avenged, as are many others my father wronged."

"Will you be laird then?" Sylvi asked.

"Will ye be my lady?" Ian grinned. "I canna do it without ye at my side."

Sylvi had never thought of taking a place as the Lady of Dunstaffnage. But wherever Ian would be, she would be. And life would be much safer for Percy and Liv. She was done with death and fighting. She nodded. "I would be honored to be at your side, so long as I'm not forced into wearing dresses and creating fancy dinners for guests."

He chuckled. "I know better than even to try. And I dinna want a woman who wears dresses and plans dinners for guests. I want the woman who has saved me, my angel, a woman with white-blonde hair wearing black trews on an arse that makes me want to grab her to me. A woman I love." He gave her a cautious gaze. "But ye know that's no' what I'm talking about."

Sylvi eyed him right back. "I really don't."

He put a hand over her stomach, his touch tentative and overly careful. His palm hovered there for a moment before he let the warmth of it cradle the swell Dunstaffnage's good cooking had put there.

"Ye're going to be a mother." His smile broke out into a wide grin. "And I'll be a da."

She stared at his hand for a long moment, her mind stunned into shock.

"Are you sure?" she asked.

Ian gave a gentle chuckle, and she knew he didn't mock her. "Percy had had her suspicions before and checked after ye were injured to ensure the babe was all right."

Sylvi continued to stare at her stomach. There was a baby in there. Something fragile and vulnerable nestled in the protective shell of her body. The offspring of a line of shieldmaidens, to be sure, after surviving the beating she'd taken from Ian's father.

How could she not have known?

But then, her courses had never been regular. She hadn't been at her full capacity since her arm had been broken. Granted, her appetite at Dunstaffnage had increased, but she had attributed it to the fine cooking. Apparently, it was a babe growing in her belly that had made her so hungry.

A baby.

Ian's brow furrowed. "Ye're crying. I've no' ever known that to be a good thing." He spoke gently, and she did not miss how his hand cupped over her stomach as if guarding the child against potential hurt. Did he think her disappointed?

Tears trailed hot down Sylvi's cheeks and stung her lip where it'd been split. "Ian, we're going to have a family. It's..." She faltered and searched for the right word before finally saying what sang in her heart. "It's so wonderful."

Ian bent over her and pulled her into his arms. "Aye, my angel, it is."

Sylvi rested her hand over the top of his, so they embraced the baby together. "But I'm still going to train. My arm was finally to the point of healing where I could."

He gingerly tilted her face upward. "Ye know I'd no' ever try to stop ye. Though promise me ye'll let yerself mend a bit first, aye?"

"And that's one of the many things I love about you." She smiled beneath the warm press of his lips against hers.

Her heart swelled with bliss, incredible completeness she had never thought possible. All the hurt she'd endured, all the years spent so filled with hate and vengeance—it all had been replaced by happiness and love.

"One more thing," Ian whispered against her mouth.

She kissed him. "Anything."

He leaned back and grinned down at her. "How much did they pay ye to kill me?"

Thirty-Five

The sun filtered from the window and cast a golden light on the battered journal in Sylvi's lap. It hadn't seemed fitting to read it before this point. Even after Reginald's death, something in Sylvi's gut had known things were not resolved.

Now, her parents had been properly avenged, and her life as a mercenary had come to a close. It seemed only fitting she ended that portion of her life the same as she'd begun it—with My Lady.

Her fingers caressed the worn leather before she pulled the cover open.

A neat script lined the yellowed page of the inside flap: *The Journal of Elsie Seymour*.

Elsie Seymour.

Sylvi ran her fingers over the name. Such poignancy seemed to require raised lettering or gilt. And yet it was flat to the page with the basic black of average ink.

She turned the page to find more neat writing.

FEBRUARY 1584

. . .

My husband and my daughter are dead.

I cannot reconcile this in my heart any more than in my head. One day my husband was at my side, our daughter cooing and happy in my arms, and the next, they are dead from a highwayman on the side of the road.

They say that while Gerald's death was intentional, that of our daughter was quite an accident. No one will give me details, no matter how often I ask.

I want to find the man who did this to them, but that information, too, is kept from me. So, I am left with no details and nothing to focus on but their incredible loss.

I keep expecting to hear Gerald's lovely deep voice in my ear, whispering his silly little love sonnets as he is so wont to do. Was so wont to do. I walk past my dear Isla's cradle and expect to see the top of her silky blonde head. And yet, each time I find it empty, the sheets smooth from never having been used. Each time I find naught but silence in my ears, it is a punch to my heart.

The healer has suggested I take to these pages to ease the melancholy in my heart, as it overwhelms me daily. I cannot eat, I cannot sleep, I cannot exist. I am nothing.

Forgive me. I find I can write no more today.

THE BEAUTIFUL SCRIPT BLURRED, AND SYLVI swallowed at the tightness in her throat. She put a hand to the small bump of her stomach. Though it had only been days since she knew, a bond had already formed between herself and the child growing within, bound by protection and love. And to lose both—child and husband—at once. The very idea of losing Ian put Sylvi on the losing side of clearing her throat from the clog of emotion.

She turned the page, reading her mentor's pain, scribed in terrible, aching detail. After months of this pain, creditors arrived, seeking payment for a life well lived and poorly managed.

In the following passages, recorded intermittently, with some spanning weeks and months between, My Lady's life fell apart, casting her downward to the threat of debtor's prison.

AUGUST 1585

I HAVE BEEN GIVEN AN OPPORTUNITY TO SAVE MYSELF, to be free of these woes I cannot handle alone and be liberated from this pain I live with on a daily basis. I can offer no details, but trust that I will no longer be Elsie Seymour. I shall abandon her as a snake sheds its skin, leaving behind a woman who had become nothing more than a shell.

What is more, I have been offered something else no one has given me—an opportunity for vengeance.

SYLVI BALLED HER HAND INTO A FIST. MY LADY understood so much more than Sylvi had ever realized.

The following entry was not until over a year later.

NOVEMBER 1586

IT IS IMPRUDENT OF ME TO KEEP THIS JOURNAL STILL, yet I find I cannot rid myself of it no matter how many times I try. It's as though burning these pages will make the memories of Isla and Gerald curl into ash and blow away.

I have uncovered the details of their deaths. Gerald was shot in the heart, and my dear Isla was dropped from a horse in the chaos. My loves, their murders senseless.

The pain of their loss stays with me, though I have been given other things to occupy my attention. It has been helpful. My instructor tells me that when I am ready to lose my suffering, I will.

What he does not understand is that it is my suffering that makes me so very good. For it is my suffering that leaves me without fear of death, and that is what makes me excel.

THE HANDWRITING IN THE FOLLOWING ENTRY WAS more slanted, less careful, as though it had been written in a hurry. Or perhaps a frenzy.

DECEMBER 1586

I have found him. The man who did this to my family, who destroyed everything I hold dear—a magistrate's son, protected by the power of his father's position.

All this time, his father knew, and he kept anyone else from knowing. Coins and lies blanketed a path of betrayal. I followed the trail into a dark window in the dead of night.

Today, I had my vengeance.

THE FOLLOWING PASSAGES WERE REMINISCENT OF THE first ones—rife with the pain of loss. My Lady suffered as Sylvi had done when she'd killed Reginald, hollow with the reality of revenge not matching the anticipation.

Killing did not bring back loved ones. It was simply more people dead. The next entry was not until nearly five years later.

MARCH 1591

A GIRL HAS BEEN FOLLOWING ME. SHE BELIEVES SHE IS being discreet, the poor dear. I know I should not get attached, and yet there is something to the pale blonde hair that reminds me of my Isla.

This girl is about the same age my daughter would have been. It may be what has made me warm to her so. Or perhaps it is the raw, ugly scar stretching the width of her impossibly slender neck.

She has obviously known pain, and in that, we are alike.

Sylvi put her hand to her heart. This was her. She was the girl My Lady mentioned in this entry. And it was she who was mentioned again and again in the following entries. Once more, they were intermittent, sometimes months or years apart, never detailing My Lady's missions, always about Sylvi.

The respect My Lady had for Sylvi's tenacity, her ability to learn quickly, the fierceness of her determination and the incredible sense of maternal protectiveness she roused in My Lady. Sylvi had to smile. Never once had any of their interactions indicated the feelings so baldly written on the page.

March 1601

The girl is finally ready to train. Or rather, I am finally giving in to her constant requests. I have tried to hold off, to keep her from this empty life I lead, and yet she stubbornly persists. The same as I was in my determination to learn more about Gerald and Isla.

Certainly, I cannot fault her, and so I will teach her.

The passages were then written more frequently, detailing the length of their sessions, their training and My Lady's immense pride for Sylvi.

Through it all, Sylvi kept her tears at bay. It was the final entry, however, that caused her to weep.

· · ·

MAY 1605

AFTER SEVERAL YEARS OF TRAINING TOGETHER, THE *girl has finally confessed to me why she works so diligently. What she has told me is too horrible even to write here.*

This poor girl has endured such suffering. And so it is here, in the place of my heart's truest confessions and lamentations, I vow to aid her in finding this man with half an ear and destroying him. Doing this, I hope, is the first step in the direction of her healing, a means of repaying her for everything she's done for me.

This young woman, who went through so much more than any child should suffer, who is the very age my own precious child would be, who somehow worked her way into my heart and helped me begin to heal. She has filled in for me as child as I have filled in for her as family. I might have become lost after Gerald and Isla, but I have been found because of Sylvi.

Epilogue

᠁

There had been a lavish wedding among them, after all—
even if it took several years for Liv to find love. But then,
she was not the typical bride, and it was not a typical
lavish wedding.

Sylvi approached the delighted couple, smiling with giddiness
she couldn't tamp down.

Liv looked up at her new husband, Beathan—Ian's Captain
of the Guard and the man she had fallen in love with over countless hours of standing watch together. They were a beautiful
couple, him with golden hair to compliment her copper sheen, his
frame almost twice the size of Liv's. They were powerful and
stunning.

She whispered something in his ear. He caught her face in his
palms and kissed her sweetly. She turned and strode toward Sylvi,
the airy white fabric of her skirts floating around her like shimmering clouds while the sun glinted off the metal breastplate she
wore.

Fianna padded along beside her, a string of small white
flowers draped around her neck. Most likely at the doing of Sylvi's
daughter, Isla. Truly, Fianna was the most patient feline in all of
Scotland.

Sylvi had initially thought to name her Elsie. But the more she thought of the journal, the more she realized My Lady would be best honored with Sylvi naming her daughter after the child she had never stopped loving—Isla.

"I'm so very happy for you." Sylvi embraced Liv.

The new bride grinned at her. "Who would have thought I would have ended up married after all these years? After..." She trailed off. She didn't need to say it. Sylvi knew how much her earlier years had caused such hurt—the sort that felt irrevocable.

A large, pink satin belly appeared between them. Percy smiled at them, her face full and beautiful with the glow of her much-anticipated pregnancy.

"I'm so glad you've found happiness, Liv." Percy rested a gentle hand on her stomach, caressing the child within. Her eyes misted with tears. "You deserve this joy, this love."

"Are you going to start crying again?" Sylvi asked warily.

Percy sniffed. "No." But even as she spoke, a tear trickled down her cheek, and she started to laugh. "I'm just so happy for you."

The women all laughed now. Percy always had been the one with the softer emotions, but a swelling belly and a joyful life had rendered more tears in the last few months than she'd most likely shed all her life. It had become a jest between them, meant with the utmost affection.

A shadow fell over the women. They looked up to find the towering form of Kyle blotting out the sun. He crossed his arms over his massive chest. "Are ye making my wife cry?"

The women all looked at one another and answered at once, "Yes."

Kyle shook his head, but a smile teased the corner of his mouth. "Then, in that case, I think I ought to steal her for a dance."

He held out his broad hand to Percy, who wiped her cheek with the palm of her hand, cast her friends a bright smile and let her husband pull her away. One large arm settled protectively on

Percy's shoulder; the other rested atop the hand she pressed to her stomach.

Liv watched them go. "Do you think we'll ever be as silly in love as those two?"

From behind Liv, Ian waved at Sylvi and drew a heart in the air, then pointed to her, winked and blew her a kiss. Sylvi laughed in spite of herself. "I think we both already are."

"And I might be a weepy mess myself soon," Sylvi added.

Liv raised her brows. "Another one? Finally?"

Isla was already five years old. Sylvi had not gotten with child again. Until now.

Sylvi settled a hand on the treasure nestled inside her womb.

A gentle tug came at Sylvi's side. She turned and found Isla staring at her with the same warm brown eyes as her father. "Da said if ye dinna dance with him soon, ye'll be sorry."

Liv laughed and shook her head.

Sylvi knelt before her daughter and stroked a length of impossibly silky blonde hair from Isla's face. "What would you do if you were me?" she asked.

Isla tilted her head in thought. "I'd make him wait a bit just to see."

Sylvi couldn't help but chuckle at this. Of course, this was Isla's answer—the perfect reply for her independent little daughter.

"But he did tell me to give ye this." Isla pulled her hand from behind her back, where a bit of wild heather wilted in the heat of her fist. "So, I think ye should dance with him."

"I think that's good advice." Sylvi kissed her daughter's head and breathed in the delicate lavender scent. "You're a smart girl."

Isla brightened. "And tough."

"And tough, of course," Sylvi agreed. "After all, you come from a long line of Norse shieldmaidens centuries ago."

"My veins run with cold blood, and my body was forged of iron," Isla recited with pride. "And I'm a Campbell to boot!"

"There's not much tougher than that." Sylvi ran a hand over

her daughter's silky head and accepted the heather. The limp stems were still warm from her daughter's hand. "It appears I have a dance waiting for me." Sylvi rose and embraced Liv once more, truly overjoyed at the pleasure on her friend's face. "I'm so happy for you."

"Thank you—and I for you." Liv squeezed Sylvi affectionately before releasing her. "Congratulations on your growing family."

Isla pulled at Sylvi's free hand all the way across the room to where Ian waited with a wide grin on his face.

"Sending a little girl to deliver your threats, Ian?" Sylvi asked in a mock tone.

He shrugged unapologetically. "She's bonnier than me." He winked down at Isla, who giggled and slapped a hug around his legs.

The instruments hummed to life, and the couples began to dance. Ian gave a playful roar and plucked Isla off his legs, tossing her lightly into the air. She gave a squeal of delight.

"I'll dance with ye next, little warrior," Ian promised. "Dances with both the lasses I love most in life. I truly am a lucky man."

He set Isla on the bench and held out his hand for Sylvi. She settled her fingertips into his palm and let him lead her to the dance floor while their daughter watched with a wistful smile on her lovely face.

"There was a day once I dinna ever think to get ye on the dance floor." Ian grinned at her. "Guess I'm that good, eh?"

"I guess you are," Sylvi conceded. "But you owe me five spars for this."

He glanced down at her stomach and hesitated.

She shot him a chastising look. "You know I'm always careful. And I trust you to be too."

He looked at her with his warm brown gaze and stroked a hand down her cheek. "Aye, ye know I'll always take care of ye and our children."

The music pulsed low and brought them together. Ian slid his hands around her waist and gently caressed her belly. "Can we start telling people soon?"

Sylvi's cheeks went warm. "I already told Liv, but I don't want too many to know. You know I hate everyone's attempts to treat me so carefully."

"They canna help but love ye, and I canna blame them for it." He stared at her for a long moment and then smiled at her. "I'm so verra happy, my angel."

She put her hands in his and let him sway her to the music. "I am too."

In a world where she had never thought to know joy again, where the need for vengeance had consumed everything in her, she had found the unthinkable. Love. Family. Happiness.

All far more satisfying ventures, which helped soothe the hurt of the past and filled her empty heart with such warmth, some days it felt near bursting.

She was, like Ian, so very happy. And she knew with certainty there was no better feeling in all the world.

Also by Madeline Martin

Mercenary Maidens

Highland Spy

Highland Ruse

Highland Wrath

Wedding a Wallflower

The Earl's Hoyden

The Borderland Ladies

Ena's Surrender

Marin's Promise

Anice's Bargain

Ella's Desire

Catriona's Secret

Leila's Legacy

The Borderland Rebels

The Highlander's Lady Knight

Faye's Sacrifice

Kinsey's Defiance

Clara's Vow

Drake's Honor

Highland Passions

A Ghostly Tale of Forbidden Love

The Madam's Highlander

Her Highland Destiny

The Highlander's Untamed Lady

Matchmaker of Mayfair

Discovering the Duke

Unmasking the Earl

Mesmerizing the Marquis

Earl of Benton

Earl of Oakhurst

Earl of Kendal

Heart of the Highlands

Deception of a Highlander

Possession of a Highlander

Enchantment of a Highlander

Standalones

The Highlander's Challenge - N W M S

Her Highland Beast - N W M S (fairytale twist retelling - Beauty and the Beast/Princess and the Pea with Scottish folklore)

About the Author

Madeline Martin is a *New York Times, USA Today,* and International Bestselling author of historical fiction and historical romance with books that have been translated into over twenty different languages.

She lives in sunny Florida with her two daughters (known collectively as the minions), two incredibly spoiled cats and a man so wonderful he's been dubbed Mr. Awesome. She is a die-hard history lover who will happily lose herself in research any day. When she's not writing, researching or 'moming', you can find her spending time with her family at Disney or sneaking a couple spoonfuls of Nutella while laughing over cat videos. She also loves research and travel, attributing her fascination with history to having spent most of her childhood as an Army brat in Germany.

Check out her website for book club visits, reader guides for her historical fiction, upcoming events, book news and more: https://madelinemartin.com